TREACHERY  AT
HURSLEY
PARK
HOUSE

Claire Gradidge was born and brought up in Romsey. After a career as, among other things, a nurse and a school librarian, she went to the University of Winchester, where she graduated in 2009 with a first class honours BA in Creative Writing. In January 2018, she was awarded a PhD in Creative Writing and *The Unexpected Return of Josephine Fox* was written as the creative element of her PhD study. An early version of the opening 3,000 words was highly commended in the *Good Housekeeping* magazine competition in 2012.

She has taught at the University of Winchester as an Associate Lecturer for eight years and has had some short fictions and poems published in *South*, *Orbis* and *Vortex*. She has been married for over 40 years and has two adult sons, a beautiful grandson and a crazy collie.

Also by Claire Gradidge

The Unexpected Return of Josephine Fox

TREACHERY AT HURSLEY PARK HOUSE

CLAIRE GRADIDGE

ZAFFRE

First published in the UK in 2021 by

ZAFFRE

An imprint of Bonnier Books UK
4th Floor, Victoria House, Bloomsbury Square,
London WC1B 4DA
Owned by Bonnier Books
Sveavägen 56, Stockholm, Sweden

A CIP catalogue record for this book is
available from the British Library.

ISBN: 978–1–83877–469–1

Also available as an ebook and an audiobook

1 3 5 7 9 10 8 6 4 2

Typeset by IDSUK (Data Connection) Ltd
Printed and bound in Great Britain by Clays Ltd, Elcograf S.p.A.

Zaffre is an imprint of Bonnier Books UK
www.bonnierbooks.co.uk

For Jessica, bright star. Love always.

Prologue

Winter Solstice

Sunday 21ˢᵗ– Monday 22ⁿᵈ December 1942, late evening

I T'S PAST MIDNIGHT, BUT THE party is still in full swing behind the blacked-out windows of the big house. Music swells into the garden each time a door is opened: singles emerging to take the air; closely twined couples strolling arm in arm, oblivious to cold and observation. The drift of cigarette smoke and the mutter of voices and laughter leaches into the night.

The two lads who are keeping watch patrol their beat as faithfully as guardsmen outside Buckingham Palace, though they've nothing between themselves and trouble but their own native wits and a stout stick apiece. For one, his route takes in the tennis court and walled garden, the tool sheds and greenhouses, the fruit stores and summer house. For the other, the coach house and stables, the well house and sunken garden, the path beyond to the water tank. On the hour and the half-hour they meet at the sundial and exchange *all's wells*, tepid tea from a flask, a dog-end cigarette.

At 12.30 a.m., only one arrives at the rendezvous. He waits a lonely five minutes, thinking jealously of the couple he's watched necking in the summer house and wishing for his own bed and his girl waiting ready in it. Then he looks at his watch and sets off to find his delinquent friend.

A chill breeze blows across the bowling green, makes the searching lad shiver and pull his scarf more closely round his neck. In the moonlight, the grass is blue-grey, the shadows sharp-honed. He calls his friend's name, *David?*, mutters a curse when an owl skims like a pale ghost over the lawn, answering his call with an interrogatory *whoo?*

The shadows are deep beneath the pergola, inky black, deceptive. In the sunken garden, a shimmer of water moves under the moonlight. Down he goes, negotiating a dozen treacherous steps.

At the water's edge, alien tessellations of black and white shift. A late lily flower, a skein of weed. *David?*

A hand, and a hank of hair.

David? he calls for the third time, but nobody answers.

1

Sunday 3ʳᵈ January 1943, afternoon

I T'S COLD ON THE BIKE, and I'm already regretting the decision not to take the offered lift to Chandler's Ford. It was meant as my declaration of independence: two fingers to the powers that be. But now, with the rain coming down in a steady drizzle and the motor bicycle's engine making ominous spluttering noises, it feels more like sheer bloody stupidity.

I ought to have asked Alf why his friend was willing to sell me the Cyc-Auto for a fiver. At that price, I should have known better. But the chap had sworn it was in good working order. 'Just what you need, Mrs Lester,' he'd said. 'Get you to work, no trouble, and you'll find it runs on a thimbleful of fuel. I guarantee you won't find a single thing wrong with it.'

And now, on my first proper trip on the beastly thing, I'm finding he was quite right about that, at least. There isn't *one* thing wrong with it – it's everything. As well as the stuttering engine and the slick tyres, it's turned out to be a beast to balance, especially with a suitcase on the carrier. I nurse it along, glad no one's around to see what a fool I'm making of myself.

The turning I want comes up on the right, beyond the thatched roof of the new hotel. I'm congratulating myself that I've only got a mile or so more to go when the engine gives out a rattling belch of blue smoke and comes to a halt. I manage to get off before the bike tips onto the ground, taking a slice out of my ankle as it falls. The last-minute things I stuffed into a basket and tied to the handlebars spill out over the wet road.

I let the bike lie while I collect up my scattered possessions. Hairbrush and comb, purse and a notebook that by Sod's Law has fallen into a patch of mud. I swipe the worst of the muck off with my glove, shove everything back in the basket. My pen and a lipstick are nestling together in a clump of grass, while the tin of shortbread Dot, my Romsey landlady, made for me, has rolled ten yards down the road. Though it's still sealed, it rattles ominously when I pick it up. It was meant as a 'thank you' gift for the couple who are going to put me up for the next few weeks, though now it looks as if it will have to be a 'sorry I broke it but it should still taste all right' kind of thing. Another muddy wipe of the glove and I'm ready to wrestle with the bike again. I heave it back onto its wheels, but there's a strong smell of petrol, and an iridescent pool of fuel sloshes across the road.

Cursing, I try to get the bike to start, but it's no good. The lane goes uphill from here, and it's too heavy to pedal without the engine. I'm tempted to abandon it, but I think about the five pounds, and what we've been told about not leaving the means of transport available for a possible enemy, and start to push.

As I walk, I remind myself of all the reasons a temporary assignment away from Romsey is a good idea. I've been working with the town's coroner, Bram Nash, for almost two years now, but there's been so little to do lately I've had to make work for myself, filing papers no one will ever need to look at again, tidying archive boxes only the spiders ever visit.

It was April 1941 when he'd first taken me on as his assistant. A girl had been murdered, her body dumped in the ruins of a bombed-out pub on the outskirts of Romsey the same day I arrived back in my home town after more than twenty years away. We'd worked together to identify Ruth Taylor and track down her killer, but events like that don't happen every day in a sleepy little town like Romsey. Though there has been other work to do, unexpected deaths that have required the coroner's attention, we both know I've not been earning my salary.

Trouble is, we can't forget what happened between us, rub along casually as colleagues, or even friends. There's always a sense of tension. It was all right when we were busy, but since things have got slack, I've found myself thinking about the personal stuff. Wishing we hadn't made such a mess of our relationship. The sex. Sometimes, I've seen it in his eyes too, in the brusque way he avoids any kind of physical contact. Any contact at all that isn't directly to do with work, come to that. We don't discuss it. How can we? I'd have to say I regret it, and I don't, despite everything. But what he feels, I can't even begin to guess.

Back when we were children, Bram and I were friends. There was a gang of us, the rest all boys, all older than me. But he was the leader, and he made them let me tag along: a little girl everyone else despised because I didn't have a father. We'd play 'Cowboys and Indians', 'Cavaliers and Roundheads', 'Pirates'. And if I was always the one who got captured, or was made to walk the plank, he'd be Abraham Lincoln, Prince Rupert, or, best of all, Cap'n Abe the Pirate King, and he'd always try to save me.

I was almost fourteen when my grandmother died and my grandfather threw me out as he'd always wanted to do. I was a bastard who'd brought shame on the family and he wanted nothing more to do with me. Not long after that, I heard the boys from the gang had all gone off to war. Jem, the policeman's son, had come home unscathed from the trenches, but my uncle, Mike, more like a brother to me; Bert, the farmer's son; and scruffy little Billy Stewart had died. Bram had been wounded, come back with a new version of his name and a face so badly injured he needed a metal mask to cover the scars. When I met him again, years later, I hardly recognised the boy I remembered. And not because of the scars, either. What he'd seen and suffered had changed him inside, given him a profound reluctance for any kind of intimacy.

But we *had* been intimate, and if it wasn't love between us, it was still more than sex. It wasn't as if I was all that trusting myself. I'd been burned too. My marriage to Richard, who'd been unfaithful so many times I'd lost count, was over long before he took his sailing boat off to Dunkirk and failed to come home. Almost three years later, I don't know if he's alive. He might have been a hero, and I wouldn't wish him dead, but I never want to see him again.

It's no bad thing to get away. I tell myself it's only post-flu depression that's making me feel miserable. That, and this crock of a bike and the rain. Ridiculous to feel as if I've been sent into exile for a second time. I'll be fine when I get somewhere out of the wet.

I'd been in bed with flu for nearly a week when the two men from some Ministry or other turned up at my digs in Tadburn Road. My bones felt as if they were made of macaroni, and every time I tried to get up I was as dizzy and sick as if I'd been at sea in a force 10 gale. I'd slept till I couldn't sleep anymore, but I was tired all the time, irritable and bored. I found myself snapping at everyone who came near, and though Dot said it was a good sign and meant I was getting better, it didn't feel like it.

So when she came upstairs that morning in a fluster to tell me two official-looking men were insisting on seeing me, I was spoiling for a fight. She offered to try and send them away, but I wasn't having any of that. I crawled out of bed, staggered downstairs in my dressing gown to see what they wanted.

I could see straightaway why Dot thought they must be on official business. Their city suits and briefcases were incongruous in her neat parlour. One, tall and thin, had an anonymous kind of face: dark hair and a polite manner. The other was more distinctive, shorter and fatter than his companion, with a straggle of hair as ginger as mine around a shining bald pate. They flashed their papers at me, too fast to read, muttered about war effort and confidentiality. The card they gave me said their names were McNaught and Jericho, but it might as well have said Smith and Jones for all I believed them.

They told me they had a proposition for me, a nice little job to keep me out of mischief. Their very words, so patronising I'd have kicked them out there and then if I'd had the strength. And though no one was crass enough to mention compulsory service, the words hung over the discussion like a rain cloud. It was almost funny, because if only they'd known, I didn't want to turn them down at that point. The idea of having a new investigation to get my teeth into, a proper excuse to get away from my job at Nash, Simmons and Bing, was irresistible.

As it turned out, it didn't really matter what I wanted, since they told me Bram had already agreed to release me. Jericho chipped in that he'd obtained leave for me to give up my firewatching shifts at the town hall, and McNaught had found me somewhere to live nearer the new job. I didn't like the idea they'd taken so much for granted, but by then I didn't have a choice. They'd told me so much about what they wanted me to do that I knew I couldn't refuse.

Late last year, secret papers had been intercepted in London. Documents and blueprints that detailed crucial modifications to the design of the Spitfire. If they'd reached Nazi Germany it would have been a crippling blow to the war effort. McNaught and Jericho's department had traced the leak back as far as Hursley Park House, where Supermarine, the firm that designed and built the aircraft, had relocated after the factory had been bombed out of Southampton. But before they could pinpoint who'd been responsible for the leak, there had been a suspicious death at the site. A boy who'd been working as a gardener was found drowned with a piece of another blueprint clutched in his hand.

When I said, Well, if you've found your culprit, what do you need me for? they pointed out he might have been part of a network. There could still be someone scheming away inside Hursley Park House, waiting for a chance to get information out to our enemies. My task was to find them. I'd go in undercover, nothing glamorous, just me doing an ordinary job and keeping my eyes open for anything suspicious.

So I agreed. Despite their high-handedness about leaving Dot's, I could see it wouldn't be practical to travel from Romsey every day. Besides which, they wanted me to integrate, to blend in. Jericho said I needed to become part of the furniture so I could keep my ear to the ground. The picture it conjured up in my head made me laugh till I coughed myself breathless; and Dot came in spitting mad and shooed them away. Reluctantly, they agreed I could have a week to get fit before I started at Hursley.

It hadn't been much of a concession. In the days before I left, I discovered they had an endless stream of things for me to do. Packages of papers were delivered that I had to read and return. Information about the work being done at Hursley Park House, the key personnel there, sketchy details about the boy who'd died. And most days there was a coy little postcard too, telling me to ring a particular number from a specific telephone box: different ones each time though it was always McNaught or Jericho who answered.

I'll hand it to them, they were clever. If they'd told me everything I'd let myself in for that first morning, I would have found a way to refuse. Especially when I discovered that it wasn't just my digs I had to leave. My orders were to cut my ties with Romsey completely, stay away from all the people who mattered in my life. Dot and her nephew Alf, Uncle Bill and his French wife Sylvie. I wasn't even allowed to tell them where I was going.

There was a special warning about Bram. A not-very-veiled threat that it wouldn't be in his interests for me to contact him. It was all wrong, but by the time I realised, I was in too deep to get out. Except for the telephone calls to touch base with them, I spent that last week incommunicado: stayed indoors as if I were too ill to go out, asked Dot to tell anyone who called that I was sleeping.

And finally, though I'd argued about it with McNaught – or perhaps it was Jericho – till the operator cut off that day's call, I dyed my hair black because they said red was too conspicuous, and accepted an identity card and a set of ration books that claimed I wasn't Jo Lester anymore, but Miss Joy Rennard, though I didn't feel the least bit of joy about it.

*

It's past three o'clock when I finally reach the Hutments, the temporary accommodation they've set up for some of the Supermarine families on the edge of Chandler's Ford. Though there's no sign of anyone around, the buildings with their mock-Tudor beams and fenced-in garden plots have an established look. Wearily, I prop the Cyc-Auto against the gatepost of number 39 and walk to the door. I'm tired, and cold, and wet, and all I want to do is get out of the rain. I knock, polite, not too much, though I'm longing to batter on the door and beg them to let me in. A long minute goes by, but no one comes. It is the right place, I'm sure of that, and it's such a small house I can't believe they haven't heard me. My mood sinks lower than low. I know I'm late, but surely they haven't all gone out and left me?

A chilly rivulet from the gutter pours down my neck, makes me yelp with surprise. I'd have thought I couldn't get any wetter or more uncomfortable, but I'd have been wrong.

Annoyed, I knock again, louder this time.

At last, I hear a shuffling noise and the sound of a bolt being drawn. The door opens, a crack at first, and then more widely. The blackout's no problem, because there's no more light coming from inside than there is out here.

'Yes?'

I can see enough to make out that the woman in the door-way is wearing a drab brown dressing gown that's reminis-cent of a monk's robe. The colour and shape do nothing for her: in the half-light the garment makes her body look boxy, solid, and her face is sallow to the point of yellowness.

'Mrs Anderson?'

'That's right.' The admission is grudging. 'What do you want?'

'The name's Rennard. I'm your new lodger.'

She stares at me blankly.

'Mr McNaught arranged it.'

'I was expecting you hours ago. Lunchtime, he said.' She puts a sour emphasis on the words. 'I hope you're not expecting me to feed you now.'

'Not if you've already eaten.' My stomach growls, loud enough for her to hear. 'I had problems with my transport.'

She peers past me. 'That thing? You can't leave it out there, cluttering the place up. It's supposed to be a footpath only.'

'Where shall I put it, then?'

She gestures impatiently into the dusk. 'Down the path here behind the house. My husband's shed. He's there, he'll show you.' She shuts the door with a bang, and another cold stream of water runs down from the gutter onto my face and neck. I look at the bags at my feet, the bike propped a couple of yards away against the fence. Even having to go back those few steps seems like too much effort, let alone exploring some ill-defined path to a hypothetical shed. But I don't have a choice. Unless I want to stay outside in the rain, I'll have to try and find it. I pick up my baggage from the step and manhandle it back onto the carrier, struggle to get enough momentum to wheel the bike along the rutted path that leads along the fence and out through a gate into the indeterminate gloom beyond.

Ahead, a long, low shape I hope is the shed I'm looking for looms out of the murk. There's a faint smell of woodsmoke and I can hear a rhythmic creaking sound which seems familiar, though I can't quite place it. With a feeling of déjà vu, I locate a door and knock, call out, 'Mr Anderson?'

The creaking sound stops, and a voice comes back: 'Who wants me?'

'My name's Rennard,' I shout, without conviction. The only thing that's better here than standing on the doorstep of number 39 is that there isn't a gutter waiting to funnel water down my neck.

'Hold on.' The door opens, and the smell of woodsmoke gets stronger. Inside, a gleam of light bleeds round the edges of what I take to be a blackout curtain a few feet inside the door and illuminates the shape of a tall man stooping in the doorway. He peers out at me.

'My word, you look wet.'

'Yes.'

He pulls the curtain further aside, and a wash of warm yellow light spills out. 'Quick,' he says. 'Come on in.'

'The bike.' I gesture helplessly towards it. 'My things.'

'Bring them in. Quick now, before the ARP warden sees us.'

With what feels like the last effort I'm capable of, I wheel the bike through the gap and into the light. I find myself in a surprisingly big space that's half living room, half carpenter's workshop. There's the smell of oil and woodsmoke, a flood of warmth from a small black stove. The light's coming from a hurricane lamp hitched on a hook above the stove, and a rocking chair is still in motion beside it.

'Let me have that.' Capable hands take the bike from me, wheel it into the shadows. 'Take your coat off, now. You'll catch your death of cold standing there.'

Half mesmerised, I do as he says. Before I know it, he's taken my coat and bustled me to the chair, pulled a pan of water onto the stove top.

'You'd like a cup of tea?' He turns, and I get a good look at him for the first time. Though I've been told he's a draughts-man in the Drawing Office at Hursley Park, he looks as if he ought to be a sailor. His pale blue eyes and thin, deeply creased cheeks with odd tufts of white bristles rightly belong on the deck of a trawler. And to add to the impression, he's wearing a roll-neck navy sweater.

'That would be lovely.'

'Sugar and milk?'

I shake my head. 'Neither, thank you.'

'You'll have sugar and like it,' he says, 'and a drop of rum against the cold.'

'You're very kind.'

He hands me an enamel mug. 'Careful, now, it's hot.'

I wrap the end of my cardigan sleeve over my fingers and take it. The warmth is like a lifeline. A deep, aromatic steam rises into my face as I sip, makes my eyes sting. 'Thank you so much. I wasn't expecting . . .'

'You met the wife, then.' It isn't a question.

I blush, start to stammer a denial.

'Don't worry. I know what she's like.'

'I think she'd been asleep.'

'I wouldn't be surprised.' He draws up a stool to the stove and sits. 'So, Miss Rennard. Or should I call you Mrs Lester? You'd better tell me all about it.'

2

Tuesday 5ᵗʰ January, afternoon

BRAM NASH LOOKS OUT THROUGH the top floor window of his office. It's another of those dull winter days that never seem to get properly light, and though it's not quite four, he's finished his work for the day. He could go home early, but there's no point. He's got nothing he needs to do there, either. He isn't even on the rota for ARP duty tonight.

His view is of roofs, bare branches. Somewhere over to his right, dirty grey smoke rises into the dirty grey sky. A train, perhaps, pulling into Romsey station, or someone with a bonfire of wet leaves. The lack of light depresses him, makes him think of mud, the sound of shelling. He wants something to do, something worthwhile. He's too middle-aged, too out of date, too *damaged*, to be of use this time around, but not so old he doesn't chafe at the inactivity. At the uselessness of being a small-town solicitor in the middle of a war, nothing more exciting to do than draw up wills or write letters in petty disputes. Business has been slow for months, it's as well

Bing's gone swanning off to a job at the War Office. Even with his other partner, Simmons, in semi-retirement since his stroke, Nash hasn't exactly been overworked. He hadn't had a leg to stand on when the men from whatever anonymous ministry it was had come to requisition Jo's services.

The men had told him she'd volunteered for the move, which had taken him aback, knocked out all his arguments before they were spoken. In some ways, it hadn't surprised him, because it had been clear for a while that she hadn't been happy about the lack of work in the office, but he'd been unsettled by the fact she hadn't spoken to him about it first. And he hadn't been able to check with her because she'd been away from the office, ill with the flu. When he'd gone to see her, Dot told him she was asleep. He hadn't believed it, but there's nothing he can do about that, either. If she doesn't want to see him, she doesn't. Perhaps it's for the best.

His secretary, Miss Haward, is still up in arms about Jo's imposed departure, even though there's no love lost between her and his assistant. It's the principle with Aggie, the affront to office prestige and her dignity. With June on compassionate leave to look after her dying husband, and the other typist, Cissie, down to half-time working since her marriage, Aggie's forever hinting at being overworked, forced to do jobs that are beneath her.

A knock at his door makes the case in point. It is Aggie, with that hard-done-by look on her face he's become accustomed to. He stifles his impatience. Perhaps he's being unfair, perhaps she *has* got too much to do. She's certainly looking flustered.

'Mr Nash,' she says. He can hear the wheeze in her breathing from the haul upstairs. She could have rung his extension, of course, but she will insist on coming up.

'What is it, Aggie?'

'There's a man.' She pats her chest. 'Downstairs. He says he wants to see you.'

'If it's a client, show him up. It's not as if I'm busy.'

'I don't know what he is,' she says, aggrieved. 'He won't tell me his business. Won't even tell me his name.'

'Another ministry man?' he asks. 'Like the ones who came about Mrs Lester?'

'Nothing like. This one says it's private. Too private for me, apparently. I don't know who he thinks he is, set down in my office like patience on a monument. Won't take no for an answer. Says he's not leaving till he sees you.'

'Intriguing.'

'Rude,' she snaps. 'I call it rude.'

'Aggressive, d'you think? Is he looking to punch my nose?'

'Nothing like that.' She's shocked. 'He's a gentleman. A bit like you, used to giving orders.'

Nash winces at the blunt assessment. He'd never thought of himself as particularly authoritarian before. His secretary must be really fed up with him. 'In uniform?'

'No.' She sniffs. 'He seems familiar, though. I've seen his face somewhere before, and not long ago, either. I just can't place him.' She drops something onto his desk that makes a sharp little sound. From where he stands by the window, he can't make out what the shapeless small blob might be. 'He told me to give you this. Said you'd know who he was.'

Suppressing the thought that she could have mentioned it in the first place, Nash moves across the room. Close to, he can see the thing is a coin, a penny that's been squashed on a railway line. It's been rubbed shiny, the old Queen's head almost obliterated. He doesn't have to pick it up, he knows if he were to turn it over the date would be 1898. The year of his birth. There's a buzzing in his ears, the whine of artillery.

'His name's George Hine, Aggie.' Without looking at it further, he slides the penny from his desk, slips it into his pocket. 'I'll come down. Perhaps you'd be good enough to let us use your office in private for a minute or two.'

He ignores the indignant sniff that this provokes, follows her downstairs.

Aggie's office faces the alley at the front of the building. It's a shadowy space in the fading daylight and he can hardly make out the shape of his visitor, ensconced in the straight-backed chair which is all his secretary allows for visitors.

'For God's sake.' Nash snaps on the light, a feeble bulb that hardly makes a difference to the gloom. He endures Aggie's shocked exclamations about the blackout, her fussing attention to the blind. Waits, pointedly holding the door open for her, till she huffs her way out of the room. Once they are alone, he speaks.

'Hine. What are you doing here?'

'Nash.' The man rises to his feet, holds out his hand in greeting.

Nash hesitates. Coming hard on the heels of his earlier thoughts about the past, the mud and blood of Passchendaele, Hine is the last person he wants to see.

'Still angry with me then?' Hine says. 'I thought you'd have forgiven me for saving your life by now. Or is it because of David?'

'Not that.' Nash moves forward, shakes the other's hand. 'I thought . . . for a minute, I wondered if you were real.'

'That's what you said then.'

'I remember.' He gives himself a mental shake. 'I'd offer you tea, but I don't think my secretary is in the mood to co-operate.'

'Doesn't matter. To tell you the truth, I'd rather have something stronger if you've got it.'

Nash hides his surprise at the bald request. 'I'm afraid I don't keep booze in the office. But we can find a pub if you like. You know what it's like in Romsey, there's always one open somewhere.'

'Not a pub, please. You'll understand I'm not too keen on public scrutiny right now.'

'My house then? It's not far.'

'If you don't mind.'

Though in some ways he does mind very much, Nash gives the only answer politeness allows. Opening the door, he takes his coat and hat from the hallstand, calls out to his secretary.

'Miss Haward, I'm off. Lock up, will you, when you're ready? I'll see you in the morning.'

At Basswood House, all is quiet. His housekeeper, Fan, will be busy at the WVS canteen for a while yet, and Billy, her son, won't be back from work till a quarter to six.

He ushers Hine upstairs to his study. The fire's laid ready, and Nash sets a match to the kindling. It's cold enough to justify the extravagance of lighting it early, he thinks, especially since he has a visitor. Remembering his civic duty, this time he doesn't switch on the light until he's closed the blackout curtains.

It's a shock when he turns, sees Hine clearly for the first time. The man's face is haggard, greyish skin drawn taut across his bones in a way that Nash associates with serious illness. 'Sit down, man,' he says. 'Before you fall down.'

His guest half sits, half collapses into the armchair by the fire. 'Bad as that, eh?'

'Worse. What'll you have? I've got brandy, or there's whisky if you'd rather.'

'Whisky, then. Brandy's too much like medicine.'

Nash forbears to say that it seems as if medicine is exactly what Hine needs. He pours a generous amount of whisky into a glass, hands it over. Pours a more judicious measure for himself.

'What's it all about, then?'

Hine drinks, a gulp that sees off half the contents of the glass. 'Don't loom over me, Nash. I've had too much of that.'

'Because of David?'

'You saw the papers?'

'Hard to miss them.' Nash shrugs. 'I meant to write to you, but I wasn't sure if you'd welcome someone like me rearing up out of the past at a time like this.'

'I'll take what help I can get, however I can get it. I'm not a fool, I know how it looks. But it's not true, you know. What they said he did.'

'You don't believe it?' Nash tops up the other man's glass, puts the decanter back on his desk. Sits down in the chair on the opposite side of the hearth.

'He was my son, Nash. I knew him through and through. After Lucy died, he and I . . . we were friends as well as father and son. Now I've lost him too.' He pauses, takes a deep breath. 'He wasn't a traitor, a spy. Quite the opposite. He was a good boy, an honest boy. An idealist.'

Nash thinks that idealism might offer a strong motivation to spy, depending on whose ideals one espouses. But he keeps the thought to himself. A question for later, perhaps.

'He'd not joined up?'

Hine takes another gulp of whisky. 'He tried. They wouldn't have him. Said his asthma was too severe. I was glad of it then, thought it meant he'd be safe. He was nineteen, Nash. Remember that? Remember being nineteen?'

Nash fishes the penny out of his pocket, leans forward and lays it on the hearth between them. In the firelight, the copper seems to glow. 'Oh, yes, I remember. I was nineteen when you brought that back to me the first time.'

'It fell out of your pocket when we picked you up from that shell-hole. I knew it was your lucky piece. I didn't want you to lose it.'

'Do you remember what I said to you when you gave it to me that day?'

'You said, I should have left it in the mud. You said if you'd been lucky, we would have left you in no man's land to die.'

'Yes.'

Hine shrugs. 'You were sick,' he says. 'Very sick. We thought you might die. I didn't take any notice of what you said.'

'I told you to keep the penny,' Nash says, 'if you thought there was any luck in it.' He nudges it with the toe of his shoe. 'Now you're calling in the favour?'

'You always were direct.' Hine frowns. 'Always called a spade a bloody shovel. But it wasn't that, not entirely. I thought . . . I didn't want to have to give my name to your secretary in case she threw me out before I got the chance to see you. You don't have children?'

'No.'

'You wouldn't know, then. But I'd do anything for David.' The colour is high on Hine's cheekbones now, an angry purplish flush. 'What happened to him was sheer wickedness, Nash. Someone killed him, held him down in that pond and drowned him. It wasn't as if it was deep, for God's sake.'

Nash sits in the chair opposite his guest. 'The Winchester coroner's verdict was misadventure, wasn't it? I heard my colleague, Mr Brown, concluded David was drunk, out of it. In that state, it's perfectly possible he drowned accidentally.'

'Colleague?' Hine snorts. 'That blind old fool Brown? I'm surprised you want to claim him. If it'd happened in your district, I don't believe you would have come to the same conclusion. You've got to help me, Nash. It was in all the papers what you did to get justice for that girl a couple of years ago. I want the same for David.'

Nash reaches forward, chucks another log on the fire. The flames burn up, set sparks glittering in the mouth of the chimney. 'All right,' he says. 'You'd better tell me about it. Another drink?'

'No thanks. It's a bit too easy to let it get out of hand these days.' He gulps down what's left in his glass then starts to speak, a recitation that seems well rehearsed. 'David was working at Hursley Park,' he says. 'For the Coopers. He went there in 1938, straight from school. He'd never been any good at book work, but he loved being outdoors. I had a friend of a friend who knew Sir George and pulled a string or two. They took him on as an under-gardener's apprentice. Not much more than a labourer at the start. But he was doing all right, gaining some knowledge, some skills. Latterly, he'd been working in the hothouses.'

'How did he feel when Hursley Park was requisitioned?'

Hine shrugs. 'Once they knew Lady Cooper was staying and would keep her staff on, he was excited about it. Spitfires at Hursley Park House? He was thrilled, thought he'd be part of the war effort.'

'Lady Cooper's staff knew who'd taken over the house?'

'Of course they did. It was common knowledge right from the start. The very first day Lady Cooper had a model of an aeroplane made of flowers put in the hall to greet the design team from Supermarine. With busloads of workers coming in every day, hangars going up in the grounds, and engines being tested, they couldn't exactly keep it secret, could they?'

'Fair point. Did he have much to do with the incoming staff? Make friends with any of them?'

'You think I haven't answered these questions before?' Hine's tone is bitter. 'No, he didn't have anything to do with the newcomers as far as I'm aware. No, he didn't make any suspicious friends. No, he didn't suddenly have more money to spend than he ought to. He did his job, came home at night, kept himself to himself. If you must know, he was disappointed. Never saw a Spitfire closer than any other lad round here, watching a dogfight overhead.'

'But he was at the party, the night Lady Cooper moved out?'

'Not as such,' Hine says. 'It's true he was there, but not as a guest. He'd been asked to do an extra shift, him and another lad. They were keeping an eye on the outbuildings, making sure there was no funny stuff going on. There'd been an attempted burglary back in June. The man started a fire in the stables to divert attention. He didn't get away with it, and the stuff was all still there, safely stowed away. Lady Cooper wanted to make sure her property stayed that way until they had a chance to get everything over to Jermyns House.'

'David told you that?'

'He did. They sent him home at lunchtime to get some kip since he'd be up till all hours. We had a meal together around five before he went back.' Hine stalls, seems lost in the memory.

'And he was OK then?' Nash prompts. 'Not worried about anything?'

'I told the police,' Hine blusters. 'I didn't notice anything wrong.'

A silence falls that Nash does nothing to break. For the first time, he thinks Hine has lied deliberately to him.

'Damn it, Nash,' Hine says at last. 'I wasn't paying attention to what he said. You know how it is. It wasn't as if I knew something was going to happen.'

'But now, looking back? Whatever it is, you need to tell me if I'm going to be any use to you.'

'I don't *know* anything. But . . . you're right. With hindsight, I can see he was a bit thoughtful, for a few days before the party. Not worried, exactly, but preoccupied. Something on his mind. I thought it was because of the move. And . . .'

'Yes?'

'He'd come home a couple of days before with some bumps and bruises. Said a branch had dropped on him while he was pruning one of the old walnut trees in the park, though it looked more like a fight to me.'

'You've no idea what it was about?'

'God, don't you think I wish I'd asked him? I didn't pry, thought it must have been something between lads, you know. Next thing I knew there were police at my door, saying he'd died. That he'd been drunk, and drowned. I couldn't believe it. I *don't* believe it. Apart from anything else, he was on duty. He wouldn't have taken a drink.'

'It was cold that night. Perhaps someone gave him a nip to keep out the chill.'

'No.' Hine shakes his head. 'I know my boy. He wasn't an old toper like me, didn't even like the taste of it. He didn't drink, and he didn't steal secrets.'

'The press reports hinted they'd found an incriminating document from one of the offices in his possession.'

'A document?' Hine scoffs. 'It was a bit of scrap paper, a torn-off corner. They tried to make something of it, but in the end the police had to admit it was nothing. Even if it had been important, there was no proof David had taken it deliberately. He could have thought it was waste paper, picked it up anywhere on his rounds.'

The sound of a door shutting downstairs makes Hine stop abruptly. 'Who's that?'

Nash checks his watch. 'It'll be my housekeeper, I expect. Fan usually gets in around now. Nothing to worry about, she won't disturb us.'

Hine struggles to his feet. 'No, no. I can't talk anymore. All I need to know is will you help?'

'I can speak to Mr Brown, if you like, see if he can shed any more light on the circumstances of David's death,' Nash says. 'But whether that will help your cause, I can't say.'

'Ask away,' Hine says. 'I'm not afraid of the truth. I know it won't – it *can't* hurt David.'

Nash is nowhere near as convinced. 'If you're sure?'

'Dead sure. I'm banking on you, Nash. I won't let it drop. David was innocent.'

Once Nash has seen Hine off into the evening, he goes back up to his study. The bright shape of the penny winks at him from the hearth. He sits to write a note to Brown. Though he's by no means convinced there's anything to investigate, he can't shake free of the sense that he owes it to Hine to try. And if he must, the sooner he gets it done, the better.

The rain comes into the trenches from every angle: more per-sistent even than the shellfire. And while if you're lucky, you can avoid the shells and the sniper fire, you can't escape from the rain. There's mud in everything – clothes, hair, boots, kit, food. No use trying to stay clean, no way to stay dry. Waiting in the wet, it almost feels like a relief when the order comes to move. He rubs the misshapen coin in his pocket between fin-ger and thumb, waits his turn to climb out of the water-filled trench and into the mud of no man's land.

Ahead of him on the ladder, George Hine grins and settles his tin helmet more firmly on his head. Behind, Mike Fox mut-ters, 'Up and at 'em, Cap'n Abe,' and then they're out in the open. The fusillade of machine-gun fire and shells is deafening, and the rain blinds him. His foot slips, and he's down on one knee, struggling to rise, conscious that Hine is ten yards ahead. Mike draws level, holds out a hand, and then everything goes silent, and he's weightless, formless, face streaming with a liq-uid that's hot and thick, and he knows he's going to die.

3

Wednesday 6ᵗʰ January, afternoon

THEY'VE FOUND ME A JOB at Hursley Park that's somewhere between being a glorified postwoman and a filing clerk-come-archivist. First thing in the morning, at one thirty in the afternoon and again an hour before the offices close, it's my job to go round collecting and delivering mail. What I collect goes back to the post room for logging before it goes out again with me on my next round, or waits for the outside postman to take away. In between times, I'm given the thankless task of trying to find paperwork someone's misfiled or sent to a colleague who hasn't remembered to return it. Or set to track down some abstruse article from a learned journal published back in 1923 that's been forgotten about till now, when it suddenly turns out to be indispensable to the war effort.

Hursley Park House is a grand old place that partly dates back to Queen Anne, though Mr Anderson says the two wings at either end were built only forty years ago, when the Coopers bought Hursley Park estate. Four storeys high, it's built of red brick with a grey slate roof. White stone pillars, like something from a Greek temple, frame the central entrance and the gable-end windows of the wings. More pillars hold up a covered porch where once carriages would have stopped for their passengers to alight, protected from the weather. It's an impressive place on first sight, though some of the grandeur is lost when the fleet of green Hants and Dorset buses is parked all along the front, waiting to ferry the workers back to Southampton at the end of the day.

Inside, it's a warren of rooms being used for offices, classical proportions cluttered with false walls and fibreboard to protect the paintwork and panelling. The grounds are the same. Every last building has some department of Supermarine squirrelled away, and there are temporary huts and hangars everywhere. Even some of the houses in the village have been pressed into use, so my post rounds have me covering a lot of ground every day.

The work is hard on the feet, and there isn't much prestige in it, but it's the perfect cover for what McNaught and Jericho want me to do. Through the course of a day, I get to visit most of the offices in Hursley Park House itself, as well as having to trek round the outlying buildings. Between times, no one knows or cares where I am – or should be. I'm virtually invisible, and practically anonymous, and the only person apart from Mr Anderson who can remember my name is the officer in charge of the post room, Mr Brennan. I wheel my little trolley around, and keep my head down, and if I take the wrong turning sometimes and arrive in a place

I'm not supposed to be, I have the perfect excuse to hand. I'm new, and I'm lost, and they smile indulgently at me and tell me the turning I should have made, and don't even think about what I might have heard or seen that I shouldn't have.

Three days in, and I've found myself a nice little corner that no one else seems to use. I don't know what the original purpose of the room is, but it's cosy, almost domestic in scale. The walls are panelled in a dark wood that I think must be oak, grown almost black with age and polishing, and floor-to-ceiling shelves on two sides are stuffed with books and folders, while the overlay of dust shows how little the space is being used day to day. There's a lovely old table, presumably banished because its uneven surface and octagonal shape don't lend themselves to conventional office use. But it's perfect for me. I've got room to pull my trolley into a corner, and then I can sit by the overgrown window with a pair of scissors beside me, and a heap of miscellaneous papers on the table to sort through as an alibi when I want to be out of the way.

I'm sitting down to my afternoon cup of tea with my shoes off and my feet on the wonderfully cool marble tiles of the hearth when I hear footsteps approaching in the corridor. The door opens. Desperately trying to shuffle my shoes back on without drawing attention to the fact that I'm barefoot in the first place, I relax when I see it's only Mr Anderson.

'Hello, there,' he says. 'You're a hard one to find.'

Though I'm living under his roof, we haven't been able to talk about anything more important than the weather since that first evening. Hilda, his wife, is always present at home, a sulky reminder that I'm there under sufferance, and as far as she's concerned, not worth the trouble I cause by being there. And if I've passed him in the Drawing Office or a corridor somewhere, we don't do more than nod a greeting to each other. I've been racking my brains wondering when – and how – I might be able to speak to him alone.

'That's the idea. How did you track me down?'

'Ways and means, you know. How are you getting on?'

'Not bad. Only got lost twice this morning.' Once was even genuine, but I'm not telling him that. However much he seems to be in the know about me, I'm wary about trusting him too much.

He hitches himself up onto the windowsill and settles in for a chat. 'And you've been all round? Met all the bosses?'

'I've been introduced to them,' I say. 'Some even looked at me when I said good morning.'

He laughs. 'You don't want to worry about that. All the better if you don't stand out.'

'I realise that.' I frown. 'In fact . . . is it safe for us to be talking like this?'

'You'd need ears like a bat to hear what we say in here. The walls are two feet thick. If you did but know it, you've picked the room with a walk-in safe for your hidey-hole.'

'I have?' But as I look round, I can't see any sign of anything out of the ordinary. 'Doesn't that make it worse?'

'Why would it?' he says. 'It's not in use. Rumour has it the key's been lost since before the last war.'

'As long as they don't ask me to find that.'

'Talking about finding things – have you met up with Mr Wakeling yet?'

'The man in the homburg hat?'

'That's the one. Never takes it off, they say.'

'McNaught told me he was ex-CID. Scotland Yard. I still don't understand why they didn't leave it to him to sort out this mess.'

'The thing is,' Anderson says, lowering his voice, 'maybe they should have. And maybe not. Because, as far as I can tell, our secret service friends McNaught and Jericho don't trust him to do the job.'

'They think he might be in on it?'

'Not that. But maybe they think he's not up to it. He comes across as solid mahogany, if you know what I mean.'

'Well, yes. I suppose he does.'

'The stories going round certainly make him out to be stupid. He's obsessed with stopping our chaps scrumping the walnuts, but then they caught him one morning with a hatful for himself. Or there's the tale about him swallowing a report about a missing bicycle, spending weeks investigating before it turned out it was a rag, and the bike hadn't even existed in the first place.'

I laugh. 'Who put him up to that?'

'Ask me no questions and I'll tell you no lies.' Anderson grins. 'On the other hand, of course, it might be professional jealousy on our friends' part. Worrying about who does what on whose turf. So bloody hush-hush the left hand isn't supposed to know what the right hand's doing. Myself, I don't think he can be such a fool as all that. A wild goose chase is damn good cover for having a poke around. I wouldn't underestimate him. He'll have his eye on you.'

'I know. He was one of the people who did look at me when we met. Wanted to know if I was coping with all the walking. Asked me if it wasn't a comedown from what I'd been doing in Swindon.'

'What did you tell him?'

'What McNaught told me to say. That I'd been bombed out in the raid last August, and had problems with my nerves, so I couldn't keep my old job with the firm. And someone had taken pity on me and sent me to Hursley because it was quiet, and this job would keep me tired enough to sleep.'

'My word,' Anderson says. 'What did he make of that?'

'He was embarrassed. I think he was afraid I'd burst into tears or something.'

'Not sure it's a good idea if it gets around you're a bit—'

'Loopy? I don't mind. Might act up on it.'

He shakes his head. 'Don't do that. It wouldn't do you any good. And besides, it's not dignified.'

I think of Hilda and wonder if he's got personal experience of people acting up.

'It's all right. I'm not thinking about having hysterics in the Drawing Office or anything like that. But if people think I'm a bit timid, they may not be on their guard when I'm around.'

'Just you remember,' Anderson says, 'don't let yourself get caught. You can't count on our friends to do the right thing by you.'

'They'd pretend they didn't know me?'

'For sure. They'd cover their backs, don't you worry.' He stands up, brushes the dust from the seat of his trousers. 'Better get going. They'll be wondering where I've got to, turning a squinny eye on me if I'm not careful.'

'See you later.'

'Yes.' He sighs. 'A word of warning. It's Wednesday. It'll be Hilda's hotpot tonight. You might want to make an excuse to be out.'

But there's no excuse I can reasonably make. As Miss Rennard, I'm supposed to be new to the area, so where can I go? The only people I'm meant to know are the Andersons themselves. I think yearningly of Dot's good cooking, and Alf's good nature. Of Joan, and Betty, and even old Mr Grey, deaf as a post, all sitting round the dinner table tonight while I'm playing silly buggers, pretending to be someone I'm not.

That night, I dream. Perhaps it's Hilda's hotpot – gristly meat of unknown origin, thin gravy with grease floating on top of it – or worse, her acid-sharp bottled rhubarb pie, but the dreams are troubled. I'm in a vast field of long grass, looking for a mouse that's eaten a hole in a black homburg hat. And then the mouse turns into an egg that breaks in my hands and I know I'll have to sneak out and bury it because otherwise I'll be put in jail for poaching. And when I get up to go outside, I suddenly find I'm in a room where the windows have bars and the door is black oak a foot thick, studded with nails like something from a cathedral, and a scrawl of graffiti that says 'Go home, you spying bitch'.

I wake, shivering in the early hours' chill, cramped in the narrow bed, hoping I haven't called out or made a noise. I can't put a light on, there's no bulb in the overhead fitting because of blackout regulations. I daren't get up and disturb the Andersons. There's nothing for it but to lie in the dark, listening to the snort of their breathing through the thin asbestos walls, trying to shake off the dream. Ridiculous as dreams always are, it still feels like a prediction of failure before I've even begun.

4

Thursday 7ᵗʰ January, morning

THE CYC-AUTO IS STILL IN the hands of Mr Anderson's mechanic pal, and there's not an ordinary bike to be had anywhere in the Hutments, either borrowed or bought. I'm having to use the bus to get to work, or walk. Though it's only a couple of miles, my daily rounds of the site mean I'm keen to save my feet if I can. The fleet of transport that brings workers up from Southampton every morning doesn't stop to pick anyone up, so my only option is to catch the public service bus to Winchester.

When my dream wakes me up at six on Thursday morning and I can't get back to sleep, I decide to get up and catch the early bus in. I slide out of bed, tiptoe through the business of getting washed and dressed. The Andersons won't be up and about for another hour. I'd been surprised to discover that Hilda works at Hursley too, though I don't know why I should be. I gather she does something in one of the offices scattered around the buildings and grounds, though I've yet to see where, and she's as close-mouthed about her work as

39

they all seem to be. But they don't need to leave until eight, since Mr Anderson has a fully functioning, standard motorcycle which whisks them both to work – Hilda riding pillion – in minutes.

I pick the last crumbs of shortbread out of the tin I brought from Dot's and let myself out into the January morning. I'm going to be early for work, but if the guard will let me in, I can probably cadge a cup of tea and a slice of toast from the canteen in the basement. It's a good place to get to know some faces, hear some chat.

The first grey light is beginning to show in the sky, and though it's not raining, a bitter wind is blowing, the kind Granny used to call lazy because it goes straight through you rather than around. I huddle in the corner of the shelter, pull my old coat closer, wishing it were thicker. I'm trying to keep one eye out for the bus without exposing myself to the full force of the wind and wondering if I've got enough coupons to splash out on something new, when I hear voices. Men's voices, urgent, verging on anger, blustering away in the cold air. I catch the odd snatch of words.

'. . . suspicious . . .'

'. . . no one's blaming . . .'

'. . . better bloody not . . .'

The voices get nearer, louder, clearer. For a moment I'm embarrassed, an unwitting eavesdropper. I cough, move out into the open, and it's not the wind that chills me, but the last snatch of words blowing across my hearing.

'. . . with Anderson, you ruddy fool. Be quiet.'

The prick of light from shielded torches shows the shapes of three people coming towards me. Though I'd only heard two men's voices, there is a woman with them as well. When they get closer, I make out more detail. The two men are in army uniform, the woman in civvies. By what I can see of her, she's very young, perhaps only eighteen or nineteen. Her pale, pinched face is enveloped in a hood of thick dark fur that makes me instantly envious. But I don't envy her look of anxiety, nor the truculent glances one of the men is giving her.

I don't recognise any of them, though I suppose the girl, at least, may be from the Hutments. And they must have seen me before if they know I'm staying with the Andersons. As they stop a few paces away, clearly waiting for the bus themselves, I murmur a greeting, which the girl and the surly man ignore. The other nods acknowledgement, but it's clear they're not keen to chat. I dig my chin down into my threadbare coat collar, try to seem unconcerned, though the way the bad-tempered one is eyeing me makes me nervous.

Mercifully, the bus comes along only a minute or two later. It's a relief to get out of the wind, and though there are plenty of seats further back in the bus, I choose one by the door, next to a fat woman with a huge wicker basket on her lap. I keep my head down until they pass, but even after the bus moves off, I can hear the sullen man's voice; a nagging undertone too low to make out the words, and feel sorry for the girl all over again.

When I stand to ring the bell, I'm surprised to find her behind me, though to my relief the men stay on the bus.

Only the two of us get off, and we turn up the road towards Hursley Park House together. Once through the security check, a fence runs along the left-hand side of the path, but the other side is open to a wide vista of parkland, with trees beyond. The silence between the girl and me feels more and more unnatural as we trudge along side by side, until I can't bear it any longer.

'It's a beastly cold day,' I say. Such a cliché, to start with the weather, but it seems harmless enough to pass muster. She mutters something in return that might be *I suppose so*, and quickens her pace.

It's obvious she doesn't want to talk to me, but my curiosity's piqued. I speed up too, pretend I haven't noticed her reluctance.

'My name's Joy Rennard,' I say, hoping she'll respond with her own name. 'I'm new to Hursley. I don't think we've met, have we?'

She heaves a huge sigh. 'I've seen you,' she says in a tight little voice. 'You're on post duties.'

'That's right,' I laugh. 'Good for the figure but not so hot on shoe leather. Where do you work?'

'We're not supposed to talk about what we do,' she says, and there's desperation in her voice. 'Haven't they told you that?'

I do know it, of course, but it's my job to try and get past that barrier. And I can play dumb as well as anyone. 'I know we're not supposed to talk to outsiders, but surely it can't matter between ourselves? We're both employed by the same firm.'

'You could be anyone,' she says. 'You could be a trick to trap me.' And she turns, and runs, haring off across the grass. Though the sky is beginning to grow lighter on the horizon, her flight comes at a point where we're out of sight of the guards at the gate, as well as the ones nearer the House. I'm the only witness to her bobbing, purposeful run. Whether she'd been intending to go that way all along, or whether I've frightened her into taking drastic action to get away from me, I don't know. But it's definitely given me something to think about as I walk on alone towards the House. Whatever the cause, she'd have been better chatting to me, pretending everything was all right. By running off, she's made me determined to find out who she is, and what her role at Supermarine is.

By Thursday morning, Nash is seething with impatience. He still hasn't heard from Theophilus Brown, the Winchester coroner, but there must be other ways he can begin to find out more about the circumstances of David Hine's death. Not for the first time, he realises how much he misses Jo. He needs her investigating skills. She wouldn't have been put off by official reluctance to co-operate. He'll have to try and think like her, make do on his own.

He has a morning appointment – yet another amendment to Mr Hollis's will – but once that pesky old man is dealt with, there's nothing he has to do that can't wait until later. Or even tomorrow, if need be. He won't even have to annoy Aggie, because today is one of the days Cissie comes in to help with the routine typing. He drops his notes for the new codicil on her desk, and when they've laughed about old Mr Hollis's ever-changing will, and commiserated about the weather, he asks her if she's heard any talk about the boy's death.

'Only what I read in the papers,' she says. 'I know they can't say much because of giving information to the enemy, but it sounded like he was up to no good.'

Though she hasn't told him anything, what she has said gives him an idea. Turning it over in his mind, he makes some bland reply before returning to his office. The news-papers were only able to hint at David Hine's supposed treachery, but perhaps they know more than they printed. And while he has no contacts with the national dailies who dropped the most salacious hints, he does know the local man quite well. So when the lunch hour comes round, he lets Aggie know he will be out of the office for a while, and sets out on the short walk to the Abbey Hotel. Barney Laidlaw should be well settled at the corner table in the public bar by now, and if he's true to form, he'll be about ready for his second pint.

Laidlaw's a big man, with the physique of a rugby player gone to seed, and a taste for lurid shirts. Today's is a mustard yellow that sits unhappily against the greenish tweed of his jacket and makes him look bilious. Poring over a newspaper, pen in hand, he's completing the crossword as quickly as he can write. Nash orders two pints at the bar and takes them over to the corner table.

'May I join you?'

Laidlaw looks up, eyes the beer. 'If one of those is for me, you can,' he says. He looks back down at his paper and his pen darts across the crossword as he fills in the last clue.

Nash sits. 'You make that look easy.'

'It is.' Laidlaw picks up the glass Nash has brought, takes a cautious sip. 'What brings you out to find me, Nash? Suppose it's too much to hope you've got some juicy case on the go? Town's as dull as ditchwater these days.'

'Nothing new. Sorry to disappoint you.'

'Just to buy an old pal a drink, then? Bit late for the spirit of Christmas, surely?'

'You're right,' Nash says. 'I'm afraid it's not entirely altruism. I want some information.'

'From a newspaper man?' Laidlaw laughs. 'That's not the way it's supposed to work.'

'Well, perhaps—'

'Yes?'

'There might be something in it for you, I suppose. Eventually.'

'That's more like it. Fire away.'

'You remember the story about David Hine?'

'The boy who drowned himself? Drunk as a lord and, by the whispers, if he hadn't killed himself, he was going to be in deep trouble.'

'Whispers?'

'Don't play dumb, Nash. You know as well as I do, there are always whispers. *Someone said, my friend heard, everyone knows* ... And the more you try to shut them up, the more newshounds like me get the scent.'

'I'll remember that.'

'I'm getting the scent right now.'

Nash ignores the dig. 'What did you hear? More than was in the papers?'

Laidlaw shakes his head. 'What's it all about, Nash? Why do you want to know? Case went to the Winchester coroner.'

'That's right. Hursley's not in my jurisdiction. Nor yours, I would have thought.'

'Near enough. And the father lives at Braishfield, so there was plenty of local interest, too. I heard a whisper—'

'Another whisper?'

'Do you want me to tell you or not?'

Nash gestures, *go on.*

'The local grapevine was chocka with talk about security, Lady Cooper's staff being unreliable. There'd been that business back in the summer when someone tried to pinch the silver, and when the boy turned up dead, I thought it might be worth my while to go along to the inquest.'

'And it was?'

'You bet. It wasn't whispers we got then, it was full volume. Mind you, it started low-key enough. Brown hadn't chosen a jury and the evidence was all routine stuff about the party and Hine being asked to stay on and keep an eye out for people misbehaving in the shrubbery. That raised a laugh, even, and I was thinking if that's all there was to the rumours I'd wasted my time. Then the doctor got up and said in his opinion the boy was so drunk he must have passed out and drowned himself. That was when Hine's father started shouting about murder and right-wing conspiracies and his son was no traitor. They hauled him out of the court sharpish, and Brown looked at me and made a pompous little speech about respecting Hine's grief and careless talk and remembering we were at war. He didn't quite say I'd find myself in jug if too much got printed, but that was the gist of it.'

'You weren't worried about that? It was you who passed the story on to the dailies?'

Laidlaw grins. 'Never trust a newspaper man to keep his mouth shut, Nash. We're a venal lot.'

'So it seems.'

'Anyway, if you ask me, that's what the father was after. That outburst of his wasn't so much about grief as anger. He was hopping mad. If I hadn't gone to the national press about it, he would have done it.' He nods towards Nash's untouched glass. 'Is that pint going begging?'

Nash pushes it over. 'All yours.'

'What's your angle, then?' Laidlaw says. 'Bribing me with alcohol.'

Nash thinks it over before answering. 'You might be right about George wanting publicity for his son's case. He came to see me a couple of days ago, asked me if I'd look into it.'

'And you said yes? What's he got on you?'

'We served together in the last war.' Nash touches the left side of his face, where the thin metal rim of his mask runs across the flesh of his cheek. 'He brought me in from no man's land when I got this.'

'That's better.' Laidlaw scribbles something in the margin of his paper. 'A story. Tell me more.'

'Not a chance,' Nash says, getting up from the table. 'Publish and be damned.'

Laidlaw finishes the beer, stands. 'Not yet. But I won't forget.'

They walk out into the street together. For once, this wet winter, it isn't raining, and a weak finger of sunlight touches the empty plinth where Palmerston's statue should be.

'Another missing person,' Laidlaw says, nodding towards it. 'Got him tucked up out of harm's way for the duration.'

'Another?' Nash says absently, missing the obvious lure.

'Your Mrs Lester,' Laidlaw says. 'Josy Fox that was. Hear she's gone AWOL too.'

'A secondment,' Nash says, deliberately offhand. 'A temporary arrangement. We weren't busy.'

'You'll miss her if you're going to investigate. Holmes without his Watson.'

More like Watson without Holmes, Nash thinks. It was always Jo who led the search for Ruth Taylor's killer. '*Am* I going to investigate?' he says aloud.

'You don't fool me.' Laidlaw taps his nose. 'Newshound's instinct.'

Nash smiles, shakes his head. 'You'll excuse me, Laidlaw. I ought to get back to work. Thanks for the chat.'

'One thing before you go—'

Nash pauses in his stride. 'Yes?'

'You might like to *chat* to a woman called Jones. Beryl, Mabel, some name like that. Lives out near your pal George somewhere. Nurse of a kind. Heard she laid out the body, was clacking on about bruises to anyone who'd listen.'

5

Thursday 7ᵗʰ January, afternoon

I'VE DISCOVERED THAT AT LUNCHTIME most of the personnel from the House are out of their offices, away down in the basement canteen having their meal. The draughtsmen from the Drawing Office have their own Mess in the grounds. By skipping my lunch, I get the perfect opportunity to snoop around more or less uninterrupted. If I take a couple of envelopes in my hand, keep a puzzled expression ready in case I'm challenged, I can still claim my recent arrival as an excuse for being where I shouldn't.

This lunchtime, I'm using the opportunity to prowl around the upper floors of the main building, looking for a coat with a dark fur collar. I've popped my head into a whole host of offices on the first and second floors, surprised at the lack of security up here, when it's so tightly controlled outside. I've heard one of the bosses hates closed doors, presume this upper level must be his domain. Most of the rooms up here are open to any passer-by, even when no one's inside.

I'm checking through a rack of coats in a side corridor on the second floor when the sound of footsteps – a woman wearing high-heeled shoes – carries towards me. I dodge into a nearby lavatory, realise my mistake almost at once as the feet stop outside the door.

'Blast,' I hear as the woman sees the toilet is engaged. Then, louder, 'Are you going to be long?'

'Sorry,' I squeak in what I hope is an unrecognisable voice. 'Tummy upset. I may be a while.'

The woman tuts. 'How inconvenient.'

I hear the footsteps recede. Not half as inconvenient, I think, as if I really were here with an upset stomach. But I don't hang around. As soon as it's quiet, I peer out, check the main corridor. No one in sight. The back stairs are nearby and I start down them cautiously. I've negotiated the first flight when I hear voices below. People must be coming back from lunch already.

I sort through the envelopes I've brought as cover, find one for the production manager's office on the first floor. As luck would have it, it's not far from the back stairs, so when I emerge with my best businesslike face on, I don't even have to pretend to be lost.

But though I get away with my snooping this time, I'm disappointed as I make my way back to the post room to get my next consignment of bona fide letters. I haven't seen hide nor hair of the girl from this morning, nor of her distinctive coat.

*

There are several ways, Nash thinks, to find out about a woman named Jones – Mabel or Beryl – who might be a nurse, and who might live somewhere near George Hine. The first is the most obvious: call George and ask him, but he'd prefer not to do that. He hasn't yet made up his mind how far he's prepared to go with the investigation. Or even if there is anything *to* investigate in the first place. Though he has to admit Laidlaw's hint at the end of their talk did seem to indicate that there might be something more to find out about David's death, something that might uphold George's theory that there was foul play involved.

Another obvious course is to look up Jones in the telephone directory. If she's any kind of nurse, the odds are she'll be in the book. But as he ploughs through the directory in his office, he can't find a likely candidate. There aren't any Joneses at all in the book in the right neighbourhood, and when he moves to the *Kelly's Directory*, the only nurse called Jones lives way off in Southampton.

Think again. What he needs is a postman, or a gossip. And straightaway that makes him think of Pete, the boy who works delivering telegrams, and fits both descriptions. He'd been instrumental in helping with the investigation into Ruth Taylor's murder when Jo first came to work for him.

Another unscheduled departure from the office, another disapproving sniff from Aggie. Now he can only hope the boy will be at the post office, and not out somewhere on his bicycle, bad news in his dispatch bag.

But all's well, and when Nash arrives at the post office, Pete is standing by the door, nattering to passers-by. By Nash's reckoning, he must be almost sixteen by now, but he's hardly any taller – and certainly no fatter – than he was at thirteen.

'Afternoon, Pete. Can I have a word?'

The boy looks wary. 'Am I in trouble?'

'Not at all. I was hoping you could help me.'

'Yeah?' The boy picks the dog-end of a cigarette from behind his ear and puts it between his lips, brings out a match from his pocket and lights it against the stone facing of the doorway. A dispiriting reek of stale smoke rises from the damp tobacco.

'That's disgusting,' Nash says. 'Here, have one of mine.'

'Ta,' Pete mutters, but he saves the dog-end anyway, pinching it out before putting it back behind his ear. 'What can I do for you?'

'I'm looking for a nurse—'

Pete sniggers.

'A particular nurse,' Nash continues. 'An older lady, I'd imagine. Her name is Jones. I've been told she lives some-where out at Braishfield.'

Pete scratches his head. 'Dunno,' he says. 'Never heard of a nurse living out that way.'

'You don't know of anyone of that name who might fit the bill? She might not be what you'd call a proper nurse.'

'S'pose it could be Auntie May,' Pete says. 'Her name's Jones. They reckon she's delivered hundreds of babies in her time.'

'Sounds promising,' Nash says. 'There's five bob in it if you can tell me where she lives.'

'Nah.' Pete shakes his head. 'For old times' sake I'll tell you for nuthin', cos I'm off out of here next week an' good riddance. Lady I'm thinking of lives up past Pucknall, along Dores Lane. Brick cottage near the turn to Farley Chamberlayne. You can't miss it. Two bloody great geese in the garden, hiss like buggers as soon as anyone gets close.'

Although he's glad of the information, Nash is sidetracked by the boy's news. 'You're leaving Romsey?'

'Joining the Navy. At last. Been wanting to go for years, you ask that Mrs Lester of yours. She'll tell you. Ma's not keen but she can't stop me now. I'll be sixteen next week.'

'I see. Well, good luck with that.' Nash can hear himself, falsely hearty to cover how appalled he feels. Pete's such a child to be going to war.

'You'll tell Mrs Lester goodbye for me?' Pete says. 'I was hoping I'd see her.'

'She'll be sorry to have missed you.' He presses the coins into Pete's hand. 'Take the five bob anyway. I expect it'll come in handy.'

Pete grins. 'That it will. Ta, Mr Nash.'

'Take care.'

As he walks away, Nash is beset by a whole raft of unpatriotic alarm and despondency. It's not his business, but he wishes there were something he could do to stop boys like Pete thinking war is an exciting adventure. But if his story won't do it, the evidence of what can happen stark on his face, nothing will. He can't dwell on it: if he's to see this Auntie May today, he'll have to get a move on. Another a quick dash into the office to pick up his messages and excuse himself yet again to Aggie; and an even briefer stop at Basswood House to collect his bicycle, and then he's on his way.

Though it's a fair distance to Braishfield, in these days of petrol rationing there's very little choice but to use a bicycle. And it keeps him fit, gives him time to mull things over as he rides. It's strange even to be thinking about getting involved in George Hine's affairs. In the years since the last war, he's done his best to avoid any contact with his old comrade. They've only met two or three times, exchanged maybe half a dozen sentences in all that time. Nash knows it's been petty of him to avoid the man who saved his life. Cutting George so ruthlessly from his life changed nothing. It wasn't as if he'd been able to avoid hearing about Hine: a man who seemed to have it all for so long – a lovely wife, a healthy son, unquestioned membership of the squirearchy. It must be all the harder for him now he's lost it all.

Nevertheless, he keeps his head down as he passes Hine's gate. When he's seen this woman – if she is the woman Laidlaw meant – he'll stop off on his way home and tell Hine what he's decided to do. Deep down, he already knows. Talking to Laidlaw and coming here isn't about proving George wrong. He's pursuing it now because he believes Hine is right: there *is* something suspicious about David's death.

There's the scent of woodsmoke in the air as he reaches the little cluster of cottages close to the turning to Farley

Chamberlayne. He gets off his bike, starts walking along the well-trimmed hedges that edge the road, separate one cottage garden from another. He's beginning to think that Pete's *can't miss it* was overly optimistic when two white shapes come hustling out, hissing aggressively as they crane their necks towards him.

He props his bike against the gatepost, pauses a moment. He can't let himself be intimidated by a goose – or even two. But their gaping beaks and oddly snake-like tongues give him pause as he puts his hand to the latch.

'You want me, love? Baby on the way? Don't think I know you.'

For a moment, Nash can't see where the voice is coming from. Then, to his embarrassment, he discovers he's been looking a foot too high. The woman approaching along the garden path is so short she scarcely seems taller than the geese confronting him.

'Ah, no,' he says, after an awkward pause. 'It's not about a baby. My name's Nash. I wanted to talk to you if I could.'

'Nash?' she says. 'Are you that coroner chap from Romsey?'

'That's it.'

'Better come in then.'

He looks at the geese. Though they've stopped hissing since the woman arrived they're still standing sentinel.

'They're as good as a guard dog any day,' she says, as if she's read his thoughts. 'But don't you worry about them. You'll be all right now they know I've invited you in.'

The front door opens into a cosy small room that's as welcoming as the geese were unfriendly. A bright fire burns in the grate, a copper kettle slung on a hook beside it. Next to the hearth, a grandfather chair is heaped with cushions. Opposite, on a table under the window, stands a great jug of holly, its shining leaves and vivid scarlet berries dancing with reflections of the flames.

'Sit down,' the woman says, indicating the big chair. 'I'll make you some tea.'

He hesitates.

'Go on.' She bustles about, pulling the kettle directly over the fire, setting out a teapot and cups. 'None of your drawing room manners here.'

He sits. 'Mrs Jones—'

'Miss, though folk mostly call me Auntie May.'

He smiles. 'I think I'm probably too drawing room for that,' he says.

'Suit yourself. What brings you to my door then, Mr Coroner?'

How can he put this without committing himself to a lie? 'It's not official in any way, but George Hine and I served together in the last war. He's asked me to look into David's death.'

'That poor boy,' she says, handing him a steaming cup of something that looks like dirty water and smells more like hay than Typhoo. 'Get that down you, now. It'll warm you up.'

He takes a scalding sip of the brew, relieved to discover that it's almost tasteless. 'I heard you prepared the boy's body for burial?'

'That's right, love. I see them into the world and I see them out again. But it's not often they're in a state like that nipper.'

'Because of the post-mortem?'

She drinks from her own cup. 'That was some of it. Great black stitches all anyhow to sew him back up where they cut him. Disrespectful. Couldn't let his poor father see that.'

'You said some of it,' Nash persists. 'Was there something else you noticed?'

'Bruises,' she says. 'Boy was a mass of bruises. I'd have said he'd been in a fight, except it can't have been a fair one. His hands were the one part that wasn't marked.'

'Interesting.' Nash thinks it through. 'And this bruising . . . in your opinion, it wasn't the staining that happens after death?'

'No. Seen plenty of that in my time, but I know the difference. Parts where he'd been lying were marked, of course, but there were bruises besides that.' She points to the left side of her jaw. 'Good big one here, there was.'

'You gave evidence at the inquest?'

She grins at him. 'Simple old woman like me? What would they want with my opinion?'

'But you attended.'

'Of course I did. He was one of our own. But you'll have heard, it didn't go too well. His dad was in such a state, shouting out in court. Not that I blame him. Seemed like they'd got something in their heads about the boy, and they were more worried about keeping that schtum than hearing the truth.'

'They?'

'There were a couple of chaps at the back of the court,' she says. 'Here, let me top that up for you.'

Before he can protest, she's poured him another cup of her patent tea. While he's not keen to drink any more of the grassy brew, it's the interruption to the story he's more concerned about. But she carries on without further prompting.

'These chaps, no one said who they were, but they had a look, sort of shifty and official at the same time. I'll eat my hat if they were there by chance. And when poor Mr Hine started shouting, it was one of them who tipped the wink to the copper on the door.'

Shifty and official is a perfect description of the men who came to requisition Jo's services, Nash thinks. Either this part of Hampshire is suddenly inundated with secret ops, or there is a link. Now what he needs is to find Jo, talk to her.

He drains what's left in his cup in one unbreathing swallow, stands up. 'Thank you for your help, Miss Jones. I appreciate it.'

'You're welcome,' she says. 'You reckon you can find out what's been going on?'

He thinks about fobbing her off, the way he did with Laidlaw, and then changes his mind. 'I'll try.'

She nods. 'Good.'

'Probably better not to mention it to anyone else,' he says. 'If you don't mind.'

'When you do the job I do in a village, you soon learn how to keep a secret.'

He smiles, but doesn't challenge her assertion. It hadn't been very hard to get her to talk, but perhaps that's because she doesn't see what she's told him as a secret.

Back in the lane, it's glimmering dusk. The sky is overcast, and though it isn't raining yet, the air is heavy with incipient fog. He wishes fervently for a better light on his bicycle, but if the lane is as quiet going home as it was coming, it shouldn't be a problem.

True to the promise he made himself on the way here, he stops at Hine's place. It must once have been a farmhouse, Nash supposes, with its thick white walls and neat cap of thatch that reaches low over the front door. He knocks, but there's no response. The house is silent, no sign of anyone being home. He knocks again, waits. Still no answer. In a way, he's relieved. He'll be able to get home in time for dinner. He's already got Aggie on the warpath with him at work, it'll be a bonus not to annoy his housekeeper as well.

As he rides on, he's thinking about what Hine said, and Laidlaw hinted. And what Auntie May – he can call her that in his head even if it's impossible face to face – most definitely told him. What it adds up to is something he's got no business to get involved with. A secret, and a suspicious death that's been written off as an accident, and a boy's name blackened.

In wartime, he should probably ignore the personal in favour of what he's led to believe is the greater good.

But he doesn't want to.

He's already had to do that about Jo, and he didn't want that either.

He's lost in his thoughts, doesn't hear the sound of a car coming up behind him at first. In this half-light he won't be easy to spot, so he pulls right into the side of the lane, gets off the bike to wait for the car to pass. The engine noise gets closer, a powerful sound that suggests it's a big car, and Nash registers the fact that instead of slowing, it seems to be revving faster. Instinctively, he steps further back onto the verge, pulling the bike in closer beside him. He's got time to think, *What does the bloody idiot think he's doing*, when a shining black shape whirrs down. He gets a fleeting glimpse of a pale face turned towards him before the car catches the back wheel of the bike, wrenching it out of his hands and knocking him off his feet. The car driver must realise he's hit something, but the vehicle speeds off.

Swearing, Nash struggles to get up. He's landed asprawl, half in and half out of a shallow ditch full of mud, while his head and shoulders are entangled in the hedge. His hat and glasses have fallen off, and thorns scratch viciously across his face as he pulls free. He stands, bruised and sore. Clambers out of the ditch onto the lane's surface, feeling the fierce twinge of a twisted ankle. It seems as if it's only been a matter of moments since the accident, but it's much darker already. He makes out the shape of the front lamp from his bike on the ground a yard away, no longer attached to the bike itself. He hobbles a step towards it, hears the crunch of glass underfoot. 'Damn.' The bulb? Whatever it was, the lamp, when he retrieves it, doesn't work.

By a combination of touch and what he can still see in the failing light, he finds his hat and part of the frame of his glasses, but the vital element – the curved plate of his mask prosthetic – is missing. Though he searches as best he can, he's afraid of putting his foot on it in the near-dark. The bike, when he retrieves it from the opposite side of the lane, is unrideable: he doesn't need light to tell the back wheel is buckled, with several spokes completely detached.

He stands, favouring his ankle, wondering what to do for the best. No point retracing his steps, he already knows Hine is not at home. It's not all that far to the Braishfield Road where there are pubs and houses, but without his glasses and mask, he's reluctant to show himself to strangers. He must be looking thoroughly disreputable. He's sure he heard his coat rip as he pulled free from the thorns, and he can feel wet mud seeping through the cloth of his trousers from hip to knee. He'll have to leg it, hope he doesn't meet anyone on the way.

He tries pushing the bike, but it's hopeless. He'll need to leave it somewhere out of sight till he can get someone to rescue it in daylight. A few yards further on, he sees a thicket of small trees on his right. He half pushes, half throws the bike into the heart of the undergrowth. If an enemy parachutist is around tonight, they're welcome to make whatever use they can of it.

At the fork in the lane, he takes the left-hand turning, reckoning it for the shorter way. He's wet and cold, but his ankle seems to have settled to a dull ache that's bearable enough to walk on, if he sets his foot down carefully. The road climbs a sharp little hill and he's perhaps a quarter of a mile from the main road when the sound of a car engine reaches him once more through the quiet of the evening. It's coming towards him this time, quite slowly, not racing along like the one that hit him. But instinct takes over, insists he should get right off the road. There's a break in the hedge and he slips through, finds himself on a building site, where a half-finished house stands in black silhouette against the sky. As he will too, if he stays where he is. Still following instinct, he crouches low behind the hedge, remembering how he'd missed seeing the nurse because he was looking too high at first. He watches as the car passes, but beyond seeing it's a black car, it's too dark now to make out any details of vehicle or driver. Feeling foolish as its rear lights disappear back down the hill, he gets up, sets off again.

As he hobbles along, he tries to reason with himself. Ridiculous to have felt apprehensive, to have hidden. Why on earth should he imagine the car – even supposing it were the same one – was looking for him? More fanciful still to think it might have meant him harm. He tells himself it was simply because he didn't want to be seen in his dishevelled state. But this isn't altogether honest. Right from the moment it happened, the idea that the car driver hit him deliberately has been lodged in his brain. Fanciful or not, it's enough to make him choose side roads and footpaths that take him away from the main route back to Romsey wherever he can. By the time he gets home, having added a good mile to the trip, he's thoroughly annoyed with himself for being so foolish.

He can hear Fan and her son, Billy, talking in the kitchen as he lets himself quietly into the house. Fan will be keeping his dinner hot, but he doesn't feel like eating, or the fuss that will follow if they see him like this. He slips upstairs to his study, pours himself a whisky. As the alcohol burns its way into his stomach, he starts to feel better. Saner.

Safer . . .

The word creeps into his consciousness, makes him angry all over again.

As he crosses to his bedroom, a voice calls from downstairs.

'Mr Nash, sir? Is that you? Didn't hear you come in.'

'Yes, it's me,' he says, thinking, *Who the hell else would it be?*

'Will you be down soon?' she calls. 'Your dinner's all ready. A nice bit of fish in white sauce.'

'Not for me, Fan, thank you. I don't want anything this evening.'

'Oh, but, sir . . .'

He pushes his door shut, just shy of a slam. He shouldn't take his irritation out on her, but he can't face Fan – or her cooking – tonight. All he wants is to take off his filthy clothes, have a wash, and perhaps another whisky. Put his feet up, and do some serious thinking. Tomorrow, he'll have to report what happened to the police, because it's not safe to have idiots like that go speeding along country lanes in the dark. But he won't say anything about thinking it was deliberate: Sergeant Tilling would suppose he'd gone nuts. With justification, because, right now, he almost believes it himself.

In the lane, a car pulls up, and the driver gets out. The bright, unshuttered beam of a torch passes across the scene of the accident. Picks out the scrape marks, the strip of cloth caught on the hedge. The light beam moves over a scatter of debris from the damaged bicycle. Picks out an alien shape, a delicate curve of painted metal. A grunt of surprise, or is it satisfaction?

A foot stamps. Lifts to stamp again.

Pauses. An idea, a bonus.

A hand reaches down, picks up the crumpled metal.

A nice touch. That'll show the interfering bastard.

6

Friday 8th January, morning

COMING TO THE END OF my first full week at Hursley, I'm starting to get the measure of the place. I can mostly find my way round, and I'm putting names and faces together, beginning to understand how the different areas intersect. All things I need to know if I'm going to find where the leak of information is coming from and stop it.

I'm not as convinced as McNaught and Jericho by the evidence against the boy who died. I can't see him being in any kind of position to steal the blueprints himself. It's true his job as an under-gardener on Lady Cooper's staff gave him access to the grounds, but he'd never have been allowed to get close to any of the Supermarine operational areas. The chain of guards protecting the restricted areas of the House would never have let someone like him inside, whatever the pretext.

The corner of the blueprint he'd had in his hand when he died is even more of an enigma. Only that one small fragment was found, and despite McNaught and Jericho's best efforts, no one's been able to suggest where it might have come from. No evidence of damaged drawings or missing copies, and the piece doesn't seem to be a match for anything that anyone would admit to knowing about. Not that they had much to go on: one curved line vanishing mysteriously off the edge of the paper, and lettering that might have said 'prop' or 'prog' before it was torn through.

In the dark hours of the night, I've wondered if it could have been a decoy, a puzzle set to test security, or another try-on like the missing bicycle. Except a boy died because of it, and that doesn't seem like any kind of a joke.

McNaught and Jericho's theory that David had been acting as a go-between seems the most likely thing. But that means the traitor's still at Hursley Park House. And it's vital they should be stopped before they can find a new way to get leaked information out to their network of spies.

So here I am, like some kind of mad dowser armed with nothing but a hazel twig, sent in to uncover the wellspring. Only I reckon dowsing would be quicker and more reliable than anything I'm supposed to be doing. It isn't like trying to find Ruth's killer, when there were obvious paths to investigate. All I can do now is watch and wait. It's just so bloody *passive*. My biggest worry is not that the betrayals are still going on, but that they're not. If David Hine's death has frightened the leaker into drying up, I'll be stuck here for the duration, caught in a totally pointless exercise and living off Hilda Anderson's horrible stews.

*

Though Nash managed to get in last evening without alerting his housekeeper to his accident, Fan makes up for it in the morning, when he comes down for breakfast. She's full of lamentations, tutting over the scratches on his face and hands.

'You put some iodine on those cuts right now,' she insists, 'or I'll do it for you. Dirty old ditch out in the country, who knows what you could get from that? There's tetanus in the soil and it's no good telling me those wounds didn't get muck in them because I've already seen the clothes you left in the laundry basket. They're wet through, all over mud. Don't know how I'll ever get it out.'

To keep the peace, and because he knows he was rude to her last evening, he dabs the places with iodine, though he washed them perfectly clean last night. But it's not the sting of the lotion that makes him wince, just the way it leaves a brown stain that only draws attention to the injuries. Fan's fierce scrutiny unsettles him too, and he's conscious that the mask attached to his standby glasses doesn't fit as seamlessly as his usual one.

He's relieved when she diverts her attention to the rips in his coat. All the time he's eating his breakfast toast and powdered scrambled egg, she laments the fact she won't be able to hide the repairs she'll have to make. He does his best to reassure her that he doesn't care, so long as she can do enough to ensure he doesn't look like a tramp, and gets up from the table as soon as he decently can.

The most urgent thing is to try and find his mask. It shouldn't be difficult to see where the accident happened in daylight. Not that he's prepared to waste half the day walking to and from the place, with his ankle still puffy and sore from last night's trek. But a call to Mercer's taxi brings him to the lay-by at the end of Dores Lane shortly after eight, as it gets full daylight.

'I'll only be a few minutes,' he says to the driver as he sets off to retrace his route. The old man nods, hunches down in his seat to wait.

He passes a farmhouse, surprised how close it is to the road. He hadn't noticed it in the dusk last evening, but when a little girl feeding hens in the farmyard calls out happily to him as he passes, he's glad he wasn't tempted to ask for help there, with his face uncovered. The child wouldn't have smiled at him then.

It's perhaps a hundred yards to the place where he ditched the bike. He hauls it back out of the thicket, dismayed to see the extent of the damage. To his untutored eye, it looks like a write-off. It won't fit in the taxi, so he props it where Wilf from the garage will be able to find it later. No need to worry about aiding the enemy, this bike's going nowhere until it's mended. Another fifty yards further on, and the site of his accident is clearly marked. A muddy scar where he fell in the ditch and several broken branches in the hedge show where it happened. There are pieces of broken metal and glass at the edge of the track, too. He stoops to examine the mess, hopeful his mask will be there, but there's no sign of it.

It takes him more than the few minutes he promised Mercer to work his way carefully up to the top of the bank, searching through the rough grass on either side. In the dense undergrowth of the hedge bottom, he finds a shred of fabric from his coat and another section of his glasses' frame, but nothing else. He stands, turns back towards the road, surveys the area. A discreet hoot of a car horn calls his attention to the waiting taxi and he scrambles back down into the lane. A final look around, but it's no good. He'll have to resign himself to the mask's loss. It will be the devil to replace. The unit that made it for him closed down years ago. He wonders, as he walks back to the taxi, what other disfigured men like him do when something happens to their prosthesis. And this war is making more damaged bodies and faces every day. What will happen to them? Perhaps it's all surgery now. Or maybe they're expected to give up, retreat from the world as too many of his cohort did.

But whatever happens, he promises himself, he won't do that.

Back in Romsey, reporting the incident to Sergeant Tilling brings the response he'd expected: outward sympathy and official concern, but offering not the faintest hope of tracking down a car Nash can't describe, let alone give a number plate of. And while Wilf has agreed to collect his bike, he's gloomy about the prospect of getting any of the necessary parts to repair it.

So when Aggie does a double-take at the sight of his face, he's shorter with her than he might be. 'Don't ask,' he says to her astonished stare. 'I'm fine.' But his ankle twinges as he walks upstairs, and he's conscious of half a dozen other places that protest as he moves.

At lunchtime, I'm thinking about the weekend ahead, and wondering what on earth I'll do with my time, when I'm called to go up to one of the offices on the second floor. A secretary with a very refined manner and a vaguely familiar voice hands me an envelope. It's been sealed with red wax, and has a Winchester address on it, with 'by hand' typed across the top left-hand corner, and 'urgent and confidential' in red above the address.

'This has to be delivered by three o'clock without fail,' the secretary says. 'You're to take it there personally and put it into the hands of the addressee yourself.'

A lot of replies spring to mind, including the obvious query about how I'll know it is the addressee when I get there, but I hold my counsel. I've already read the superscription, and it suits me very well to be going to the office in question, armed with a good reason to speak to the person it names.

'It's somewhat unusual,' she says, and I tag her voice now as the woman who'd called through the lavatory door yesterday, 'but Mr Brennan tells me you are the best fitted of his staff to carry out the task.' She hands me another couple of envelopes, equally well sealed, though without the 'urgent' tag. 'You can take these too, since you are going to Winchester, but deliver them after the other. That one is the most important.'

'Ah ... You realise I don't have transport of my own,' I say.

'It's been taken care of,' she says. 'There's a van going back to the city shortly, the driver has been asked to drop you off. You'll have to make your own way back, but there won't be any urgency about it. The post manager has given permission for you not to come back to the office afterwards, though he will expect you as usual tomorrow morning.'

I wonder why the driver couldn't drop the letter off and save me the trip, but she answers that before I can ask.

'It's the baker's van,' she says. 'I trust you've no objection?'

'No.' I think it's more than odd, but it won't do to say so.

'And you're clear, this envelope must not leave your hands until you give it to Mr Brown?'

'He's expecting it?'

'He is, yes. Now, do hurry. The van's waiting for you at the front security post.'

I run down to the post room, the envelopes in my hand, and grab my coat and bag. The post manager nods at me but says nothing as I call my goodbyes.

It starts to rain as Nash walks down the hill from the station towards his Winchester counterpart's office in Westgate Chambers. The coroner has agreed to see him this afternoon as a matter of professional etiquette, but the letter that was waiting for him at the office this morning made it plain the interview was being granted under sufferance. Brown may have an eminent reputation, but he's not known for harbouring doubts about his decisions. It's going to be tricky to get the man to open up about his findings with regard to David Hine's death.

Nash is almost at the Westgate when it begins to rain. It's been such a sodden wet winter, so dank and miserable it reminds him of his time in France. The sleety drizzle chills his face and soaks into his elderly raincoat, raising the smell of mothballs from the long-stored fabric. Not for the first time this morning, he curses the careless driver of last night's incident.

It's about time, Nash thinks, as he emerges from the arched footpath under the Westgate, that something positive should happen. Perhaps Brown will be helpful after all, and he'll discover there is a simple explanation for the state of David Hine's body. Or perhaps, he thinks, as the distinctive bow front of the solicitor's office comes into view, pigs might fly. He's anticipating the joy of getting in out of the rain when a woman comes out of the door, turns away down the High Street. Though he doesn't get even the briefest glimpse of her face, he's immediately convinced it's Jo. Something in the way she moves, the way she carries her head.

Instinct takes him hurrying past the office after her, despite the rain, the nuisance it will cause if he's late for his appointment with Brown. Ahead, the woman has picked up speed. She's almost running. Common sense says it's a natural enough reaction to the weather, but the same instinct that prompted him to follow her is insisting now that there is something wrong: that she's deliberately trying to get away from him.

He could call out to her, but he doesn't want to draw that kind of attention to them both. He quickens his own pace, ignoring his ankle's protest. Determined to catch her up, he's aware how irrational his behaviour must seem to a bystander, and worse, how threatening it might be from the woman's point of view, if it isn't Jo.

A blink, a moment's inattention as a young man with a large umbrella bumps into him, cutting off his view of her. With a grunt of apology, he sidesteps, but so does the man, and for a moment they dance a futile little jig on the pavement before Nash can get past. But there's no sign of the woman now. He's lost her, vanished into the murk.

'Damn.' He isn't aware he's said it out loud until an old lady passing by turns and startles at his piebald face, tuts disapproval.

Surely Jo can't have disappeared so thoroughly in a few seconds?

He walks on, more cautiously now. A narrow passageway opens to the right and he glances into its shadowy maw. Against all expectation, the woman he's followed has stopped only a few yards into the alley. But she's angled away from him, poised to run, one hand against the wall as if to steady herself.

He hesitates, moves forward a step, careful not to box her in. Now he's close, he's not as sure. 'Jo?' he says softly. 'It is you, isn't it?'

She turns fully towards him, hand at her throat. Her face is blank, the scarlet lipstick and hard pencilled brows so *not* like the Jo he knows that the words of an apology rush into his mind. He only just manages not to say them aloud.

It is her, yet it's not. There's something so different about her, he can't work it out straightaway. Then he realises. The strands of hair stuck to her wet cheeks where they have escaped her bedraggled felt hat are dead black, as harsh as her pencilled brows.

'Bram,' she says. 'Whatever have you done to yourself?'

He wants to ask her the same question, because of course, it *is* Jo. The moment she speaks, there's no room for doubt. Despite the hair and the harsh makeup that alters her face, makes her look ten years older, it couldn't be anyone else.

'Fell in a ditch,' he says. 'What about you?'

She pushes the dark strands off her cheek. 'Fell in a vat of hair dye. Hideous, isn't it?'

What can he say? *Yes, it's hideous?* Better not. *What the hell's going on?*

He settles for a politer version of the last, speaks at the same moment she does. He doesn't quite catch what she says, the words swallowed up in the echo of his own voice, but he thinks it might have been, *What are you doing here?*

'What am *I* doing here . . . ? God, Jo, I could ask you the same. And why on earth did you run away?'

'Oh, Bram,' she says. 'Couldn't you just bugger off? Pretend you haven't seen me?'

The tone of her voice is normal enough, but there's something anxious, almost hunted in the way she's looking at him, checking past him to the street beyond. It makes it impossible for him to leave her here, at the mercy of who knows what. He shakes his head. 'You know me better than that.'

A gust of wind whips a flurry of rain into the alleyway and he sees her shiver. 'Come on,' he says. 'Let's get in the dry, somewhere we can talk. What about the tea room in the High Street?'

'I'm not supposed to—' She breaks off, tries again. 'I can't afford . . .'

He doesn't think it's money she's talking about. 'To be seen with me?' he says, incredulous. 'Pick somewhere quiet, then. I'm not going to let you go until we've had a chance to talk.'

She hesitates a moment, then, 'Kingsgate,' she snaps. 'Under the archway behind the cathedral. It'll be dry there. Meet me in twenty minutes. Don't follow me.'

Another darting glance. Almost before he realises, she's gone, slipping away down the passage towards the further end, where the brighter shape of its exit gives out onto a backstreet.

Twenty minutes doesn't give him enough time to go back to Westgate Chambers and keep his appointment with Brown, but that's too bad. He'll deal with that problem when he has to. For now, he's focused on meeting her, finding out what's going on. He turns back into the High Street, makes his way towards the cathedral. But even as he's hurrying down the hill, he can't help wondering if she'll actually be there. The way his luck's running, she's probably used the lure of a rendezvous as a means to shake him off.

*

I'm swearing to myself as I walk away. Another bloody mess I've got myself into, and nothing to show for it but embarrassment. First, Mr Theophilus Brown, Winchester's snooty coroner, had made me wait for ten minutes before he condescended to come out of his office and collect the envelope. And when he did, he'd taken it from me with a look that suggested I might have compromised or contaminated it simply by bringing it. He'd examined the seals minutely, nodded dismissively. Not even a thank you.

Like a fool, I'd hoped I might be able to pump him, or one of his staff, for information about David Hine but he hadn't given me a chance. He'd stood watching, disapproval in every line of his face, until I was out of the office door. But whose curiosity he'd wanted to thwart, I couldn't tell. He could hardly have known what I wanted to ask. Perhaps his vigilance was just to make sure his office staff couldn't quiz me about the delivery I'd made.

And then to run straight into Nash . . .

It'd been instinctive – but stupid – to try and get away from him. I knew he must have seen me, knew as soon as I bolted he'd be bound to follow.

It felt as if I'd conjured him up by thinking about him. I'd been wishing he'd been the coroner in charge of Hine's case instead of Theophilus E. and smarting from the way the Winchester man had acted. Thinking Nash would never have been so rude. And then there he was, large as life and . . .

For a moment I'd been so glad to see him. Until I remembered McNaught and Jericho telling me not to contact him.

Hinting that if I ignored what they said, there'd be consequences: that he'd be the one to suffer for any failure on my part.

I *should* stand him up. Once I've found my way through the warren of backstreets and delivered the other two envelopes, I should catch the bus straight back to the Andersons' place, but the idea doesn't appeal. For one thing, I don't have a key, and my hosts won't be home till after six. I could stop off at Hursley, pretend I hadn't remembered I didn't have to go back to work. But I won't do that either. I can't leave Bram waiting at Kingsgate, thinking I've tricked him.

Despite the way it was between us before I caught the flu, I want . . . I *need* to see him. I need to know what he thinks about the way I left, whether he blames me for leaving him in the lurch. And I'm curious to find out what he's doing here in Winchester. It occurs to me that if the coroner wouldn't talk to me about the boy's death, he might to a colleague. Do I dare ask him to find out?

The rain's coming down in stair rods now, and there's hardly anyone out on the streets. I'm sure no one's interested enough to follow me in this. I keep my eyes open just the same, sneaking looks behind me, or trying to pick up reflections in windows as I pass. A couple of times I catch a glimpse of someone, but it's never the same person twice, and I'm feeling safe enough to make my way towards Kingsgate. I can still cut back to the High Street and bus station if I pick up a follower. A glance at my watch shows the twenty minutes are almost up. My deliveries have brought me further from the centre than I thought, and I start to worry Nash won't wait, even if he bothers to come at all.

The triple archway of Kingsgate is empty when I arrive. The streets around are as deserted as if the air-raid siren's sounded, and everyone's disappeared into a shelter, though I know it isn't that. It's the rain.

I stand, wondering what to do. Trying to get my breath. Trying not to feel disappointed. He *hasn't* come.

I'm walking away when I hear my name called.

'Jo. In here.'

'Here' is the porch of St Swithun's Church, where a wooden stairway leads up to the strange little chapel built over Kingsgate itself.

I slip inside, trying not to look shifty.

'Come on,' Nash says. 'It'll be warmer upstairs. I've had a scout round and there's no one up there. And the way the stairs creak, we'll have plenty of warning if anyone decides to come in. You can pretend you're doing the flowers.'

'Flowers? In January?' I shake my head as I follow him up the stairs. But he's right, the creaking treads mean no one could creep up on us unawares. 'And what'll you do?'

'Pretend I'm an eccentric tourist, of course. A collector of unusual churches.'

That seems more believable than the flower story, at any rate. It certainly feels odd, to be going upstairs into a church, passing the bellrope on the way, coming into a surprisingly spacious room at the top. It smells of candle grease and old wood, but though the light is dim through the rain-washed windows, there's a feeling of warmth and welcome.

Bram takes off his hat, slaps it against his thigh to shake off the worst of the wet. I wish I could do the same, but ladies who come to church to do the flowers don't take off their hats. Even when there aren't any flowers to do. And besides, I don't want him to see the full horror of my hair.

He gestures to the nearest pew. 'Shall we sit?'

I edge my way in, take a seat. Look ahead, not at him, though I feel the give of the long wooden bench as he lowers himself down, decently distanced, at the other end of the pew. It feels wrong to be thinking about death and secrets in this sacred space. But a sense of calm seems to seep down from the boat-arch beams of the roof, comforting despite my soaked clothes, the awkwardness of the situation.

'Tell me,' Nash says, 'what brings you to Winchester? And why are we hiding in a church, soaking wet, when we could be having a cup of tea in the Cosy Café?' There's a resigned kind of humour in his voice, and something deeper, too. Not anxiety, exactly, though I can't think of another word for it.

'I'm supposed to stay away from you. From everyone in Romsey. Everyone I know.' I gesture at my face, the grim makeup. 'You're not meant to recognise me.'

'It'd take more than black hair and a bit of red lipstick.'

'So I've discovered,' I say bitterly. 'McNaught and Jericho will be disappointed.'

'Ah, the gentlemen who were adamant you'd volunteered to join them. Should you have told me their names?'

Startled, I turn to face him. I can't tell what he's thinking. '*Volunteered* to join them? Is that what they told you? I wouldn't rely on them for the truth, not even about their names. I don't suppose they're any more real than the one they've saddled me with.'

'I see.' He raises his eyebrow. 'So, am I allowed to know who I have the pleasure of catching pneumonia with?'

'Joy Rennard,' I say through gritted teeth.

He laughs. 'What bright spark thought of that? You'd only have to speak French to guess, Josy *Fox*.'

'It was nothing to do with me. A *fait accompli*.'

'It's a comedy, then, Jo? The way you ran away, I thought it was something serious.'

'It *is* serious,' I say. There are things I can't tell him, my signature's on forms that mean I'll never be able to tell him. But I have to find out about David Hine, and Bram's my best hope for that now. 'A boy died. That's why they wanted me to . . . I'm supposed to investigate . . .' I pause, hard up against the no-go area. 'They found me a job, a public face. So I can . . . snoop around without anyone knowing what else I'm doing there.'

Bram grins. 'You're working undercover?'

'It's not funny.'

'No.' He sobers. 'It isn't. When I caught up with you just now, you looked frightened, Jo.'

'Not frightened, exactly.' Though I suppose I am. What can I tell him? 'Trying not to be obvious.'

'I suppose that explains it. The name, the hair. And the allergy to your old friends.'

Friends, I think. Oh, God, much more . . . But under everything else, he *is* a friend, and though I'm not sure right now who I can trust at Hursley or the Hutments, I know I can trust him.

'It's complicated. Because where I'm working . . . it's . . .'

'Undercover,' he repeats, no hint of amusement this time. 'I get the message.'

There's a rustle of noise from outside, and I freeze. 'What's that?'

Nash listens a moment. The rustle comes again. 'Wait.'

He stands up, goes to the door. Opens it a fraction and peers out. Then opens it wider, claps his hands. An answering rattle of wings. 'Pigeons,' he says. 'Like us. Taking refuge from the rain.' He comes and sits down again. 'You're all on edge, Jo. And this isn't the place to talk.'

'I know. But it's all there is right now.'

'Best make it quick then. This time.'

I blink at the inference, but somewhere inside I feel comforted. 'The job . . . I came into Winchester this afternoon because they wanted me to hand-deliver some urgent outside mail.'

'To Mr Brown?'

'I can't say.' I shake my head, miserably.

He frowns. 'This is going to be awkward.'

I make up my mind. 'But I can say I was hoping to talk to someone there about the boy who died. There was an inquest and . . . I thought your colleague might be able to help.'

'And he couldn't?'

'Never got a chance to ask.'

'And your pseudonymous friends won't help?'

I look away. 'Strictly speaking, it's not what they're interested in. I'm supposed to take it on trust that he drowned by accident. When he was drunk.'

The long silence that follows is broken only by the steady drip of water from the hem of my coat onto the polished oak floor. I don't know what I've said, but something has clearly unsettled him.

'I know you can't tell me, but if I were to guess—' Nash frowns, as if he's having as much trouble picking his words as I am. 'Might it be David Hine's death you wanted to ask Brown about? Because if so, you may be interested to know that's why I'm here too.'

'Really?' A spark of hope leaps in my chest.

'Mmm.'

Our eyes meet, and for the first time in ages, much longer than I've been exiled in Hursley, I don't feel alone. The old connection is there. A sense of understanding, of being understood.

He sighs, looks away, breaking the link between us. 'And now, you see, I think I can guess why they recruited you. Was it something to do with a certain scrap of paper? I don't like it, Jo.'

Nor do I, but . . .

'How do you know about that?' I've started to shiver, and the words jitter through my teeth before I can smooth them out.

He shrugs. 'It's a long story, and now's not the time for it.' He gestures at my dripping clothes. 'I was serious about the pneumonia. Especially when you've only just got over the flu.'

'I'm all right.'

'You're not,' he says decisively. 'If you don't want to be seen in the café with me, that's fair enough. But go on your own and get yourself warm and dry. I'll make myself scarce. As long as you don't trek all the way back to Hursley like that.'

'I didn't say . . .'

'You didn't have to.'

I want to tell him everything. I want to run away before my traitor mouth can speak another word. But in the end, the idea of getting warm and dry wins out, and I resort to commonplaces. 'What about you? What will you do?'

'Never mind about me. I've got things to do. People to see.' He smiles, wolfish, almost a little smug. 'Your unhelpful Mr Brown, for one, if he'll still see me. I should have been with him an hour ago.' He gets up from the pew, moves into the centre aisle. 'I'll let you go first,' he says. 'Give you a couple of minutes to get clear.'

'Thanks.' Feeling relieved and foolish, I scoot out of my seat and move to go past him.

'We need to talk properly, Jo. Seems we have interests in common.'

'All right.' I go to step away, but he reaches out to detain me, takes hold of my wrist. The heat of his hand is surprising against my skin.

'Not so fast,' he says. 'You're not going to disappear until I know how I can get in touch with you.'

My mind races through the options. A letter addressed to me at the Hutments or Hursley Park House would be bound to raise suspicion. And there's nowhere I can take a telephone call in confidence. 'You'll have to let me call you,' I say.

'Make sure you do.' He lets go of my wrist. 'And make it soon, because otherwise I'll come looking. And I'm fairly sure I know where you've gone to earth, Miss Rennard.'

7

Friday, later

BACK AT WESTGATE CHAMBERS, NASH is pleasantly surprised to discover that Mr Brown will still see him, despite the earlier missed appointment. A motherly secretary relieves him of his wet coat and hat and brings a pot of coffee to an office that feels almost tropical after the chill outside. He's intrigued to note an envelope like the one Jo told him about folded into the waste-paper basket by Brown's desk, red wax seals broken. What he'd give for a few moments alone with that. But there's no chance. However benign Brown seems, he's got nothing to add to what Nash already knows about David Hine's death. His opinion is fixed.

'The pathologist found nothing out of the ordinary,' he says. 'He stated that the boy was obviously drunk. The smell of alcohol was noticeable when the stomach was opened and, in his opinion, he thought Hine had imbibed the equivalent of three double whiskies.'

'His father told me David didn't drink,' Nash puts in.

'Which has no adverse bearing on my conclusion,' Brown says, not a bit deterred. 'On the contrary, it gives weight to his state of inebriation. No doubt his unfamiliarity with strong drink reduced his capacity to tolerate alcohol on that occasion. A perfect rationale to explain why he was incapable of saving himself when he tripped into the water.'

'I was told he was badly bruised.'

Brown raises his eyebrows. 'Really? I wonder who might have told you that?'

But two can play at Brown's refusal to discuss any new information, and Nash says nothing.

'The location where the boy was found,' Brown continues after an expectant pause, 'was in a lower part of the garden, reached by a number of steps. In my opinion, Hine's perimortem injuries are consistent with a precipitate fall down those steps, and subsequent stumble against the raised edge of the pond as he overbalanced into the water.'

'I suppose it could have happened like that.'

'Take my word for it, Nash, you don't want to listen to his father's ravings about murder. In my opinion, the man is most definitely a habitual drunk, however abstemious his son might have been in the normal run of things. Now, if you'll forgive me . . .'

His coat is at least dryish when he finds himself out on the street, and it's stopped raining, so that's a plus. Though his interview with Brown hasn't been any more productive than he feared, something in the way his colleague refused to admit any contradiction in the evidence about David

Hine's death makes him think Brown isn't being straight with him.

And with Jo involved too in this business, he's determined to carry on with his investigation. He thinks he can guess where she's working, though he won't ask. He has to respect her need not to tell him, though it worries him to think what McNaught and Jericho have got her mixed up in. But, for now, it's enough to know that they're on converging paths about the boy's death. He'll have to try and look out for her as best he can. The main difficulty is how they're going to meet, to talk, to share their information. Because if she can't come to Romsey, and he can't go to Hursley, where the hell *can* they meet that's safe, and discreet and, above all this miserable winter, out of the rain?

In the Cosy Café I've finally warmed up and dried out. I've worked my way through a whole pot of tea, watered down so many times it's almost water itself; and filled up on a not-half-bad version of Woolton pie. Too much swede and a heavy hand with the Marmite, but some surprising nuggets of parsnip among the cauliflower and carrots almost make up for it. To finish, there'd been stewed prunes and custard. If none of it had been as good as Dot's cooking, it was certainly a whole lot nicer than anything I've had at the Andersons'.

All through the meal, I've been thinking about Bram. Worrying away at the problem about how to meet him again without it getting back to McNaught and Jericho's mob.

I wouldn't put it past him to do what he said and come looking for me at Hursley.

I suppose I shouldn't have told him my new name. But the whole complicated push-me pull-you mess of feelings when I saw him made it seem important he should know who I am. That I trust him.

More than that . . . Seeing him after an absence has sharpened what I feel. The heat's still there for me, inconvenient as that may be. And as little welcome to him, no doubt. But I'm not ashamed, though I probably should be. Lusting after him in a church . . . In the steamy little café, I feel a surge of blood to my face, hope no one's noticed.

'Meal all right?'

I come back to the present to find the waitress beside the table. Apart from the two of us, the café is empty. I glance at my watch, surprised to find it's almost five o'clock.

'Oh, yes. Fine, thank you.' I stand up, shrug back into my coat. 'How much do I owe you?'

'That'll be one and sixpence.' She casts a glance towards the kitchen, where, by the sound of it, someone's washing up. 'What did you make of the custard?'

'The custard?' I hand her two shillings. 'I thought it was good. Nice and creamy.'

'Only' – she glances at the kitchen again – 'we've had complaints, see. People saying they could taste it.'

I raise my eyebrows. 'Taste what?'

'Goats' milk,' she says. 'Fair turns my stomach.'

'Goats?' I can't keep the smile out of my voice. 'Really?'

But she must mistake my tone. She shudders, lowers her voice to a whisper. 'The missus has a cousin up Oliver's Battery that keeps goats. He's got a little cart for the goats to pull, deliver the milk. I hate it when they come here, beastly things with their yellow devil eyes. And the smell . . .'

I sling my bag over my shoulder. 'I like goats,' I say mildly. 'And, I promise, I didn't notice anything wrong with the custard.'

'Good of you to say, miss.' She rummages in her apron pocket for change, hands me sixpence.

I hand it back. 'Thank you.'

'Thank *you*, miss,' she says.

It starts to rain again as I leave the café. But I don't take much notice. My mind's elsewhere. Remembering other rainy days, and goats.

It's raining, it's pouring, the old man's snoring . . .

I hate wet days, stuck in the cottage, nine of us if Grandfather's home. We kids get on his nerves, me especially. Better if we can find somewhere else to go. So when Mike sneaks off to find the gang, I tag along behind.

We can't play at Jem's today. His dad's a policeman, he was on duty last night. He'll be sleeping and we'd have to creep round like little mice.

Can't go to Billy's. His house is even smaller than ours.

Bert's? We can get lost on the farm, there are outhouses and barns everywhere and no one to bother us. It's my favourite place, I'd vote to go there every time if it wasn't for

Bert being so mean. But today it's all right and he says yes, even to me.

We start by playing hide-and-seek in the stacks of straw bales in the barn. 'Fluffy's had kittens,' Bert says. 'Give you a penny if you can find them.' But if he knows where they are, he'll tell his dad. And then Bert's dad will drown them in a bucket, give Bert thruppence.

When it's my turn to hide, I burrow deep between the stacks. I'm littlest, I can get furthest in. Straw goes down my neck, scratches my legs. One false move and I'll be squashed like a beetle. Fluffy's there in her nest, purring over three blind kittens. I wouldn't tell on her for a thousand quid. Bert pinches me hard as I come crawling out, but he won't make me cry. He'll never find her, he's too fat to get where I've been.

Then it's off to see the animals. Feeding the chickens, scrumping flaked maize from the feed store. 'It'll swell up inside till you burst,' Bert jeers, after we've all eaten a handful.

Cows with their gentle eyes and sandpaper-rough tongues lick my hands for salt. Pigs, noses deep in swill, whiffle for lumps of potato, soft-grunting to each other like they're talking.

'Dare you to pat old Billy Goat Gruff,' Bert says. 'He ripped a man's belly open once with his horns.'

By the time the boys have all had a go, jostling and yelling, egging each other on, the old Billy is seething. Only Abe's managed to touch the beast.

'Your turn, Josy Fox,' Bert sneers. 'Hope you're not frit.'

'Shut your trap,' I say. 'Shut your traps, all of you. I'll do it.'

And I do, creeping up quiet and slow, dredging a few pieces of the stolen flaked maize from my pocket. 'It's all right,' I tell the goat softly. 'I'm not gonna make fun of you.'

He eyes me, the strange rectangular pupils looking sideways for the threat. I hold my hand out flat, the way Mike showed me for horses, feel the velvet lips pick the maize carefully off my palm. With my other hand, I rub the bony crest between his horns, stroke down his nose. He rears up, butting his head against my hand.

'That's cheating,' Bert shouts. 'I never said you could feed him.'

But I don't care. For a moment, it feels like magic, the beast and I playing our own game, and neither of us losing.

The rail journey from Winchester to Romsey is tedious, forcing a change at Eastleigh. While he's waiting for the connection, a swirl of sooty smoke makes Nash sneeze. As he fumbles in his raincoat pockets for a handkerchief, he damns the weather, Jo's intransigence, and the lack of a direct route between towns that are less than ten miles apart. He finds what he's looking for in his right-hand pocket, brings out the square of linen to wipe his nose. But even as he's doing it, his left hand discovers something alien tucked in the bottom of the other pocket. A small, hard shape that feels as if it's wrapped in paper.

His first thought is that it must be something left over from the last time he wore the coat – years ago, probably. He fetches it out, wondering what it can be. It's a flat packet, less than the size of his palm, wrapped in what appears to be a blank sheet of good quality writing paper. Puzzled, he finds himself making deductions even as he begins to unwrap it. The paper feels fresh and crisp, looks clean. It can't have been in his pocket all that long.

One more fold, and he's staring down at what remains of the mask he lost last night. Half an eye – half *his* eye – stares back at him.

His brain, his thought processes, come to a juddering halt. He can't believe what he's seeing, what he's holding. How can it be . . . ?

The delicate copper substrate has been folded sharply in two, the contours flattened. The paint has cracked and flaked from the upper surface. Half persuaded it must be a delusion, he turns it over in his hand. But it's real, and all he can think for a moment is that the damage is deliberate, not something that happened in the accident last night.

Someone touches him on the shoulder, and he closes his hand protectively over the mask and its wrapping. Turns. It's a woman, a railway porter, and he sees that the train he's been waiting for is standing at the platform. 'If you want this train, sir, it's about to leave.'

Like an automaton, he thanks the woman, pushes his left hand and what it holds back into his pocket. The third-class compartment is crowded, and he elects to stand as the train rattles on its way. He must be suffering from some kind of shock, because every thought seems to take an age. Only the physical reality of the mask, the shape of it, sharp-edged under his fingers, tells him he's not imagining things.

This morning, he looked for it in the lane, but it wasn't there. Not lost, as he thought, but taken.

By whom?

There's only one logical answer to that. The driver. Who else knew what had happened but he and the person in the car? Who else could even have known where to look?

They must have gone back, searching for something. For him?

Finding the mask. He runs his finger over the sharp folded edge. Breaking it. But why?

Why?

Never mind why, who? Who could have put it in his pocket? Who's he seen today, been in contact with?

He goes through them all in his head. Every man Jack of them, no matter how unlikely.

Fan? No. Apart from anything else, he's as sure as he can be there was nothing in his pockets but his handkerchief and gloves when he set out from home this morning.

Old Mercer, Wilf? He's seen them both this morning, and they both have access to cars, the possibility of obtaining fuel. But he can't believe either of them was out in Dores Lane last evening, amusing themselves by knocking him off his bike.

Someone in the office, Aggie, or the caretaker, Fred? Though they might easily have handled his coat, neither of them could have been driving that car.

On the train to Winchester, he'd had a seat to himself. And once he got to the city . . . Jo.

No. Not her. That's one thing he is sure of.

Brown and his secretary?

Maybe. But *why* . . . ?

8

Saturday 9th January, morning

GOOD NEWS IN THE MORNING. Mr Anderson's mechanic friend, Reg, knocks on the door as I'm about to leave for the bus. A grizzled little man with oily black hands, he nevertheless turns out to be the most welcome of visitors. He's brought the Cyc-Auto back and it's fixed. When I try it, I find it's better than fixed: it's transformed. The engine runs smoothly and even the balance seems better. Not only that, he's got hold of some fuel from the transport depot at Hursley Park, filled up the tank. I'm so pleased I could hug him.

'How much do I owe you?' I ask, hoping I'll have enough ready cash to meet the bill.

'You keep your money, m'dear,' he says. 'Happy to help.'

'That doesn't seem right. You must have spent a lot of time on it.'

'My little hobby,' he says, winking at me. 'Nothing I like better than tinkering with an engine.'

'Well, perhaps I can buy you a drink one day?'

'I never say no to a pint of bitter,' he says. 'You can find me in the Dolphin most evenings after work.'

'It's a date.'

When I go inside to let the Andersons know what's happened, my pleasure in the morning is somewhat dampened by Hilda's snide remark that tonight I'll have no excuse for not getting back in time for supper. I bite my tongue not to say something I'll regret, and leave straightaway. I'll be even earlier this morning, but better that than alienating my landlady completely.

The irritation soon fades as the bike whips me down the lane towards Hursley. It may not have all that much power, but the route is mostly downhill. By the time I get to the village, I'm grinning like an idiot, even though every bit of exposed skin is tingling with the cold. It's wonderful to have freedom of movement again.

There's hardly anyone around when I reach the village centre. I'm thinking it will be good to get into the post room early and make a start on the backlog of deliveries that are sure to be waiting for me, when I hear a clanking sound, see a glimmer of light moving about on the far side of the road. Curious, I pull up directly opposite the place where the back lane goes up towards Winchester.

I make out the shape of a man walking alongside a low cart pulled by two pale-coloured animals smaller even than Shetland ponies. If I'm not mistaken, this must be the goats' milk man on his rounds. Delighted, I prop the bike and cross the road.

'Now then,' the man greets me. His accent has a country twang to it, but it's not local.

'Good morning,' I say. 'What lovely goats.' And they are. A matching pair of little white darlings with silky fur and the amber, slit-pupilled eyes the waitress called devilish.

'Ah,' he says.

'Is it all right if I stroke them?'

'Ah.' A man of few words.

I rub my hands down their noses, feel the way they butt instinctively at my palms, exactly as I remember from childhood. I laugh, press back.

'Doesta know goats then?'

'When I was a child, I used to play on a farm where there were goats. It was a dare to go and stroke the billy.'

He nods.

'Someone said you had a farm at Oliver's Battery. Do you keep a lot of goats?'

'Ah.'

'Would you mind if I came to see them?'

He shrugs. 'Nay, lass. Come if tha like.'

Encouraged to get more than a one-word reply, I ask him where he lives.

He jerks his head to the lane behind. 'Mile'n a bit back along. Ask for Sam. Anyone'll tell thee.'

I give the goats a final rub. 'I'd better let you get on.'

'Ah. Work t' do.'

He clucks a giddy-up to the goats and they move along the village street. I have to wait to cross as the first of the fleet of buses bringing staff to Hursley Park House careers down the road. But I'm smiling. I've got a perfect excuse to do what I was going to do anyway. All I'd need to make it perfect would be a pocket full of flaked maize.

Nash drops in at the garage on his way back from the office. He catches Wilf at his lunch, a gory-looking sandwich in his hand.

'Tomato sauce,' he says in answer to Nash's look of enquiry. 'Makes the cheese ration go further.'

Nash is flummoxed. 'Really?'

'Excepting I haven't got any cheese.' Wilf grins as if he's told a great joke, balances what's left of the sandwich on the edge of the grimy bench beside him. 'Gotta make do with what you've got.'

'And what have I got?' Nash asks. 'Anything like a working bike?'

Wilf shakes his head. 'To be honest, Mr Nash, I don't think it's worth repairing. Apart from the damage to the wheel the frame's been knocked right out of true. Even with the best I can do, I reckon it'd be like riding a crab.'

'Damn,' Nash says. 'Not your fault, of course, but I was hoping—'

Wilf grimaces, takes a fidgeting look at the clock on the back wall of the garage. 'I could try, but I can't promise anything. And it'd be a while. I've got a lot on at the mo.'

'Oh, don't waste your time on it. As you say, it's probably not worth it.'

'You sure?'

Nash nods, sighs. 'Yes. What do I owe you for your time picking up the bike yesterday?'

'Well, I was thinking, what do you want to do with the bits? I could use them for spares if you don't want 'em. We could call it quits.'

'Fair enough,' Nash says. 'Let's do that.'

'Thanks.'

He looks so pleased Nash wonders for a moment if he's got an ulterior motive. Perhaps the bike's not as bad as Wilf says, and he'll get it back on the road again some day. But he can't worry about some day. He needs a bike now.

It's a chilly morning, and by eleven, when I drop the last items of post off at the Drawing Office, I'm cold and hungry. The problems with Hilda yesterday and this morning mean I haven't eaten since my meal at the Cosy Café. Though I'd usually go to the canteen in the basement of the main building, the hut that houses the one for the Drawing Office is temptingly close.

Inside, the warmth and scent of food envelops me, makes me feel almost light-headed. Three long tables take up the middle of the space, while rows of smaller tables for four are arranged down each side of the hut. At this between-meals time of day, only a few of the smaller tables are occupied, people chatting over a hot drink, or reading a newspaper. I thread my way to the counter, more interested in what there might be to eat than who is around when I notice Hilda

Anderson is sitting at one of the tables. She hasn't seen me yet, and I almost decide to leave before she does. Then I see who she's with and change my mind. It's the girl from the bus stop. To confirm it, the coat with the fur collar is draped over the back of her chair.

At the counter, a woman in a floral overall greets me. 'What can I get you?'

'Whatever you've got,' I say. 'I missed breakfast this morning.'

She tuts. 'You've missed it here, too, love. And I'm sorry, but we don't start lunches till twelve.'

My heart sinks and I hope she won't hear the way my stomach is growling. 'A hot drink then? I'm not Drawing Office staff. I'm not sure I'm allowed to be here at all.'

'Don't want to worry about that,' she says. 'Might be different at lunchtime when we're packed out. But you're hardly going to take someone's place right now. What about some cocoa?'

'That would be lovely.'

'Got a fair old job with the post, haven't you?' she says as she's making my drink. 'Enough to make anyone hungry.' She glances over her shoulder. 'I could maybe find you a bit of bread and dripping if you like?'

'Oh, I'd like.'

She pushes the mug of cocoa across to me. 'You go and sit down, love. Take the weight off. I'll bring it over in a tick.'

The chocolate smell is heady, and I can't resist a scalding sip as I cross to the table where Hilda and the girl sit. Now, seeing her for the first time in the light, I see how pretty she is. Elfin features and bright blonde hair that looks natural rather than coming from a bottle give her a film star glamour. The women look up as I approach and I smile as if I'm sure of a welcome, though, by the expressions on their faces, that's the last emotion either of them feels at seeing me.

'You won't mind if I join you?' I say, as if I haven't noticed their hostility. I put my mug down, pull a chair to the end of the table so Hilda's on one side of me, and the girl on the other. 'I haven't been in this canteen before.'

'Huh.' Hilda glares at me. 'It's for Drawing Office staff.'

'I know. But the woman behind the counter said it was all right.' I smile at the girl, though it doesn't feel genuine even to me. 'We met the other day on the bus,' I say. 'I didn't catch your name.'

'This is my goddaughter, Anita,' Hilda says before the girl can speak. 'We work together.'

'Tracers?' I say, mock innocent. I know there's only one woman in the Drawing Office itself.

Hilda shakes her head. 'None of your business. Come on, Anita.'

They get up from the table, and the girl shrugs back into her coat.

'Nice to meet you,' I say to her.

Anita flinches, casts a quick glance around without ever meeting my eye. 'Yes.' It's the baby voice I remember. 'Bye.'

'Bye. See you later, Hilda.'

From where I'm sitting, I can't see out of the window, but I shuffle round into the seat the girl vacated and watch as they walk away from the canteen. They don't go towards the Drawing Office or the associated huts but turn onto the south path that leads to Hursley Park House itself and beyond.

I'm pretty sure Hilda isn't employed anywhere in the House, because I've been into all of those offices several times this week. And I've searched there for the girl too, without success. They could be heading for the old stables, a warren of departments I haven't fully sorted out in my head, though the easiest way to get there from this end of the site is to cut round the back of the House.

Which leaves the Experimental Hangar, way down by the south entrance. Of all the secret parts of the establishment, it must be the most secret. It's where the developmental work goes on, the modifications and refinements that keep our aircraft flying and fighting better than the Luftwaffe's. Perhaps that's why Hilda's taciturn, and the girl seems frightened to death about revealing something.

I can't help wondering what's brought them up to the main site. The hangar's got a canteen too, so they're certainly not taking the nearest option for their tea break.

'Here you are.' The woman from behind the counter puts a plate down in front of me, breaking my train of thought. But it's more than worth it when I see what she's brought. The plate's heaped with slices of what looks astonishingly like fried bread, crisp and golden from the pan. I can't remember a time when there was fat enough left over to have fried bread. The savoury scent is almost overwhelming, and I feel my mouth water.

'That's wonderful,' I manage to say without dribbling.

'There's only a bit of salt to go with it,' she says. 'But it's not bad if you eat it while it's nice and hot.'

I don't think of anything else, except doing that, until there are only crumbs left on the plate. Replete and warm again, I'm ready to go back to work. But, as I stack my mug and plate and take them back to the counter, I can't help but think how useless I am as a spy, when all it takes to distract me from my investigations is a plate of fried bread.

First stop when Nash gets into town is the cycle shop. But his best intentions are thwarted, because it's closed. A note on the door says, 'Closed due to staff illness. Reopening Tuesday 12th at noon'.

Another setback. He's good and tired of those, of feeling helpless, a target of circumstances. And of more than circumstances, if his ruined bicycle and mask are anything to go by.

He stands, pretending to be casual, surveying Market Place. He doesn't feel as if he's being watched, but then, how would he know? The clichéd sixth sense that's supposed to warn someone when they're being observed? He doesn't have it – or at least, he doesn't have it now.

'Afternoon, Mr Nash. You're a bit early for duty, aren't you?'

The voice makes him jump. He looks round to see Pete beside him. So much for his efforts at surveillance. He glances at his watch, surprised to see the time. He'd almost forgotten he has an ARP shift this afternoon, and the entrance to the warden's post is just across the road.

'I was after a bike, actually. But the shop's closed.'

'Ain't you still got that nice Claud Butler?'

'Sadly not. Had a bit of an accident after blackout the other evening.' He glances at his watch again. 'I suppose I might as well go in,' he says. 'What about you, Pete? It's a long time since we've seen you at ARP dispatch.'

'Bit of a loose end, see. I'm off tomorrow, and me mum's fussing fit to bust. Thought I'd come and say cheerio to old Jim and Miss Margaret.'

'Good idea.' They cross the road together. 'We might even find you a farewell cup of tea and a biscuit.'

Pete grins, props his bicycle against the wall by the door to the ARP post. 'Wouldn't say no.'

The bike must be twenty years old and its paintwork is shabby, rust showing through in patches. But it's demonstrably in working order, and the tyres look almost new.

'What are you going to do with your bike when you go off to sea?'

'Got a mate wants to buy it off me. Couple of fellas, actually. Haven't made up me mind yet who gets it.'

'Best offer?' Nash says.

'Reckon so.'

'What if I were to double it?'

'Double?' The boy looks startled. 'You don't want an old rattletrap like this, surely?'

'I need a bike, Pete. As soon as possible. And I'm not fussy as long as it gets me where I want to go.'

Pete shrugs. 'It's your funeral. Best offer I had was fifteen bob.'

'I'll stand by what I said. I'll give you thirty.' It's probably unfair to outbid Pete's friends like this, but Pete seems more than happy.

'It's a deal.' They shake hands on it. 'D'you want it now?'

'That'll leave you with a long walk home.'

'Nah. I'll catch the bus.'

'It would be a great help, if you're sure?'

'Aye aye, sir,' Pete says. Grins. Gives a mock salute. 'Just practising.'

Inside the ARP post, the other wardens greet the boy like the long-lost friend he is. Margaret's soon bustling around making tea, fetching out the best biscuits for the boy. Nash smiles to himself, remembering Pete's complaint about his mother's attentions. He doesn't seem to mind a fuss here.

When Nash has taken handover from Jim Fox, Pete's ready to leave. He pays the boy his money, wishes him well. There's nothing much happening, Jim says, so if Nash doesn't mind, he'll push off early. Plenty to do in the wireless trade.

Nash agrees, writes in the log heading for the start of shift. Not that there's anything else to report. Jim was quite right. There is absolutely nothing to do until it's time for the evening rounds. He has a book stashed in his desk for moments like these, and Stan and Vic Wild, the other wardens, are always ready for a game of cards, but he wants something active, not more sitting around. If he'd been at home, he could have gone to his workshop. He's started the fiddly job of trying to repair his damaged mask already. The copper's much trickier to work with than the silver he's used to. It needs annealing after every few hammer strokes, but he's determined. Mending it, getting it back to wearable, feels like the best way of defeating the malice that damaged it.

He frets at the inaction but he can't pace in here, Vic and Stan will think he's gone mad. He goes outside, examines the bike he's bought. Perhaps he *is* mad, now he looks at it properly. He has to hope that when he gets the dirt off, it won't turn out to be too much worse than he originally thought.

Inside the warden's post, he hears the telephone ring. Sod's Law, of course. Soon as he turns his back . . . He hurries in. Stan's already answered the call, but he beckons Nash over, scribbles something on the pad of scrap paper they keep by the phone. Nash makes out the words 'Sergeant Tilling. Personal', as Stan says, 'Here he is now,' and hands over the receiver.

'I need to talk to you,' Tilling says, before Nash can speak. 'It's rather urgent.'

'Happy to talk,' Nash responds, 'but I'm on duty here at the ARP post till ten.'

'Wild said you weren't busy,' the sergeant says in a faintly accusing tone. 'Can't you get away for half an hour or so?'

'You can't come here?'

'It's regarding an ongoing criminal investigation. It wouldn't be appropriate.'

'Hang on a minute.' Nash covers the mouthpiece, speaks to Stan. 'He wants me to go down to the police station now.'

'What's it about?'

Nash shrugs. 'I've no idea.' Faint quacking sounds issue from the telephone. 'I'd better go.' Then, speaking into the phone again, 'I'm on my way. Yes, goodbye.'

He replaces the receiver, picks up his coat and hat. 'I shouldn't be long,' he says to Stan. 'But if anything urgent comes up, ring me at the police station.'

'As long as they don't take you in,' Stan jokes.

'My conscience is clear.'

But as he walks down the Hundred towards the police station he has a twinge or two. Have his very preliminary investigations into David's death triggered some kind of response from the authorities? Worse, could his meeting with Jo have alerted her bosses?

When he's shown into Sergeant Tilling's office, it turns out it's neither of those. Or not directly. Against everything the policeman said yesterday when Nash reported the accident in the lane, now Tilling's interested. He wants to go over everything again in detail.

Baffled, Nash repeats his account of the accident. What he saw, what he didn't. He doesn't add the sequel of the mask, the policeman would probably think he's making it up. And anyway, it doesn't seem relevant to the direction of Tilling's questioning, which becomes more and more accusatory.

'Look, what's this all about?' Nash says when Tilling asks to inspect the healing scratches on his face and hands.

Tilling completes his survey, sits back in his chair. 'Well now, Mr Nash. It's about your friend George Hine. You say you called at his house at around 5 p.m. on Thursday? It was dark, of course.'

'The *house* was completely dark, I told you. There was no response when I knocked, so I presumed he was out.'

'You didn't notice if there was a car parked at the property?'

'No,' he says instinctively. Then, 'You're not suggesting it was George who hit me?'

'No, Mr Nash. Quite the reverse, in fact. I'm wondering if you did see him. Quarrel with him, perhaps? Land a punch or two?'

'What?' He stands up. 'What's this all about? Is George saying I hit him?'

'Calm down, Mr Nash. Sit down. Your friend Mr Hine is saying nothing, I'm afraid. He was the subject of a serious assault sometime between 3 p.m. on Thursday and 7 p.m. yesterday. His housekeeper came back from her day off to find him unconscious and badly beaten. He's unconscious still, in hospital. We're trying to establish when the attack happened.'

'And you think I—?' He stops, considers his position. 'Are you intending to arrest me, Sergeant Tilling? Because if you are, I'll ask a colleague to come and represent me before I say any more.'

'No, sir. Just trying to establish the chain of events. And you happen to have made it known you were in the vicinity at the crucial time.'

Nash rubs his hand across his face. 'Some part of the crucial time,' he says tartly. 'If there's any doubt in your mind, I'm not averse to having my injuries assessed by a properly qualified member of the medical profession. I'm sure they'd corroborate my statement about how they occurred. And no doubt the marks where the car hit me are still observable in the lane.'

'Yes, sir. We have observed them.'

'And you think—?' he says again. Stops, again. He wants to ask all sorts of questions, but he doesn't dare, because the answers are going to put ideas into Tilling's head. Things like how they know the assault happened after three on Thursday? Because if anyone saw George then, it's possible they saw him too. It must have been about three when he passed Hine's house on the way to Auntie May. Had George been found inside the house, as if he'd known his assailants, invited them in? Or outside, victim of a less personal attack? Do they have physical evidence of the attackers, footprints, fingerprints, blood?

God, that's the last thing he can ask. There will be traces of his presence at Hine's house. His footprints, perhaps even his fingerprints. He can't remember now if he took off his gloves when he knocked at the door. He's conscious of the silence, the gap Tilling has left for him to fill. 'What exactly is it you're thinking, Sergeant?'

'Hypothetically, sir, you could have been knocked off your bike by Mr Hine, followed him back to his house and had a fight with him.'

It's all too absurd. 'Not even hypothetically. The car that hit me was going away from Hine's house, not towards it. I told you that when I reported the accident.'

'Yes, sir. You did.'

'Look, I'm sorry to hear about George. Really sorry. But whatever happened to him was nothing to do with me. I'm sure, when he wakes up, he'll tell you so.'

'If he wakes up. At the moment, it's by no means certain.'

Nash feels sick. 'It's as bad as that?'

'Yes, sir. He was very cold when they found him. They think he must have been lying unconscious a good few hours.'

'But why?' He stops. Time to put an end to this nonsense. He can think of one very unsettling reason why George might have been targeted. 'I take it, it wasn't a burglary gone wrong? Nothing like that?'

Tilling shakes his head. 'That's not a question it would be proper for me to answer, sir. Not when it concerns an ongoing investigation.'

'What a lot of nonsense. We're on the same side here, Sergeant. If it wasn't a burglary, don't you think it might be relevant that George had asked me to follow up on David's death? That he was stirring up trouble about it? When I reported the accident to you yesterday, I told you that was why I'd been in Braishfield in the first place, to try and find out what had happened.'

'And I told you, Mr Nash, sir, that it was inadvisable for you to be making any kind of investigations into that.'

'All right, you did. We both know you don't approve of my activities in that area, past or present. But leave that aside for a minute. Doesn't what's happened to George make you suspicious? What if he's right, and David was killed? Isn't it possible the attack on him is a consequence of his refusal to accept the coroner's verdict?'

Tilling grimaces, shakes his head. 'Don't you think you're letting your imagination run away with you, sir? Young Hine got drunk and drowned. Simple as that.'

'It doesn't seem nearly as imaginative as your thinking I might have assaulted George,' Nash says drily.

'But there, if you had' – Tilling looks directly at Nash – 'you would say that, wouldn't you?'

He's had enough. He stands up. 'Are you going to charge me, Sergeant?'

'No, sir. Not at this moment.' The policeman stands up too. 'But I'm going to warn you that any attempt on your part to interfere in our investigation into this matter will be considered very detrimental and could result in charges against you.'

'And that's the official view, is it? I thought it was a citizen's duty to help the police.'

'Help us by keeping out of it, sir,' Tilling says. 'These matters aren't for civilians. You don't have the evidence.'

Nash bites back the retort, *And nor do you.* Instead, he bids the sergeant a chilly goodbye, and leaves.

As he makes his way out of the police station, his mind is a jumble of competing thoughts. There's anger at Tilling's hypothesis, an underlying anxiety for George. A feeling he's missed something, forgotten something he knows that would throw light on what's happened. And he's certain now that the car which hit him on Thursday evening did so deliberately. George's attackers? It's the only thing that makes sense. He's been targeted because George asked him to investigate David's death.

9

Saturday, afternoon

PORT LANE IS NARROW, AND just out of Hursley village it runs uphill between steep banks that prove how old this road to Winchester is. How many travellers have come this way. But this Saturday afternoon, I seem to be the only one.

The Cyc-Auto putters along steadily, the noise of the engine beating back from the banks, wrapping me up in a bubble of sound. Further on, the sound – and the banks – dwindle as the roadway levels out, and through the thread-bare winter hedges I get a view of the downland on either side of me. Nothing moves within my line of sight except for a huddle of rooks picking over a scoop of ploughland; a bird of prey hovering over the ridge. It's hard to believe that Hursley's less than a mile behind, and that only a bit further in the other direction, the bustling city of Winchester waits. Apart from my presence, this might be a medieval scene, so little of the modern world intrudes.

But the impression doesn't last. Soon, the lane passes between two houses – a thatched cottage on one side and a newer-looking, brick-built house on the other. There must be people here, because smoke rises from the chimney of the cottage, but I can't see anyone around. A few yards further on, I come to what turns out to be the first of a succession of army huts. I'm beginning to think I've wandered into a restricted area, but, as I get closer, I see the hut's far from new. There are chintzy curtains at the windows and chickens peck around. It must have been here since the last war. A range of mismatched sheds and the pervasive smell of pig suggest it's now being used as a farmhouse.

The road rises in front of me, with a scatter of huts on either side. They all seem to be occupied as housing, while the ground around each shows they're mostly being used for small-scale farming. A stack of hay here, a stand of sorry-looking cabbages there. More chickens, even a couple of cows. But no goats, yet. And still no one I can ask.

While I've come to find Sam, the goats' milk man, I'd wondered if this might be a good place to meet Bram out of the way of prying eyes. But though it's quiet enough and could hardly be more secluded, there's no sign of anywhere we could meet. No pub or café, I haven't even seen a shop or bus stop. It's a long way from Romsey when the only transport's a bike.

The road takes a sharp bend to the right, still rising, and then comes to a T-junction. I debate with myself whether to turn right or left, choose left rather than double back. Still no shops, but, as the road levels out, there's a post office sign. I stop the bike, get off and manoeuvre it onto its stand. It's good to be able to stretch, to listen to the quiet after the buzz of the engine.

The post office is a bungalow at the side of the road. Though it must be closed at this time on a Saturday afternoon, a note on the door reads, 'Paraffin sales at back door, please knock', and a hand-drawn arrow points round the side of the house. I follow the sign, and find myself at a half-glazed, green-painted door. There isn't a knocker, but I tap on the glass and wait.

A young woman appears. 'Is it paraffin you're wanting?' she asks. Then seeing my empty hands, 'You have to bring your own can, you know.'

'Not paraffin, no. Sorry to disturb you. I wondered if you could help me? I'm trying to find a man called Sam who keeps goats.'

'Sam?' She looks surprised. 'You're the second one today. I told the other fellow, he doesn't sell milk at the gate.'

'It's not for milk either,' I say. 'I'm visiting.'

'Oh, well, in that case I suppose . . . Turn right out of here, then keep on the road for about half a mile. Sam's place is straight in front of you. You can't miss it.'

I thank her, return to the bike. As I pass the junction where I'd decided to turn left, I think how typical it was that I'd chosen the wrong way. The thought echoes, something about right and wrong choices that sits uneasily in my head, feels unlucky. But I rationalise it, telling myself I probably wouldn't have come this far if I had chosen this way, since I've apparently left all the dwellings behind. Now it's woodland on one side and fields on the other. I'd never have guessed there might be more houses down here.

The road winds round, comes to an end. And I've arrived, exactly as the woman in the post office said. Another pensioned-off army hut, with the goat cart I saw dimly this morning standing in front of it. Relieved, I stop, park the bike. Beyond, a muddy-looking yard stretches towards a range of low wooden buildings. I don't know whether to knock on the hut door or just go looking for the goats' milk man when I hear voices coming from the far side of the yard. Sam's other visitor must still be here, I think. My earlier unease resurfaces. What should I do? Wait, or leave altogether? It's not as if I had a firm invitation.

As I hesitate, it becomes obvious that there's an argument going on. Someone's shouting, sharp-accented, nothing like Sam's slow burr. A tethered sheepdog in a kennel beside the hut gets to its feet, whining and straining at the rope that holds it.

I don't know what I can do, but if Sam's in trouble I shouldn't turn tail and run. Warily, I move towards the open entrance to the buildings. It's dark inside, so I can only make out shapes. A tall man and a shorter one, and behind them a row of white goats tied to a rail.

'All right, you bastard,' the sharp voice shouts. 'I was trying to do you a good turn. You'll be sorry when I get a requisition order for these bleedin' goats and you lose the lot.'

'*If* tha does,' Sam says.

The man throws a punch and Sam goes down. A clanking sound, and a bucket tips over, sending a white swoosh of milk onto the ground. Instinctively, I move towards the men, but Sam sees me and shouts, 'Nay, lass, stand clear. Go'n let Lady off. She'll soon settle un.'

I run, afraid of what might happen while I'm away. When I get to the dog, she's growling under her breath, but she's focused on the entrance to the barn, not me, so I dare to untie her. As soon as the rope slackens, she's off, barking aggressively. Seconds later, a tall man in khaki dashes out of the shed, and the release of tension makes me laugh out loud as the dog nips at his heels, herding him away like an unruly sheep. He casts an evil glance my way as he darts past, and astonished, I recognise him as the unpleasant soldier from the bus stop the other morning.

I hurry across to the barn, expecting to see Sam still on the ground, but he comes to the doorway as I get there. He watches a moment before whistling the dog back to his heels. It's the first time I've seen him in full daylight, and I'm shocked to see how old he looks. Though he's a wiry little man, he moves carefully, as if his joints hurt.

'Are you all right?' I say, stupidly. Of course he's not all right. He's been punched, fallen over.

'Ah. Never bother about me, lass. I'll be grand.'

'What was it all about? What did he want?'

'Wanted to buy me goats,' Sam says. 'For the army, sez he, but I reckon t'was all cack. They're not bred for meat anyhow. Nowt on them for eating. They're milkers.'

'I've seen him before,' I say. 'He's a nasty piece of work. He was arguing with someone then, too.'

'Well known for it,' Sam says. 'Bit of a bad do, losing the milk. I'll be short tomorrow.'

'You'd finished milking?'

'Pity of it.' He sighs. 'Time t' let them out.'

'Can I help?'

He looks at me dubiously. 'Wouldn't want thee to spoil tha good clothes.'

'Nothing to spoil,' I say. Which is true enough. My coat's on its last legs, and my shoes are my most sensible pair, easy enough to clean if they get mucky.

He shakes his head. 'Nay. Stay there.'

He goes off into the hut, comes back carrying a khaki coverall coat like the one he's wearing and a pair of canvas galoshes. He holds them out to me.

'Put them on. That'll keep thee decent.'

The coat's big enough to go over mine, and the galoshes slip over my shoes with room to spare. 'I look like a proper farmer,' I say, rolling back the sleeves so my hands are free. 'What do you want me to do first?'

'We'll take the beasts t' the back pasture,' he says. 'Out of sight while yon gowk's about.'

In the barn, he gives me the halters of half a dozen goats, takes the rest himself. 'I'll go first,' he says. 'The others'll follow right enough.'

And they do. He leads his goats and me up behind the woodland to a rising slope of rough grass and scrub that's got a rudimentary wire fence around its boundaries. We come to a gate, half collapsed on its hinges. Sam nudges it open with his hip.

'When tha's inside, tha can take the ropes off,' he says. 'Leave the halters, mind.'

I release the last goat, give her a pat as she skitters off to join her fellows. 'Will they be OK here?' I ask. 'Won't they stray? There isn't much of a fence.'

'They'll be right,' he says. 'They're hefted.'

He pushes the gate up and drapes a rusty bit of chain round the post.

'Hefted?' I say. 'What's that?'

'Means they know where home is,' he says. 'The old ladies in the herd teach the young ones. They don't stray far any day.'

I think about that. About having the sense to know where home is and envy the goats. 'Not like you, then?' I say. 'You sound as if you're a long way from home.'

'Ah, well. Came here with the Army in the last lot. It was a vet'nary hospital for hosses then. Never left. Reckon I got hefted too.' He laughs. 'Promised us an acre and a cow, tha knows, but I never did take t' cows.'

'Is this all of your stock?' I ask him. 'Just these goats?'

'Got a few does inside that're near their first kidding. And a billy, of course.' He eyes me as doubtfully as he had earlier about my clothes. 'I'll need to bring some watter for these. Will tha wait?'

'I don't mind carrying a bucket or two.'

'If tha's sure?'

'Of course.' But it is hard labour, pumping the water up from the well in the yard and I'm glad when the old oil drum on pram wheels is finally full. Sam pushes the peculiar-looking contraption and I go in front to open the gate for him. Back in the field, we make our way to the far corner, where a long zinc trough stands next to an open-fronted animal shelter.

'Keep clear, lass,' Sam says as he levers the tub over to fill the trough. I step away, ease my back from the task.

My eye is caught by a small shed on wheels, its curved tin roof red with rust. It's backed into the woodland skirting the field and rickety-looking steps go up to the half and half door. 'Is that a gypsy caravan?'

'Nay, yon's a shepherd's hut. T'was all sheep up here back along till the army took it over. Lambing time, shepherd slept out with the flock.'

'Sounds romantic.'

'What it is, is damned cold,' Sam says. He looks at me, tuts. 'Tha looks fair clemmed thaself. Reckon we'd better get inside. I'll make thee a brew.'

But the light's fading fast, and I'm none too confident about riding the Cyc-Auto in the dark. I need to get back to Chandler's Ford, though I don't like to leave him.

'Will you be all right?'

'Ah. I'm grand,' he says as he had before.

I'm not sure I believe him, but I don't know what else I can do. 'I should go, then. I could come back tomorrow if you'd like some help?'

'Tha must have better things t' do?'

'No. Not really.' I start to take off the coverall he lent me, shiver as the chill seeps in.

'Nay,' he says. 'Don't shed tha coat. Keep it to go home. Bring it the next time tha comes.'

His words warm me better than the coat. For the first time since I left Romsey I haven't had to keep my guard up, weigh my words. Despite the nasty incident with the soldier – or perhaps because of it – Hursley, McNaught and Jericho, even Bram haven't mattered. But as I ride back through the lanes, it all creeps back. Anxieties, connections, speculations. I might not have seen the billy goat, but I somehow feel my nerve has been tested all the same.

10

Saturday, afternoon and early evening

AFTER HIS RUN-IN WITH TILLING, Nash goes back to the ARP post but he's even more restless now than before. What Tilling's told him about the assault on Hine plays over and over in his mind. In the end, he knows he can't wait until tomorrow to find out how he is.

A telephone call to the local hospital confirms George is a patient there, but they won't tell him anything. Frustrated, he asks Vic and Stan to cover him a bit longer so he can go up to the hospital, see if he can find out any more in person. But though he gets as far as the ward, the ward sister won't let him in. He stretches a point, tells her he's Hine's solicitor, asks her to inform him when George wakes. She ums and ahs a bit about that, but in the end she agrees. Admits they don't have anyone else to tell, since George has no traceable next of kin.

But it turns out his visit isn't a waste of time after all. As he's leaving, a faded-looking woman of uncertain years arrives. Her eyes are red with weeping and she's struggling with a suitcase. It's second nature for him to offer help. The case isn't so much heavy as awkward, but she thanks him over and over, as if he's undertaken some Herculean task.

'Where are you headed?' he asks her.

'The men's ward,' she says forlornly. 'My employer, he had a terrible accident. Well, to tell the truth, he got beaten up. He's in a coma. The ward sister told me I had to bring his things. Pyjamas and stuff. Asked specially for his razor because they can't get the blades. Oh dear. I put in his dressing gown and slippers as well, that's why the case is so heavy. I wanted him to have them, even though they say he might never . . .'

She starts to cry again, noisy sobs that rack her skinny body. He sits her down on a bench in the corridor, hands her his handkerchief. When she grows calmer, he says, 'You wouldn't be George Hine's housekeeper, by any chance?'

'Oh dear, yes, I am. Edna Stone. *Miss* Edna Stone. I've been Mr Hine's housekeeper nearly fifteen years. You know him, do you, sir?'

'Yes.' Now's not the time for complicated explanations. 'I came up to the hospital because I heard he'd been injured. My name's Nash. I'm a solicitor here in town.'

'*You're* Mr Nash? Mr Hine said you used to be friends. He came to see you about Master David, didn't he?'

'That's right. I've been trying to find out what happened.'

'And now this,' she says with a fresh bout of sobbing. 'I don't know what things are coming to these days, I really don't.'

He tries to console her.

'I want to see him,' she says when the tears ease, 'but I don't think they'll let me. Even when I'd come up in the ambulance with him yesterday, I couldn't go in.'

'That's a shame, but I'm afraid you're right. They won't allow any visitors. Look, why don't you wait here? I'll deliver the case for you, and I'll ask about you seeing him. If they say you can, I'll come and fetch you straightaway.'

'All right.' She twists the sodden handkerchief nervously between her hands. 'Thank you, sir. That sister, she frightens me. I didn't take to her at all.'

Nash doesn't take to the senior nurse much himself when she once again refuses to allow him past the ward door. 'I told you, only next of kin,' she says, eyeing the case suspiciously. 'I don't know where his housekeeper expects us to store that thing. Stupid woman. Surely you could take it away with you?'

'Afraid not,' he says. 'I think that's a job for his next of kin.'

He ignores her stuttered protest, makes his way back to Miss Stone.

'What you need,' he says to her, 'is a cup of tea. Unless you'd prefer something stronger?'

She looks up at him, pale eyes swimming with tears. 'Oh no,' she says as she gets to her feet. 'I couldn't do that, sir. I'm Chapel, you see.'

'A cup of tea it is, then. I suppose there'll be somewhere we can get one here?'

'I'd rather not stay here, if you don't mind, sir. This place . . .' She swallows. 'I don't care for hospitals. They make me feel all hot and bothered.'

'Fair enough.' He takes her elbow, steers her out of the building. 'We'll have to go back into town for tea, then,' he says. 'But I'm afraid I don't have a car. I came up on foot this afternoon.'

'I don't mind a walk, sir. T'isn't that far.' She does seem stronger now she's out in the fresh air. As they go down the hill, she tells him she's staying with her sister in town.

'To tell you the truth, sir, I was that scared after what happened to Mr Hine I couldn't bear to go back to his place last night. I went to Susan's after we brought him in to the hospital. My brother-in-law took me to fetch the master's bits and pieces this morning. I couldn't have stood to go there on my own, not even in broad daylight. I will have to go back, I know, but dear me, I don't know when. Or even *if* I can. There's all that blood wants cleaning up.' She shudders, comes to a dead halt. 'But the police said . . .'

'Don't think about that now,' he says, urging her forward as tactfully as he can. 'It's too cold to be standing about. I'm sure we can get someone to help you sort things out when the time comes.'

He'd set out from the hospital with the intention of taking her to the Palmerston tea room in Market Place before he has to go back on duty. But after her initial rally, she's now looking far too pale and shaky for his liking. They'll pass Basswood House on their way, and it seems ridiculous not to stop there and give her a chance to recover. Though she looks startled at the suggestion, he persuades her easily enough once she knows his own housekeeper will be there. As he lets them in through the front door, he wonders wryly whether he has such an unsavoury reputation that she doesn't feel safe with him. Or perhaps it's all men. Even as he takes her coat, steers her towards the kitchen where it will be warmest, another thought strikes him. Perhaps it's experience that makes her afraid? Surely *George* wouldn't have . . . ?

The kitchen door opens as they approach. 'Mr Nash? What's happened? I thought you were on duty?'

'I was,' he says, 'and I'll need to get back soon. But I heard Mr Hine had been badly injured so I went up to the hospital to see how he was.' He urges Miss Stone forward. 'This is Edna, his housekeeper. I met her at the hospital, promised her a cup of tea. She's had a very upsetting time, and it's beastly cold outside. I know you won't mind if we come into the kitchen to warm up.'

Fan hesitates, and he can see the dilemma in her face. She doesn't like him in the kitchen, thinks it's not proper. But she won't like the idea of someone of her own status being entertained in the drawing room either.

'Of course, sir,' she says, after a moment. 'Come on in. The kettle's nice and hot on the range. It'll soon boil.'

However rigid Fan may be about the proprieties, she's a motherly soul underneath the starch. Miss Stone visibly relaxes now she's in the care of a woman. He's tempted to leave the two of them together, but there are things he urgently wants to know that Edna may be able to tell him.

'Sit down with us, Fan.' His tone makes it an order, because otherwise she will refuse. 'I've got some questions I want to ask Miss Stone, and I'm sure she'd be glad of your moral support.'

Though his housekeeper looks surprised, she complies.

'Questions?' Miss Stone looks as if she'd like to bolt. 'If it's about poor Mr Hine, I told the police, I don't know anything about what happened.'

Nash considers how to frame what he wants to say without alarming her – or Fan – unduly. If either of them knew he'd been questioned as a suspect, they'd be horrified, if for different reasons. And he doesn't have the time to explain.

'I've talked to the police,' he says. 'And I wasn't able to help them much either. But you see, I may have had an encounter with the same folk who hurt Mr Hine. I got knocked off my bike on Thursday evening, not far from George's house. Though the police won't commit themselves to anything, I think it must have been around the time he was attacked.'

'Oh dear,' Miss Stone says. 'That's dreadful. I'm so sorry.'

'Nothing to worry about. Not like what happened to George.'

'Oh dear, no,' she says. 'That was awful. Ever since I found him I can't stop thinking about it. Seeing him the way he was. And so cold, it was shocking. Right there on the hall floor. I thought he was dead for sure.'

Fan gets up, but it's only to go to the woman who's started to cry again. 'It must have been a nasty shock,' Fan says to her. 'Now, have a sip more of this tea. I'm sure Mr Nash won't ask you any more questions if it's going to upset you.'

He intercepts Fan's glare, shakes his head. 'I'll try not to distress you, Miss Stone,' he says. 'But anything you could tell me would be a help.'

The woman mops her eyes, pats Fan's hand. 'It's all right, dear. I know Mr Nash is doing it for the best.'

'The police seemed to think George had been attacked on Thursday afternoon or evening.'

'That's right. Oh dear. He'd let me go after lunch on Thursday to help my sister. She's had this flu that's been going around, and she was worried about the housework. My brother-in-law, he's not fussy, but Susan, she'd worked herself into a real old state, and they were afraid she was going to have a relapse, so I said I'd come over and do a bit of laundry and that. Cook a couple of meals so she could rest.' She draws a hitching breath. 'If I hadn't gone early, maybe . . . If I'd been there with Mr Hine . . .'

'I'm glad you weren't,' Nash says, as gently as he can. 'And I'm sure George would be too.'

She looks at him, horrified. 'You think they might have hurt me as well?'

Before he can find a suitable answer, Fan jumps in. 'Don't dwell on it, Edna. You weren't there, that's the main thing. All that matters now is to make sure the animals that did it get caught.'

'Miss Stone.' Nash pulls the woman's attention back to himself. He's acutely conscious of how time's passing. It's not fair to expect Vic and Stan to cover for him much longer. 'You said George was in the hall. How did the attackers get in, do you think? Were there signs of a break-in?'

'When I got home I went in through the back like I always do,' she says. 'Everything seemed just as usual from outside. I wasn't expecting to see a light because of the blackout, but when I got inside it was pitch dark and ever so cold. The range had gone out, and Mr Hine never lets it do that. I went through to see where he was, thought perhaps he might've got sick with the flu. But soon as I turned on the light in the hall, I saw him. Couldn't think what had happened at first. Looked like he'd fallen down the stairs. Oh dear. But as soon as I got close I could see it was more than a fall. There was so much blood . . . So I rang the exchange and they sent for the ambulance and police.'

She patters to a halt, takes a deep breath, starts again. 'Like I said, I went off with him to the hospital, then this morning, that Sergeant Tilling comes round to my sister's, asks me all sorts of questions. He said there was no sign of a break-in. Poor Mr Hine must've opened the door to whoever it was, let them in. Said he thought there was probably two of them, maybe more. There were footprints, see, not outside but . . .' Another deep breath. 'In the blood. Sorry to go on like this, sir, I don't know what's happened to me. I couldn't hardly put two words together when the sergeant was asking me.'

'It's the shock,' Nash says. 'You'll feel better when you've talked it out.'

She looks at him so gratefully he feels like a hypocrite. Talking's never helped him.

'One last thing,' he says. 'I know it must have been very difficult since David's death, but was George acting as if he was afraid of something? Had he fallen out with anyone lately?'

'No, Mr Nash, not really. He was cross with that coroner chap, of course. And well, with the police, too, because they said poor Mr David was stealing things from his work. But there, I mean, they wouldn't have hurt him.'

'Last question, I promise,' Nash says. 'There was nothing stolen?'

'Oh dear.' She looks anxiously at Nash. 'I hope I haven't done anything wrong but ... the police asked me that and I told them no because I didn't think there had been. They made me check last night, and I admit I wasn't too thorough because I was afraid the ambulance was going to leave me behind. But all the stuff I could think of, the housekeeping money in the kitchen, the silver in the dining room, none of that had been touched. Even the few bits of the late Mrs Lucy's jewellery were where they ought to be. But this morning, see, when I was getting his things, I did notice there was something gone.'

'Yes?'

'He had this watch,' she says. 'Mostly he wore his father's old pocket watch but someone'd given him a watch for his birthday. Last April, it was. Funny-looking thing, all dials over the face but he was as pleased as Punch with it at first. Then, I don't know why exactly, but he stopped using it. Left it up on his dressing table gathering dust. It wasn't broken or anything because he used to keep it wound up and it went all right. Only this morning, when I went to get his hairbrushes to take in, it wasn't there.'

'You're sure? George couldn't have moved it himself? Put it somewhere else?'

'Well, he might've done, I suppose. I couldn't swear it was there Thursday, because I only had a quick flick round in the morning. Made the bed and that, but I'd given the room a thorough doing the day before so it didn't need much. But I am sure it was there on the Wednesday.'

'That seems odd,' Nash says. 'Do you know who gave it to him?'

She opens her mouth to speak, closes it again without saying anything. Bright colour floods her face. 'I don't know if I ought to say. It's not my place to gossip.'

Fan gives her a little shake. 'You tell Mr Nash if you know. It won't go any further with him.'

It's not a promise he'd have made, but he doesn't contradict her. 'It might be important,' he says.

'Oh dear, well, if you think so. I don't know, exactly. But he was seeing someone for a while. A woman, I mean. Never brought her home that I know of. Course, he would have been entitled to if he'd wanted. Mrs Lucy's been dead for almost five years now. Do you think I ought to tell the police, sir? About the watch, I mean.'

Nash sighs. 'I think you probably should.' He looks at his own watch, stands up. 'You've been very helpful, Miss Stone. But I must get back on duty now. Can I walk you to your sister's first?'

'No need of that,' Fan says. 'Edna'll have a bite of something to eat with Billy and me. He can make sure she gets back safe.'

'Is that all right with you, Miss Stone?'

'That'd be nice,' she says. 'Thank you.'

'It's I who should thank you.' He holds out his hand to her and she shakes it timidly. 'If you remember anything else, anything at all, or if you're worried, you can always come back to me. If I'm not about, Fan will help. Or you can come to the office. You know where that is?'

'Oh dear yes. You're very kind. I'll do that, of course I will.'

He says goodbye as Fan practically shoos him out of the door. 'Don't worry,' she says when they're out of earshot. 'I'll look after her. Just you get yourself back on duty before it's dark.'

11

Sunday 10th January, early morning

SUNDAY MORNING, AND THERE'S SNOW. Even before I venture out of bed, I can tell. The light that filters around the edge of the inadequate curtains is whiter, with a cold blue edge almost like moonlight. The air is still and cold, and when I get up to look, the windows are iced up inside, frost patterns dissolving with the warmth of my breath. Outside, a sparkling thin glaze covers every surface. From where I stand, no footprint mars the white near the Andersons' house, but I can hear the excited whoops of children playing somewhere outside, answering the same snowy siren call I remember from childhood.

Eight years old, frost licking at my fingers, my nose, my bare knees. The soft shuffle of falling snowflakes. Out with the gang, trying to be the first to trample footprints across a virgin landscape. Abe's got new rubber wellingtons and Bert's hand-me-downs are well greased, but Jem and Mike and me are still in our ordinary old boots, wet through in a wink, but we don't care as we run through the fields.

Dodging the splatter of snowballs. Gotta keep out of the way of Bert's, they've always got a stone in them. Building a snowman on the lawn at Basswood House, heaping the snow up higher than I can reach. Rolling a ball round for the head, getting bigger and bigger. Abe lifting it up into place, putting in coal for the eyes, an old pipe of his dad's in its mouth. Cups of cocoa in the stables after, the snuffle of Mr Nash's bay mare in my ear.

Making a slide on Mile Hill, trampling the white into messy sludge. A cuff round the ear from Grandfather when he slips and no supper if we don't shovel it clear before he gets home.

The itch of chilblains as toes thaw by the fire, the stink and burn of the wintergreen ointment Granny rubs in.

But it's not wintergreen I smell as I shiver my way through a cat's lick wash this morning, and dress hastily. It's the rare smell of bacon frying. I go through to the kitchen, nose practically twitching. Mr Anderson and Hilda are there before me, sitting at the table, a rasher of fat bacon and slice of toast on each of their plates, empty porridge bowls pushed to the middle of the table. Though Mr Anderson is fully dressed, Hilda's still in her drab brown dressing gown.

'Good morning,' I greet them. 'It's a cold one again.'

Mr Anderson looks up, grins when he sees me. Even Hilda manages to raise a smile.

'What?' I say with injured dignity. 'What's funny?'

'Look at you,' Mr Anderson snorts. 'Have you got all your clothes on at once?'

He's nearly right. I'm wearing two jumpers under my jacket, and two pairs of socks on my feet. I've tucked my slacks into the outer ones, a knee-high, luridly striped pair in orange and pink that Dot knitted from her stash of recycled wool, intended only as bedsocks.

'Not at all. I took my pyjamas off.' And that was a sacrifice.

'Could be a lot worse,' he says. 'What'll you do then?'

'Stay in bed,' I mutter. 'Shall I help myself to porridge?'

'Yes, do, dear,' Hilda says. 'Mr Anderson and I have had ours. You can take as much as you want.'

I'm reeling from the endearment, half expecting there'll only be a scrape left, but I do her an injustice, because they've left me plenty. But an empty frying pan shows there won't be any bacon for me, so I fill my bowl, sit down to eat.

'What are your plans for today?' Hilda, again. She shrugs closer into her dressing gown, but she sounds quite friendly. Perhaps she's finally thawed towards me, despite the weather. 'Mr Anderson will be working in his shed, and Sunday's my one day of rest. I'm afraid I'll have to ask you to look out for yourself until this evening. You can make yourself a sandwich to take with you if you like.'

'That's all right. I'll get out of your hair as soon as I've finished eating.'

I hadn't made any real plans, except to think vaguely of taking the coat back to Sam, or scouting for somewhere Bram and I could meet. But it seems whatever I do, I'll need to do it away from the Hutments. I remember Hilda's unwilling reception of me last week, the impression I'd woken her from sleep at almost four in the afternoon, think shudderingly of the cold. Perhaps I should have left my pyjamas on after all.

'If you'll excuse me, then,' she says, getting up from the table, 'I'll see you later. Put your bowl in the sink when you've finished.'

Mr Anderson waits till the door shuts behind her before he speaks. He keeps his voice down, not quite a whisper, but low enough to be sure she won't hear him. 'Don't go wandering about all day in the snow,' he says. 'You'd better come down to the shed with me.'

Though there's nothing flirtatious in the offer, it makes me bristle. He probably means it kindly, but I get the feeling there's something patriarchal, a *keep you where I can see you* purpose in the offer. That's something I'd spend all day in the snow to avoid. The idea of hiding away, the look of it, is too feeble to contemplate. The cold outside is nothing compared to the chill there'd be if Hilda found out I'd been closeted away with her husband all day. If I go to Sam's there will be something for me to do. I might even get to see the billy goat.

'Thank you, but no. I've got things I want to do.'

Anderson looks suspiciously at me. 'As long as whatever it is doesn't take you back to Romsey. You know what McNaught and Jericho said about that.'

For a moment, it almost feels as if Hilda and he have changed places, like the figures in a weather house. She's being friendly, so it's his turn to be stern.

'No,' I say. 'Don't worry. I remember.' Though I haven't quite finished my porridge, I've lost my appetite. I push away from the table. 'I'll get my things.'

I don't care that the warmest hat I have is a match for the socks and looks more like a tea cosy than anything a person ought to wear. Or that the gloves are striped as well, though not in matching colours. I bundle on my coat, wind a mercifully plain scarf round my neck, and go back to the kitchen on my way out.

Neither of the Andersons are there at first, but as I'm folding Sam's coverall into a bag, Mr Anderson comes in. He blinks a bit when he sees me, but he manages not to laugh, so that's a plus.

'I'm sorry about this,' he says, with an open-handed gesture that's almost apologetic and seems to include the weather, my clothes and my temporary banishment. Perhaps it's only because he's worried he'll have to answer to McNaught and Jericho if I break the rules that makes him act the heavy-handed father. He nods towards a paper-wrapped parcel on the kitchen table. 'Your rasher,' he says. 'I made you a sandwich.'

'Thanks.' The parcel's still warm as I add it to my bag. Feeling less sore towards him, I smile. 'I need to grab my bike from the shed. Can I have the key?'

'I'll come down with you,' he says, shrugging into his coat. 'I was on my way there anyway.'

Outside, it's not much colder than it was indoors. The snow crunches under our feet, dry and powdery. 'What will you do in the shed all day?' I ask him, more to keep things friendly than any real wish to know.

'I've got a cupboard to build,' he says as we arrive at the shed. 'Hilda's friend along at number 90 wants it for her daughter's bedroom.'

'That'll keep you busy.' I concentrate on backing the bike out of its corner, checking the fuel, but his answer makes me pause.

'I've got the wood all cut ready,' he says. 'Won't take long to put it together. But Anita wants me to paint it. Khaki'd be easy enough but the girl wants pink. Don't know where I'm going to find that unless I can mix it up from the stuff I've already got.'

'Anita? Is that Hilda's goddaughter? She introduced me to her yesterday in the Drawing Office canteen.'

'That's her. Hilda said you'd seen them. She was put out that the tea place down at the hangar was closed.'

One mystery solved. Hilda and the girl *do* work in the Experimental Hangar together. It still leaves the question of why Anita had run off when I tried to talk to her on Thursday morning, though. I'm wondering if I ought to tell Mr Anderson about it, maybe ask if he knows who the soldiers might have been, when he says:

'Nice little girl, Anita, despite her fancy ideas. Hilda and me, we think a lot of her and her brother. He's in the army, stationed up at the transit camp in the Park.' He turns deeper into the shed, running his gaze along a shelf of paint pots. 'Now then,' he says, but he's not talking to me anymore. 'What am I going to do about this pink?'

I take my cue and leave. As I start the Cyc-Auto up out-side, I make up my mind. With Hursley Park House closed for office staff, I've got a day off too. I can't do anything to investigate today. I'll make the most of my time and look for somewhere Bram and I can meet. Then I'll pop over to see Sam, return his coat. But first things first. As soon as I'm well out of sight of the Hutments, I stop the bike, fish the sandwich packet out of my bag. Later, I may wish I'd saved it, but, right now I just want to eat my bacon sandwich while it's still warm.

In the old stables at Basswood House, Nash keeps warm enough in the heat of the fire he's lit to work on the repairs to his copper mask. He's managed to straighten out the folded metal, even bring it back to some semblance of its former shape, but it needs more than that. It has to fit. And it has to fit well. But the measurements are so precise, the metal so thin, he's far from sure he can achieve it. In the past, he's managed small adjustments, touched up the paintwork, even replated the inside surface when the silvering wore thin, but this, a complete rebuild, feels as if it may be a step too far for his skills.

He broods as he thinks about the complex business of making the mask in the first place. The decision made in 1918: there was nothing more surgery could do for him. The visits to the 'Tin Noses' unit, swathed in unnecessary band-ages to avoid scaring the public. The brutal business of tak-ing an impression, the panicky smother as they covered what was left of his face with plaster of Paris, a tube up his nose so he could breathe, the heat of the plaster as it set. Then the wait till they'd made a mould and cast the mask. Worst, perhaps, of all, the painstaking sessions when the mask was finished. Putting it on for the first time, feeling the alien metal press against flesh and bone. Sitting, nauseated, in a full flood of light as they scrutinised his face and painted the mask to blend perfectly with his skin. Knowing he should be grateful, feeling only resentment and self-disgust.

But that's all done and past: over. He fingers the battered metal. Except it isn't. Won't ever be. It's what has made him who he is. Thinking about it makes him feel as sick with himself now as he had been then. A man who would cut off his friend, his rescuer, rather than be reminded of his indebtedness. A man who can't commit himself to any gentle emotion, who's still afraid to let anyone get close.

He gives himself a mental shake. It's no good to dwell on the past. There's a practical problem to be solved, and perhaps what he needs is to think beyond the obvious. If working with copper's too difficult, he could try silver. He knows how that behaves. He has only to figure out a way to use the spare mask as a pattern. Fill it with clay or cast it in sand. But he's only got one chance to get it right. He can't risk damaging it. And as much as he sometimes feels the prosthesis is a curse, he knows it's also his freedom.

I'm feeling smug as I zip back along Port Lane this afternoon. I've scouted out a good place for Bram and me to meet. The White Horse at Ampfield is perfect – not too far from

Romsey, not too close to Hursley. There's a fire, dim lighting and lots of quaint little oak-beamed corners where people can hunker down in privacy. It's perfect. I'll phone him later and let him know.

But, for now, I'm looking forward to seeing Sam. There's a weak sun shining which makes everything sparkle, taking the edge off the chill air. I'm grateful Hilda and Mr Anderson won't expect me back until nightfall. With my wheel marks the first in the snow all the way up the lane, I feel like an explorer abroad in new lands.

I should have realised sooner, I suppose. Wondered why there weren't any tracks in the snow from Sam's goat cart going down to Hursley and back. But I'm lost in the moment, and if it crosses my mind at all, it's only to think the loss of the milk yesterday must have made it impossible for him to do his usual round. It isn't until I draw up outside his place, register the silence when I knock, that I start to worry.

There are boot prints criss-crossing the snow in the yard, but I can't see anyone in the building where Sam milks the goats, and Lady's not tied up at her kennel. I poke my head into the sheds I didn't visit yesterday, where the billy goat and the does near to kidding look up from their pens and scrutinise me with a kind of benign curiosity. I can see their mangers are half full, and they've got water. Sam's obviously been here not long ago.

Back in the yard, I wonder if he could have gone out. It'd have to be to church on a Sunday, I suppose, but it must be getting close to the time he does the milking, if yesterday's anything to go by. He wouldn't want to be late with that, and the goats aren't in the shed. Even as I think it, I realise that's the answer. He'll have gone up to the top pasture to bring in the goats.

The theory's proved by finding his footprints leading out beyond the barn towards the field. All one way. That must mean he hasn't come back yet. I'll nip up and meet him.

From the gate, I can see a huddle of goats over in the far corner, milling around by their shelter. No sign of Sam, though, and the snow's too uneven here in the field for me to make out a track. The only place I can think of where he might be is the shepherd's hut. I walk along the fence line till it comes into view, but the door's padlocked shut. Puzzled, I look across at the goats once more.

'Sam,' I call. Hear my voice echo back faintly from the hill-side, 'Am . . . am . . .'

Lady barks, the sound coming from the spot across the field where the goats are. As they shift and move, I think I can see a dark shape on the ground.

Sam.

Stumbling over the rough grass, I run towards the gaggle of animals. And there he is, the old man down on the ground beside the water trough. The dog's close beside him, and the way the snow's melted around them both shows she must have been lying there, guarding him. She looks at me warily, but she doesn't stop me coming closer. His eyes are closed, and he's got a nasty-looking cut on his forehead that's obviously bled a lot though it's stopped now. There's blood on the edge of the trough, too. Stripping off my coat, I kneel beside him. Reach out and touch him, praying he's not dead.

He stirs as I tuck my coat around him. Though he's not dead, thank God, he's almost as cold as a corpse. They told us at the first aid course that casualties lose most heat from their heads so I take off my hat, pull it gently down over his sparse hair. I'm rewarded by a groan.

'Sam?'

'Eh, lass.' He opens the eye that's not stuck shut with dried blood. 'What's t' do?'

'I could ask you that,' I say. He struggles to sit, and I prop him against my shoulder. 'What happened?'

'Don't rightly know,' he says, catching his breath as he tries to straighten his legs. Despite his wellington boots, I can see one foot is twisted at an alarming angle.

'Keep still,' I tell him, trying to sound calm, though inside I'm scared. It looks as if he's broken his leg, and I'm not strong enough to carry him down to safety. He can't stay here, but there isn't a house anywhere in sight to get help.

'Came t' make sure goats' watter hadn't frozen,' he mutters. 'Must'a slipped, knocked m'self out. What time is it?'

Trying not to jar him, I peer at my watch. 'Five to three.'

'Hellfire. I set out hours ago.' He struggles again to get up. The movement makes him shudder, but whether with cold or pain, I can't tell.

'We have to get you into the warm,' I say. 'I can't carry you, though.'

'Get the goat cart,' he mumbles. 'That should do the trick.'

Sliding on snow, I make my way as quickly as I dare to the house, grab the cart from in front. No time to waste looking for the harness, even if I thought I could catch the goats to pull it. It's light enough for me, these few hundred yards. He's still sitting stubbornly upright, one arm tightly round Lady's neck. I steer the shaft of the cart to one side, half guide, half lift him till he's sitting on the baseboard. He leans back, eyes closed, sweating from the effort of moving, though his skin's clammily cold.

'I'm afraid it'll be a rough ride,' I say as I push the cart into motion. My biggest worry, though, is that once I get it moving on the slope I won't be able to hold it back with his weight dragging it forward.

From a distance, it would probably be amusing, the way the goats follow us down in a little procession. But the grey pallor of his skin's no joke, and the way his injured foot flops with the movement of the cart means I'm not in the mood for laughing. My first aid's no match for the damage he's done to himself by the fall. I have to get help.

With a huge effort from us both, we struggle our way indoors, though he drops like a stone into a chair by the range and I know I won't be able to move him any further on my own. The fire is almost out, but I riddle the ashes, add some knobs of wood and coal from the scuttle and open the dampers as far as they'll go.

'Need a drink,' Sam says. 'Throat's dry as dust.'

'Better not.' I pat his hand. 'Just in case.'

I don't like to leave him, but I must get help. 'Where's the nearest phone?' I say. 'We're going to need an ambulance to get you to hospital.'

'Post office. Tha'll need to knock for the lass.'

'All right.' And then, though it doesn't look as if he could stir if his life depended on it, 'Stay put. I'll go and phone. I'll be back as soon as I can.'

It's freezing on the bike without my outer clothes, but it doesn't take long to get to the post office. Round at the back door I knock furiously, resenting every second it takes for the woman to answer the door. But it's my fault. If I'd come to Oliver's Battery this morning, maybe this wouldn't have happened. Or at least, I would have been here, saved Sam from hours lying in the snow.

When the woman comes to the door, I explain. Beg her to ring for an ambulance. 'It's urgent,' I say. 'Will you explain where they need to go? I don't even know the address.'

She nods. 'You'll wait for them?'

'I will,' I say. 'But not here. I don't want to leave him alone too long.'

The fire's roaring up the chimney when I get back, and there's a bit of pink in Sam's face. He seems to be asleep, and I try not to wake him as I stoke the range again, shut it down to a trickle of heat and wait.

12

Sunday, evening

T HE TELEPHONE RINGS AT EIGHT o'clock. It's Fan's evening off, so Nash puts down the book he's reading, makes his way into the hall to answer it. There's an undercurrent of alarm as he wonders who could be ringing at this time on a Sunday evening. He hasn't heard a siren; it won't be ARP duty calling.

'Bram?'

He recognises her voice at once. It's Jo, but she sounds almost as distracted as when they'd met in Winchester.

'Of course. What's wrong?' Because it's clear something is.

'You said I had to ring or you'd come looking for me.'

'Well, yes. But it's only been two days. You surely didn't think I'd mean you to turn out on a snowy evening to call me?'

'No, no. I was going to ring you earlier, suggest a meeting, but things happened and it got late . . . too late now.'

'Probably,' he says. 'Unless it's very urgent?'

'No,' she says, but he's not entirely convinced. 'I thought it would be good if we could talk. But now I'm stuck out at

Oliver's Battery, looking after a herd of goats, and I don't know how long I'll need to be here.'

'Goats?' In deference to the stress in her voice, he avoids the obvious *you're kidding*, says, 'You've lost me, Jo.'

'It'd take too long to explain. But until Sam's better, I'm going to stay here. Mr Anderson's not very pleased but . . . oh. I shouldn't have said that.'

Another clue? He notes it down for future reference. And then, who's Sam? But all he says is, 'Are you all right, Jo? You're obviously upset.'

He hears her take a deep breath. 'I'm fine. I've never looked after goats before, but Sam's told me what I need to do. I even managed to get them milked without too much trouble. But it does feel a bit like being stranded at the back of beyond.'

'Where exactly are you?'

'Exactly?' She laughs. 'I'm ringing from the post office now. Sam's place is about half a mile down the hill at the end of a road going nowhere.'

He looks at his watch, makes up his mind. 'Do you want me to come?'

'No.' But something in her voice makes him think she'd have liked to say yes. 'Anyway, how would you get here?'

'That's my problem,' he says. 'Don't worry about it. I'll be there as soon as I can.'

I don't get a chance to answer before he puts the phone down. I thank the woman at the post office yet again, get wearily back onto the Cyc-Auto. All the way back to Sam's, I'm cursing myself for letting Nash hear my anxiety, exasperated that he thinks he has to act like some old-time hero riding to the rescue. But I'm relieved, too. I've begun to realise what I've let myself in for by saying I'd look after the farm, and I'm by no means sure I'm equal to it. Not to mention the job I'm supposed to be doing. It's a different kind of anxiety there, frustration that I've made so little progress. Maybe if I can talk to him, he'll help me see the way forward, even if I can't tell him much. Because whatever else lies between us, I can rely on him, not just to hear what I *do* say, but to read between the lines to what I don't. It hasn't always been a good thing, but this evening, I'm glad of it. I feel bad about dragging him out all this way on a cold night, but if we're to meet, there isn't any choice.

It had been instinctive to promise Sam I'd stay and look after his goats. As we'd waited for the ambulance this afternoon, his animals were his only concern. When he'd said *I can't ask the neighbours to look after them*, the words *I'll do it* were out of my mouth before I thought. After that, I'd been too busy getting him to tell me what I'd need to do to think about what the promise would mean. And then, when Sam had been taken off to hospital, there was so much to do. Milk the goats, give them their feed. For a first time, I managed all right, though I don't think I got half the milk Sam would have done. And it took me so long. I'll have to get quicker, but there are going to be an awful lot of early mornings and late sessions milking by lamplight ahead. Because I have to fit it round my job at Hursley Park, and it's obvious Sam isn't going to be back in action for quite a while. Though he'd pro-tested, the ambulance men had insisted on cutting him out of his boots before they put him on the stretcher, and when it was done, even I could see his right ankle was broken.

Waiting again now, waiting for Bram, I feel like an inter-loper in this quiet space. Though Sam told me to make myself comfortable, I don't feel it yet, though I have explored the hut he's made his home. The kitchen must be where Sam spends most of his time when he's not out on the farm, judging by the way everything is put handily close to his chair by the fire. The table is set with a place for one, but most of it's taken up with a Tilley lamp and a stack of *Farmers Weekly* news-papers, an old accumulator wireless.

Beyond the kitchen, there's a sitting room with mis-matched furniture that looks as if it's never used, and a single bedroom. Best of all, there's an indoor lavatory and wash-hand basin with a single cold tap. Sam told me how to pump water up to the tank in the roof to service these, but if I'm careful, I shouldn't have to do it every day.

Furthest away from the kitchen and the warmth of the range, a big room has been set out as a dairy. I'd dealt with the milk there this afternoon, scrubbing the wooden drain-ing boards and sink, straining the milk into gallon churns, leaving it to stand on a cold slate slab to wait for the morn-ing milk round. The list of addresses in Hursley where Sam delivers the milk is pinned up on the wall, with how much, and which days, pencilled in. That shouldn't be too hard. But what I'm going to do about getting the milk to Sam's cousin's café in Winchester, I don't know. I can't see how I can possibly fit that in with my day's work.

It's a problem that will have to wait. I can't solve it now. At least his cousin will hear what's happened. The hospital's bound to inform her because she's his nearest relative. That was one awkward telephone call I hadn't had to make, thank goodness. Just as well. The call to Mr Anderson had been difficult enough.

The recognised way to get a message through to anyone in the Hutments is to ring the public call box on the corner and wait until someone answers, ask them to fetch whoever it is you want to speak to. I'd done that, asked the public-spirited soul who answered to fetch Mr Anderson for me and rung off: given him time to arrive at the telephone box before ringing the number again.

It took a couple of goes before he actually answered, and when I finally managed to speak to him, I thought he'd be sympathetic. But he sounded put out when I told him I wouldn't be back that night. Perhaps it was because he'd been interrupted in his painting, or perhaps it was the old McNaught and Jericho angle. Whatever it was, it didn't make it any better that I couldn't really answer his questions about Sam. He tried to persuade me it's nothing to do with me, that I should go back to the Hutments tonight. There was a lot more of the early morning irritation in his voice than the later, kindly provider of bacon sandwiches.

But he wasn't the only one annoyed by then. The sheer indifference to Sam's plight and the implication that I have to be supervised every minute of the day, made me all the more determined not to give in. In the end, he'd had to concede: I'd stay the night, do what needed to be done, and we'd talk about it at work in the morning.

I look at my watch. It's almost nine, nearly an hour since I rang Bram. Anxiety washes over me. How the hell will he find the place? It was hard enough in daylight, and now, in the dark and the snow, it'll be next to impossible. But there's nothing I can do to help him. I can't even show a light to guide him.

I prowl around the kitchen. Lady eyes me from her place on the rug by the fire. Though she seems to have accepted me, she's still wary. She's waiting too, waiting for Sam. Unkind as it may be to think it, I hope she's the only one who's going to be disappointed this evening.

My stomach cramps. Granny would've said it's hunger making me feel sick. Perhaps if I could eat something, I'd feel less anxious. It is a very long time since that early morning sandwich. I find the heel of a loaf, a dish of pale butter, more than I've seen for years in one helping. Sam must make it from the goats' milk, I suppose. There's tea, and sugar, a bag of oats, and all the milk I can drink. Porridge for breakfast again, then, but for now, it seems like too much trouble.

I fill the kettle, put it on the range. Think about making toast, but I can't settle to eat. All the time I'm listening, trying to pick out the sounds that might have meaning from what – as far as I know – are the usual noises of the night in this place. I'm so far away from everything else up here that

I feel uneasy. What if the soldier were to come back tonight? Could Lady and I between us frighten him off?

I'm wondering whether to distract myself from imagined fears by turning on the wireless, when Lady pricks up her ears. She gets up, patters across to the door. Stands, head cocked, expectant. She seems eager, rather than hostile, and I take it as a good sign. She wouldn't be like this if it was the soldier come back.

I fetch my torch, put on my coat and hat. 'Come on, then,' I say to her, 'good girl. Let's go and see.'

Outside, the moon's up but it's only a few days old, hardly more than a nail paring of light in the sky. It hasn't snowed any more, but the frost has hardened the earlier fall into icy ridges that show the tracks I've mostly made myself, going back and forth from the post office. It's too cold to stand still, so I walk up the hill a little way. It's so quiet I can hear every footstep, every breath. Even the sound of the dog's paws on the snow.

Dimly, I start to hear a different noise. Is it wishful thinking? The breeze soughing through the woodland? But Lady's staring up along the road intently too. It's wheels, the sound of bicycle wheels crunching in the snow.

A shape comes into view round the corner, gets larger, clearer. Though the rider's face is muffled up with scarves and a hat, I catch the gleam of moonlight on glasses. It has to be Bram.

Something inside me starts to shake. 'Thank God.' Until I hear it, I don't realise I've spoken aloud.

He swings off the bike, unwinds the scarf from his face. 'You were right when you said it's the back of beyond.'

'Come on in,' I fuss. 'You must be frozen.'

But Lady's standing in front of him, not growling, but making it plain she doesn't intend to let him pass.

'Friend,' I say to her. 'Good girl, it's all right. Friend.'

She doesn't move, continues to stare at Nash, blocking his way.

'She doesn't seem convinced,' he says. 'Perhaps this will help.' He puts his hands on my shoulders, leans forward. Cold lips touch mine, briefly. So briefly I don't have time to react before it's over.

He's never kissed me like this before. Hardly ever kissed me at all, even the times when we've had sex. Confused, more than confused, I look away, reach out to the dog. 'Good girl, Lady. Let us in.' And she does.

Inside, the warmth hits me and I shiver. I can't meet Bram's eye as I take his coat and hat, hang them up with mine. 'Kettle's boiling,' I say inanely, though that's blindingly obvious from the fact the kitchen is filled with clouds of steam. 'I'll make a hot drink. There's only tea, I'm afraid.'

'Tea's fine,' he says, rubbing his hands.

'And toast?' I witter on. 'I was going to make toast. You can have butter, we've got a lot of that . . .'

'Take it easy,' he says. 'It was just a kiss.'

I can't think of an answer. Don't even try. Just try to pretend it didn't happen. But I'm suddenly aware of how it might seem, fetching him out on a night like this, meeting him in an empty house. What if he thinks . . . if he supposes I've brought him here expecting sex? My face flames. 'Toast,'

I say again, taking care not to look at him. 'Sit down, get yourself warm. Won't be a minute.'

I busy myself making tea, cutting doorsteps of bread. I stick the first slice on a fork, open the range door. 'Here, hold this. Don't let it burn.'

Once the bread's toasted and buttered, and the tea's poured, I'm feeling calmer. Though there's only one chair, I pull what must be Sam's footstool to the other side of the fire, settle down. As I tuck ravenously into my food, I've stopped feeling awkward with Bram. Something about eating together does away with the embarrassment.

'I'm amazed you found me,' I say, through a mouthful of toast. 'You didn't even let me give you directions.'

'It wasn't too difficult. You said you were at the post office when you phoned. So once I found that, all I had to do was ask the woman there for directions.'

'But even then . . . ? God, I've disturbed her so many times today. She must have been furious when you turned up.'

'Furious?' he replies. 'I didn't get that impression at all. Curious, maybe. In fact, she seemed quite gratified by all the excitement.'

'Poor Sam.'

'Sam.' He offers the last corner of his toast to Lady. 'Tell me about Sam.'

So I do, right from the beginning when I met the goats' milk man in Hursley. As I'm telling it, it doesn't seem possible that was only a couple of days ago. It seems like a lifetime.

When I get to the bit about the soldier, Bram frowns. 'He made threats?'

'I suppose.'

'And now you're here alone.'

'I've got Lady.'

'Hmm. I'll reserve judgement on that. Go on.'

I skip the bit about the Andersons this morning, tell him about visiting the White Horse at Ampfield, thinking that would be a good place to meet. And then how I'd come up here this afternoon, found Sam out in the field with Lady beside him, the goats looking on.

'What if I hadn't come? What if he'd been there all night?'

'But he wasn't,' Bram says. 'No good getting yourself worked up about maybes.'

'I had to say I'd stay. You do see that?'

He grins. 'Jo to the rescue.'

'That's you, surely?' I say. 'Coming here tonight.'

He shrugs. 'Pure selfishness. I'm supposed to be investigating David Hine's death, but I'm not getting very far. Then Barney Laidlaw said the other day – you remember him, the reporter? – that he thought we were like Watson and Holmes. When you called, it seemed like my cue. I thought if I could talk things through with you, you might be able to help me see a pattern. As it is, all I have is some worrying incidents and disconnected facts.'

'I'll help if I can, of course I will.' I'm not sure I believe that's why he came, but I am stupidly gratified by the idea that someone from Romsey sees us as a team. That Bram might think it too, might have come here tonight for the same kinds of reasons I'd wanted to see him.

'Oh, I think you can,' Bram says. 'You're looking at David's death from the other end of the chain.'

'Even if that's true, I can't tell you much about . . . well, my end of the chain. Not only because I'm not allowed. Mostly because I haven't worked out where it might be. I'm still groping around in the dark.'

'Me too,' he says. 'But I thought if we talked things through we might get a glimmer of a lead. Why don't I tell you about my end of it?'

Just as I'd laid out the story of my meeting with Sam, now Bram tells me how he got involved. About David's father asking him to investigate because he didn't believe his son was a traitor, or that he'd died in a drunken accident. And now the father's in a coma, attacked in his own home by unidentified assailants. Bram plays down his own accident in the lane that same evening, but I'm horrified.

'They targeted you,' I say. 'You know they must have done.'

'Perhaps.'

I frown, studying the scrapes and bruises on his face. I hadn't thought about it till now, too caught up with my own selfish problems to take proper notice. More than the damage to his skin, though, I can see the prosthesis he wears beneath the left side of his glasses is not the usual one. Now I look properly, I can see a difference. A more obvious line between metal and flesh, something not quite right about the painted skin tone.

'Your mask. Did it get damaged too?'

He's silent for such a long time, I think I must have gone too far. Trespassed on his private territory, his own secrets.

'I wasn't going to tell you, but I suppose I'll have to.' He smiles, but his heart's not in it. 'When the car hit me, my glasses came off. I couldn't find them, or my mask, in the dark. I knew I'd have to go back in daylight to look. When I did, the next morning, it wasn't there. I searched as best I could, but in the end I had to give up, admit defeat. Accept it was lost. Then, on Friday, when I was in Winchester, on my way home from meeting you, I put my hand in my coat pocket and there it was. It wasn't a mistake, it couldn't have been there all the time. It wasn't the same coat, for one thing.' He pauses again. 'It had been . . . broken. Deliberately folded in two. Nothing in the accident could have caused it. Someone broke it, wrapped it up in paper like a present. There was a man I'd run into, literally bumped into, just before I caught up with you. I didn't think anything of it then, but now I think it must have been him.'

'Why? Why would anyone do that?' And then it hits me. 'You must have been followed.'

'Yes. *Before* I met you.'

'Oh, Bram. And you were worried about me?'

He scrubs his hand across his face in the old, familiar gesture. 'I don't think,' he says slowly, 'it was about your end of the chain, if you want to put it like that.'

'Whether it is or not, you're right. It is all linked up. David's at the centre of it.'

'Oh yes, it's about him. What happened to him. It all comes back to that.'

We talk late into the night. Fruitless discussion, most of it, because we each want the other to give up the investigation. Bram tries to persuade me to resign from my commission from McNaught and Jericho, argues I don't even know who they are, what government organisation it is I'm working for. And it's true, I don't, but I do know that the documents I've signed mean I can't get out just like that. I have to see it through.

I'm more worried about what happened to him. Who might have been responsible for his accident. The mind that conceived that vile trick with his mask is a dangerous one. It's devious, and cruel: more subtle than the attack on David's father. But it's linked, it has to be. I don't believe the attack on Mr Hine was about the theft of a watch. It seems much more likely it was because he'd kicked up a stink about what happened to his son. His death, and the official conclusion that David had been part of a plot to get secrets out of Hursley Park House. And by asking Bram for help, Hine has made him a target too.

Though I try to persuade him not to investigate anymore, I know it's no use. Bram won't leave it alone. He can't, even though he hasn't signed anything. For him it's his own innate sense of doing what's right.

We talk it round and round. Even though I have to hedge about the leak of information, it's obvious he's worked most of it out for himself. The piece of paper in David's hand, what Mr Hine shouted at the inquest. He knows all that matters, and neither of us can succeed in our investigation without encroaching on the other's enquiries. But while I'm up against one adversary in my hunt for the leaker, it seems possible Bram has two. Two sets of people trying to stop him finding out what happened. David Hine's killer, or killers. And McNaught and Jericho's cohorts, hell-bent on keeping their secrets safe at all costs. What am I going to do if they're the ones responsible for the attack on Bram?

It's three o clock before we finally come to a halt. Yawning, Bram gets up to leave.

'No.' Like Lady earlier, I stand in his way. 'I'm not letting you go off at this time of night.'

'I'll be fine.'

I'm too tired to be tactful. 'Like you were the other night?'

'Like I was coming here.' There's an edge in his voice, too. 'Don't play the fool, Jo. Let me get on.'

'You can stay here, get some sleep,' I say. 'A couple of hours, anyway. I'll wake you when I get up. It'll be early, because I'll have to feed the goats, get the milk round done.'

He shrugs. 'I'm too tired to fight. Where do you want me to kip down?'

'You can use the bed in Sam's room. Or the sofa in the sitting room if you'd rather.'

'And you?'

'I'm staying here in the warm. With that chair and the footstool, I'll be fine.'

A quick wash to get rid of some of the day's grime, and I'm ready to sleep. I've found some blankets, tatty round the edges and smelling of mothballs, but good enough for the night. One for Bram and one for me, I think hazily as I set them by the range to warm.

I'm intending to listen out for him, take him a blanket when he's finished his own preparations for the night, but though I tell myself I'm only sitting down for a moment, I fall asleep like falling down a well, all of a piece. I must be dreaming when I think I feel hands tucking me gently into a warm blanket, hear a voice murmuring, 'Goodnight.'

Though he's tired, Nash finds it difficult to sleep. Everything is unfamiliar. The lack of noise: nothing stirs in the countryside beyond the hut. The chilly little room where his unknown host usually sleeps: seems like Jo certainly made the right choice, picking the warm kitchen to sleep in. The hard bed he's lying on: it's been moulded to a shape that definitely doesn't match his. Rolled up in a single blanket because it feels like an intimacy too far to actually get into the bed, his mind races with speculation. So many questions unanswered, and perhaps, unanswerable.

13

Monday 11ᵗʰ January, very early

I T'S LADY WHO WAKES ME, snuffling her nose into my face barely two hours after I fell asleep. I'm cramped, and when I try to stand up my right leg buzzes with pins and needles. Hobbling, I let the dog out into the yard, turn up the Tilley lamp. Fill up the kettle and put it on to boil. I refuse to start work until I've had a cup of tea.

Sleep doesn't want to let me go, despite the icy air coming in as I wait for Lady to finish her business outside. I splash my face with cold water, scrub my finger round my teeth, wishing for toothpaste and a brush. But at least it doesn't take a minute to be fully dressed, ready for the day. Just put on my shoes, my jacket and I'm done. Though that's a problem in itself. I don't think my Sunday-on-the-farm attire is going to go down very well at Hursley Park House.

I pour the tea. A cup for Bram, an old tin mug for me ready to take out when I go to the goats. The door of the bedroom's ajar, and I can hear the quiet sound of Bram's breathing. It seems a shame to wake him, but I promised. I tap on the door, go in.

He doesn't wake at first, even when the pale wash of light from the kitchen touches his face. He's laid down in his clothes the way I did. But he's had to take off his glasses, of course. And his mask.

I've seen him without it before, once or twice. The hollows where a shell fragment sheered away part of the bony structure of his left temple and brow, obliterated his eye. The scars where the doctors did what they could to reconstruct his face. It doesn't shock me or disgust me, but this morning it does make me want to cry.

I'm still standing there like a soft great idiot when he wakes, opens his eye and looks at me. The moment of unbearable intimacy, the vulnerability vanishes. He sits up quickly, reaches for his glasses.

'It's . . . it's almost half past five,' I stammer. 'I brought you a cup of tea.'

'Thank you.' His tone is brisk as he takes the cup from me. 'You on your way to the goats?'

'Yes. Bram . . .'

'I should probably say goodbye now,' he says. 'I'll have to get going as soon as I've had the tea.'

'Right. Of course.'

'I'll be in touch.'

'But . . .'

'We'll need to meet again, some more civilised hour. I'll leave a message at the post office for you. Or you can ring me.'

'Yes.' I seem to be stuck on monosyllables. 'I'll do that.'

I turn to leave, get to the door before he speaks again. 'Take care, Jo.'

'And you.' My voice breaks. The sense that there's danger out there, waiting, nearly overwhelms me. I daren't look back at him or I won't be able to leave.

A creak of bedsprings as he stands, a step. Then I feel his hands on my arms as he pulls me into a hug. 'We'll get through this,' he murmurs.

And now I really can't look at him, because I *am* crying. 'I know.'

A moment more of comfort and temptation. 'Soon,' he says, I think he says, and then he lets me go.

All the way back to Romsey, Nash is thinking of how he'd woken to the sight of Jo's face. The look on her face. It's as well there isn't any traffic on the roads until he's almost back in town, because he's no real memory of the actual journey at all.

He's glad of a bath, a change of clothes, and if Fan's realised he's been out all night, she doesn't say so. She serves up his breakfast on the dot of eight as usual, brings the newspaper and an envelope.

'Post's early,' he says.

Fan shakes her head. 'Hasn't come yet. Someone must have put that through the letter box early on.'

'Right.' The envelope's addressed to him but it's not been stuck down. Inside, there's a page torn from a leaflet for the Methodist Church just down the road. Turning it over, he sees a message pencilled on the back.

Dear Mr Nash,

I'm sorry for writing to you like this, but not having all my things here at my sister's I am having to make do with what I can find. I ought to have told you something else about Mr Hine's watch on Saturday but I was too ashamed to say anything because I never ought to have known about it at all if I hadn't been putting my nose in where it shouldn't have been. But I was troubled because I hadn't told you so I prayed about it in chapel this evening and I've been guided to put aside my pride and tell you what I know. The watch had writing on the back '*George from B April 1942*' and a funny little drawing. As far as I remember, it was a circle with something that looked like a lightning bolt in it. I don't know if it's important, but I thought I better own up to having looked. I am ever so sorry I didn't tell you before, I hope it won't have caused any trouble with your enquiries. Mr Hine is still the same they say. I pray he will come round soon and tell us all who hurt him.

    Yours sincerely

    Edna Stone (Miss)

Well, well, he thinks to himself. Whatever have you got yourself into, George? Because if he's not very much mistaken, Miss Stone's description of the engraving on the back of George's watch sounds awfully like the symbol for Mosley's British Union of Fascists. The party's been proscribed since 1940, when Mosley and his cronies were interned, but it would seem there are still some people who haven't forgotten.

'Porridge this morning.' Fan's voice breaks his train of thought.

'What?'

'Porridge,' she repeats. 'I had to make it with water today, but there's a bit of jam if you want it.'

'I'll pass on that.' As he eats his plain porridge, he thinks of the big jug of milk on the table at Sam's and hopes Jo is having a better-tasting breakfast than he is.

By ten o'clock I've finished a lighter-than-usual first round of deliveries at Hursley, made my way back to the post room. After my early morning start with all the jobs at Sam's, I feel as if I've done a whole day's work already. At least there hasn't been any more snow to make life more difficult. But there's still the rest of my day at Hursley to get through before I can even make a start on this evening's milking and feeding. It makes me yawn to think about it. At some point, I'll have to face Mr Anderson, too, and judging by his attitude yesterday, I don't think he'll be very happy about the idea I'll be staying at the smallholding while Sam's away.

Longer than that, the thought whispers. Even when he gets back, Sam won't be able to return straightaway to the farm work. But I can't worry about that now. Right now, my problem is trying to work out how I'm going to fit in a trip to Chandler's Ford to pick up some clean clothes. If I have to wait till after work, I won't finish the rest of the work before midnight.

There've been plenty of raised eyebrows at my slacks already. Among them, the post manager's, so when I take him his morning cup of tea, I'm hoping I'll be able to persuade him to give me a couple of hours off. His eyebrows raise even further when I outline what's happened, explain I need to fetch some things from the Hutments if I'm not to go around in slacks all week.

'You're a dark horse, Miss Rennard,' Mr Brennan says. 'I thought you were a stranger here. But you seem to have got yourself very involved with your fellow man in a short space of time. Or should I say your fellow goats?'

He obviously means it as a joke. I smile, though it's really not funny from where I'm standing. But I can tell the truth when I say I'd never met Sam before Saturday morning, and I certainly hadn't planned on turning into a goatherd.

'Very well.' He looks at his watch. 'If you go on now, I'll get Jim to do the mid-morning sorting. Just make sure you're back for the one thirty round. You'll have to make up the time, mind. No lunch breaks for you this week, missy.'

I can live with that, as long as he doesn't want me to stay late. As I go to fetch the bike, I'm trying to decide what I'm going to do about getting into the Andersons' house, since I don't have a key. I'm wary of asking Mr Anderson. If it's anything like yesterday's conversation, it'll turn into some long haggle about me moving out. But Hilda? She might not mind. She's never been keen on having me there. She'll be glad to see the back of me.

The security guards outside the Experimental Hangar are used to seeing me come and go, but I leave the bike out of sight so I don't have to explain all over again. If they think I'm on official business, that's all to the good.

Inside, there's the smell of oil and paint, other chemicals I can't identify. It's the largest single area Supermarine have here at Hursley Park, open from the wooden planking of the floor to the metal rafters that support the roof. Rows of overhead lights send bright shadows fanning out in every direction: up into the murky spaces of the roof and down across the rows of workbenches and shrouded shapes of aircraft wings and tails, mysterious part assemblies. A row of desks and drawing boards is squashed along one side, under the lowered section where the roof slants down.

The man I usually speak to, the hangar foreman, is up a ladder inspecting something I don't even try to look at. A chap in dark overalls ambles over to speak to me. 'What can I do for you, love? More post for us?'

'Not yet. I wanted to speak to Hilda Anderson if I could. It's not official, but—'

He doesn't wait for me to finish. 'Sure. She's probably over at her drawing board. Help yourself.'

After a week working at Hursley, I've got used to the relaxed atmosphere in this, the most sensitive area of the establishment. At first I'd been surprised, but I assume that the way the hangar's set out, with everyone pretty much in full view of everyone else working there, means it wouldn't be feasible to get up to anything shady. But this time it's not a matter of simply handing over a bundle of mail and leaving. Now I'm free to move deeper into the building, I can see that people working at the desks are partly screened from the rest of the staff. I negotiate my way past various bits of machinery and desks littered with drawings and paperwork to reach the row of drawing boards and finally catch sight of Hilda, right at the far end. No sign of her goddaughter, though.

Hilda frowns when she sees me approaching. 'What are you doing here?'

'Could I borrow the key to number 39? Mr Brennan has given me time to go and fetch some clean clothes.'

She tuts. 'Can't it wait until this evening?'

'Well, perhaps it could if I was going to come back to yours tonight. But I won't be. Not sure when I will, actually. I certainly can't leave while Sam's still in hospital.'

'That's the man with the goats?' she says.

'That's right. Someone has to look after them. Anyway, can I have the key for an hour or so?'

She reaches for her big black handbag. 'I suppose so. I don't know what Mr Anderson will say.'

'Be honest,' I say. 'You don't even like me being there.'

For a minute, I think she's going to start on some indignant denial, but there's almost a smile on her face as she hands over the key. 'I never said that.'

'No, but it's true. This way, you won't have to worry about me for a while.'

'You'll need to keep up the rent,' she says, 'that was the agreement.'

There's certainly no love lost between us if that's her only concern. 'All right.'

'And I'll want that key back before the end of the day, mind.'

'You'll get it. Oh, perhaps you could let me have my ration book, too? I'll need it.' If looks could kill, I'd certainly be feeling a pinch right now.

'Haven't got it with me,' she says quickly.

'Fine, tell me where it is and I'll pick it up when I'm back at the house.'

Another hard look before she rummages deep in her bag again, slaps the book down on the table. 'I've used your meat ration,' she says belligerently. 'You won't get any more this week.'

I smile. 'One of your hotpots? Hope you and Mr Anderson enjoy it.'

'There's no need to be snide. I'll see you later with that key.'

'OK.' I flip her a wave, thread my way back through the crowded section and out into the main part of the hangar.

'All right, love?' the man in dark overalls asks as I pass. 'Sort it out, did you?'

'Yes, thanks. No Anita this morning?'

He shrugs. 'Sent her off with a headache. Feeling sick, you know. Girls' stuff.'

'The smell in here must be hard if you're not feeling well.'

'Smell?' He looks around as if he expects to see a pile of rotting fish or a heap of manure. 'What smell?'

I laugh. 'I suppose you can get used to anything.'

But I'm glad to be outside in the clean morning air again as I make my way back to the bike. Time's pressing on, and so must I.

For once, Nash's appointment book is full today. He doesn't get a chance to think anymore about what he's learned from Miss Stone's letter until lunchtime. Perhaps she's made a mistake with her description, but he can't ignore the possibility she hasn't.

As someone whose half-Jewish parentage is well known in the town, Nash has come up against his share of antisemitism. But the implication that there is – or recently has been – an active fascist organisation operating somewhere in the area is disquieting. The date on the watch suggests as much, though it could, he supposes, be a private matter between George and whoever 'B' might be. Miss Stone seemed to think the watch had been a present from a woman. The fact that George had stopped wearing it might suggest he was no longer involved with whomever it was. But whether or not that's true, it doesn't mean his political views will have changed.

If George is a fascist, or has been, Nash thinks, does it make a difference to what he does now? Whether or not he goes on investigating David's death?

He's positive the boy's death wasn't an accident. But if the son shared his father's views, it might well throw a different interpretation on how he'd come by the scrap of paper found in his hand when he died. Though George had been adamant that David was no traitor, his definition of what that might mean could be very different to Nash's own.

And if he factors in Jo's mission at Hursley, what she *hasn't* said about her interest in David Hine, that's another piece of evidence for what's going on. She can't be there as a direct result of the boy's death, or she wouldn't have been able to talk about it. The obvious conclusion is that she's been asked to investigate the security breach. And who's more likely to be in the market for stolen aircraft secrets than Nazi Germany?

Restless, he paces across his office, stares out of the window at the rooftops of Romsey. Like anywhere, it has its faults, but he loves the place. It's in his blood, a visceral connection. Though he knows there are as many bigots as saints living within its walls, it's home, and he doesn't want to be anywhere else. But it does shock him to think of organised hatred festering somewhere under its surface.

He can't let politics deter him from trying to find out about the boy's death. But he's beginning to see this isn't a question of trying to track down a killer in the same way he and Jo had hunted for Ruth Taylor's murderer. It's not a simple pursuit of someone with a private motive for murder: some humdrum quarrel over money or a girl. What lies at the heart of David Hine's death is much bigger, much more dangerous.

The attack on George suggests as much. The removal of the watch, with its evidence of extremism, proves it.

He needs to proceed warily. Any investigation risks stirring up trouble, but this time the risk may not be his alone. It could touch anyone he speaks to. People he's already spoken to, like Auntie May and Miss Stone. If he'd known, he'd have thought twice about involving them, but it's too late now. He can't go back and change things. He can't even go and see them, warn them, because if he is being watched, that will do the very thing he wants to avoid, and draw attention to them. Miss Stone's probably safe enough while she's staying in town with her sister, but Auntie May is more exposed out in her cottage with only the geese to guard her. He'll have to think what to do to alert her. He could write to her, perhaps, though it'll be difficult not to sound ridiculously melodramatic.

But the hard truth is, if he is to find out what happened, he will have to keep looking for witnesses, asking questions. Because all he's got now is suspicion and a nasty feeling in his gut: what he needs is solid information.

Laidlaw's his best option for that. If there's anything dodgy going on, he's bound to know. And Nash doesn't feel too worried about asking him. The reporter is big enough, worldly-wise enough, to take care of himself.

A glance at his watch. No time for a leisurely drink in the pub with Laidlaw today. Pumping him for information – if he has any – will have to wait. His next client is due any minute. He'll have to call Barney later, see what he knows.

But even as he goes back to his desk, takes up the paperwork for the client's case in a boundary dispute, he's thinking of someone else. Someone who's never far from his mind.

Jo.

What about her? If he's in deep with his investigation, she's in even deeper with hers. Her vulnerability alarms him, alone on that farm in what even she admits is the middle of nowhere. He'd been uneasy enough about her before, squirrelling away in Hursley in some role he only half understands. But she's so stubborn. Nothing he could say last night had made the slightest difference to her determination to continue with her assignment. And nothing, either, was going to make her break her promise to look after those damned goats.

There's one thing about this unsettled life: it doesn't encourage unnecessary possessions. It only takes me a few minutes to pack up my things and get back on the road to Oliver's Battery. With one eye on the time, and the knowledge that Hilda and Mr Anderson will be dining off my meat ration this week, I hack off a couple of slices of bread to make into a sandwich when I get to Sam's.

Though Port Lane is as deserted as ever, there are people around as I come into the settled area. A woman nods to me as I pass the first smallholding, and a bit further up the road, a man waves purposefully from a gateway on the right, shouts something that might be 'Hang on there.' So I pull up, leave the engine running. I can see that the pasture beyond the gate must be the field that leads up towards Sam's holding, and the roof I can make out on the far side might even be his.

The man who shouted is a stout little red-faced chap, and he takes his time crossing the road towards me. But he's

smiling, so I wait, though I'm conscious of the minutes tick-
ing by faster than I'd like.

'You the girl looking after Sam's place?' he says.

Girl, I'm not, but I admit I did stay last night at Sam's. 'My
name's Rennard,' I tell him, feeling guilty at the lie. 'I was the
one who found Sam yesterday.'

'That's right,' he says, as if I might not have remembered.
'Della up at the post office told us you called the ambulance.
Bust his leg, she said.'

I'm uncomfortable discussing Sam with this man I don't
know. 'I think so.'

'It's a good community up here. We look after our own.
Not that we're nosy, nothing like that. We don't interfere. If
you're getting on all right, so much the better. We've all got
plenty to do. But if you need anything, you holler. Help with
the goats, anything like that. That place up there' – he points
to the roof I thought might be Sam's – 'is where you'll find
me. It's in a bit of a dip so you can't see it from Sam's, but I'm
not far as the crow flies. Evans is the name. Harry Evans. You
ask anyone if you're worried.'

'Thanks.' I feel a bit ashamed of myself for being suspicious. 'I'll certainly bear it in mind. If the does start to kid
while I'm here on my own, I'll definitely need help.'

'Not to worry, they mostly manage all right by themselves.
But you call if you need me.' He taps his nose. 'It's a bit of a
secret, but if you promise not to tell . . . ?'

I laugh. 'All right.'

'We have a system. If you get in trouble, all you've got to do is find a good big pot or pan and something to hit it with, and you give it a good old whacking and someone'll come along before you know it. Dunno why Sam didn't try it yesterday.'

He was knocked out, I think. That's why. But I don't say it, I just laugh again, tell him I understand. 'Mr Evans?'

'What can I do for you?'

'Do you know anything about a soldier hanging around up here? The first day I came to see Sam he was at the farm. Sam said he'd been trying to buy the goats for meat.'

'That'll be Adam Fisher,' he says. 'Horrible kind of chap. He's over at the transit camp, does something in the stores there. He's always sniffing around for stuff. Don't believe a word of it if he tells you it's for the Army. Black market, more like. Dunno how they let him get away with it.'

'I'll be careful.' In a way, I'm relieved. If he's often about, used to being refused, maybe his threats are just hot air. I'd hate to think he had a specific grudge against Sam. 'I must get on,' I say. 'Just going to drop my things off at the farm, then I have to go back to work.'

'Righty-ho,' he says. 'You remember what I say, though. Glad to help if you need it.'

It fits the bill to say 'I will,' since I definitely shan't forget. Though it would be nice to think I won't need help in such a hurry I can't just go and knock on Mr Evans's door. Raising the whole neighbourhood seems a bit extreme.

By the time I've ridden round the loop of roads to Sam's, it's almost time I was on my way back again. I dump my things in the kitchen, stoke up the range and damp it right down. With any luck it will still be alight when I get back. Lady comes with me as I make a round of the goats, check they're all right, and then it's back to her kennel for her, and me for the road. I haven't even managed to put butter on my bread, so I eat it dry as I zip back to Hursley.

I screech into the post room as the half-hour clicks over on the clock. Mr Brennan nods. 'Just in time. Jim's put it all ready for you. Off you go.'

I've got the key to number 39 in my pocket. When I get to the hangar with the afternoon post, I ask permission to give it to Hilda. Casual as before, I'm waved into the interior reaches where she works. There's no one in the section as I pass through, and Hilda's not at her drawing board either.

I'm struck by how many documents are piled round her workplace, a great jumble of paper lodged on every available flat surface, and overspilling onto the floor. I scoop up a couple of drawings before I tread on them, plonk them back down on her desk. I'm curious, of course, but I try not to look it. It seems as if she's copying drawings from a large master diagram, enlarging parts of it into more detailed sections. I don't know enough to gauge how sensitive they are: to my untutored eye they could equally well show some vital component of the latest aircraft or a dustbin.

Though there's no sign of Hilda, her handbag is still hanging on the back of her chair. She won't go home without that, so she must be coming back. I put the key in the pen tray, where she can't possibly miss it, and slip away before she catches me. It's a bonus not to have to face her again today.

There's internal mail for Southend House, which means I have to go off the Hursley Park site and across the main road through the village to deliver it. I'm on my way back when I see a girl in a very familiar coat running down the road towards the pub. It's Anita, her headache apparently cured. She flings herself into the arms of a tall man lounging against the corner of the building. The soldier again, Adam Fisher. Oblivious to any watcher, they engage in a film star-style kiss, and I wonder what Hilda would say if she knew the sort of company her goddaughter is keeping.

It's food for thought for me, anyway.

14

Monday, late afternoon and evening

'I HOPE I HAVEN'T CALLED YOU at an inconvenient moment, Laidlaw. I'm after some more information.'

'I told you last time, Nash. Reporters gather information, they don't give it away.'

'I remember. But think of how smug you'll feel if something you tell me leads to an arrest in the case we discussed the other day.'

'You're being very cagey.'

'The telephone isn't ideal for what I want to ask, but I haven't had a chance to come and see you today. And it is rather pressing.'

'Go on.'

'I wondered if you might have something in your archives – or more recently, come to that – about local friends of the Baronet of Ancoats.'

'The ... You mean Mos—?'

Nash cuts in quickly. 'That's right.'

'You're getting in deep waters if that's where you're looking.'

'I was hoping I was wrong.'

'You know what they say about hope. But you're right, better not be too explicit on the blower.'

'Could we meet up later? Have a chat?'

'Can't do it tonight. Gotta cover a council meeting. What about tomorrow lunchtime?'

'I suppose it'll have to do, if that's the earliest you can manage.'

'Well, it is, but . . . I've got a file that might interest you. I could drop it off at your place on my way home. Not the office. Can I trust that housekeeper of yours not to get nosy?'

'Of course.'

'All right then. But don't let it out of your sight. And I want it back tomorrow, without fail.'

'It's a deal.'

'You owe me a pint, Nash. Better put it in your will, just in case.'

Though Laidlaw laughs as he hangs up, Nash is left even more uneasy than before. He'd been hoping his friend would tell him he was imagining it all: chasing some crazy mares' nest of suspicion.

Because I'm still in my old jumper and slacks, I don't need to go into the house before I start on the farm work. I know if I go inside, sit down in the warm, I won't want to turn out into the cold again. I run the Cyc-Auto into the lee of the barn, light the lantern and set to with Lady beside me for company. There's milking and feeding, watering and mucking out. At least the goats in the field don't need that. Sam didn't say to keep them in so I don't. They don't seem to mind the cold, and they have straw in their shelter. But they do need fresh water and fodder because there's not much for them to forage on while the snow's still patchy on the grass. Once I've finished that and scrubbed down the dairy, it's late. So late I don't think I can be bothered to feed myself. I'll give Lady her supper, have a cup of tea and a wash, and then it's bed for me.

But when I let myself into the kitchen, the first thing I notice is the smell of food. I think I must be hallucinating, but as I light the Tilley lamp I see there's a big saucepan keeping hot at the back of the range. On the table, there's a bowl with four eggs and a note.

> *Soup for you keeping hot. Save you a job tonight. Della at the post office says the hospital says Sam's doing fine. Annie.*

I've no idea who Annie might be, but, as far as I'm concerned, she's a saint. Even more to be blessed when I go to stoke the range and find the coal scuttle's full and so is the wood basket. I feed Lady, wash hands that are chapped from the cold already, and ladle out a big helping of soup. It's as thick as a stew, with leek and potato, carrots and parsnips and split peas. If I'm not too greedy, there will be enough for tomorrow as well.

As soon as I start to eat, I realise how hungry I am. And, as the warmth of the food spreads through my system, how cold. I'd like a nice chunk of bread to go with the soup, but I've eaten what I took from the Andersons, and there's none left here after last night's toast. Butter in plenty, but nothing to spread it on. I put the eggs and soup carefully away in the larder. I need to conserve my resources in case there's no chance for me to slip into the village tomorrow to buy food since I'll have to work through my lunch hour. But I need to try. I can't rely on good angels to provide a meal for me every day.

I ache all over from the unfamiliar exercise, and I need to lie down. I'll use Sam's bed tonight, I think. I can't be fiddled with changing sheets, but I can lie on top of the covers like Bram did, and I should be warm enough. I'll have two blankets instead of one. If I leave the door to the kitchen open, some warmth will trickle through to the rooms at the back.

It troubles me that there's no lock on the outside door to the yard. Last night, it didn't seem to matter. But tonight, even with Lady to keep me company, it does make me feel nervous. I can't even wedge the handle with a chair because it's a round knob, not a lever. In the end, I have to settle for building a tower of pots and pans inside the doorway. There will be plenty of warning if anyone tries to get in.

If it was late when I sat down to eat, it's early for bed. Not much after nine, but I'm so tired I could sleep on a clothes line. In Sam's room, I turn off the Tilley lamp, open the curtains to a faint gleam of moonlight in the west. Roll myself in blankets and lie down. And, for a moment, before I slide into sleep, I catch the smell of bay rum: Bram's scent, like another tiny hug.

Nash sits late in his study, sifting through the documents Laidlaw has sent him. There are cuttings from national and local press going back to the 1930s.

Mr Mosley's London debut – 'For he's a jolly good fellow' greets the young man from two thousand throats.

British Union of Fascists launched – Sir Oswald tells follow-ers 'prepare to sacrifice all'.

Mosley gives fascist salute with Mussolini at Palazzo Venezia.

Hurrah for the Blackshirts – Rothermere backs Mosley. 'The new age requires new methods and new men!'

Sir Oswald speaks in Leeds – audience swept away by magnificent oratory.

Sunday Dispatch *sponsors Blackshirt beauty competition.*

Blackshirt brutality – hecklers at Mosley meeting badly beaten.

Mosley – 'the forces of Jewish corruption must be overcome'.

Battle of Cable Street – working-class people oppose the evil of fascism.

Mosley interned under Defence of the Realm regulations.

Remembering Mosley's ability to rouse an audience makes depressing reading, though there's comfort in his fall from grace. But Laidlaw's handwritten notes make it clear he believes there's a local group of supporters who haven't dispersed or given up their allegiance, but simply gone to ground. He names a councillor, a clergyman, a company director. Most disquieting of all, a senior policeman. None of them high up enough in Mosley's party to have been arrested like him – or even questioned – but Laidlaw's been keeping records that show they're still meeting: still, by inference, working for their cause.

The main focus of the reporter's investigations appears to be the occupant of a house called Limeshard Gate at Braishfield. There's an article torn from a society magazine about the building of the house back in 1928, when it had been hailed as a marvel of modernist architecture. The pictures show a house as square and white as a sugar cube, set down within an equally uncompromising square of high white walls. Built for an industrialist from the Midlands who died of a heart attack before it was completed, his widow, Mrs Ilse Reed, lives there now in what the article describes as semi-retirement. She's a woman of taste, judging by the interior of the house, less brutal than the exterior. In addition to the article, there's a blurry photograph, which looks as if it's been taken without her knowledge. A woman of a certain age, but not old enough to be in any kind of retirement, who's been snapped as she crossed Market Place in Romsey. Moving fast, if the out-of-focus image is anything to go by; stylishly dressed, cheekbones sharp enough to cut.

There's no indication of when the snapshot was taken, though it would appear Laidlaw's had her in his sights for years, following the rumour that she'd stood as a candidate for Mosley's New Party somewhere in the North. He's logged visits to her house by each of the men he's suspicious of, some of them very frequent, though she doesn't appear to be part of the area's usual social circle. Even from the poor photograph, she's a stunner, and Laidlaw's obsessive record of her movements makes Nash wonder whether the reporter's interest is more personal than professional.

He can't call to mind ever seeing the house on his travels through Braishfield, though it ought to be obvious, so white and square, and so very much not a run-of-the-mill country cottage. It has to be well off the beaten track. Nevertheless, she must be a neighbour of George's. Nash turns the pages of the notes warily, expecting at any minute to come across Hine's name. He's more relieved than he would have guessed to reach the end and find no trace of him.

Yet by Miss Stone's evidence there's the inscription on the watch. The symbol that sounds suspiciously like the BUF emblem. If only he could have seen it for himself, judged for himself.

Now he's read Laidlaw's file, he's no clearer. No nearer the truth. There are still so many questions, so many ifs.

If the description is accurate.

If it means what he thinks it does.

If George *was* involved with the fascists, why isn't he in Laidlaw's notes?

If David shared his father's beliefs, could he have been smuggling secrets after all?

One final question. Not an *if*, but a *who*. Perhaps the most important question of all.

Who the hell is 'B'?

At first, I don't know what wakes me. I can't tell what time it is: there's only starlight outside, gleaming on the retreating snow. I make out Lady's dark shape as she stands beside the bed. Whatever it is, she's heard it too. I'm beginning to think it must have been a false alarm, a passing fox that's disturbed the dog's sleep, when I hear it. The crunch of boots on snow, and a voice. A man's voice, and he's not even trying to be quiet.

'The old bugger's in hospital.' A laugh, as a flicker of torch-light sweeps through the window. 'Place is deserted. Just right.'

'You sure, Kipper? Don't want to end up in the glasshouse.'

'Who's gonna know? We'll have his bloody goats and away, no trouble.'

Beside me, Lady's giving out a low, continuous growl. 'Shh,' I whisper, laying my hand on her muzzle. 'Quiet, there's a good girl.'

Quick as I can, I pull my slacks and jumper on top of my pyjamas, shove my bare feet into my shoes. Two voices. And one of them, I'm pretty sure, belongs to the soldier who was here the other day. Adam Fisher. I don't know what I can do against two men, but I know I'm not going to let them steal Sam's animals without a fight. In the kitchen, I pick up the poker. A silly weapon, but there's nothing else I can locate in the dark, and I daren't light the lamp. It'll spoil my night vision, and anyway, I want to scare them off, not beat them up. If they see it's me, a woman on her own, they'll fight rather than run.

Edging past my booby trap of pans, I remember what Mr Evans told me. I don't want to raise the whole community, but I will if I have to. I pick up a cast-iron frying pan and open the door. Lady streaks out across the yard, the rumble of her growl rising in pitch. I run after her, yelling and shouting, trying to sound like a whole host of avenging guardians rather than just one woman.

'Who's there?' one shouts.

I see them now, dark figures with shielded torches in the doorway of the barn where the penned goats are kept. I run and duck, still yelling. It doesn't occur to me till the last minute that if they're soldiers, they could be armed. Lady barks, and one of them shouts in pain.

'Fucking dog bit me. Shoot it, Chalky.'

There's a shot, and it feels like my heart stops. My feet certainly do, for a split second.

Lady.

A tall man, who I'm convinced now is Fisher, is still grappling with the dog and cursing, so Lady's not dead. The one with the gun turns towards me.

They must have opened the billy's pen, because I see a shape rear up behind him. He staggers forward, his aim going wild as he's butted from behind.

Momentum keeps him moving, stumbling past me. I manage to catch him a glancing blow. His arm, I think, nothing vital, but he squeals like a pig, runs off across Mr Evans's pasture.

Only one of them now. I'm hoarse with shouting, shaking with adrenaline and nerves, but I won't give up. I drop the poker, take a better grip on the pan. With the goat and the dog behind him, and me in front, I reckon he's outnumbered. But just as I think I've got him cornered, a strident voice calls out. Mr Evans, I think, and I turn, taking my eyes off the man. The next moment I'm down on the ground and he's off, back across the field the way his mate went.

'Damn.' I've bumped my elbow and wet snow is seeping through the seat of my trousers. Mr Evans is beside me, all concern, but I wish he hadn't bothered. It would have been much better if he'd tried to stop my assailant. But by the time I'm up on my feet and he's reassured I'm all right, it's too late. Both men are long gone.

The night's over before Mr Evans and I manage to restore order on the farm. The billy, overexcited, is having too much fun to co-operate. He obviously doesn't rate my skills as a goat herder. He's determined to get out into the field with his harem and it takes all our efforts, Lady and Mr Evans more efficient than me, to get him to go back in his pen. Half a bucket of food pellets helps, though I'm not sure what Sam would say about that. He keeps the billy on a low diet when he's inside, and the pellets are for the does in kid.

When we finally get him settled, it's getting on for five. Though I don't think the men will come back again tonight, I'm glad when Mr Evans accepts the offer of a cup of tea. I'm almost sure he's been enjoying the excitement too, which is more than can be said for me. I'm still quivering inside from the memory of the gunshots, my fear for Lady. And for my own skin, come to that.

'Now, then, girl,' he says, 'what are we going to do about this little hoo-ha?'

'Do?' I'm confused. 'What can we do?'

'By rights, we ought to report it. Wasn't just a bit of petty thieving tonight, was it? There were shots fired. You were lucky you didn't get seriously hurt.'

'Thanks to you.'

'Huh. Thanks to me, they got away. Reckon you could identify them?'

'I thought I recognised the tall one's voice. That soldier who was here the other day, Adam Fisher. But I never saw either of their faces.'

'Me neither. Odds are it was him, but—'

'I know.' The thought of having to wait for a policeman to arrive, explain all over again seems like far too much effort for no possible gain. And there's the issue of McNaught and Jericho. They won't be pleased if I draw attention to myself. 'Honestly, I don't think it'll do any good to report it. The police have got enough to do.'

'Grieves me to let a toerag like that think he's got away with it,' he says. 'But I have to agree with you. It's all guess-work unless you saw his face. We'd just be stirring up a hor-nets' nest for ourselves.'

It's probably already stirred, I think. 'The trouble is . . .'

'I'll buy it. What?'

'I'll be at work all day. I'm worried what might happen if they decide to come back in daylight.'

'Don't fret about that. I'll have a word with the neighbours. We'll keep an eye on the place, make sure no one's hanging about.'

'I'm grateful, but it's a lot to ask.'

'But you're not asking, are you? I'm telling you. Like I said this afternoon, we look after our own.'

'I know Sam will be grateful.'

'Of course he will. But don't forget, while you're up here, you're one of ours, too. You do what you've got to do, and we'll do what we can to help.'

I'm too tired to argue, and the day's not even begun. 'That's a relief, thank you. Oh, and while we're talking about people being looked after, who's Annie? Her soup was terrific. A real lifesaver.'

'My sister,' Mr Evans says, yawning. 'I better get back to her too, or she'll be wondering what's happened to me.'

'Thank her for me.'

'I will. You take care of yourself, girl, and we'll take care of Sam's.'

After he's gone, I sit for a minute at the table, willing myself to get up, get on. Feed the goats. Make sure the water trough in the field hasn't iced over. Get the milk down to Hursley. Come back, wash and dress, something a bit less shocking today than trousers. I tell myself I shouldn't feel so tired. I've had almost six hours' sleep, what more do I want? I catch myself nodding, stand abruptly. The world sways giddily. I'm more than half asleep, but it'll be cold enough outside to wake me properly.

'Come on, Lady.'

With part of my mind, I notice she seems stiff as she gets up. The rest is occupied with puzzling out why there should be a red blotch on the blanket that forms her bed. With a sick jolt, I understand what it means. I didn't even check to see if she was all right. Just assumed because she made no noise, went on fighting, that she was uninjured. Full of remorse, I drop to my knees.

'Here, good girl.'

She comes to me. Now I'm paying attention, I can see she's having difficulty moving one of her back legs. I run my hand as gently as I can down her dark fur, feel wetness. My hand comes away sticky and red. Her fur's very thick, and it takes a moment to part it down to the skin, trace the damage. Relief washes over me as I see the source of the bleeding, a long graze over her hip. It's bad enough, but I was afraid it might be a deep wound with the bullet still inside.

There's enough warm water left in the kettle to clean her up a bit. 'You and Sam,' I say to her as I work. 'What a pair you are. Both of you with a bad leg now.' She licks my hand, waves her tail lazily. 'Perhaps you'd better stay here in the warm this morning.' But she's more of a trouper than I am, because as soon as I go out of the back door she's at my heels, ready for work despite her injury.

15

Tuesday 12th January, morning

'AGGIE, DO WE KNOW ANYTHING about a woman called Reed?' Nash asks his secretary the next morning. Society gossip is right up her street: if there's anything to know about a celebrity, local, national or international, she'll know it. And her memory is phenomenal for clients, past or present.

'Reed?' She pulls open a drawer of the card index cabinet in front of her. 'Reed. We did the conveyancing on a house for a woman named Reed. Two years ago? Three? Here it is. Miss Elsie Reed. Took a place on Winchester Hill. Not one of your clients. Mr Bing handled it.'

'Elsie?' It's tantalisingly like Ilse. Perhaps the widow no longer lives in Braishfield.

'That's right. She's a retired schoolteacher if I remember rightly. Nice old thing. She and her sister moved from Brighton. Do you want me to find the file?'

'No need. That can't be the woman I'm thinking of.'

She picks out another card. 'There's Daniel Reed, not sure what his wife's called. He worked for the railway. We got him compensation – oh, it must have been ten years ago.'

Nash smiles. 'No. This Mrs Reed is a rich widow living out at Braishfield.'

Aggie sniffs, purses her lips as she refiles the cards, snaps the drawer shut. 'That one,' she says contemptuously. 'Not one of our clients. And I certainly hope you're not thinking of taking her on, Mr Nash. We don't need people like that on our books.'

'Like what? Come on, Aggie, spill the beans.'

'I thought you didn't like gossip, sir.'

'Perhaps not, as a general rule. But you know what they say, rules are made to be broken.'

'Well.' She folds her arms, leans over her desk towards him. 'Thing is, it's not so much one story you hear about her, as lots of them. Nasty spiteful things she's done, people she's upset.'

He pulls the client chair close. 'I'm listening.'

'She's supposed to be rolling in money, but she doesn't pay her bills. Just before the war, she ran up a huge tally with the butcher's in Bell Street, months' and months' worth of meat and all the best cuts. When he eventually asked her to pay, she refused, said she'd had sausages from there that had given her food poisoning. Sausages! When would someone like her eat sausages? It was all steak with her, until he sent in his bill. But she told him if he pressed for the money, she'd let everyone know his meat was bad. Threatened to blacken his name, even take him to court. He had to back down, let it go, but it nearly broke him. And he wasn't the only one. A lot of tradesmen have said she bilks them if she can, they don't do business with her anymore unless she pays on the nail.'

'Perhaps she's not as well off as people think.'

'It's not the point, though, is it? If she can't afford things, it's not fair to trade on her position to get them. Other people can't do it. And shopkeepers certainly can't afford customers like that, especially nowadays.'

'True, but is that the worst you know of her?'

'Not by a long chalk. She can't keep a maid. Must have had ten or a dozen in the last couple of years. Won't give them a reference, either, never mind why they leave. The little girl who's at the greengrocer's now, Rosie Smith, she was out there for three months. On probation, the woman told her, she'd get paid if she suited. But it turned out she didn't get a penny, because the woman chucked her out in the last week over a broken cup.'

'She doesn't get involved with anything in town? Women's Guild, WVS?'

'Not her. Do something to help? She even managed to wangle her way out of taking evacuees, though she's got that great big house and only her in it. Claimed she had exemption because she has delicate health.' Aggie snorts. 'Delicate health, my foot. Have you seen her?'

Nash shakes his head. 'It's why I'm asking you.'

'It's true she's not in town very often, but when she is! The clothes she wears, like something out of Hollywood. She either had the best wardrobe in England before the war, or else she's got a line in black market coupons. She's not buying utility issue, that's for certain. And I bet she's never had to make do and mend either. Swanning around like Lady Muck. Anyone would look good if they could afford stuff like that.'

He makes a sympathetic noise. He knows how sensitive Aggie is about the enforced economies of war, especially when it comes to clothes. She's an only child, and her elderly parents are dependent on her to support them. But if the worst she knows about Ilse Reed is that she's tight with money and profligate with clothes, it's not particularly shocking.

'No . . . followers?' he says, deliberately choosing ambiguity.

'Huh.' Aggie sniffs again. 'If rumour's to be believed, she's a lot fonder of her men servants than her maids, though they don't seem to last any longer. They're not local though, not like the girls. Word has it she brings them down from the East End of London, young chaps all muscles and no brains to chauffeur her and goodness knows what else . . .' She stops, colour rising in her face. 'You can guess.'

'She's got a bit of a reputation, then?' If it was just sex, he still wouldn't be overly shocked. He's got a bit of a reputation himself if it comes to that. But the description of her men servants as musclemen from the East End does give him pause for thought.

'You could say that. And you could ask where she gets the petrol for that big old Wolseley of hers, because that's another mystery with rationing the way it is. She must know the right people, because she's not doing essential war work anywhere round here.'

'Not one for us then,' he says lightly, getting up from the chair.

'Certainly not. Has she approached you?'

He shakes his head. 'No, don't worry. Her name came up in connection with something I'm doing for George Hine. I'm not thinking of taking her on as a client for Nash, Simmons and Bing.'

Which is true enough, he thinks. But though he may not want her as a client, he does need to approach her if he's to follow his line of enquiry. Though what he's going to say to her, he doesn't yet know. He can hardly go knocking on her door, asking if she's a Nazi. Casually enquiring if she's come across his old comrade George at some illegal meeting. But he will have to find an excuse of some kind, though if she's a Mosleyite, it's going to be an awkward confrontation in all sorts of ways.

I've got a lovely mindless job, inserting articles and press cuttings into glassine envelopes and filing them in the appropriate folders. Just what I need after the disturbances of the night. Hidden away in the room with the safe, I can spread the papers out across the table. While my hands are occupied with cutting and sorting, my mind's free to work on my own problems. The only drawback is that Mr Anderson knows where to find me, and we still haven't had the talk about me staying on at Sam's that I know must be coming.

I don't mind being away from the Hutments, in fact, it's a bonus. But I have to admit that the whole business of looking after the farm is a problem. The goats' milk round is the worst. I can't keep on walking down and back to Hursley village every morning before I come to work, it takes too long. Not to mention the wear and tear on shoe leather and my feet. If only I could get it onto the Cyc-Auto, but even with a basket on the carrier, I couldn't fit in the three one-gallon churns I need. I'm trying to think my way through it, my eyes on the middle distance, scissors in one hand and a half-cut-out item about fine pitch propellers in the other when the door bangs open.

I jump, nick the tip of my finger with the scissors. 'Ow.' I drop the scissors, put the article down before it gets bloody. 'You startled me.'

'So I see,' Mr Anderson says, shutting the door behind him. 'Guilty conscience?'

'What have I got to feel guilty about?'

'You tell me.'

'If you mean me moving out of the Hutments, why should I feel guilty about that?'

'You're supposed to stay where I—'

They say attack is the best form of defence, and I cut in before he can complete his sentence. 'Can keep an eye on me? Is that what McNaught and Jericho told you? Not to trust me?'

'I was going to say, look out for you,' he says mildly. '*That's* what they told me. My job's to look after you, try and make sure you don't come to harm.'

'Sorry.'

Now I do feel guilty, up to a point. This is friendly Mr Anderson, the one who pops out of the weather house when the sun shines. If I hadn't seen that flash of chill on Sunday morning, realised what he could be like, I might have wanted to tell him about last night. Perhaps it's a good job I did see it, because there are all kinds of reasons why it would still be unwise to confide in him. I don't know him well enough to know where his loyalties might lie if it came to a test. They'd have to be with Hilda, surely, who doesn't like me at all, and who's definitely fond of Anita. Anita, who's mixed up with Adam Fisher, who might be the man who tried to get me shot last night. What was it E. M. Forster said? If it came to the choice of betraying his country or his friend, he'd hope he'd have the courage to betray his country. If Anderson knew what happened last night, he'd probably put his foot down about me staying at the farm. And if he knew I'd seen Bram twice already, he'd almost certainly report it to McNaught and Jericho as a breach of security.

'Are you all right?' His voice breaks through my thoughts, and I realise how long I've been silent.

'What? Yes, yes. I'm just tired.' I force a laugh, try to sound matter-of-fact. 'You wouldn't believe I'd have the energy to get into trouble if you could see what it's like up at Sam's. I'm getting up before five to feed and water the goats, bring the milk down to the village. Then when I get back in the evening it's another slog to do the milking, and feed and water all over again and muck out.'

Anderson scratches his head. 'That's it,' he says. 'Why on earth take it on? It's not as if you know this chap. You don't owe him anything.'

'You can't walk away when someone's in trouble.'

'Not sure about that. It's no good if you're tiring yourself out with this farming lark so you can't do your job. You have to remember what you're here for. Your priority is finding out who's getting secrets out of Hursley Park.'

I'm tired, it's true. And I'm tired of this . . . interrogation. I'm thoroughly fed up with the way he's standing while I'm still seated. Looming over me. It has the same daddy-knows-best authority that annoyed me on Sunday.

'Look, Mr Anderson. What difference does it make where I spend my evenings? Unless you think that the traitor is someone from the Hutments, I'm not going to be doing any investigating in Chandler's Ford, am I?'

'Ssh, not so loud.'

I hadn't realised how much my voice had risen. 'I thought you said the walls were three feet thick here?'

'Two feet,' he says drily. 'Don't exaggerate.'

'All right. I take your point about the investigation. But truly, the clues have to be here, at Hursley.'

'They do.' He sighs, perches on the edge of the table. Immediately, it feels as if the tension in the room eases. We're colleagues again, not schoolteacher and naughty pupil. 'The bosses are going to expect a report from me soon. What can I tell them?'

'You don't have to tell them I've moved out,' I say. 'I'm still paying the rent. And I'll be back when Sam's recovered.' That'll be weeks, I think. Maybe even months. It makes me tired even to consider it. And, God, what will I do if I haven't found out where the leak's coming from by then?

'If that's what I can't tell them, what can I say?'

'Say I'm making some progress. I've got some leads I'm following up.' Attack, I think again. Not defence. 'Ask them what they know about the coroner in Winchester. Mr Brown.' It's a shot in the dark, but that oh-so important letter intrigues me.

'I can do that.' He gets up. 'I'll be in touch.'

'Fine.'

At the door, he hesitates. 'Just remember, if you need to come back, you can. Don't worry about Hilda. Her bark's a lot worse than her bite.'

'Thanks.'

When he's gone, I can't retrieve that lovely feeling of almost-floating mindlessness from before. I put my head down on the table, but there's no danger I'll go to sleep. My mind is whirring with what's been said. If I've been cagey, avoided giving him straight answers, he has too. It's not good to feel he doesn't trust me, but then, I don't entirely trust him either.

Nash can't wait till lunchtime to speak to Laidlaw. And in any case, he doesn't think the public bar of the Abbey Hotel is the right place for the discussion he wants to have. When the morning letters have been dealt with, he takes the envelope with Laidlaw's files inside and goes along to the *Romsey Advertiser* office.

There's a girl Nash hasn't seen before at the reception desk. A pert brunette who welcomes him with a beaming smile and a 'come-on' attitude that would be easy to misinterpret. When he asks if it's possible for him to see Mr Laidlaw she doesn't ask his business or his name, just sashays off to the back office. He notices she doesn't bother to knock, but goes straight in. Behind her, the door doesn't catch, but springs ajar so he can hear what she's saying, her high voice carrying clearly to the outer office.

'There's a gentleman for you, Barney.'

Laidlaw's reply is a low rumble. Though he can't make out the words, Nash guesses it must be to ask who his visitor is, because she says, 'I forgot to ask his name. Very polite, but he looks a bit funny. He's got these horrible thick glasses. I think he must have something wrong with his eye.'

The scrape of a chair. The door opens wide and Laidlaw comes bounding out, the girl trailing in his wake. 'Nash. I thought it must be you.'

'A fairly safe bet from the description?' He doesn't want to embarrass the girl but she ought to realise how easily she can be overheard.

Laidlaw turns to her. 'There you are, Noreen. I've told you before, you have to make sure the door's shut before you're rude to visitors. Nash here's a solicitor. He'll have you for libel if you aren't careful.'

'Oh, I'm sorry. I didn't mean . . . I wasn't . . .'

'Don't let him tease you. It's not libel if it's true.'

He can see her working it out, the dawning look of embarrassment. 'Really, don't worry,' he says as he follows Laidlaw to his office. 'No bones broken.'

Once they're inside, Laidlaw takes exaggerated care to make sure the door shuts and stays shut. 'Noreen's a good girl,' he says. 'An ornament to the front office, but a bit slow.'

'She seemed bright enough to me. Just not very tactful.'

Laidlaw grins. 'She's eighteen. She'll learn. You've come about the file, of course?'

'That's right.' He takes the wodge of papers from his briefcase, puts it onto Laidlaw's desk. 'I didn't think the pub was the right place to talk.'

'True enough.' Laidlaw pulls the file towards him, puts his hands protectively over it. 'Sit down, man. Tell me, what's your interest?'

'Since reading your file,' Nash says, 'I think it's probably Ilse Reed.'

'What about her?'

'Exactly. What about her?'

'You said you'd read the file.'

'That's all?' Nash pushes.

'What more do you want?'

'Looks like you've been observing her for months, but it's a bit thin on detail, isn't it? Unless your journalistic skills have suddenly failed you, I'd guess you know plenty more.'

Laidlaw bristles. 'Like?'

'My sources tell me she's a mean woman, who wears beautiful clothes but lives at other people's expense and takes lovers from the lower classes.'

'Wow. Whoever your sources are, they obviously don't like her much.'

'And you do?'

'Now, wait a minute.'

'You've documented her as a fascist, but you seem to be defensive about her. I'm wondering if your sympathies might lean that way.'

'You must be joking. I'm practically a card-carrying communist.' Laidlaw blows out an exasperated breath. 'But I suppose you're right. There is something about Ilse Reed that . . . Have you seen her, Nash? In the flesh, I mean, not my poxy little photograph.'

'I wasn't even aware of her existence till I read your file.'

'Quick work then if your sources filled you in since last night.'

'Newspaper men aren't the only ones with contacts.'

'Obviously not. You'll have to introduce me.'

There's a knock at the door. Laidlaw gets up and crosses to the door, pulls it open. 'What is it, Noreen?' There's irritation in his voice, and Nash sees the girl shrink back.

'I thought you might like coffee,' she says. 'You and Mr Nash. I've put it all ready on a tray.'

'Oh, yes, all right, bring it in.' Laidlaw holds the door while she fetches the tray. 'Put it on the desk, there's a good girl. Then off you go. No more interruptions, though. Not till Nash and I are finished.'

'OK.' She casts a glance at Nash, smiles with a ghost of her former come-hither manner. 'I get it.'

When the door's firmly shut again, Laidlaw says, 'Where were we?'

'I think I was questioning your loyalty. Your motives for following Ilse Reed.'

'You're a rude bastard, you know that?' Laidlaw grins, hands him a cup of coffee. 'Do you want sugar? Sweeten you up?'

'It's fine as it is.' He takes a sip. 'Mmm. She makes good coffee, your Noreen.'

'Don't change the subject.'

'All right. You were suggesting that I'd succumb to Ilse Reed's personal magnetism if I saw her in the flesh.'

'What?' He thinks about it. 'I suppose I was.'

'And you have?'

'Seen her, yes. Succumbed? No. I don't think so. But she really is an extraordinary woman, Nash. I'd heard the stories, like you. And I hate her politics, but there's something about her that transcends it all when she's actually in front of you.'

'*La belle dame sans merci*?'

'Just that.'

'I'll take it as a warning, then.' Nash leans forward, taps the file on Laidlaw's desk. 'The names in here. You're certain they're all part of Mrs Reed's right-wing group?'

'Oh yes, no doubt about it. And they're still active, despite the ban.'

'And that's all of them, you think?'

'I didn't say that. There were more sympathisers locally, before the BUF was proscribed. But when Mosley got interned, they seemed to fade out of the picture. I can't say I believe they've changed their views, but they aren't actively engaged as far as I can tell.'

'You don't mention George Hine.'

'Hine? Should I? Wait.' Laidlaw's much quicker than his receptionist. 'Are you saying you've got a line on the fascists because of that business with his boy?'

Nash hesitates. If Jo were around, he could share his thoughts with her and know with absolute confidence that what he said wouldn't go any further. But to feed a newshound like Laidlaw has its dangers. 'Not exactly, no. You heard he'd been attacked?'

Laidlaw nods.

'This is not for publication,' Nash says. 'Really, Barney, it can't go any further. People might get hurt.'

'All right.'

'His housekeeper tells me Hine had been wearing a watch with a symbol like this on it.' He picks up a pencil from Laidlaw's desk, sketches the symbol on the corner of the file.

'Phhuh. Not much doubt about that. How have I missed him?'

Nash shrugs. 'You tell me. Hine must be a neighbour of Mrs Reed's. Could they both be secret fascists and not know each other?'

'Anything's possible, I suppose, but I wouldn't have thought so.'

'But you hadn't identified him as one of her group?'

'Not a sniff. Damn, I must be slipping.'

'As long as it's slipping, and not covering. What would you do if there was a story, and it involved your bewitching Mrs Reed?'

'Print it,' Laidlaw says so quickly that Nash has no doubt it's the truth. 'I hate the bloody fascists, whoever they are.'

Nash gets up from his chair. 'Fair enough. I'd better get moving, Barney. I've got things to do, and I'm sure you have too. A paper to put to bed. That's what they say, isn't it?'

Laidlaw laughs. 'It is. All the better if I could wake it up to a story about fascist plots.'

'One last question?'

'Fire away.'

'This policeman you name. Could he be the tip of an iceberg? Or is he the only one, do you think?'

Laidlaw hesitates. 'If I were you—'

'Yes?'

'I'd go very carefully.'

It's Nash's turn to laugh. 'You're getting old, Barney. Old and cautious.'

'Better than old and dead. You watch your step. Don't want to be printing your obituary in the next edition.'

16

Tuesday, afternoon and evening

M Y DAY IMPROVES ONCE MR Anderson leaves, though I can't get back to my mood of peaceful, couldn't-care-less pottering. Time to show my face in the post room. It's nearly lunchtime so I'm not surprised when Mr Brennan calls me over as soon as I walk through the door. After what he said yesterday, he's bound to have something for me to do.

'Miss Rennard.'

'Mr Brennan?'

'It's twelve thirty. Time you went to lunch.'

'I thought you said I—'

'Yes?'

'You said I should work through my lunch hours this week, to make up for yesterday.'

'Did I?' He looks serious, but there's a twinkle in his eye. 'And there's the missus, complaining I never put two words together.'

'I can go?'

'Better had. You're skinny enough already, can't have you fading away. Mind, if I need you another day, I'll expect you to do the extra.'

'Of course.' I grab my coat, get out before he changes his mind. Though I'd be glad of something to eat right now, the more pressing problem is getting stocked up for my meals at Sam's. I know already I can't have meat, and when I check my ration book it looks as if Hilda's used at least a fortnight's worth of my points. I'll have to make do with whatever the little shop at the south end of the village can supply. Though I'm ashamed of myself, I take the Cyc-Auto rather than walking. I should save the fuel, but right now, saving time seems more important.

The village shop's one of my stops with goats' milk and the woman there greets me like a friend. I hand her my ration book, explain what's happened. Ask her if I can register with her from now on. She looks at the book and shakes her head.

'You haven't got much left for this week, dear. All your meat and fat's gone.'

'It doesn't matter,' I say, thinking guiltily of the bowl of butter at Sam's.

'You've still got a bit of cheese. Hmm. You won't worry about milk, of course, but I can't let you have any sugar or tea.'

'Never mind. What about bread? Have you got any to spare?'

'This time of day it's nearly all gone. I've got a couple of cob rolls if they're any good to you.'

'They'd be lovely. Does Sam usually have bread from you?'

'Small loaf Wednesdays and Saturdays,' she says. 'Want me to keep them for you?'

'Yes, please.'

'You can take it when you bring the milk. That's what Sam does. Now, have you got a bag? No? All right, you can borrow one from me.' She brings a string bag out from under the counter, starts to pack up my goods. 'Long as I get it back. Don't know if you'd fancy it, but I've got a little jar of fish paste you could have. It's not on points.'

'I'll take it. Thank you. You're very kind.'

'Well, it's a shame. Someone's done a real fast one on you with that ration book. Never mind, we'll get you straight next week.'

'What do I owe you?'

'Ninepence ha'penny. Make it ninepence, the rolls are a bit stale.'

Heartened by her kindness, I pay for my provisions and leave. As I putter back up the drive, I'm congratulating myself that I've still got twenty minutes left to have some lunch.

I park the bike round the back of the stables. The string bag has got caught round the bars of the carrier and I'm fiddling about, trying to free it when I see Anita scurrying towards the sunken garden. Curiosity piqued, I abandon my shopping and follow at a discreet distance.

In summer, there would have been plenty of cover for someone like me, intent on spying. But this time of year, with most of the greenery reduced to bare branches, there's very little to shield me from view. Cautiously, I keep to the back of the denuded pergola, peering down into the sunken garden as best I can. The flower beds are mostly as bare as the branches, but spear-like green leaves rustle at one end of the pond where David Hine died. I can't see Anita. With only the narrow shelter of a clipped cypress to shield me from view, I move forward, convinced I've lost her.

'I told you, I can't do it first thing, Addy.'

I pull up short just in time. That's Anita's voice, babyish with a hint of a whine.

'Thought you said you loved me?' And that's Adam Fisher, not a shadow of doubt. I'd know his aggressive tones anywhere.

'I do, course I do. But I won't have a chance till lunchtime.'

'Twelve sharp then. Not a second later, or we're through.'

'Don't say that . . . Oh, Addy, give me a kiss.'

'All the kisses you want when I get the stuff.'

'Addy . . .'

And now I see him, Adam Fisher, striding away. He takes the steps at the far end of the garden two at a time and is gone without a glance behind, though I can hear – and I'm sure he must too – that Anita has burst into noisy sobs.

I'm torn. I don't know what's going on between her and Fisher, but it sounds bad. I'm trying not to jump to conclusions, but, at the very least, it seems as if Anita's being coerced by Fisher. His reference to 'stuff' sounds more like the black market than secrets, but I can't ignore the possibility it might not be. She could be the source of the leaks; she'd have the opportunity. I've seen how casual the access to plans seems to be in the Experimental Hangar where she works.

I should report what I've heard to McNaught and Jericho at once, but the only way I have to do it is through Mr Anderson. And I don't trust him to do it, knowing his fondness for the girl. He might warn her off, then I'd never get the evidence I need to free me from this damn task.

So I'll keep quiet. Make sure I'm here, tomorrow, at twelve. Find out for myself what's going on. Time enough then to make my report.

Late on Tuesday afternoon, Nash makes his daily visit to the hospital, hoping to be allowed to see George Hine. The ward sister, that stern gatekeeper, must surely go off duty sometimes? But whenever that happy day might be, it isn't today. She's there in her office as usual, polite but uncompromising. Hine still can't have visitors. In a way, Nash is reassured. If he can't get to George, presumably no one else can. Tilling might be sceptical, but Nash can't help thinking his friend might still be in danger if his attackers believe he can identify them.

The thought persists as he ploughs through the daily rigmarole. How is he? – the same. Has he woken? – not yet. But there's an extra question he needs to ask.

'I wondered, have there been any new enquiries about him?'

The ward sister adjusts the starched cuffs at her wrists. 'I'm surprised you should ask, Mr Nash. What earthly business is it of yours?'

He falls back on the half-truth from before. 'As George's solicitor, I'd be failing in my duty if I neglected to follow up any lead that might result in tracking down his next of kin.'

She unbends a little. 'Well, I suppose I can tell you someone did telephone yesterday asking about Mr Hine. A young man. He didn't give his name. Equally, I wasn't at liberty to give *him* any information.'

It's no good. He'll have to risk taking her into his confidence. 'Sister, can I be frank with you?'

'I hope you've been nothing else.'

'Until the police track down George's assailants, I believe he's at risk. Even here, in your care. Especially since he hasn't yet been able to communicate what he knows about the attack. Whoever did it has a vested interest in ensuring he doesn't recover.'

She nods. 'That aspect hadn't escaped me, Mr Nash. Indeed, I believe the police questioned you yourself about what happened?'

'Touché.' He can't help but smile. 'Well, if you're as efficient in keeping everyone else away from George as you are in protecting him from me, I don't think I've anything much to worry about.'

She might almost smile in return. 'Depend on it,' she says. 'Now, I must get on. The consultant's round is due in five minutes exactly.'

He's passing the porters' lodge when the enquiry hatch snaps open. It's Jo's estranged grandfather, Joseph Fox. The man's a phenomenon, still working despite his age. Still unforgiving, full of spite towards Jo and himself. Nash gives a curt nod of acknowledgement but keeps on walking. He's not looking for a fight today, and fighting is all he and Fox ever seem to do.

'Nash.' Peremptory. And then again, 'Mr Nash.'

He stops, turns. 'Mr Fox.'

'What've you done with my granddaughter?'

'Jo?'

'That's the one,' the old man says with heavy sarcasm. 'The bastard. Hear she's deserted you.'

'I wonder who told you that?'

'Talk of the town. Wouldn't be the first time though, would it? She's a great one for running away. Always has been.'

'It's not my understanding she's run away,' Nash says. 'Nor, for that matter, that she left of her own will all those years ago. That was you, wasn't it? Banishing her while she was still a child because of her birth.'

Fox sneers. 'That's her story.'

'Was there a point you wanted to make? Only I've got plenty to do.'

'Get you,' Fox says. 'That's not what I heard either. Folk say your little firm is going to the wall, that's why she's left.'

'Just gossip.' He tips his hat to the old man. 'You don't want to credit all you hear. Shall I tell Jo you asked after her?'

'You could tell her *someone's* been asking after her, if you like. Someone with a legal right to know. See what she makes of that.'

'That's it? No name?'

Fox grins. 'That'll do for now. She can come and ask her old grandad if she wants any more.'

The hatch slams shut. Nash walks away. The old man was undoubtedly trying to get under his skin with the jibes about Jo and the business. And perhaps people *are* talking. But it's the last comment that worms uneasily in his mind. Who could have been asking about Jo who'd have a legal right to know? The police? The ministry men? Why would they go to old Joe Fox for information?

I get through the evening work at the farm quicker today. I'm better at handling the goats, even the billy seems friendlier after the excitements of the night. I'm finishing in the dairy, scrubbing down the draining boards, when Mr Evans calls.

'Got a message for you from Sam.' He holds a piece of paper out towards me.

'I can't take it for a minute,' I say. 'My hands are wet. What does it say?'

'You want me to read it to you?'

'Yes, please. If you don't mind.'

As Mr Evans reads, I can almost hear Sam's laconic speech. '"*Dear lass, going to need your help a bit longer. Sending me out but not home. Have to stay with cousin Ada. If kids come they need names starting with N. Regards, Sam. PS Ada says people complaining about milk at the café, so don't send this week. Save you a job anyway. Get Annie to show you what to do with the extra.*" Whoah. That's a bit of a facer.'

'You could say that.' I shake the wet out of the scrubbing brush, dry my hands.

'Can you stay?'

I shrug. 'I can't go, can I? Leave the goats? You've all got enough to do.'

'Suppose we could split the animals up, share them round for the time being.'

'No.' I remember what Sam said about the goats knowing where their home is. 'I can manage.' I yawn.

'Looks like it,' Evans says.

'No, really, it's all right. The only real problem is the milk round. If I could find a way to get the milk down to the village with the bike it would save such a lot of time. The goat cart's all very well but I have to walk down with them and then come back here to settle them again before I can go to work.'

'Well, my dear, what you need is a bodger.'

'A bodger? What's that?'

'Properly speaking, it's a bloke who makes chairs out in the woods, but, in this case, it's me. Someone who can bodge something up for you. Give me a hammer and nails and a few old bits of wood and I'll make you anything you want. You show me this 'ere bike and I'll sort it out for you.'

I take him to the barn where the bike's parked.

'I've seen the goat cart often enough,' he says. 'Does it have to be that big? Do you need all that room?'

'Not really. Just enough to hold three one-gallon churns.'

'Right. Leave me the lamp and go and have your tea. Bring me a cuppa in an hour or so, I should have it done by then.'

I'm too grateful to argue with him. If he can fix something up, it'll make all the difference. If not, he'll deserve a cup of tea for trying, even if it does use the last of Sam's ration.

I cheat a bit, because it's not quite an hour when I go back to the barn. I'm curious to see what he's doing, and anyway, if I stay in the warm any longer I'll go to sleep.

'There now,' he says as I walk into the light with his mug of tea in hand, 'just right. What do you think?'

He steps back and I see Cyc-Auto has sprung an appendage. A dinky little cart with a square base and low rail mounted on what look like two pram wheels. Connecting it to the bike is a long, curved wooden bar which arches over the back wheel and is fixed somehow to the saddle post.

'I know it looks a bit of a beast,' he says. 'Had to make do with what Sam had got lying about, but it should do the job.'

'It looks . . .' I shake my head. 'I don't know how you've done it, Mr Evans, but it looks like salvation to me.'

'Steady on,' he says. 'What would the vicar think? Now then, you can unbolt this bar from the back here, if you don't want the cart trailing along behind you when the milk round's done.'

'If that's a bodge it's got to be the best in the world. I could hug you.'

He grins. 'I'm not stopping you. So long as you don't spill my tea.'

It's a very different kind of hug from the one I got from Bram yesterday morning, but it's warm and it's human, and I don't know about him, but I feel all the better for it.

'There,' he says, patting me awkwardly on the shoulder before he lets me go. 'Glad I could help.'

I'm about to try and tell him how grateful I am when I hear the sound of booted feet. Instantly, I'm back in the panic of last night. I can feel my heart race, the blood drain from my face. 'Who's that?' I whisper.

'Hey, don't get upset. It's all right. That's Bill, doing his rounds.'

'Bill?'

'The neighbours and me, we're going to have a stroll round after dark, make sure that Fisher chap's not hanging about. You see, look, Lady's wagging her tail. You hear anyone around, and she's not worried, you know it's one of us.'

'But . . .'

'Call it a sort of ARP,' Evans says. 'Your own private raid protection.'

The kindness is almost the last straw. Another word and I'll cry, and I don't want to do that and embarrass us both.

'There now,' he says. 'You get off to bed. Bill and I'll tidy up here and then we'll be off ourselves.'

I nod, speechless. Click my fingers for Lady, go inside. When I shut the door, I finally notice what I should have seen earlier. Someone's fixed sturdy bolts top and bottom. I push them home, lean back against the door. Then, because I can't fight it anymore, I do cry.

Nash has racked his brains for a way to scrape up an acquaintance with Ilse Reed, but he can't think of anything. It's not as if he can disguise himself, and by what he knows, she's unlikely to respond to an appeal on behalf of charity, real or invented. His only recourse is honesty.

> Dear Mrs Reed,
>
> You may be aware that a neighbour of yours, George Hine, was attacked and seriously injured on Thursday last. As his friend and solicitor, I'm anxious to discover any evidence which might lead to the apprehension of the culprits.
>
> I wondered if you may have seen or heard something that day which might aid my enquiries. Perhaps you would be good enough to spare me a half-hour of your time to discuss this?
>
> Yours sincerely,
>
> A Nash

As he seals the envelope, stamps it ready for posting, he doesn't know what he expects by way of a reply. If he gets one at all, of course. Whether it will mean more if she refuses to see him than if she agrees. But it's in the lap of the gods now. He'll have to wait and see.

17

Wednesday 13th January, late morning

I GET TO THE SUNKEN GARDEN with ten minutes to spare before Anita or Fisher are due to arrive. As I ease my way into a space behind another of the little cypresses that shielded me from view yesterday, I'm feeling positive. A good night's sleep and being able to do the milk round using the Cyc-Auto have made all the difference. Even Mr Brennan seemed surprised at how quickly I'd got the post done, and he'd barely raised an eyebrow when I asked to go to lunch early.

It's a dim morning, the air dank with fine rain. Crouched down in my old grey coat and with a dark scarf pulled round to hide the whiteness of my face, I don't think they'll see me. I've chosen to watch from the far end of the garden, because that's the route he chose yesterday. It's him I'm going to follow if I can. I suppose it's most likely he'll head out across the park towards the transit camp, which will be awkward, because there's no cover for miles. I'll have to keep my distance, hope he won't spot me in the mizzling rain.

Footsteps on the path. I freeze, not daring to breathe as Fisher passes by, close enough to reach out and touch. He clatters down the steps and I hear him curse as he sees Anita isn't there.

In my head, I echo his curse. If she doesn't come, I'll maybe never know what's going on between them. His boots ring on the crazy paving: it seems he's confident – or arrogant – enough not to care whether anyone knows he's here. A minute passes, then another. He's muttering now, and I catch the word 'bitch' as he comes nearer to my hiding place. His pacing seems concentrated towards this end of the garden, and I'm afraid he's going to leave without completing whatever transaction was supposed to happen. I'm trying to make up my mind whether to follow him if that's the case, when I hear the rustle of lighter steps, hear Anita call.

'Addy, oh, Addy, I'm sorry. I thought I'd never get the old witch to leave me alone.'

'Have you got the stuff?' Fisher's voice is harsh.

'Here it is.'

I'm longing to take a look but they're really close, and I don't dare move.

'It's all here?'

'Like I promised. Oh, Addy . . .'

'No time for that now, I'm already late, thanks to you.'

'When will I see you?'

'Tomorrow maybe or Friday. No, get off me. Let me go.'

I shrink back as he comes rushing up the steps towards me. Wait as long as I dare before inching out of my hiding place. I hope Anita's gone too, but I can't wait. I mustn't risk losing sight of Fisher.

As I emerge onto the path above the garden, it seems as if I have left it too late and Fisher's gone. But when I look to my right, away from the House and park, I catch a glimpse of him as he turns into the tree-lined lane that borders the site. I hurry after. It's beginning to rain harder, but I'm glad of it. Fisher's got his head down against the weather and he seems oblivious to everything except covering the ground as fast as he can. He moves at a lope, just short of running, and I can barely keep up. A couple of hundred yards further on, and he veers right again, takes the path that leads out towards Ampfield woods.

At first it looks as if he might be heading for the boathouse by the fish ponds, or even the lodge nestled into the trees at the edge of the wood, but he passes both by without a glance, keeps on going.

Once through the gate by the lodge, he plunges deep into the woods. As we go further in, I start to lose my sense of direction. I think we're heading west, or maybe north of west, but I've no idea where that will take us. The rain's less troublesome here within the shelter of the trees but Fisher's still moving fast, head down, purposeful. I'm having even more trouble keeping up with him now. While the track he's on is a good straight path, grassy underfoot and relatively easy walking, it runs so straight I can't risk using it. He'll see me for sure if he looks back. I have to keep in the lee of the trees where the undergrowth is thicker and the ground is rough. It's as well we've had a wet winter, everything is green and soft and I don't need to worry too much about making a noise as I pass through. I get a few flicks across my face from low hanging branches, and scratches on my legs from brambles, but I keep doggedly on. Though I lose sight of him every now and again, I manage not to lose him altogether. Despite the numerous tracks that cross ours, he doesn't deviate from his beeline through the woods.

We must have been walking for ten minutes or more when he suddenly pulls up, turns half towards me. I stand stock-still, willing him not to see me.

For a moment it seems he must have picked up the feeling he's being followed, but then I see he's turned this way to light a cigarette, shielding the match from the wind with his hand. The smell of smoke reaches back towards me, and though I gave up smoking months ago, the scent in the rain-washed wood makes me long for a cigarette myself.

Fisher reaches into his battledress jacket again, and I get the first glimpse of what he's carrying. He keeps it close to his body, out of the wet, and it's too far to make out details. But I can see it is something flat, light coloured. An envelope, perhaps? No, the way he riffles across the top edges makes me think it must be folded papers.

It still could be something to do with the black market that's brought him out here, I suppose. But it seems much more likely this is how the secrets get out. I feel sick with the knowledge. If I'd reported it yesterday, the information he's carrying would have been safe. But there's nothing I can do now. It would be suicide to try and stop him on my own. The only thing I can do is make sure I see where he goes, who he meets. Then, if I'm quick, and report back straightaway, Anderson may be able to get a message to McNaught and Jericho in time to stop the information going any further.

I watch him tuck the papers carefully back into his jacket, throw down the cigarette end. And he's off again, moving quickly as before, long strides I can't match. I scramble along as best I can, keeping him in sight, keeping me out of it.

The trees begin to thin in front, and there's a criss-cross of tracks leading away from the one we're on. Fisher takes a path that's still heading in the same direction, but curves away from the grassy track. For the first time since we came into the woods, his boots crunch on gravel. I'm wondering how I'm going to follow him here, when I realise that the brightness I've been seeing through the trees is not simply where light is coming in across more open ground. It's reflecting off a wall, a high white wall, clean and square.

I take a chance, duck across the track, go to ground in the trees beyond. Skirting along the gravel path, it's easy enough to follow the sound of Fisher's boots. The wall turns a corner and it's obvious now that this is an enclosure for some kind of building. It's impossible to see what: the wall's too high and as soon as I move further away for a better perspective, the trees cut off any view. Another corner, and I can see a pair of tall, black, solid-looking wooden gates. Fisher's standing to one side, obviously waiting to be let in. Anticipating the moment when the gates open, I try to manoeuvre to a vantage point where I'll see inside. But instead, a domestic-sized door inset into the left-hand gate cracks open and all I see before it closes again behind Fisher is a glimpse of a man in a dark uniform.

There's no time to lose. Desperate to get my bearings, I weave through the trees parallel to the building's driveway. There must be a road ahead, because the way we've come through the woods can't be the main route to this place. But it's no good. After a few yards, I come to a field boundary. There's no cover to go any further, and hedges bisect my forward view. All I can do is turn round, get back to Hursley as quick as I can.

I run as much of the way as I can manage. It must be a mile, and I wouldn't have thought I could do even half of it at speed. But it seems, when I have to, I can. I take the track, in too much of a hurry to try and hide, though apart from a startled-looking roe deer which goes bounding off with a flash of white rump, I seem to be alone. There's no sign of anyone following me, though I stop to look back over my shoulder a dozen times.

I've no idea what time it is, whether I should be back at work. It doesn't matter, I go straight to the Drawing Office.

'Mr Anderson,' I pant as I crash in through the door. 'I need to speak to Mr Anderson.'

Half a dozen heads look up from their drawing boards. One, a tall man with an air of authority, gets up, comes over to me.

'You look as if you're in a bit of a state, love,' he says in a tone that I think is meant to calm me down, but only makes me even more frantic. 'What's wrong?'

'Mr Anderson, where is he? I've got to speak to him. It's urgent.'

'Well, I'm sorry, love, but you can't. He's not here.'

I take a deep breath, try not to scream. 'I can see that. I need to know where he is.'

He shrugs. 'I can't rightly say.'

'Please. It's important.'

'You're the one who's been lodging with him, aren't you? If it's something important, why don't you nip down and talk to Mrs Anderson? Hilda. She's in the Experimental Hangar.'

'I know where she is. It's Mr Anderson I want.'

'Look, love, I probably shouldn't tell you but I will. He's been sent up to Castle Bromwich on an assignment. Just this morning. He's on his way there right now.'

'Oh, God.' Since I arrived at Hursley, I've had no way to get in touch with McNaught and Jericho myself. It all has to go through Anderson. Something to do with keeping lines of communication secret. 'Did he leave a message for me?'

The tall man shakes his head. All he says is 'No,' but by the expression on his face it might as well be *Why on earth do you think he would?*

The realisation brings me up short. If I don't take hold of myself, I'm going to completely blow Anderson's cover as well as my own. I can't think of a rational excuse for the state I'm in, the urgency. But the tall man solves that problem for me at least. With a return to his soothing tone, he says, 'Have you had an accident on that ruddy bike of yours? They're lethal, those things.'

'That's it,' I say, hoping the lie won't show in my face.

He pats my arm. 'Look, go and get yourself tidied up a bit. Nip into the canteen here, have a cup of tea.'

'I can't. I need to . . .'

He misunderstands my anxiety. 'Don't you worry, I'll give Brennan a ring, tell him what's happened. When you've calmed down a bit, go and see Hilda, eh? Only don't turn up like that, she'll have fifty fits.'

I'm on the brink of protesting when I think better of it. Much better if I don't have to excuse myself to Mr Brennan. The lies will be better coming from this man. And I need time to think, to work out what to do. 'All right. Thank you, I will.'

In the lavatory attached to the Drawing Office canteen, a tiny mirror shows me why the tall draughtsman thought I might have come off the Cyc-Auto. There are red marks where branches have slashed across my face and my hair's a fuzzy mess. Granny would have said I look as if I've been dragged through a hedge backwards. Which is fair enough, I suppose, because I pretty much have.

I splash my face with cold water, finger-comb my hair into some semblance of order. My legs are scratched, spotted with mud. It's as well I didn't put on stockings this morning, they'd have been in shreds. I mop myself clean with my handkerchief, brush twigs off my coat. Another survey in the mirror shows me looking more normal, but inside I'm in turmoil, my thoughts as jumbled as before.

When I come out of the lavatory, I still haven't decided what to do. Though I know, realistically, there's nothing I *can* do until someone from McNaught and Jericho's department contacts me, it doesn't seem right just to wait. To go tamely back to my job and sort letters. Even though I have to accept today's secrets are lost, what of the future? How am I going to get the message out, stop future leaks?

As I stand hesitating in the entrance way to the canteen, Jim from the post room bustles in, my handbag in his hand. 'There you are,' he says. 'Blimey, you look bad. Must have been a nasty accident.'

'What? Oh, yes ...'

'Buck up, girl. The boss sent me to find you, give you this. Thought you'd be making for the canteen. Go on, take it.' He thrusts the bag towards me. 'Don't leave me standing here with it in my hand like a great lemon.'

Puzzled, I take the bag. 'What ... ?'

'He said to tell you to go on home. Get a bit of rest. We'll manage this afternoon.'

I can't keep up. 'Mr Brennan's given me the afternoon off?'

'That's right. Bloke from the Drawing Office said you were proper shook up. Brennan's not a bad old stick, you know. He means well.'

'He doesn't want me to go back to work?'

'Not ... this ... afternoon,' Jim says with heavy patience. 'Way you are, you wouldn't be any good anyway, would you?'

'Um . . .'

'Look, get on home. That bike of yours, can you still ride it?'

'Yes.' If only he knew.

'Well, bugger off then. See you tomorrow.'

'Right. Thank you.'

I stand staring as he leaves. A glance at my watch shows it's barely one o'clock. It doesn't seem possible. It feels as if the whole afternoon has gone by, but, in reality, that hectic chase through the woods and back has taken hardly any more time than my lunch would have done.

Now what am I going to do?

I need to think.

A cup of tea, the draughtsman had suggested, and it seems like a good idea. The canteen's busier today with people still eating lunch, but the woman behind the counter remembers me, tells me it's all right if I stay. I could have something to eat today, she says, but I refuse. I couldn't eat if she paid me. I feel sick with anxiety. It's my fault, all my fault. If I'd told Anderson what I'd seen yesterday, none of this need have happened.

My fears that he might ignore what I'd seen to protect Anita seem petty now. He could still have made sure Fisher was stopped.

I should have tried to stop Fisher myself. Would have, if I'd known Mr Anderson was going to be sent away today. But then I'd probably be out in the woods somewhere now, a cooling corpse that would never be found. I give myself a mental shake. It's pure self-justification and melodrama to think like that.

What the hell was that place Fisher led me to? I don't know where we got to. There was nothing identifiable except that one incongruous square of white walls. I'll need a map to work it out. That glimpse of a man in uniform was unsettling. I didn't recognise it as belonging to any of the armed forces. He could have been a servant in fancy livery, I suppose, but that's pretty rare these days.

What if it's some kind of official establishment? A secret department? It'd be a real kick in the teeth if it turns out to be where McNaught and Jericho hang out. If Fisher's not a villain after all, but on the side of the angels, working to trap Anita?

But I can't believe that. He's such a vile specimen. The way he hit Sam and came after the goats. Got Lady shot . . . None of that's what I'd expect if he's on the level. Far more likely he's up to no good.

And it's no good either, me sitting here. I have to do something. Though as I take my cup back to the counter, I still don't know what. Should I tell someone here, at Hursley? But who? McNaught and Jericho made it very plain I shouldn't speak to anyone about my task here except Mr Anderson. The police? There's Mr Wakeling, the ex-CID man over in the stables, but Anderson seemed to think he wasn't to be trusted. With my supposed history of nervous trouble, would he even listen to me?

There's only one person I can trust.

Bram.

The thought of talking to him gives me purpose. I collect my bike from behind the stables, hitch up the cart Mr Evans made me. While neither bike nor cart have a mark on them from my supposed accident, they're both muddy enough from this morning's trip down Port Lane to be concealing any amount of damage. The rain's still keeping most of the staff within doors, and as I wheel the bike down the driveway to the security post, no one comes close enough to examine the bike or me. I turn onto the main road through the village, make for the telephone box. I rummage for pennies, dial the number for Nash, Simmons and Bing. Miss Haward answers almost at once.

'It's Jo,' I say, 'Jo Lester. Is Mr Nash there? I need to speak to him.'

'Good afternoon, Mrs Lester,' Miss Haward says with pointed courtesy. 'I believe Mr Nash is in his office. If you'll hold on, I'll try and put you through.'

It seems like an age before I hear a click on the line, and there's his voice. 'Jo?'

'Bram, is there any chance . . . ? Could we meet, do you think? I'm sorry to be calling on you again, but I need your advice.'

'No need to apologise,' he says. 'When and where?'

'As soon as you can. But where, I don't know. I daren't come to the office in case I'm seen.' Though thinking about it, perhaps that would be the best way to alert McNaught and Jericho.

'Hmm. Not a good idea, I agree.'

'The other day I was going to suggest the White Horse at Ampfield, but it'll be closed by the time we get there.'

'It can't wait till after six?'

'I'd rather not. Apart from anything else, I've got the afternoon off, but I'll have to get back to the farm before then.'

'Tell you what, I'll meet you there anyway. In about half an hour, say. I know the landlady slightly, she's a good sort. She'll probably let us use the back parlour if we ask her nicely.'

'All right. Half an hour.'

As soon as he's rung off the doubts begin. What have I done? It's all very well running to Bram, but what can I actually tell him? So much of what's happened is about the part of the job I can't discuss. But like it was in Winchester, I've made the arrangement. I can't stand him up now.

18

Wednesday afternoon, later

ALL THE WAY TO AMPFIELD the cart bumps along behind the Cyc-Auto, the empty churns rattling together. I should have left it at Hursley, because now everyone I pass, looks. Most of them laugh. A couple of children even run along beside me, giggling and catcalling in the rain. If this doesn't get back to Hursley, or worse, to McNaught and Jericho, it won't be lucky, it'll be a miracle.

It's a relief to pull off the road in front of the pub. My watch tells me it's not quite closing time, but Bram won't be here yet. It's twice as far for him to come, and he hasn't the benefits of the Cyc-Auto's motor to help him. I park the bike as unobtrusively as possible, go inside. Though the landlady will probably turn me out at two, I can at least wait in the dry until then.

There's not much light inside because the windows are quite small and the sky's overcast. But the fire burning in the inglenook casts a welcome glow of warmth into the room. Two men sit playing cribbage at a table near the fire, while a solitary chap at the bar is taking advantage of the illumination from the lights over the optics to read a newspaper. Neither he nor the card players take any notice of me, but the landlady nods.

'Your gin and tonic's on the table,' she says. 'Over in the corner.'

I look. The table in the corner is about as far from everyone else in the room as it's possible to get. There's a settle with dark green cushions and, on the table, not one glass but two.

'Excuse me?'

'It's all right,' she says, 'Mr Nash telephoned.' She winks. 'Take the weight off. He won't be long.'

I don't know which is most welcome. The chance to get my wet coat off, sit somewhere warm, or the first mouthful of my drink. On balance, it's probably the alcohol, and I bless Bram and the landlady both. For a minute I can let go of my anxieties, still the spiralling thoughts. I hope Bram isn't going to be too long, or I'll be hard pushed not to drink his gin too.

The two men at the table finish their game, get up and leave. Not long after, so does the man with the newspaper and I'm left in solitary state.

'If anyone asks,' the landlady says, 'remember I haven't charged you for the drinks. As soon as Mr Nash gets here, I'm going to turn the lights out and shut up shop. Then I'm going upstairs to put my feet up. OK?'

'Sounds perfect.' The gin's definitely gone to my head because I couldn't care less about anything.

The door opens.

'Oh look,' I say. 'Here he is. Right on cue.' I can feel the silly smile on my face, but I can't stop it.

His raises his eyebrow. 'You've got her drunk already,' he says to the landlady.

'Nothing to do with me.' True to her word, she's locking the door behind him as she speaks. 'Just one drink, like you said.'

'Hey, I'm here, you know.'

Bram takes off his coat and hat, hangs them to dry next to mine. Comes to the table, eyes the untouched glass. 'One drink,' he says as he sits next to me. 'Are you sure?'

I lean my head back against the settle, close my eyes. 'Try it. It's good. But I don't think it's a standard pub measure.'

Even with my eyes closed, I'm conscious of what he's doing. His movement as he picks up his drink, tastes and swallows. Tastes again.

'I see what you mean.' A tiny moment of silence, then he says, 'You look all in, Jo. What's happened?'

I start to laugh. I think I'm going to laugh, and then it turns into a sob. 'I brought you all this way, and I can't tell you.'

Beyond my eyelids, there's only the red glow of firelight.

'I'm off then,' the landlady calls. 'Give me a shout when you're ready to go.'

'Sure.' That's Bram. 'Thank you.'

The click, click of a cigarette lighter, and I open my eyes to the bloom of a candle flame.

'Pretty,' I say. 'Oh, Bram.' And already the alcohol's leaving my system, the lovely lethargy fading. 'What am I going to do?'

'You're going to sit here quietly,' he says, 'and I'll pour you another gin. But it'll have to be a small one this time.'

'Trying to loosen my tongue?'

'Just to relax your mind. There's no hurry. We've got all afternoon.'

'I'm here under false pretences,' I say very carefully, because the words seem to have become very slippery in my mouth. 'It's all bloody lies.'

I let my head roll so I'm looking at his profile in the candlelight. Because of the way we're sitting, it's the unspoiled side of his face. And it hits me all at once. How dear he is to me. How much I want him to hold me. Kiss me. That fleeting tease of contact on Sunday night has woken so much.

A kind of desolation sweeps over me. The physical isolation this second exile from Romsey has imposed is hard to bear. I'm homesick for my life, for the people who share laughter with me, give me a hug. Dot and Alf; Uncle Bill and specially his wife Sylvie, my French aunt, whose kisses of greeting and hugs of farewell are like a mirage in the desert of my current existence.

I thought I'd be better away from Bram, from the mess we've made of our relationship. But all that's happened is now I know I can't do without him.

It's not about sex. If it was only that, it would be simple. Like that night in the Blitz, when we met by chance before ever I came back to Romsey. We slept together – or didn't sleep – while London burned around us. We're adults, we can do what we choose. Even if I don't know if I'm a wife or a widow, my marriage was over long before Richard sailed off to Dunkirk with his damn yacht and didn't come home.

For Bram and me, the problem is love. Living it. Living with it. His fear of getting involved and my need to be independent mess everything up.

There was a kiss once, the sort of kiss I need now. The Christmas of 1914, before my grandfather kicked me out for good. I was thirteen, and the war they'd promised us would be over by then was sending grim news home every day. Uncle Bill had joined up, was away with the army, waiting to be sent to France, and upstairs, confined to her bed, Granny was slowly dying.

She'd given me Nell's dress to try on. Green velvet, faded in the folds it had been left in for all of the thirteen years of my life. But soft still and smelling of the lavender it had been packed with. I'd never knowingly met Nell, my mother. Grandfather had banished her when I'd been born because I didn't have a father, and my birth shamed them all.

Granny had smiled when she'd seen me in the dress. 'Growing up so fast, sweetheart,' she'd said. 'You look a fair treat,' and for a few minutes I'd been happy, basking in her pleasure. But when I went down to the kitchen, Grandfather had taken one look.

'Take that whore's dress off, you little bastard,' he'd said. I didn't see his hand come up, didn't expect the punch in the face that knocked me down. He'd thrashed me scores of times in the past but never like this, so ... *personal*, somehow, so obvious.

I'd scrambled up off the floor, run. Sobbing and snorting from my bleeding nose, face throbbing in the cold.

It had been years since Abe's gang had last met. The boys and me, the lone girl, the baby. The boys were too grown-up now for playing pirates and climbing trees, and most of them were at work. But it was Abe – as we'd called Bram then – who I'd run to, the same as I have now. Abe, who'd been our leader. Abe, because he always knew what to do.

Treading softly up the steps to the front door of Basswood House. Seeing the firelight through the front room window, the swags of holly and mistletoe. Mr and Mrs Nash, with gaily wrapped presents on their lap. Abe, standing by the Christmas tree with another present in his hand.

This is how Christmas is supposed to be. The contrast with what I've left at the cottage hurts more than my face. I change my mind. I won't be like some Dickens orphan, begging at the gate. I want to run again, even further, even faster. But it's too late. Abe's seen me. Even though I don't pull the bell handle, he comes to the door.

'Josy. Whatever's happened to your face?'

Close to, I hardly recognise him. It's months and months since I last saw him. Away at his posh school, he's grown. A stranger. At three years older than me, he's nearly a man.

'It doesn't matter,' I say. 'I didn't mean . . . Happy Christmas.' I turn to go.

'No, you don't.' He grabs my hand, pulls me inside. 'You're freezing.'

In their big kitchen, warmth hits me. I stand, mute and shivering, while he mops the blood off my face.

'Was it your grandfather?' he says. 'The old devil. You're going to have a hell of a black eye.'

'It doesn't matter,' I say again. The only thing I can seem to think of to say.

'Of course it does.' He rinses the cloth he's used to wipe my face, offers it to me. 'You should try and get the blood off your dress.'

I push the cloth away. 'Too late,' I say. 'It's spoiled anyway.'

'Come and sit by the range. We'll put the kettle on. Just hang on a tick while I speak to my mother and father.'

I look up at him, shy all over again. 'You were opening presents. You shouldn't . . .'

He touches my face very gently, cradles my bruised cheek. 'Be quiet,' he says. 'Just rest.' And leans forward, kisses me on the mouth.

A brief kiss, sweet, almost chaste. A kiss that soothes the hurt of my grandfather's hating, the pain of Granny's slow dying. A kiss that's comfort, and not being alone anymore.

'Jo. Jo, I'm sorry, but you'll have to wake up.'

There's warmth, and there's firelight, but Christmas is over, and it's 1943, not 1914. And I'm not thirteen any longer. My head's on Bram's shoulder. I sit up with a start, feel my head spin. 'God, how long have I been asleep?'

'Half an hour or so,' he says. 'You needed it. But if we're going to talk—'

'Yes.' My mouth is dry, and though there's still some liquid in the glass in front of me. I push it away. 'No more gin.'

'I suppose you haven't eaten.'

'It doesn't matter. I'll have something when I get back to Sam's.'

'Tell me what you can,' he says. 'I'll guess the rest.'

He's a good listener. He doesn't interrupt as I pick over the bones of the story. He frowns over Fisher's late night visit to the farm, though even then he doesn't say anything, just nods for me to go on. The bit about Anita is hard to get across without giving details he shouldn't know, but I manage. It isn't till I tell him about Fisher's arrival at the white-walled establishment that he finally cuts in.

'Where were you exactly?' he says.

'I don't know. Not exactly. That's the problem. It was about a mile through the woods. There are a lot of paths but Fisher kept to the same one nearly all the way. The place with the white walls was in the woods, but it couldn't have been far from a road because the last bit of the track had been gravelled for a driveway. It was obvious the gates were meant for vehicle access. You could bring a car or lorry through the woods, I suppose, but there was no sign anyone had.'

'You're sure Fisher was up to no good? And it's to do with why you're undercover?'

'Oh, definitely. He's a wrong 'un. And the other? Yes. It's because of that. Oh, I wish I had a map.'

'If you came a mile west of Hursley, you wouldn't be far from here.'

'I don't think so. We turned right into the woods. I know I said I'd lost my sense of direction, but we must have been heading more north than this.'

'Hmm.' He reaches forward, picks up his glass from the table. But it's a play for time because he doesn't drink.

'What have I said?'

He draws a long breath, puts the glass down again. 'I suppose it's my turn to level with you. But I don't want you to jump to conclusions.'

'OK.'

'I've discovered something disquieting about George Hine. I don't know if it's relevant to what happened to him, or to David, but it looks as if George was one of Mosley's lot at some point.'

'A fascist? I can see it would be upsetting but . . .' Then it begins to dawn on me. 'If David was too, it might have given him a motive.'

'I said, don't jump to conclusions. It might mean nothing at all.'

'You don't think that, or it wouldn't be worrying you. And you haven't told me everything, either. What does it have to do with me following Fisher north rather than south?'

'North and west from Hursley takes you towards Braishfield. About a mile as the crow flies – or a woodland track leads – you come to a lane with some cottages and farms. It's where George Hine lives.'

'Is it where you were when you got knocked off your bike?'

'Just there, yes. And it's where a woman who's said to be at the hub of a surviving fascist group may also live. I don't actually know where, but I've seen a picture of her house. A place called Limeshard Gate. It's a very modern white block of a place, surrounded by equally white walls.'

'Oh.'

'Exactly. Oh. You may like to know yesterday I wrote to her, asking for an appointment to meet.'

'What? Bram . . . Why would you?'

'Because I don't like what happened to David. Or George. Never mind the politics.'

'But if she's . . . if it . . .' I stop, try and work it through. If this place is where a fascist group meets, and Fisher went there with papers Anita took from the Experimental Hangar, it makes a horrible kind of sense. 'You know, I caught a glimpse of a man when the door opened. He was wearing a black uniform,' I say bleakly. 'That's what he is, isn't it? If this woman's a fascist, he's one of the Blackshirts. Oh, Bram, you mustn't go.'

'I very much *must*,' he says. 'You're not the only one who can take risks in a good cause.'

'I didn't mean . . .'

'What are you intending to do now about this man Fisher? Will you report what you know?'

'That's why I came to you,' I say. 'Because I needed advice. I can't report it. I don't know how. The person I report to, I found out, he's been sent . . . well, somewhere else.'

'No forwarding address?' he says lightly.

'It's not a joke.'

'Sorry. I can see it isn't.'

'I suppose, sooner or later they'll realise. He'll get in touch or . . . someone will.'

'Seems a pretty inefficient kind of an operation, leaving you unsupported.'

'I've been a failure till yesterday,' I say. 'I'd got nothing to tell them.'

'But he knew then there was something in the wind?'

'No.' I hunch forward, put my head in my hands. 'He didn't. I didn't report to him yesterday because . . . well, there were reasons. Complications.'

'And now you can't, even if you want to.'

I sit up, twist to look at him. 'Right. A total failure.'

He smiles. 'I wouldn't say that. We're not beaten yet.'

We? There's hope in that word. 'We're not?'

'Maybe it's a good thing,' he says. 'It's a pity about Fisher, if he's got away with – whatever it is, today. If you'd reported it yesterday, it's true, you'd probably have stopped him, but that would be all. If we can prove he's linked to this group, it might be much more significant in the long run.'

'I suppose.'

He puts an arm round my shoulders, draws me close. 'Don't sound so dismal,' he says. 'We can do it.'

'All right.' For a moment, I let myself rest in his warmth, his certainty. 'I'll buy it. You're off to visit this woman, this what's-her-name, this Mata Hari . . .' I don't know what makes me say it. I don't like the way the words echo. But Bram doesn't seem to mind.

'That's what I've heard.' He laughs. 'I'm looking forward to meeting her.'

I struggle free of his arm, sit up straighter. 'You will be careful?'

'Her name's Ilse Reed,' he says. 'She's supposed to be irresistible. But if she supports that evil bastard Hitler, she could be Helen of Troy served up naked on a silver platter and I wouldn't stir.'

'That's not what I meant. It's not your morals I'm afraid for.'

Now he really laughs. 'Oh, Jo. I know. I will take care.' He looks at his watch. 'Half past four. We should both get going.'

'You'll . . . let me know what happens?'

'Of course. We'll need to work out what to do if she's what I think she is and your friend Fisher's involved.'

'He's no friend of mine.'

'No. But seriously, Jo. You need to take care too, up on that farm on your own. I don't like it.'

'Mr Evans has got all that sorted with his bolts and patrols. Don't worry about me.'

'Evans?'

'One of the neighbours.'

'Fair enough.' He gets up, fetches my coat from the rack. Holds it for me while I slip it on. 'I still can't contact you at Hursley?'

'I don't think you'd better. Keep to what you said before. Leave a message for me at the post office at Oliver's Battery.'

'I could always send you a telegram.'

'You could, care of Sam's.'

'Talking of telegrams reminds me. Pete said to tell you goodbye. He turns sixteen this week. He went off at the week-end to join the Navy.'

'Oh, damn. I was hoping he'd change his mind.' I watch as Bram takes out his wallet, pulls out a note. Puts it under his glass on the table. 'The landlady told me not to pay for the drinks.'

'Hire of the room,' he says. 'Worth it for the warm.'

He calls up to her that we're leaving, unbolts the door. 'After you.'

Outside, it's stopped raining, but it's dark already.

'Will you be all right?' Bram says. 'Riding in the dark?'

'I've got used to it now. What about you?'

'I'll be fine. It's Pete's bike, I'll have you know. Sturdy as they come.'

It's hard to leave, so I have to do it at once. As I rattle and bang my way back to Sam's, I think of trust. He's told me his plans, been careful not to delve into mine. He gave me the woman's name, knowing I'll have to pass it on if I get a chance. And that would wreck his investigation. I think of his arm around me, and sleeping on his shoulder. No kiss, but it's plenty to be going on with.

19

Thursday 14ᵗʰ January, morning

FIRST THING ON THURSDAY MORNING, I go to find Hilda. It's early enough that work hasn't started, and I have to wait almost quarter of an hour before she arrives. I hadn't thought about the difficulties she might have getting in without Mr Anderson, and I suppose she must have had to use the bus. I'd have expected Anita to be with her, but she's not. I wonder what's happened to the girl, but that's not a priority at the moment. What I have to find out is when Mr Anderson will be back.

Hilda huffs when she sees me. 'Hear you made a fool of yourself yesterday. Had to be sent home.'

'I was upset, but everyone was very kind.'

'You wanted Tim? Something about a message.'

For a minute, I'm thrown. I've never heard Mr Anderson's first name before. 'Ah, yes, I wondered if he'd left me a message. Something I'd asked him about.'

She huffs again. 'Barely had time to speak even to me,' she says. 'The bosses whirled him off to the station with hardly a by-your-leave.'

'I'm sorry. It must be difficult for you.'

'Hmph. Isn't the first time and I don't suppose it'll be the last.'

'When do you expect him back?'

'I don't expect anything,' she says. 'And if you had any sense, you wouldn't either. Not with this lot. Bosses don't care how awkward things might be for a person.'

'Have they told you how you can get in touch with him?'

She blows out a huge breath of exasperation. 'Look here,' she says. 'If it's any of your business, I probably won't hear from him till he turns up on the doorstep again. He'll be kept too busy to mess about with letters. And for the record, I don't appreciate hearing people snigger behind my back because you got into a paddy when you found out he'd gone. Leave a message for you? Why ever would he? You chose to leave us. Now bloody well leave us alone.'

The extension in Nash's office rings. Nash hopes it's Aggie, to tell him his next client has arrived. Instead, she asks him if he'll take an outside call.

'A woman named Reed.' Aggie sniffs. No doubt she's remembering the conversation they had on Tuesday. 'Says it's a private call.'

'By all means put her through, Aggie. If Mr Sharp turns up, tell him I won't keep him long.'

He waits while the buzz and click of the line tells him Aggie is grappling with the intricacies of putting the outside caller through.

'Mr Nash?' a female voice says. 'This is Ilse Reed. I got your letter.' If he'd been asked to categorise her by voice alone, he wouldn't have guessed Mrs Reed to be an enigmatic beauty. Her rather croaky tone suggests a dowager rather than a woman in her prime.

'Thank you for calling me, Mrs Reed,' he says.

'I was intrigued, Mr Nash. Devastated, of course, to hear about Mr Hine.'

'Yes. It's very shocking.'

'Indeed. You wanted to see me?'

'That would be very helpful.'

'You know, of course, I very rarely take part in any kind of social interaction. But in this case, I think I should make an exception. Can you manage short notice?'

'Whatever's convenient for you, Mrs Reed.'

She gives a strange chuckling laugh. 'So kind. Three this afternoon?'

'Admirable. I appreciate it.'

'Do you know where to find me?'

'I believe it's somewhere along Dores Lane?'

'Not exactly. Perhaps I should send my car for you?'

'That's a very kind offer, but I don't need to trouble you with that. I have my own transport.'

'Well, then. We're rather off the beaten track, I'm afraid. Just beyond the road to Farley, you'll see a turning marked Dove Lane on the opposite side. Are you familiar with it?'

'Not familiar, exactly. But I should be able to find it,' he says, though he knows perfectly well where it is. He's been poring over maps ever since he spoke to Jo.

'If you take the turning there, we're at the end of the lane. Just where it goes into the woods.' That disquieting laugh again. 'The house is called Limeshard Gate. You can't actually see it from the lane, however. We have rather a high wall, I'm afraid. We've always been rather security conscious. Such a good thing, when you think of poor Mr Hine.'

'Yes.'

'I'll see you later then.'

'Thank you, Mrs Reed. I look forward to meeting you.'

'Of course.'

The line cuts as she hangs up. Rings again almost at once. Aggie, again. 'Mr Sharp's arrived, sir.'

'Good. I believe I'm right in saying there's nothing in the appointment book this afternoon?'

'That's right.'

'Fine. Well, if anyone calls, I'll be out.'

'All afternoon, sir?'

'I shouldn't think so. But better put a line through it, just in case.'

'Very well. Can Mr Sharp come up now?'

'Give me a minute, Aggie, and then you can send him on up. Thanks.'

As he's turning to a new page in his daybook, he notices the doodles he's made while he's been talking to Ilse Reed. A series of boxes. Or perhaps they're bricks in a wall. They're blank as yet, whatever that might mean. It's to be hoped that after this afternoon, he may be able to fill some of them in.

Without Mr Anderson to report to, I'm free to do whatever I think best in terms of my investigation. It's a kind of relief in a way. Though I tell myself it shouldn't make any difference what it was Anita gave Fisher yesterday, that she's a traitor if she's passed anything at all out of Hursley Park, it doesn't feel like that. I'd be more than happy to see that thug Fisher locked up, but I'm squeamish about the idea of getting her in trouble. It's almost a relief I can't give her name to the authorities yet, though I'll have to, as soon as McNaught and Jericho catch on and send me another minder.

I've got to keep a close eye on her, though. Try and persuade her to tell me about it, the hold Fisher's got over her. Though I don't doubt he's the one who's put her up to it, she'll still be the one who has to pay.

The only two places in Hursley Park I know where I might find her are the Experimental Hangar and the sunken garden. I don't fancy trying to catch her at work, with Hilda ever present. Though I'm not much keener on the idea of coming face to face with Fisher again, he did say he might see her today. And the garden's where they meet, so it's worth a try.

When Mr Brennan tells me to go to lunch, I slip off to the sunken garden. And if today I'm seeking, rather than hiding, there's no law against me eating my sandwich in the garden if I want to. Though whether Anita will turn tail and run if she sees me there, I don't know.

But I needn't have worried. She's there, all right, huddled up in the corner of a bench. And she's crying again. She doesn't even hear me coming.

'Anita?' I sit at the far end of the bench, not to crowd her. 'What's wrong?'

She skews herself round so her back is turned towards me. 'Go away.'

'Not while you're upset like this. Can't I do something to help?'

'No. Leave me alone.' Her sobbing sounds more heartbroken, more desperate than before.

Even if I didn't have an ulterior motive, I don't think I could leave her like this. 'Is it something to do with Adam?'

'No,' she wails.

'Look, shall I fetch Hilda for you? Would you like to talk to her?'

'No.' She swivels round, raises a furious face to me. 'Don't you get it? I want to be left alone.'

I get it. And I see why. Where she's been crying and rubbing at her eyes, her makeup's streaked into blotches. But if it once concealed the fact she's got a black eye, now it doesn't.

'Did he do that?' I say gently. 'Adam, I mean.'

She turns her face away. 'I fell down,' she says sullenly. 'That's all.'

'So you might have done, when he hit you. You didn't get that in a fall.'

'Oh, leave me alone.' She drags her sleeve across her face.

'Here.' I give her my handkerchief. 'Why don't you come with me and get tidied up a bit? We can sit in the canteen and have a hot drink. You'll feel better.'

She dabs at her eyes. 'Ow.'

'Careful.'

Blows her nose. 'Oh, all right. You win. But I'm not going down to the hangar.'

'All right. Come on, we can easily slip in the canteen here.'

With her face washed and powdered, fresh lipstick and mascara applied, Anita looks a lot better. But there's no real way to disguise the bruising round her eye. She gets a few curious looks as we find a table in the Drawing Office canteen, but no one says anything.

'You stay here,' I tell her. 'I'll get the tea.'

I don't like leaving her alone, afraid she'll think better of my company and bolt, but she's still there when I come back with two mugs of tea and a couple of biscuits on a plate.

'Do you want to talk about it?' I say, as I set the mugs down.

She shakes her head. 'It won't do any good. Anyway, it was my fault.'

'Your fault? How?'

'I was late, and he was in a hurry. He didn't mean to do it.'

'All the same, he shouldn't have hit you.'

'I don't mind that,' she says with quiet desperation. 'But he promised . . .'

'Mmm?'

'He said he'd see me today and he didn't come.'

'Anita, you can't . . .'

'What?'

'You can't really want to be with a man who hits you?'

'What do you know?' She picks at a biscuit, breaking it into crumbs. 'I love him. He's, he's *everything* to me. You probably don't know what that means. You've got to be twice my age and you're still a Miss.'

'I've had my moments,' I say mildly. 'You can't always judge by appearances.'

'Oh, what's the use?' she bursts out. 'He's probably finished with me anyway. And after all I've done . . .'

I don't reply at once, let the silence hang between us. Then, 'What have you done, Anita?'

'Nothing,' she says as she pushes up from her chair. 'Nothing that's any of your business.'

'Anita . . .'

But she's gone, storming off between the tables to the exit. If I'd ever thought I'd made a mistake about what happened yesterday, now I know better. She *has* done something she shouldn't because of Fisher, and she knows it.

Nash sets out in good time for his meeting with Ilse Reed. It amuses him to imagine her reaction to his arrival on a scruffy old bicycle, when he could have been transported in comfort in her car. Better transported than knocked down by it, he thinks. But that's jumping the gun. Just because she can run a car doesn't mean she had anything to do with what happened.

When he gets to Dove Lane, he climbs off the bike and walks. The track is well gravelled, with hedgerows on either side. At first, he gets glimpses of fields beyond the hedges, but then the lane curves and he's walking between trees. Ahead, there's the first glimmer of white. As he approaches, the wall rises up in front of him, split by a pair of high black gates exactly as Jo described.

He doesn't fancy leaning his bike against that pristine whiteness but parks it instead against a tree on the opposite side of the lane, crosses to ring the bell. The door is opened straightaway by an athletic-looking young man of perhaps eighteen or twenty wearing a black shirt and trousers. One of Mrs Reed's East End bruisers?

'Mr Nash?' The voice is pure cockney, confirming Nash's guess.

'That's right.'

'This way.'

The door shuts behind him. The house is directly in front, centred between the outer white walls, equally white and square itself. A row of grey spikes, like dragon's teeth, define the roof line in a way that reminds Nash of a medieval castle's crenellations. A paved path runs straight to a glossy black front door, while a driveway kicks round to the side of the house, presumably to a garage. Everything in sight is perfectly straight-edged, monochrome except for the viridian green of the close-cut grass on either side of the path.

It's been designed, Nash thinks, to overawe the visitor, even intimidate them. For himself, it's the feeling of being penned in he doesn't like: the sense he's being watched every step of the way as he walks towards the front door. The impression is uncomfortably underlined by the way the young man in black paces along in total silence beside him, giving the impression more of a guard than a servant.

Once inside, the discomfort fades. The young man tells him to wait, disappears behind a white-panelled door.

The house is surprisingly welcoming. The spacious hall is filled with light, from the opal glass chandelier overhead to the gleaming, asymmetric patterns of grey and white tiles on the floor. A red-carpeted staircase ascends to the upper floors, and the quiet tick of a clock is the only sound.

Nash waits for several minutes, a ploy, he guesses, to keep him on edge. Like the guarded approach to the house, the occupant of this place doesn't intend her visitors should feel at ease. He resists the urge to pace or fidget, stands studying a gilt-framed portrait of a man uncannily like the late King George.

'My darling husband.' Without the interference of the telephone line, the croaky tone is rather softer.

He turns, sees his hostess at the top of the stairs. 'Mrs Reed.'

It is a staged entrance, perfectly executed as she pauses for him to look up at her. He understands at once what Laidlaw meant about this *belle dame*. From his position in the hall, she seems like a young girl, a slender figure in a leaf-green dress, the epitome of spring. Her hair is platinum blonde, shingled close to her shapely neck in a style that was popular twenty-odd years ago. On Ilse Reed, it looks like the height of fashion.

After a moment, she comes stepping lightly down the stairs. If her voice gives the impression of an older woman, her movements are definitely those of a young one. Younger, perhaps, than she actually is. Seen close to, it's apparent she's neither particularly old nor very young: rather a woman in her prime. Somewhere around his own age, in all probability. He registers the scent of tuberose, an explosion of flowers, heady and expensive.

'Mr Nash, I presume,' she says as she reaches the bottom of the stairs. 'My dear man, has no one taken your coat and hat? I don't know what has happened to servants these days.' She claps her hands, calls, 'Bertholdt.'

A young man appears, very similar in almost every respect to the first. But this one is blond, rather than dark-haired.

'Wherever have you been hiding, Bertholdt? Take Mr Nash's coat and hat at once.'

'Sorry, madam.'

The name may be Germanic, Nash thinks, but this young man's as cockney as the first. If he was christened Bertholdt, he'll eat the hat that's just been taken out of his hands.

'Come in, come in,' Ilse Reed says, opening double doors that lead into a sitting room where a fire burns in a grey stone hearth. The mantelpiece is chunky stone, unornamented except for a pair of elegant vases in jade green. 'Do, please, sit down.'

They seem to have bypassed the usual pleasantries of greeting, and he's aware she's managed to avoid the conventional gesture of offering him her hand to shake.

'Thank you.' He chooses an austere-looking armchair away from the fire, where a window gives out on to another perfectly plain expanse of lawn.

'Bertholdt shall bring us coffee,' she says, 'unless you would prefer tea?'

'Not at all.'

'The best cups, Bertholdt. And some of the little almond cakes.' She tilts her head, with an expression that somehow manages to convey a sort of pleasurable melancholy. 'My cook is a wonderful *pâtissière*, I'm sure you will enjoy them. A small luxury, you know, in these hard-pressed times.'

It feels like a sly little trap she's set for him. To see whether he'll wave away the idea of luxury – almost certainly black market, or jump greedily in. 'Indeed,' he says, meaninglessly, resolving to eat nothing if he can possibly help it.

'Bertholdt tells me you arrived on a bicycle.' She could scarcely have sounded more astonished if she'd learned he'd come by camel. 'So intrepid of you, and so virtuous. But you really should have let me send the car.'

'It was no trouble,' he says. 'A pleasant ride on a dry afternoon.'

'Tell me,' she says, 'what news is there about dear Mr Hine? I was terribly distressed to hear what had happened to him.'

'I can't tell you very much. To the best of my knowledge, his condition remains unchanged.'

'He's still unconscious?'

'I'm afraid so. Do you know him well?'

'I told you, Mr Nash, I have very little social contact.' She smiles, flutters her eyelashes in a mime of shy fragility.

He isn't taken in for a second. This woman's about as far from frail and shy as anyone he's ever come across.

She speaks again, still with that self-deprecating air. 'I've been something of a recluse since my darling husband passed away.'

'I had hoped' – he leans forward, plays the earnest supplicant for all he's worth – 'that as a neighbour, and, shall we say, a woman of discernment from George's own social milieu, you might have known something about his family.'

She shakes her head sadly. 'Why, no. Like me, he knew the pain of widowhood, of course. He lost his wife several years ago. And then that terrible business with his son a few weeks ago. One might almost say he had very little to call him back to life.'

'Not me,' Nash says. 'I'm hoping for his full recovery.'

'Of course. Ah, here's Bertholdt at last. That's right, put the tray on the cabinet. Serve Mr Nash first, no, no, I insist. How do you take your coffee? Sugar and cream?'

'Black, thank you. No sugar.'

Bertholdt sets a small table alongside Nash's chair, puts down an almost translucent white cup and saucer with an intricate border of gold, a tiny plate of the same pattern. With a deft shake, he unfolds a linen napkin, spreads it ceremoniously across Nash's lap. Then comes the coffee, aromatic and

dark, shadowing the cup as it fills. Before Nash has had time to protest that he doesn't want anything to eat, the young man wields a pair of silver tongs to put a sugar-coated pastry onto the plate.

Nash waits while the young man performs the same operation for his mistress, dosing her coffee with both sugar and cream.

'Please, don't wait for me,' the woman says. 'Your coffee will get cold.'

It's true, the thin china does let the heat seep away more quickly than the cups he's used to. Nash takes a sip. The coffee tastes as good as it smells, a rarity these days when nine times out of ten it turns out to be made with chicory essence. Yet it's difficult to enjoy the drink when he's conscious his hostess is watching him closely, as if she's waiting for him to react in some way.

'I congratulate you on your coffee,' he says. 'You must have a secret supplier.'

Her lips twitch amusement. 'It's all a question of who you know. But I'm glad you like it. And of course, things always taste better when they are elegantly served, don't you agree? The china, for instance, is particularly close to my heart.'

There's that same sly air of a waiting trap. She's obviously determined to draw his attention to some aspect of her hospitality he's missed. He looks more closely at the cup in his hand. The pattern in the gold banding he'd registered as a Greek key design is emphatically not. On closer inspection, he can see it's an intricately entwined pattern of swastikas. He's sure she will have seen his jolt of distaste, the elaborate care with which he replaces it on the saucer.

'The fylfot is a Sanskrit good luck symbol, you know,' Ilse Reed's croaky voice mocks. 'The set was made specially for me in France. I refuse to be shamed into not using it because of its associations.'

Shame? Nash thinks. It's nothing like shame she feels. It's pride, deliberately flaunting the symbol in his face. Anger rises inside him at her manoeuvres.

'I don't suppose many people would think first of good luck,' he says drily. 'Not these days, at any rate.'

'Of course, you served in the last war. Perhaps you hold a grudge?'

'Not for that, no. But I'm sure you're aware that I'm unlikely to feel any sympathy with the Nazi regime.'

'Because you're a Jew?'

It's too much. 'Because, God help me, I believe in democracy and justice, not the rule of a bloody tyrant.'

She raises exquisitely plucked eyebrows in mock surprise.

'I won't apologise,' he says, as he gets up from the chair, 'because I think you've been trying to make me lose my temper since I arrived. I'm only sorry you've managed to achieve it.'

She smiles with such delight he's tempted to slap her. 'Mr Nash. How naughty you must think me.'

'I think you're a very clever woman, Mrs Reed. Now, if you'll excuse me?'

'Of course. I am rather exhausted by our little tête-à-tête. You'll forgive me if I don't see you out? Bertholdt, Mr Nash's hat and coat, please.'

Nash is waiting impatiently in the hall for the servant to reappear with his things when a door opens at the top of the stairs and a man emerges.

'Bette,' he calls, 'have you got—' He stops abruptly as he sees Nash. 'Oh.' Then he turns abruptly, disappears once more behind a slammed door.

'And good afternoon to you too,' Nash mutters to himself as Bertholdt brings his coat.

'Beg your pardon, sir?' the young man says sullenly.

'Nothing.' If he thought he'd get an answer, Nash might have asked who the man was. But it doesn't matter, because he thinks, even from that brief glance, he knows. He'll need to check with Laidlaw's picture files, but he's pretty certain it's the Mosleyite clergyman: dressed in tweeds and masquerading as a country gentleman, seeming very much at home.

Once outside, it's a relief to feel he can breathe freely, his anger beginning to subside. He's never felt such malice as Ilse Reed projects: the dragon's teeth on the roof of the house are far more truthful about the occupant than the pale elegance of its interior. She's like a spider inside a rose, waiting to kill.

So it's hardly a surprise to him when he finds his bicycle has acquired two flat tyres while he was inside. He stands staring at the closed black gates, wondering whether it's worth the devilment of knocking and asking for a lift back to

Romsey. But though part of him is tempted, he's not willing to step back into Ilse Reed's domain.

It's another long walk for him, then. But it's not been a wasted effort. Though he can't be sure why she invited him to call, unless it was to show him how little she cares for his investigations, it's clear she planned every aspect of the meeting. From keeping him waiting, to her determination to make him notice the pattern on the cups. He might have thought she meant it as a test of his sympathies, except for her obvious knowledge of his heritage.

But for all her efforts at directing the meeting, there are a couple of things which escaped her control. He knows now she has someone in her household called Bertholdt, and that she rejoices in the nickname Bette. Two 'Bs'. Two possibilities for the dedication on the back of George's watch.

He doesn't rule out Bertholdt as a candidate. George's preferences are no business of his. But he'd guess Bertholdt would be unlikely to have the funds to give lavish presents like the watch Miss Stone described. And if Aggie's right about the longevity of Ilse Reed's servants, he's unlikely to have lasted that long in Mrs Reed's employment.

So Bette it is, or could be. He needs to tread carefully, not from fear of her, the influence she wields, but because he would so like to see her brought down. Her and her obnoxious politics. But he'll need evidence, not emotion, if he's to do that.

20

Friday 15ᵗʰ January

WHEN I'D GOT BACK TO Sam's place on Thursday evening, I found an envelope on the kitchen table, with a pencilled note above my name – or rather, my pseudonym – in ink. *Della at the PO asked me to drop this in for you. HE.* Tearing open the envelope, I'd discovered a message from Bram, taken down verbatim by the woman in the post office, so brief he could have sent it as a telegram for ninepence. *Meet you Sam's Saturday 4 p.m. News to share. Bram.* I'd been relieved, thinking it must mean he'd got back all right from his meeting with Mrs Reed, but I'd still lain awake half the night, trying to puzzle out what to do next.

Until I'd come to work at Hursley Park House, I hadn't realised how much freedom I've had, with Bram as my employer. Not only when I'd started working as his assistant, way back when we were investigating Ruth Taylor's death, but ever since. Interviewing the bereaved, researching the history of a property or tracing an heir. Different kinds of tasks, but the principle's the same. He'd let me know what needed doing, leave me to get it done. But now, having to juggle the day-to-day routines of my cover job with trying to investigate is a nightmare. At first the role of delivering Hursley Park's internal mail had seemed like a good idea, giving me access to the whole Supermarine site, but now it seems impossibly restrictive. It's hard to make any progress with the investigation when I'm still having to keep to the post room schedules under Brennan's eagle eye. I wish McNaught and Jericho could have found me a job that left me more freedom to act independently.

Just thinking about the ministry men makes me anxious. How the hell can I get in touch with them? I can't see any way to stop Fisher except with their help. I've nothing that a policeman would consider evidence against him.

If only Mr Anderson had left me a message . . .

In the dead of the night, I've thought of all the possible permutations. Perhaps he *did* leave a message, but with Hilda, and she hasn't passed it on. I know she's not fond of me, but I can't see why she wouldn't. Just to get me into trouble? But she'd have to know not getting it would cause trouble. She'd have to know what I'm doing at Hursley Park . . .

That sets a whole new set of wild geese flying for me to chase in the dark. Would Hilda suppress a message to protect Anita if she suspects the girl's involved? Could she herself be involved? The mastermind of the operation?

That one makes me laugh, but stranger things have happened.

What if Mr Anderson really *didn't* leave a message because he forgot, or didn't care what happened, or because it's him who's involved? What if he knows what's going on, but isn't willing to let the people he loves be found out?

Nastiest of all, what if it's all been orchestrated by McNaught and Jericho? If they told Mr Anderson not to tell me how to reach them? What if it was them who spirited him away in the first place?

And I'm back to the beginning. Who to trust? Who to tell? It feels like it's all coming to pieces in my hands: an uphill struggle to keep the pieces of my life separate. Joy Rennard, Jo Lester, Josy Fox. I'm like a quick-change actor in a farce, trying desperately to remember which disguise I should be wearing as I come through the door.

This morning, it's been especially hard to stay in character. Sorting the post, I keep on drifting off, still trying to make up my mind what to do. Wondering what news Bram has to share. It's a relief to start the round, the rhythm of walking somehow clears my mind of the dross.

It's good to be out in the daylight, I seem to spend so many of my waking hours in the dark. After all the rain and the snow, it's a lovely day for January, mild and still. A mist softens the view across the parkland to the north of the house. Somewhere beyond, I know there's the army transit camp where Fisher works, but from here it's camouflaged by the trees around Merdon Castle. A pheasant calls, a harsh *cuuk cuk* of sound. For a few moments, I can imagine myself a thousand miles away from secrets and death and the war.

And then an engine starts up in one of the testing sheds, and the illusion shatters. Get on with the job, the one they pay me for. Deliver the letters, the internal memos, the specially sealed packets of photographs and drawings.

I'm on my way from the photographic studios in the stables back to the main House, when someone taps me on the shoulder. It makes me jump, because with all the racket from the engine, I hadn't heard anyone approaching.

It's Reg, Mr Anderson's mechanic friend. 'Hello, Miss Rennard,' he mouths at me.

'Hello.' I bellow it, but I don't think he can possibly hear. Redoubling my efforts, I shout, 'I'm feeling guilty about you.' The last three words emerge into a sudden silence as the engine is switched off. Red-faced, I smile. 'Sorry.'

'Guilty?' he says. 'What for, m'dear?'

'I promised you a drink and I've never had a chance to do it yet.'

'Got your hands full, I've heard.'

'Mr Anderson told you about the goats?'

'Yeah.' He laughs. 'Fancy yourself as a shepherdess, do you?'

'Not exactly. But what I'd do if you hadn't mended the bike I don't know. I owe you more than one drink.'

'Like I told you, it's no trouble. Heard you had a bit of a tumble, though?'

'What?' I'm about to deny it when I remember the assumption the man in the Drawing Office made about me having had a bike accident, my acquiescence in the lie. Embarrassed,

I fiddle with my hair to avoid meeting his gaze. 'Oh yes. Nothing serious. I was shaken up a bit. The bike's fine.'

'Still going all right, then?'

'It's brilliant. Running really well. I don't know what you did to it but it doesn't even seem to be using much fuel.'

'That's good. But don't you worry if it does get low. Bring it along and we'll sort it out for you. Essential travel, you know.'

'That's kind of you, but I'm all right for the moment. Look, what do you do at lunchtimes? I know it's not the same as after work, but you could probably manage a swift half at the Dolphin, couldn't you? Wartime beer's nearly all water anyway.'

He grins. 'Better not let the landlord hear you say that. Go on, then, it's Friday. I don't see why not.'

'I'll meet you there, shall I? Half past twelve all right for you?'

'Suits me. If I'm late, make it a bitter.' He winks. 'And you can make it a pint. I drink fast.'

The engine starts up again, makes it impossible to reply except with a thumbs up. Silly as it might seem, I'm looking forward to it, relaxing in the company of someone who doesn't expect anything more of me than a glass of beer.

Since the office personnel has been reduced to a minimum, it's Nash's habit to go down for morning coffee to Aggie's office on the ground floor. Today's one of Cissie's days, so it's quite a cheerful session, especially once he's managed to reassure his secretary that Ilse Reed is never going to be a client of theirs. 'I'm nowhere near posh enough for her,' he says. He can't tell them any details of what happened, but he makes a story of the lovely interior of Limeshard Gate, has them laughing about Bertholdt's fancy touches with the table napkin and the silver tongs when the phone rings. For once, he answers it himself, much to Aggie's disapproval. But it's just as well, because the call is for him.

'Mr Nash?'

'Yes?'

'It's Sergeant Tilling, Mr Nash.'

'Yes?'

'I believe you're Mr Hine's solicitor?'

'In a manner of speaking.'

'Is that a yes or a no, sir?'

'I told you last week, George Hine asked me to look into his son's death. You warned me against it, I believe.'

'Look, sir, I've got a difficult situation here. Don't make it any harder.'

Apprehension grips Nash, strikes cold in his belly. Time to put hostility away. 'All right, Sergeant. I certainly consider myself to be acting on George Hine's behalf. You'd better tell me what's happened.'

'There was a fire at Mr Hine's property last night. Despite the fire brigade's prompt attendance, I'm sorry to say there's been a lot of damage done. I obviously can't ask Mr Hine to come along while I make a search of the premises, but

I need somebody there to represent him. His housekeeper says she'll do it, but only if you'll come too.'

All that faffing about, Nash thinks. Tilling only had to say Miss Stone had asked for him, wouldn't have mattered whether he was George's solicitor or not. 'I'll come,' he says. 'Of course I will. When are you going?'

'Right away, sir. We'll pick you up in a few minutes.'

By the time Nash has explained to Aggie and put his coat on, Sergeant Tilling is at the door.

As they walk down the alley to where the police car is waiting, Nash asks, 'Do you know what happened, Sergeant? How did the fire start?'

'Petrol, sir. That's what the fire officer thinks.'

'Deliberate, then?'

'Oh yes. No doubt about it.'

At the police car, Miss Stone's already installed in the car, a young uniformed policewoman at the wheel. Tilling ushers Nash into the back seat next to the nervous woman, gets into the front with the constable. No more chance to question the policeman for the moment.

'Oh dear, Mr Nash, thank you for coming,' Miss Stone says. She's perched on the edge of the seat, so when the car starts with a jerk she's thrown off balance. Nash grabs her arm, stops her from sliding into the footwell.

'Easy, Constable,' he hears Tilling say. Echoes it himself as he helps Hine's housekeeper to settle back in her seat.

'Try and relax for a minute,' he says. 'We'll get there soon enough.'

'It's been such a shock. First Mr Hine and now this. Whatever is he going to say when he knows what's happened? His lovely house.' Her voice breaks.

'Your home too,' Nash says gently. 'I'm so sorry.'

'Yes, yes,' she says. 'All my little bits and pieces will be gone, I'm afraid. But I won't be homeless or anything. I can stay with Susan as long as I need. I just worry about Mr Hine.'

'We'll sort that out when the time comes.'

'So wicked. As if Hitler's bombs aren't enough. Whoever could have wanted to do it?'

Nash has a grim feeling he knows. Not that he's willing to say so at this stage. It's all speculation based on the thinnest of threads: an overheard nickname. But he doesn't need to answer, because as they come round the corner by Pucknall, the acrid smell of burning reaches into the car, and they see the devastation the fire has caused in front of them.

Miss Stone lets out a muffled shriek, reaches for Nash's hand.

The roof structure and first-floor walls have collapsed almost completely, though the brick chimney stacks and gable ends remain. As soon as the car pulls up, Tilling gets out, opens the rear door. 'You stay here for a minute, Miss Stone. Constable Shaw will look after you. Mr Nash and I will go and see what's what.'

At the obvious cue, Nash gets out. In the open air, the acrid smell is intense, a mixture of scorch and wetness. And underneath that, the chemical stink of petrol. They move forward a few paces before Tilling holds up a hand, brings them both to a halt. From here, Nash can see the house looks relatively intact at ground level, though the porch is gone, the paint on the front door blistered. Smoke and soot stain the white cob walls and there's ample evidence of the fire brigade's work. Great heaps of straw are piled up against the walls where they pulled down the thatch to stop the fire from spreading, and shallow pools of water puddle the ground. Everything seems very quiet. Only the tick of the car's engine cooling and the muffled voices of the women inside break the silence.

'It's bad, sir, I'm afraid,' Tilling says.

'Yes. Looks as if the fire was started in the thatch over the front door. Easier to reach there, I suppose.'

Tilling looks sideways at Nash. 'That's what the fire chief said.'

'Sergeant Tilling, let's get one thing straight. You asked me to come here as George Hine's legal representative, and to support Miss Stone. Fair enough. But if you're still enter-taining ideas that I'm some kind of suspect in the attack on George, or this' – he takes a deep breath, levels the annoy-ance out of his voice – 'then I'm afraid I'll have to decline to say anything more without my own legal representation.'

Red suffuses Tilling's face. 'No, sir. I'm leaning more to your theory now. That Mr Hine has been targeted because of the trouble over his son. But, of course, if you were willing to volunteer information about where you might have been last night, I would be grateful.'

'I had an evening shift at the ARP post. Eight till mid-night. You could ask Vic Wild if you want corroboration.

Incidentally, we didn't receive any report of a fire during the evening.'

'No, sir. The call came in just before 2 a.m.,' Tilling says stolidly.

'I was in bed by then. No witnesses.'

'Thank you, Mr Nash. Now then, what do you reckon to the idea of vigilantes?'

'Targeting George because they believe his son was a traitor?'

'That's my thought at the moment.'

The truth's a long way from that, Nash thinks, if he himself is right. 'It's possible. But I still think it's more likely he's been targeted because his son was murdered. The killer would have plenty of reasons to prevent further investigation.'

'You're still questioning your colleague's conclusions, then, sir? You don't believe his verdict that David Hine died in a drunken accident?'

'No, I don't. What's happened here makes me all the more convinced of it. I'd lay odds this is because someone thinks George has evidence that would incriminate them. First, they beat him up to try and cover their tracks. And then, in case there might be something material, something he'd written down perhaps, they burn his house. The question is, are they right? If so, and they're lucky, the fire will have destroyed it. But it could be we'll be the lucky ones. That search of the premises you said you wanted to make, it's more important than ever, don't you think?'

'You may be right.' But Tilling makes no move towards the house.

'Is it safe to go in?' Nash asks.

The policeman sighs. 'So the fire officer says.'

'What are we waiting for, then? Better get on with it.'

'Yes, all right. We'll hold off calling the woman in until we've had a bit of a look-see.'

Inside, the smell is overwhelmingly of smoke, though the chemical mix of paint and petrol is strong in the hallway. It catches the back of Nash's throat, and he pulls up a fold of his scarf to filter the worst of it out. Fire burns up, he thinks. Whoever did this didn't reckon with that, because despite the damage in the upper floors, down here, the rooms are relatively unscathed. Only the smell and the sullen drip of water indicate what's happened to the structures above.

I arrive at the Dolphin ahead of Reg. Put in my order for a pint for him, half for me. I'm not much of a beer drinker, but I probably shouldn't have gin at lunchtime, judging by what happened the other day with Bram.

While most of the customers are men I don't recognise, there are a couple of faces I know from the accounts department at Southend House. The pub's quite busy already, but I manage to find a couple of seats and shuffle into place. While I'm waiting, the door opens and Adam Fisher comes in.

A roar of greeting rises from a group of men standing at the bar. He goes across to them, and there's a lot of backslapping and laughter. He's got his back mostly to me, but I do notice when he gets something out of his pocket, passes it across to one of the men. I get a flash of colour as whatever it is circulates round the group. Judging by the tone of their laughter, it's a girly picture of some kind.

My attention's distracted from the men as Reg joins me.

'Sorry I'm late, m'dear.'

'Not by much. Your beer hasn't even had a chance to go flat yet.'

'Cheers,' he says, picking it up. 'Here's to you.'

'Cheers.'

Another great shout of laughter goes up from the group. Reg glances over, shakes his head. 'Not much of place for a woman,' he says. 'Uncouth lot.'

'It's not our lads, thank goodness,' I say. 'They're playing darts. That lot's swapping dirty postcards, I think.'

'And that lout Fisher's right in the thick of it. I might have known.'

'He was the one brought the cards, I think.'

Reg takes a deep pull at his beer. 'He's enough to put you off your pint.'

'Do you want to go?'

'Let him chase me off? No. Chap like him? Wouldn't give him the pleasure.'

It seems like a good moment to see what I can find out about Fisher. Reg certainly doesn't seem to be a fan. 'Go on,' I say, 'tell me about him. I love a good gossip.'

He laughs, but there's a sour note in it. 'Wouldn't sully your ears with most of what I know.'

'No?'

'It's not just the shady deals,' Reg bursts out, 'though that's bad enough these days. Proper unpatriotic. Don't know how he gets away with it. Slippery as an eel, he is.'

'I'd heard he was a bit of a wide boy.'

'All of that. And he thinks he's a proper Romeo into the bargain. Oh, he's got the looks for it all right, it's what he does with them . . . Led my youngest girl a merry dance. Wouldn't listen to her old dad, finished up breaking her heart over the bloody man. 'Scuse m' language.'

'I've heard worse.' Said worse, too. 'She all right now, your daughter? No permanent harm done?'

'She's fine, thanks for asking. But I tell you, Miss Rennard, if he'd done what you'd call permanent harm, he wouldn't be walking around in one piece now. It's not nice to see your children upset, however much they think they're grown up.'

'Your daughter's lucky to have a father who thinks like that.'

'Huh,' he scoffs, but I can see he's pleased. 'Not what she'd say.'

'Anyway, changing the subject. Did you see Mr Anderson before he got sent away?'

'Tim? No. Hilda was proper put out.'

'Me too,' I say. No use pretending, I already know he's heard about the supposed accident. 'He was meant to be giving me a message.'

'Oh?'

'You old fraud,' I say, smiling. 'I know very well everyone's wondering what message.'

'Well, there's bets on it, you know.'

'Bets? What about?'

'Most of them reckon you were going to ask to go back to the Hutments, cos you'd had enough of the goats.'

'Not a chance. I love the goats.'

'And a few, well, they've got dirty minds.'

I laugh and mean it. 'Mr Anderson and me? Not in a million years. He's not my type.'

'A couple of weird ones, then. Someone said maybe you had a secret boyfriend somewhere and Tim was acting as go-between.'

Not as easy to laugh this time, but I manage it. 'No boyfriend.'

'Drug habit, and Tim's your supplier?'

'Not even close. No drugs either.' Out of the corner of my eye, I see Fisher make his way to the door.

'Last one then.'

'This yours?'

'You got me.'

'Go on.'

'Well.' He grins. 'Thought you might be asking him for my street address, so you could come and spirit me off on that bike.'

'That's it,' I say. 'You win.' Nonsense, of course. He's made it up on the spur of the moment, the way I was doing with my answers. But it does make me wonder what his guess might really be.

He laughs, downs the end of his pint. 'Thought so. Better be getting back, though, m'dear.'

'All right. I'll walk with you.'

We emerge onto the main street through the village. The quickest way is to take the path that goes up from Southampton Lodge, past the Experimental Hangar, so we turn that way. But before we get that far, we see Fisher again. He's on the opposite side of the road, by the long flint wall that runs round the grounds of Southend House. He seems to be having a heated argument with a young man in the dark uniform of a chauffeur, though there's no sign of a car. The young man pushes Fisher in the chest, and the soldier stumbles back.

'I wonder what's going on?' I say. 'Looks like Fisher's getting the worst of it for once.'

'Serve the nasty little devil right.'

The young man pushes Fisher again, forces him to step into the road. They keep coming on, the young man the aggressor, Fisher in retreat.

'Hold up,' Reg says, 'you don't want to get involved in this. Shall we cut back the other way?'

I shake my head. 'Call me nosy, but I want to see what happens.'

The two men are perhaps twenty yards away on our side of the road when the young man delivers a push that sends Fisher sprawling on the ground. They're close enough now to hear what's being said.

'You better get it Monday,' the young man snarls, 'or you're a dead man.' He stomps back across the road, casting

a hostile glance over his shoulder at us. At this range, there's something familiar about him, but I can't think what.

When I turn towards Fisher again, he's up on his feet, brushing himself down. The look on his face is pure hatred. He spits in the young man's direction, flicks Reg and me a two-fingered salute that's the reverse of Churchillian and sets off at a run on the path towards the House.

'What was all that about?' Reg says. 'Sounds like Fisher owes him money.'

'Something like that. I'm wondering . . .'

'What?'

'He's in a hell of a temper. If someone crosses him now . . .' I'm thinking of the sunken garden, and Anita waiting for him, perhaps. 'What's the time, Reg?'

'Quarter past one. You going to be late?'

'Not yet. But I'm going to run, if you'll forgive me.'

I take to my heels, chasing Fisher for a second time. He's well ahead, I can only just see him in the arch of trees over the footpath. I bless the fact that I've got my post-round shoes on, because I have to go all out not to lose him.

Off the main path, through the network of trails meandering among the specimen trees of the shrubbery. I've lost sight of him completely now, am following him by sound until the low wall surrounding the sunken garden comes into view. I stop short to get my breath. Don't want to fall foul of that temper myself if I can help it.

I hope I'm mistaken, and Anita won't be there. Because the way Fisher looked, he'd black anyone's eye who got in his way this afternoon. And I'm guessing that what Fisher needs to produce by Monday isn't money. Because I think I've worked out where I've seen the young man before, or one very like him. The last time I chased Fisher through woodland, to Limeshard Gate.

Just when I think everything's going to be all right and I can get back to work, I hear a man's voice, raised in anger. A cry. Not tears this time, but pain and fear.

I rush forward, caution forgotten. Fisher's got Anita by the shoulders, is shaking her to and fro like a rag doll. I go sweeping down the steps two at a time, and with surprise on my side, manage to push him away from the girl.

'Get off her, you bully. Leave her alone.'

'You again,' he says. 'You bitch. You followed me.'

'Yes. I know what you did to Anita last time.' We're eye to eye, and I daren't blink or look away. It's like confronting a mad dog.

He clenches his fists. 'I'll do you as well if you don't get out.'

'Not a chance.' Behind me, the girl is sobbing again. 'Because Anita might not want to report you, but I will.' It's an empty threat, because I want to catch him red-handed, smuggling secrets, not get him hauled up on a petty assault charge.

He pushes his face towards me. 'Don't threaten me,' he says. 'Or you'll find yourself in deep shit. I know where to find you, don't forget. I owe you one already, you and that bloody dog.'

'Interesting,' I say. 'I was sure it must've been you, *Kipper*, but I couldn't prove it. Now I've got a witness who's heard you admit it.'

'You bitch . . .'

I'm bracing myself, because I'm sure he's going to hit me this time, when I hear a voice calling.

'Miss Rennard? Joy? Where are you?'

It's Reg, and I call out 'here' as loud as I can.

Fisher swears under his breath, but not so quietly I don't hear the obscenity.

'You fucking wait,' he says, louder. 'I'll have you.'

Reg comes into view at the top of the steps. 'Fisher,' he yells. 'I warned you.'

Another two-fingered salute, and Fisher's gone.

Reg stops beside me. 'Are you all right?'

My legs are trembling with reaction and I'm afraid to move in case I fall down, but I tell him, 'Fine. It's Anita I'm worried about.'

She's got a bloody nose and her hair's all anyhow from where Fisher manhandled her.

Reg shakes his head. 'You get the girl up to the medical room, and I'll go and tell security what's happened. They'll track him down.'

'No!' Anita wails. 'Please, no. You mustn't.'

'Don't be silly,' he says indignantly. 'Can't let him get away with it.'

Her sobs rise, verging on the hysterical.

'Leave it, Reg. Just for now. I'll get her calmed down.'

'But Fisher—'

'I'll deal with him, I promise. If you want to do me a favour, tell Mr Brennan I've been held up. Say Anita's had an accident, or something. She won't want talk about this going all round the House.'

'All right,' he says reluctantly. 'You take care of that girl.'

'I will. And Reg?'

'Yes?'

'Thank you. Reckon you saved my bacon.'

He looks at me, eyes narrowed. 'No such thing,' he says. 'I'd back you against that bastard any day. More to you than meets the eye, that's for sure.'

21

Friday afternoon and early evening

B Y MIDDAY, NASH BEGINS TO feel as if he's been pok-
ing round in the wreck of George's house half his
life. There's been nothing to find that might give the
police a lead to the arsonists, or to confirm his unvoiced theory about Ilse Reed's henchmen. He's emptied George's desk
of papers, but as far as he can tell without closer inspection,
there's nothing particularly extraordinary or revealing. Paid
and unpaid bills, bank statements, a few photographs. One,
in a tarnished silver frame, shows George with a woman who
Nash supposes must be Lucy, his late wife, and a smiling,
lanky boy of perhaps twelve or thirteen. David, of course. It's
the first time he's seen the young man's face, and it gives him
a jolt. Brings the investigation of his death into focus: a real
person lost, not simply a puzzle to solve.

The image is faded enough that it must have been dis-
played in sunlight for some time but the tarnish and its
banishment to the depths of Hine's desk speak of more
recent neglect. In a gesture he doesn't entirely understand,

Nash polishes the frame on his sleeve, stands it back on top of the desk.

He shoves the ragbag of paperwork into George's briefcase, goes through to the drawing room, where Miss Stone is still engaged in her self-imposed task of packing up the contents of a large corner cabinet. Mr Hine's treasures, she called them, insisting they must be salvaged. After the first tearful shock of coming inside, the housekeeper's proved remarkably resilient. The small triumph of discovering some of her own bits and pieces intact in her sitting room behind the kitchen seems to have given her strength. More than he would have credited her with. More, perhaps, than he'd wish right at this moment, when all he wants to do is get out. As she fusses around, wrapping what seem like innumerable tiny objects in pieces of rag and paper she's salvaged from the kitchen, the only thing he can do to speed up the process is to help.

'These things are special to Mr Hine,' she says, handing him a wrapped bundle to stow away in the basket she's using to collect the treasures in. 'I know he'd want us to take care of them.'

'What are they, exactly?'

'Oh dear, I'm not an expert, of course, but Mr Hine calls the little ones with holes in netsuke. Japanese, he says, some kind of fastening for clothes. Buttons or the like. They're all different things, see, animals and that. Clever little carvings. This white one's ivory, a mouse with a hazelnut.'

'Right.' Nash yawns. 'Excuse me. The air's really poor in here. We ought to get out soon.'

'Yes.' But she doesn't seem to have taken in what he's said. She's delving deep into the back of the lowest shelf in the cabinet. With a cry of discovery, she pulls out a small green object and passes it to him. 'Look, here's the dragon jug.'

With the eye of faith, Nash thinks, it might be a dragon of some kind. Though it's bigger than the netsuke and obviously no kind of button, he can't think what it could be used for. A tablespoon of cream, perhaps?

'Mr Hine calls that celedon ware. It's one of his most precious things. Because of the lovely green colour, see? Like jade, but made of china.' She's still rummaging about, busily bringing out more of the tiny objects and putting them ready to wrap. 'There was a pair of vases the same colour, he gave them to Mrs Lucy one Christmas. Very plain, but so pretty. Used to be on the mantelpiece, then not long after she died one disappeared. He said it got broken and he took the other one into his study. He keeps it on the desk. Didn't you see it?'

'A vase? No.'

She gets up, goes pattering off into the study. 'Funny, I can't see it anywhere,' she calls. 'Oh dear. Whatever can have happened to it?

'Perhaps it got broken too?'

She pops back into the drawing room, the photograph in her hands. 'Oh, I hope not. First one then the other ... that'd be like an omen. They were very old, you know. Rare. Mr Hine said they came all the way from China. Look, you can see one there in the corner by Mrs Lucy's hand.'

The light's somewhat better in here, and though the picture is faded, now it's been brought to his attention he can make out a shape he's half expecting to see. A shape he's seen not long ago, one of a pair gracing a grey stone mantelpiece.

'Rare, you said?'

'Oh dear, yes. Very rare. Mr Hine said they were the only vases like it in England.'

'Miss Stone, did you tell Sergeant Tilling about the watch?'

'I did.' She looks at him conspiratorially. 'Not about the words on the back, though. Didn't want him thinking badly of Mr Hine, him being a widower and all.'

'I don't think he'd have been shocked. But I do think you should tell him about the vase now, too.'

'You think it's been stolen? Oh dear.'

'It's possible.' More than possible, a near certainty. Not that he could prove it. George might have given the vases to Ilse, exaggerated their rarity. 'Now, look, let's finish these last few pieces and get out of here. It's not healthy breathing in all this sooty damp air.'

Anita flatly refuses to go to the medical room. It's all I can do to persuade her to let me clean her up a bit before she goes back to work. Instead, I take her to the quiet room Mr Anderson calls my hidey-hole and make her promise to wait while I go in search of water to bathe her face and a cup of tea.

When I get back with both, courtesy of the basement canteen, I'm half expecting she will have vanished. But she's there, sitting exactly as I left her, slumped into a chair. She looks up at me as I enter, so miserable it seems that she's past tears. With a sense of déjà vu, I wet the cotton cloth I've borrowed from the canteen, hand it to her.

'Come on, give your face a wipe. You'll feel better.'

She does it, listless. Her face is puffy with tears and the latest blow, her pretty elfin features eclipsed. She looks such a child even my unmaternal heart is moved.

'What was it this time, Anita? Why did he hit you this time?'

She hands the bloodied cloth back to me. Shrugs. 'Dunno.'

I'm sure she does know, but I don't pursue it for the moment. 'You must see, you can't keep defending him. What would have happened if I hadn't come along?'

'Don't care.'

'Don't be silly.' I want to shake her out of her apathy into some kind of defiance. 'He's just a bloke, and a nasty one at that. You'd be better off without him.'

She scowls at me. 'That's all you know, Miss Clever. I need him. He's promised to marry me.'

A horrid thought occurs to me. 'Anita? Are you pregnant?'

'What if I am? It's none of your business.'

Oh God, but it is. I feel the cold sweat creeping down my back. If I get Fisher and this girl arrested for espionage, what's going to happen to them? To her baby? It's a capital crime. 'And Adam's the father?'

She sits up straight, eyes blazing. 'Of course he is. What sort of girl do you think I am? We're going to get married, I told you.'

'Have you told anyone else? Do your parents know?'

'No.' She shakes her head. 'And don't you go blabbing to them, either.'

'Of course not.' Another thought occurs to me, remembering the stink in the Experimental Hangar. 'Is it safe for you to be working in the hangar, Anita? All those chemicals?'

'What do you care about me or my baby? I know what you think, just another stupid girl who's got herself into trouble.'

'I don't think that.' It isn't entirely a lie. If I condemn her, I condemn my mother too. The stupidity isn't so much about getting pregnant, as in the choice of partner. 'But I do think you'd be safer with your parents than with Adam.'

Now she does cry again, great sobs fetched up from deep inside. 'I know, I know, but what can I do? I'd have to give my baby away.'

I put my arm round her. 'How far are you along?'

'Nearly five months, I think,' she says between sobs.

'You haven't seen a doctor?'

'No.'

'Well, that's the first thing to do, isn't it? Come on, crying like this can't be doing you or the baby any good. Have some of the tea, try and calm down.'

'If you were me, what would you do?'

'I don't know. I think . . . if it were me, I'd do anything I could to keep my baby with me. But I know that isn't easy. I'm' – I usually say '*a bastard*' because I hate the mealy-mouthed expressions some people use, but it would hardly do now – 'illegitimate myself. Brought up by my grandparents.'

'And it worked out all right?'

'I survived.' I try to smile reassurance. Because it's true, I did survive. 'I'd rather have been with my mother, though.'

She gulps back another sob. 'I don't know. Suppose I should thank you really, but ... You've been nicer than I thought ...'

The door bursts open, and there's Hilda, like an avenging angel. 'Anita, my poor girl.' She rushes over, practically knocks me out of the way. 'Reg told me that animal Fisher had hit you. That brother of yours has got a lot to answer for, bringing a fellow like him home to his family. Just you wait till Tim hears.'

Just when I thought I'd got her to stop, now Anita starts to cry again.

'And you,' Hilda says, looking at me. 'Why didn't you take her to the nurse? You should have come and found me yourself.'

'Auntie Hilda,' Anita gasps. 'It's not her fault. I told her not to.'

'Huh. Anyone with a grain of sense wouldn't take any notice of that,' Hilda says. 'Anyway, you can push off back to work now, can't you? Leave this poor child with me. I'll look after her.'

'If that's what Anita wants?'

The girl looks up at me, eyes swimming. 'It'll be all right,' she says. 'I don't mind, Auntie Hilda.'

'OK. But if you want me, if you want to talk, you know where to find me.'

'She doesn't need you,' Hilda butts in. 'She's got her family and me if she wants to talk to anybody.'

'Auntie Hilda.' Anita reaches out to me, takes my hand. 'I'm sorry, Miss Rennard. For everything. You won't say . . . ?'

'I won't. But you should.'

'Oh, get on with you,' Hilda says. 'Enough riddles. Go and mind your own business, do.'

Outside, I make straight for the lavatory. Not because I need to use it, but because I urgently need somewhere private to look at whatever it is Anita's put in my hand. A crumpled piece of paper she must have fetched out of her coat pocket, palmed to me under Hilda's nose.

After dinner, in the quiet of his study, Nash prepares to tackle the papers he's brought back from Hine's house. He hasn't had a chance before. The police car had brought him and Miss Stone back to Romsey and he'd left her in the capable hands of his housekeeper. Then there had been the business of arranging for George's property to be secured, finding someone who could get the downstairs windows and doors boarded up, fix a tarpaulin over the remains of the roof to keep out the worst of the weather.

This rummaging through Hine's private life is not a job he's looking forward to, but he can't put it off any longer. He pulls the briefcase he brought back with him open, takes out the first handful of stuff. It reeks of smoke, catching in his throat, still raw from this morning's stint at the house. The smell is nauseating.

He flicks through the papers, dividing them into separate heaps. Thank God George doesn't seem to be much of a hoarder, there's nothing here that's more than a few months old. Enough to fill in his tax form, no more. Copies of letters he's written to Theophilus Brown before and after the inquest, with the same impersonal compliments slip received in reply stapled to each. Four notes from friends sending condolences over David's death, another suggesting he's well rid of a son who was a traitor. Two more express pious satisfaction that Lucy hadn't lived to see the day her son was disgraced. Frowning, Nash wonders why George kept them. To keep the wound open, to fuel his anger? Even more of a mystery is why anyone should think it their duty to write such sanctimonious twaddle to a bereaved man.

He's almost at the end of his task, the dwindling stack of papers to be sorted dwarfed by the tidy piles of those already done, when he hits gold. A half-sheet of writing paper, handwritten. A difficult, ornamented handwriting full of loops and swirls, extravagantly punctuated. Despite his first thought, it's not another letter of condolence or blame.

> *G, naughty boy! Breaking that lovely pair to please me!! I won't refuse, I'm no such fool! But perhaps I can hope one day they will be reunited? B.*

There's no date, no other superscription, but he can't help wondering if the 'lovely pair' might refer to the vases. If so, they're reunited now. Did that happen before the attack on

George as a freely given gift, or after? Was the second one taken, like the watch, as spoils of war? There's a deep and abiding anger growing inside him. And it isn't only evidence of a link between George and Ilse Reed. He pulls open his desk drawer, takes out the square of paper that his mask was wrapped in, lays it next to the note on the desktop. Though it's not proof that would be accepted in a court of law, to his naked eye, the two pieces of paper are undoubtedly the same.

It's nearly ten o'clock before I'm finally able to sit down at the table in Sam's kitchen with a plate of toast and Marmite, a mug of tea. It's been a pig of an afternoon. First the shock of knowing Anita's pregnant, then Hilda's scolding. Just to finish it off, when I'd finally got back to the post room, Mr Brennan had treated me to an interminable – though I have to admit, justifiable – lecture about reliability. And all the while the note Anita had passed me was burning a hole in my pocket, my mind. *Imperative you contact Mayfair 273 before you proceed further.* The note from Anderson. She must have had it all along. If I hadn't helped her today, perhaps she'd never have given it to me at all.

I had to presume she'd read it. I spent the rest of my afternoon wondering whether she could have understood what it meant, or if she'd suppressed it out of sheer awkwardness, to get me in hot water. Whatever her intention, my dressing-down from Brennan meant there'd been no possibility of getting away during the afternoon to make the call. Increasingly impatient, I'd watched the hands of the clock crawl towards 5 p.m. And then right at the last minute, Mr Brennan had sent me to the archive office to find the stamp ledgers from 1941. As I scrabbled through the dusty shelves in search of the elusive books, I cursed, thinking it was a job that could quite as easily have waited till the morning. Or next week, come to that. But I couldn't complain, because I'd promised last week I'd work late if he needed me to.

In the end, I'd got away only half an hour late, made straight for the telephone box in Collins Lane. It had seemed to take forever for the operator to reach the number, my stomach churning with nerves. What would McNaught and Jericho say when they knew I'd been operating without Mr Anderson to report to since Wednesday? That I'd probably let secret information pass to the enemy without even trying to stop it.

But I didn't even get as far as telling them anything about it. When the number finally went through and I announced myself, the conversation was very short.

'Mr McNaught?'

'Jericho.'

'Mr Anderson's been relocated.'

'Yes. We were getting concerned about you.'

'The note he left didn't reach me till today. I need to tell you—'

'Where are you calling from?'

'The telephone box in Hursley.'

'Not secure.'

'There's nowhere else. It's important.'

'Sunday, 10 a.m. Westgate Chambers in Winchester. You know it?'

'Yes, but—'

'Use the side door.'

A purr as the line is cut off, then the operator's voice. 'You've been disconnected, caller. Do you want me to try the number again?'

'No need, thank you.'

Not no need: no point. Chances are the telephone won't be answered if I ring it again. I've no choice but to wait, turn up as instructed. Meanwhile, there's another new puzzle in my head. Westgate Chambers is where the unhelpful Mr Brown has his office. That random shot in the dark I'd asked Mr Anderson to check on seems to have hit gold.

My supper finished, I rouse myself from the warmth of the kitchen. A final check of the goats, then I'll turn in. I whistle up Lady, light the lantern and go out into the dark.

In the goat shed, there's a rustle of movement unusual at this time of night. They don't seem disturbed in the way they were the night Fisher and his friend attacked, but there's definitely something going on.

I pass the lantern across the pens. The billy's in and safely settled, his eyes dark and inscrutable in the golden light. Next, the does. One, two, three, are up and moving around in their stalls at a time when I'd expect them to be lying down, contentedly chewing the cud. The fourth is down, her head in a corner, but she's not resting. She looks up at me, makes a mewing sound as her belly heaves. One glance at her tail end and even I can see she must be in labour. God, just the end of the day I need. What am I supposed to do? I've never been present at any kind of birth before.

I could run for Mr Evans. The goat heaves again, and a dark glistening shape appears. Too late to do anything but stand and stare, fascinated and horrified in equal measures.

I've heard about having hot water and towels ready at a human birth, but if goats need them too, there's no time to fetch either. The goat strains again, and more of the kid appears. Instinct takes me into the pen beside her as she pushes, the shape changing and shifting as it slithers out, the kid still trapped inside the birth sac. Now I can see what I'd want a towel for. I take off my jacket and the cardigan under it, use the rough wool of the cardigan to wipe the kid's face clean. For a grim moment I think it must be dead, and then it sneezes, opens its eyes. Bleats, a sound of protest uncannily like a human baby's cry.

The doe noses round, begins to lick the kid, and I feel a ridiculous sense of pride as the wet-dark fur turns pale under the mother's tongue. Almost at once it's struggling to stand, its own survival instinct urging it to move. I've done nothing except ruin a perfectly good cardigan, but I'm as pleased as if I've performed the miracle single-handed. Except I still don't know what to do next for the mother and her baby. I need Mr Evans's expertise.

I put my jacket back on, leave the lantern safe on the hook above the pen. Torch in hand, I'm ready to go, but I take one last look to check all's well. Lady's sitting beside the pen, apparently on watch. I'm sure she knows better than I do, and she's calm enough, so I take it as a sign it's safe to go. I tiptoe out into the night and down to Mr Evans's place. I'm wondering whether I'll wake the whole household if I knock when the door opens and he comes out.

'Hey,' he says. 'Are you all right? I was on my way to you. Late night patrol.'

'I'm fine. Better than fine, really,' I say, the words tumbling out with excitement. 'One of the does has given birth. I was there. I didn't know what to do but I think she's all right. It was . . . magical. Only I've no idea what I should do for her now. If there's anything she needs or . . .'

'Slow down,' he says. 'If she's managed on her own, chances are everything's all right. But I'll come and take a look, though sheep are more in my line.'

'I never thought . . . Could there be more?'

He laughs. 'It's often a pair,' he says. 'Sometimes even three.'

'Oh, help. Three?'

For a stout man he moves fast, and by the time we get back to the shed, I'm almost running to keep up. As soon as we get there, I see he's half right, because now there are two tiny white kids in the pen with the mother, who's up and feeding already.

'Two,' I say. 'How do you know if there are more to come?'

'She's telling you. When she's up and feeding like that, she's done.'

'What do I do now?'

'Did you look to see if the first one was a doe or a buck?'

'No. Why?'

'Doesn't pay to rear the males when it's a milking herd.' He leans over the side of the pen, picks up one and examines it. 'That's good. A doe.' Then he lifts the other. I don't know how I can tell, but I'm sure this is the kid I saw born.

'Buck,' Mr Evans says, shrugging. 'Bad luck. Want me to knock it on the head for you?'

I snatch it from him. 'You mean, kill it?'

'Of course. Sam would.'

'No.' I'll answer to Sam when I have to. The buckling's fur is soft and warm as it nuzzles at my neck, searching for milk. 'You can't kill it. I helped it take its first breath.'

'Well, give him back to his mother, then. If you want him to survive, he needs to feed.' He sounds disgruntled. 'Easy to tell you're no farmer. Can't afford sentiment in this business.'

I put the little kid down by his mother, watch as he latches on to a teat, tail wagging as he feeds. I hope the dim light hides my flush. I know Mr Evans is right, but I can't help feeling the way I do. In some indefinable way, the kid is mine, a life I helped begin. I think of that horrid minute when I thought it wouldn't breathe, the joy when its chest moved. I couldn't bear to see its life ended less than an hour later. 'I know, but . . . What do I need to do for them now? Should I clean out the pen?'

'Not tonight. Let her settle with them. Put in a bit of extra straw for the kids. You'll find she'll clean up, eat the afterbirth. You could give her some molasses water if Sam's got any molasses. Hang on.' He rootles about on the shelf while I fuss about, putting in handfuls of fresh straw around the little goats.

'Yep, here we are. Now then.'

If his pragmatic attitude to the male kid shocked me, I bless his competence now as he sorts out the drink for the doe. 'She'll need extra feed, too,' he says. 'What about the others? Any of them ready to go?'

'Tonight?'

He laughs again. 'It's nearly always night-time. Nature's way when the predators are asleep. Let's have a look. No, you're all right. Don't think you'll have any more excitement tonight.'

'Thank goodness. And . . . well, thank you, Mr Evans. I'm sorry if I was rude about the buck.'

He pats me on the shoulder. 'Never you mind. You're not doing a bad job, for a townee.'

It's almost a compliment. Yawning, I take my leave of him, watch him go back down the hill. One last look at the goats, and it's time to turn in. The little glow the kid's birth lit in me is still burning, accompanies me to bed. Buoys me up enough that I don't even get round to worrying before I fall asleep.

22

Saturday 16ᵗʰ January, morning

IT'S PROBABLY THE STRANGEST METALWORKING job Nash has ever done. Creating a new mask for himself out of silver since the original copper shell had proved beyond his skills to salvage or remould. Using the spare as a pattern to sand-cast the new mask, wondering what his mother would say if she knew he'd melted down two of her best teaspoons for the metal. Planishing the shape into a perfect fit, hour after hour of painstaking work. That had been tricky enough, refining the edges so they would merge seamlessly with the surface of his face and yet not cut in. But the business of painting it had been trickier still. Staring into the mirror, trying to identify the colours he needed to replicate his skin tones, transferring what he saw onto the metal. Trying to make sure it would be more restrained self-portrait than pantomime dame. By the time he'd finished, his patience, and the little pots of matt enamel he'd been given years ago to touch up the original mask, were almost exhausted.

But though he hopes never to have to do anything like it again, he's pleased with it now it's finished. It's not quite as thin as the copper, a bit heavier to wear, but his glasses hold it well enough. It's a strange feeling, putting it on and going out to confront the world in a face he's made for himself, reclaimed from the wreck. Strange, and oddly satisfying. Perhaps he should have done it years ago. His mood gets a further boost when Fan, who sees him most often, doesn't seem to notice anything when he appears at the breakfast table. If it passes her scrutiny, it will probably fool the world as much as ever he needs to. And it's certainly one in the eye – he grins to himself with fierce satisfaction at the wordplay his mind offers – for the person who broke the original.

Ilse Reed. It feels like the kind of thing she would have done, but it could as easily have been one of her henchmen. It had definitely been a man who'd slipped the broken mask in his pocket in Winchester in the rain. If only he'd taken more notice at the time. He's got no memory of the man's face, not even of his build or clothes. He'd been too focused on following Jo.

Destroying the mask had been such a petty crime, spiteful and small. Next to David's death, insignificant. The thought sobers him. Almost without realising it, his investigation into what happened to the boy has been sidelined by Jo's secret mission. Important as that might be, for him it's a side issue. He's in no doubt it's the reason David died, but it doesn't tell him who the killer is. Whether David was a go-between, or an innocent bystander, caught in the wrong place at the

'Here you go.' He cuts a big slice, plops it onto a plate and hands it over.

It's dark and crumbly-moist, and I can see there are currants in it. 'Fruitcake? Is Fan a magician?'

'Do you know, I think she's the worst cook in England. I spend half my life with indigestion. But she bakes like an angel. In peacetime this cake is a triumph, full of dried fruit and spices. These days she has to make do with what she can get, but it still comes out pretty well.'

'Mmm.'

He's watching me with amusement. I'm trying to eat nicely, aiming for the impression of nibbling like a mouse, rather than gobbling like a pig.

'Aren't you having some?'

'Watching you eat is much more fun.'

'It's hard work on a farm,' I say defensively, much more pig-like than mousy as I collect up the crumbs on a fingertip and lick them off.

'I can see. You've got thin, Jo.'

'Everyone's thin these days.'

'Want some more?'

Oh, yes. I could eat the lot.

I shake my head. 'I'll save it for later.' Which is presumptuous of me, I suppose, because he might not be meaning to leave it.

'Fair enough. Now. We need to get down to business. I'd better tell you about the fire at George's house first.'

'A fire?'

'On Thursday night. The police took me round there yesterday.'

'Was anyone hurt?'

'Thankfully not. The house is bad, though. The thatched roof's completely gone, and the first floor is pretty well gutted.'

'What happened? Was it an accident?'

'No. Arson. The fire officer confirmed it. Said the blaze had been started in the thatch by the front door. The place reeked of petrol.'

'That's awful. Another blow for Mr Hine.'

'Not that he knows about it yet. I feel sorry for his housekeeper, she's lost her home and her job. She'll be in limbo until George can sort things out.'

'He's still unconscious?'

'Yes. At first I thought he was bound to recover, but the longer he stays in a coma, the more I begin to wonder if he ever will.'

'I'm sorry.'

'Me too.' He looks more than sorry, as unhappy as I've ever seen him. 'I wish—'

'What?'

'Nothing really. Regrets are futile. But I've wasted a lot of time.'

'It's only been a couple of weeks.'

He smiles, but his heart's not in it. 'Not the investigation. The years and years I avoided George. Blamed him for saving me.'

'I don't understand.'

'It doesn't matter.'

'Yes, it does. Tell me.'

'He was the one who rescued me when I was wounded.' He rubs his face. 'I wanted him to leave me, but he wouldn't. I couldn't forgive him for it.'

I get it, I really do. I'm not surprised he'd shunned his friend for saving him. It's all part of that lonely pride that won't let him get close to anyone. I hurt for him, knowing how bitter he must have felt. May still feel. But a glance is enough to tell me not to venture further. The barriers are up. *No entry.*

'You're doing all you can now,' I say, as matter-of-fact as I can make it. 'Finding out what happened to his son. He knows that.'

'Hmm. In point of fact, he doesn't. I'd only said I'd think about it.'

'But you are doing it. Investigating. Taking the risks.'

'Determined to make me feel better?'

I shrug. 'Just saying what I think. You haven't told me about your visit to Mrs Reed yet.'

'Stamping on my foot to make me forget I've got a head-ache? All right.'

As Bram tells me about his visit to Limeshard Gate, I find myself hating Mrs Reed from the very first mention. I bite my tongue on the comments I'd like to make about her supercilious behaviour. But when he gets to the bit about the swastikas on the coffee cups, I can't keep quiet any longer.

'And she's walking around free? That's monstrous.'

'A very elegant monster, but I agree. Thing is, if we get it right, she won't be free much longer.'

'We have to get it right, Bram. Fisher and that woman . . . it can't go on.'

'You don't need to convince me. Ilse Reed isn't just right wing, she's an out-and-out Nazi.'

And George Hine was her lover, I think. If he shared her views as well as her bed, the reason Bram and he had kept apart so long might not have been all one-sided. But it doesn't seem tactful to suggest it at the moment.

'Bram, the way she drew your attention to that pattern. Such a petty thing to do, but risky, surely? Wasn't she afraid you'd report her?'

'I don't think she cares. In the file Laidlaw showed me, there were names of her contacts, members of her group. Influential names, some of them. You remember Superintendent Bell?'

'How could I forget him? He's one of them?'

'If Laidlaw's right.'

'The way he was when we caught Ruth's killer, I can believe he's a Nazi.'

'At this stage, it's all supposition, Jo. Don't get carried away.'

'But it would explain why Mrs Reed isn't afraid of displaying her sympathies, if she thinks she's got a policeman in her pocket.'

'It may just be arrogance.'

'Doesn't matter, does it? She's going to get a nasty shock either way.'

'This is where your story comes in?'

'Yes. I'm back in contact with McNaught and Jericho. I've been summoned to report to them tomorrow.'

'You'll have plenty to tell them.' He's looking better now, not so pinched and sad. 'They should be able to round up Fisher and his girlfriend, anyway.'

'I don't know how I feel about that, Bram. About Anita, I mean. I don't know if I want her to be arrested.'

'Going soft, Jo? You wouldn't let Ilse Reed get away with it because she's a woman, would you?'

'It's not about being a woman. Anita's hardly more than a child. She's naïve, and Fisher's got her completely under his thumb. He beats her up, I've seen it. And she's pregnant.'

'Ah.' He sighs. 'I'm afraid it may not make a difference.'

'I thought . . .'

'Go on. I'll buy it.'

'If we have a plan, if I can present it to McNaught and Jericho tomorrow, sell it to them, we might be able to do some kind of deal. Immunity for her if she co-operates.'

'It's an idea. What have you got in mind?'

I tell him about Fisher, the young man who'd threatened the soldier, the threats he'd made. And how I'd thought he might be the man I'd glimpsed at Limeshard Gate. How I'd followed Fisher, stopped him from taking out his temper on Anita.

'That's where it gets a bit iffy,' I say. 'I think he must have been asking her for the plans or whatever he needs to deliver, but I don't know for sure. But assuming it is, and we can get

Anita to help us, we could catch him in the act of taking it to Mrs Reed.'

'Even better if they caught him handing it over to her. Without that, and with Superintendent Bell in the picture, she'd probably get away scot-free.'

'There's a lot of ifs, I know. But we can try.'

'You think the girl would co-operate?'

'I might be able to persuade her if she believed we'd help her. That you would.'

'Me?'

'I thought . . . you could represent her, the way you did for me back then. You got me off the hook.'

There's a long silence. The only sound comes from Lady, who's woken up and is chewing a bone by the fire. After what feels like an age, he speaks.

'We'll have to see, Jo. All this playing spies, it's important, but it's not my first priority. That's to find out why David died, and who killed him. I owe George that. I've gone on with it because everything points to someone involved in this business of treachery. But I couldn't represent this girl if she's responsible for David's death.'

'Oh, Bram, if you saw her you'd never think it could be her.'

'She could be shielding Fisher.'

My turn to be silent. 'Yes. I accept that. She could. She's in love with him, but she's frightened of him, too. There might be more to it than his violence. But you know I'd never expect you to do anything against your conscience.'

He smiles, a proper smile this time. 'OK. We'll call it a qualified yes, shall we?'

'Thank you.' My stomach gives an enormous growl. Even Lady looks up from her bone, surprised. 'Sorry.'

'Good Lord,' he says. 'How long is it since you ate?'

I gesture to the table. 'You saw me eat cake.'

'An hour ago.' He looks at his watch. 'More than that. Two hours. It's past six already.'

Disappointment kills appetite, sits in my belly like a stone. 'You have to go?'

'I didn't say that. You have to eat, Jo.'

Red-faced, it's my turn not to be able to look at him.

'What's up? What have I said?'

'You must want a meal too, and I've nothing to offer you. Only a choice between a fish paste sandwich or Marmite on toast. Hilda – Mrs Anderson, where I was staying till last week – she'd already had my rations when I took my book back, so I can't get anything else till Monday. And you know what it's like queuing for anything off ration. What with work and the farm, I haven't had a chance.'

'What a mean thing to do.'

'I'm glad to be out of there. She's another terrible cook. But it's been a bit of a struggle. And it's embarrassing to bring you all this way and not be able to give you a proper meal.'

'We've got bread, and we've got cake. What more do you want?'

'Steak,' I say longingly. 'Roast chicken. Fish and chips.'

'Stop it. It's tea for two, and like it. Get the kettle on.'

In the end, digging around the back of the cupboard Sam uses as a larder, I find a Colman's tin with a scrape of mustard powder left in the bottom, and half a bag of flour. They're both well past their best, but with butter and milk, the chopped-up rind of cheese that's all that's left of my ration, I achieve a kind of rarebit sauce that's not too bad on toast. It might not be the food I've been dreaming of, but with that and the cake, there's enough to silence hunger.

We've finished eating, sitting over the last cup of tea out of the pot when Bram makes a comment about being lucky to have milk and butter.

'Here's to the goats,' he says, raising his teacup in mock tribute.

'The goats. Oh my God. I need to check on them.'

'I thought you'd finished for the day?'

'Well, I have, more or less. But one of the does had kids last night, and I need to check on them. Make sure none of the others have gone into labour.'

He pales. 'You sound like a proper farmer.'

'Not what Mr Evans says.' I shrug into my coat, heel off my slippers, shivering as I put my feet into cold wellington boots. 'Come with me. The babies are really sweet.'

'I think I'll leave it to you.'

'Scared, Captain Abe?'

The old taunt hits home, and he reaches for his coat. 'That's a low blow, Josy Fox.'

'Well? Are you coming, or not?'

'Any sign of birth happening, and you won't see me for dust.'

'It's a deal.'

Outside, it's a cold, clear night. The moon's waxing to full, bright in a sky as dark as velvet. There's been no more snow, but frost sparkles underfoot as we crunch across the yard. In the shed, it's warm from the animal bodies, smelling of straw and clean goat: musky and not unpleasant, at least to me. Even before the lantern light falls on the pens, it's so peaceful I can tell Bram's not going to get a shock tonight. Only a soft dialogue of bleats between the new mother and her babies breaks the silence. I probably shouldn't disturb them at all, but I can't resist.

'Look,' I say quietly. 'Aren't they pretty?'

He leans his folded arms on the edge of the pen, watching the kids do what I've discovered they like to do best; irresistibly drawn to climb on anything and everything available. The piled straw round the edge of the pen, their mother, each other.

'Hmm.' There's a chuckle in the sound. 'They're very silly.'

'They make me feel better.'

I'm standing on his left, his blind side, and I can't see his expression. Equally, he can't see me. For once, in the lamplight, while he's absorbed in watching the goats, I can study his face without seeming rude.

'Is that the mended mask?' I say. 'It's looking much better than the other one.'

He turns his face sideways to look at me. 'You think?'

323

Feeling bold, I touch a fingertip to the edge where metal meets flesh. 'Much smoother.'

'In point of fact, it's new. I made it myself.'

'That's amazing.'

'No choice. I don't think anyone does this kind of work anymore. It's all plastic surgery for today's casualties.'

I can't forget what he said earlier: wishing George Hine had left him in no man's land. It's upsetting to think of him, not even twenty, in such despair. It's lodged itself in my head, a silent swirl of snow on every warm thought, a stone in my chest.

'Would you . . . ?' I begin, before my courage runs out. 'If they offered now, would you want . . . ?'

He smiles. 'Don't tear your heart out over me, Jo. I'm OK. After all this time, the only thing I'd want is binocular vision, and even the best surgeon can't manage that.'

'Oh, Bram. You see clearly enough. You've always seen through me.' My own two eyes are wet as I bend to touch my lips to his, a tentative offering. Without breaking contact, he straightens. His arms go round me and the kiss turns real.

'Goat magic,' he says at last. Though the kiss is over, he's still holding me close. I can feel the beat of his heart, the pulse of my own. 'Are you sure this isn't a mistake?'

'Not at all sure,' I say, as I slide out of his arms, take his hand to lead him back to the house. 'But that's for tomorrow. Come on.'

*

In the far reaches of the night, Nash wakes to the unfamiliar sensation of another body outlined against his own. It's not something he's tolerated in the past: he's always made sure his liaisons don't include the intimacy of sharing sleep. Even on those singular occasions with Jo, this has never happened before.

In a stranger's narrow bed, by the last of the moonlight, he watches her sleep. Her head rests against his shoulder, the tickle of her breath feathers against his skin. He thinks about what he said to her last evening about wasted time. Here's another relationship he's put off, denied, belittled, because he's been too afraid to risk commitment.

The moonglow fades, but he doesn't sleep. He's daring to think of the future. Things can change. *He* can change. Gentle, not wanting to wake her, he touches his lips to her hair.

'Mmm?' She stirs, blinks her eyes open in surprise. 'Oh, my. You're still here.'

'Shh. You don't have to wake yet.'

'What time is it?'

He turns his head to look at the luminous dial of the bed-side alarm clock. 'Not quite five.'

'Good.' She yawns, makes a nuzzling movement against him. 'Another half-hour,' she murmurs, and is instantly asleep.

Nash folds her a little closer to his body.

Things are going to change.

23

Sunday 17ᵗʰ January, morning

WHEN I WAKE, IT SEEMS I must have dreamed Bram's presence beside me in the night after all. There's no trace of him now. I'm alone in the bedroom, and I can't hear any sound from beyond the room that might suggest he's somewhere in the house. But there's no time to brood. A look at the clock shows me I've overslept. It's nearly seven, and shocked, I shoot out of the warmth of the blankets and into the cold morning air. In the haze of making love, I must have forgotten to set the alarm.

Just as well it's Sunday, I think, as I head into the frigid little lavatory for a pee and a quick splash of a wash in water that's practically freezing. And there's not much of it, either. I must remember to pump some more up into the tank later.

As I get dressed, I try to avoid thinking about Bram, where he might be. How he might be feeling. Embarrassed? Regretful? This morning, early, when I woke to find him there, I should never have gone back to sleep, as if I could take it for granted he'd stay. Sex is one thing, but sleeping together, the bond it creates, is quite another. And something, from experience, he avoids.

I'm trying to work out whether I've got time for a cup of tea before I go out and see to the goats. I've got to be in Winchester by ten. If Bram has gone, I won't have time to contact him again before I go. We didn't properly work out what we were going to do about Fisher and Anita, Mrs Reed. I don't regret last night, but it's going to be awkward if I haven't got my plan straightened out for McNaught and Jericho.

I'm pulling on my thickest jumper as I go out into the kitchen. Blinded by the wool over my head, it's the warmth that hits me first. Bram must have stoked the range.

'Tea's poured,' he says. His voice makes me jump. 'I heard you moving around.'

Struggling free of the jumper's tight neckline, I turn to see him get up from the chair by the fire, an open copy of *Farmers Weekly* in his hand. It's the most incongruous picture I could ever have imagined. This is all territory that's strange to me. I don't know how to react. 'Doing some research?' I say, keeping it light. 'Anything useful about goats in there?'

He shakes his head. 'Not so far.'

I pick up my cup of tea, take a reviving mouthful.

'It's a bit anaemic,' he says. 'You're all but out of tea.'

'I know. But it's hot and wet, that's all that matters.'

He grins and I blush. 'Bram!'

Dropping the newspaper on the table, he crosses to me. Pushes a strand of hair off my face. Much as I'd like to prolong the moment, I turn to the stove, set about putting oats and milk in a pan over the lowest heat, ready for breakfast once the morning work is done.

'I can't get used to you with black hair,' he says. 'I hope it's not permanent.'

'I hate it too, but it's already growing out. And if we catch Fisher and his lot tomorrow, I won't need to dye it again.'

'What time are you due in Winchester?'

'Ten o'clock. Good job there's no milk to deliver today. But it's still going to be a hell of a rush to get everything done. You should have woken me.'

'I thought the sleep would do you more good. Anyway, I can help.' He gestures towards the paper on the table. 'After all, I've read up what to do.'

I look at him. Even though he's wearing yesterday's clothes, he's as neat and tidy in his white shirt and dark suit as always. 'You're not exactly dressed for it.'

'You don't think the goats will appreciate my office get-up?'

In the back of my mind I register how strange it is that we should be talking like this, as if nothing's happened, nothing's changed between us.

'I don't think the goats will mind, but you'd better put on one of Sam's coveralls, if you're sure. We'll have to get on.'

It certainly helps when he tackles the jobs I struggle with: pumping the water into the barrel to take to the goats in the field, lifting sacks of feed. And as we work through the morning jobs, it's a chance to talk, decide what I'm going to say to McNaught and Jericho.

'Will you tell them about us?' Bram says as we finish up, make our way back down to the house.

'Us?'

'That we've discovered our separate investigations are connected.'

'I suppose I'll have to. How else can I explain about Mrs Reed? I'd never have known about her without you.'

'Doesn't mean they won't be aware of her, though. They'd surely have as much information as Laidlaw.'

'I suppose so. Though when they recruited me, they seemed pretty clueless. I got the impression they didn't know anything about the local situation.'

'Well, tell them what you have to. I'm not worried for myself, but you should be careful, Jo. After all the warnings they gave you about staying away from everyone in Romsey, they're not going to be pleased to find we've collaborated.'

Inside, I take off my boots and coat, start to wash my hands at the sink. 'I'm hoping they'll be so keen to wrap the thing up they won't care. Damn.'

'What is it?'

'The water's run out. I should have pumped it up to the tank in the roof.'

'I can do it. You get your breakfast.'

I dry my hands, put out three bowls of porridge. One each for Bram and me, a third for Lady. 'Don't worry about it now. Come and sit down.'

A hasty look at my watch shows I've got less than half an hour if I'm to get to my meeting on time. 'One odd thing.'

'Yes?'

'I don't think I said where I'm meeting McNaught and Jericho?'

'I don't think you did.'

'Westgate Chambers. Your friend Mr Brown's office.'

'That is odd. You think he's working with them too?'

'Would he . . . you know, have agreed to cover up the facts about David's death if they'd asked him to?'

Bram shrugs. 'I would have thought not, but I don't know him that well. I suppose he might. Look, you're going to have to make a move or you'll be late. We've got a lot of unfinished business still.'

'Yes. What will you do?'

'I need to get home, I suppose. And I'll have to call in at the hospital, see if there's any news about George. I wish I could do more to help today.'

'Not much you can do about McNaught and Jericho. And I'll be better seeing Anita on my own. But I'll ring you, as soon as I've seen her.'

'Fair enough.'

An awkward moment. So much unfinished business between us. The pressures of getting the morning work done have tided us over this far: no time to discuss what happened between us, ask him why he stayed. It seems as if something's changed, but I'm afraid to question it. Fragile as a cobweb, perhaps it's all my imagination that his presence here this morning is significant. In the end, I settle for neutrality. 'Take care.'

'And you. Jo . . . ?'

Do it fast, I think. Like ripping a plaster off a wound.

'Later, Bram. We'll talk about it later.'

As the Cyc-Auto putters off away up the road, my mind's so full of him that I don't think of the meeting ahead, nor of anything else until I reach the Westgate.

Although Nash feels scruffy after his exertions of the morning, he's as clean as cold water and carbolic soap can make him. Since it's on his route, it seems like the sensible option to call in at the hospital on his way home. He's under no illusion that the ward sister will let him in, especially at the outrageous hour of ten thirty in the morning, but she's often more informative when he visits in person than when he rings. Even so, he's unprepared for her almost cordial invitation to him to step into her office as soon as he appears at the ward door. He can see how busy they must be, nurses intent as they bustle past with bowls of hot water and shaving mugs. Canvas screens, buff or blue and one set of scarlet, shield some of the beds from view, oddly decorative splashes of colour in a setting that's otherwise predominantly white.

'I shouldn't keep you, Sister,' he says. 'I wanted to know how Mr Hine's doing.'

'Yes. Come in, Mr Nash. Sit down.'

There's nothing different in her tone, it's as brisk as ever. But when she shuts the door firmly behind them, he gets it. Something's wrong.

'He's worse?'

'Sit down,' she repeats.

'Dead?'

'I'm afraid so. I did try to telephone you.'

'Yes.' He answers automatically. 'I was out. When did it happen?'

'Just after six this morning. It was rather sudden, I'm afraid. The doctor thinks it was probably an embolus.'

'No question of – interference?'

'No, Mr Nash. There was no one on the ward at the time but my nurses.'

'Where is he now? His body?'

She frowns. 'On the ward, still. Most irregular. When I couldn't get hold of you, I informed Sergeant Tilling of Mr Hine's death. He insisted the body shouldn't be moved until you'd seen it. In your official capacity as coroner, he said. There will have to be an inquest?'

'Oh, yes. The proximate cause of death may be an embolus, but the wider cause is the attack. His death makes that murder.' He runs the regulations through his mind. His personal relationship to George shouldn't disbar him from conducting the formalities. 'I'll need to speak to his doctor, and Sergeant Tilling.'

'I understand this is difficult for you, Mr Nash, as you were his friend, too. But I'd be grateful if you could do what you need to do as coroner as soon as possible. It disturbs the other patients to keep a dead body on the ward so long.'

'Of course.' He gathers his scattered wits, pulls on his official persona. 'I'll do it now.'

'That would be most helpful. If you're sure?'

'Yes. Take me to him.'

It's not a surprise when she leads him to the bed behind the scarlet screens. With utmost discretion, she parts the frames so they can slip inside without revealing George's body to anyone in the ward.

It's not Nash's first body, by any means. It's not even his first with whom he has had a personal relationship. But for any number of reasons, the sight of George's face, inscrutable in death, hits him hard. Patched as it is with wounds that will never heal, yellowing bruises that will never completely fade, yet there is something in it now that recalls the young man Nash served with: the cheerful hero who brought him back from death.

The pity of it, the waste, has him swallowing emotion. But there's a job to do. 'I'll need to look at his other injuries, Sister.'

'Yes.' She pulls back the sheet. Someone, one of the nurses or perhaps the doctor who came to pronounce life extinct, has straightened Hine's body in the bed, arranged his arms so his hands are crossed on his chest.

'And the gown, I'm afraid.'

She glances at him, startled. 'Surely you don't need . . . ? Won't the doctor's records be enough?'

'I have to see for myself.' But whether it's his duty as coroner or his penance as a friend which prompts him, he hardly knows. And when she's complied, helped him to inspect the marks of the attack stark on George's body, he still doesn't know.

'Thank you. If I could have a few minutes alone with him?'

She pats his arm. 'Of course. I'll be in my office when you're ready.'

He stands a moment, a minute . . . who knows? His mind's a perfect blank beyond the sense of regret, of waste. Then, softly, so he won't be heard by anyone but the dead, he says, 'George. You were right about David's death, it was murder. But you can rest easy. We'll get the bastards responsible. Won't be long now.'

I get to Brown's office on the dot of ten. I'm expecting someone to greet me when I knock on the side door, but time passes and there's no sign of a response. I'm not sure what to do. I knock again, try the door handle. It turns and the door opens easily. There must be someone inside, surely? Otherwise Brown's office has the worst security I've ever come across.

The reception area where I remember waiting before is empty. The lights are on and it's warm enough that my cold face stings at the change in temperature. There's a bell on the reception desk, and I ring it hard. The sound seems to get swallowed up, lost in the empty space. 'Hello?' I call. 'Is there anyone here?'

Nothing. If they think I'm going to hang around half the day for them, they've got another think coming. But it wouldn't do any harm to wait a few minutes, get a bit warmer. I pull my hat off, scrape my fingers through my hair. What is this all about? Though there's some comfortable seating for waiting clients, much more welcoming than Miss Haward's austere space, I can't relax enough to sit. I pace the space, three steps from reception desk to the window, four from the outside door to the stair.

If I was nervous before, now I'm beginning to feel almost scared. If it's not a test, could it possibly be a set-up? How would I explain my presence to anyone other than the secret service men? I'm beginning to think I should get out while the going's good, when I finally hear footsteps on the stair. It's the one who calls himself Jericho. Unmistakable with that doughy complexion, the sparse straggle of ginger hair.

'About time.' Tension dispelled, I'm furious.

'Sorry to keep you waiting,' he says, but it's only words. There's no regret in his voice. 'Come on up to the office. We're ready for you now.'

I follow him up a stairway that's nothing like the one at Nash, Simmons and Bing. Wide, shallow steps, a stair carpet that looks like the best Axminster. Not the long trek upward, either, like Bram's. The office Jericho leads me to is on the first floor, with a brass plate on the door which announces the usual occupant is Theophilus E. Brown himself.

Inside, though, it's McNaught who's waiting. I'm surprised to see he's grown a moustache and beard since I last met him. It makes him look much more distinguished, and much more conspicuous. In his trade, it seems an odd thing to do.

'Come and sit down, Miss Rennard,' he says, maintaining the fiction he himself set up. 'Make yourself comfortable.

You've got a lot to tell us, I believe. Now, shall my colleague get you a cup of tea? Or would you prefer coffee?'

'Don't soft-soap me,' I say. 'What was all that about downstairs? Not answering the door, making me hang around. You're lucky I didn't pi—go home.'

'Had to be sure you weren't bringing unwelcome company.'

I glare at him. Though I've every intention of not falling for his routine, I am thirsty. 'I'll have a cup of coffee, if you've got it. Milk, no sugar.'

'That's better,' he says. 'Coffee for me too, please, Jericho. You know how I like it.'

'I suppose I've got to wait till he comes back before I give my report?'

'No need to be truculent, my dear. It only makes me think you've got something to hide.'

I sit back in my chair, wishing I hadn't said I'd have a drink. But he's probably got a point. Even though they've made me cross, I don't need to return the compliment. If I'm going to get them to agree to my plan, I should at least seem more co-operative. It seems like another age before Jericho's back and all the fuss with distributing cups is over.

'Now, then,' McNaught says. 'Off you go. You won't mind if Jericho takes notes?'

'I don't know what Mr Anderson told you before he was sent away.'

'Not very much. He was rather worried about you. Something to do with goats?'

'Not important,' I say. 'It's Fisher I need to tell you about.' So I do, conscious of the sound of Jericho scribbling somewhere behind me. I tell them how lax security seems in the Experimental Hangar, and, inevitably, I have to tell them about Anita. Her involvement with Fisher. Overhearing their quarrel, the arrangement they'd made for the next day.

'You knew she was passing documents to him?'

'No, of course I didn't. I didn't know what he was asking for. From the way they'd spoken, it could have been something to do with the black market. Stores or something.'

'Components?'

'I didn't even think of that. I knew I couldn't get in touch with you so I made up my mind to be there for their meeting. Even then I didn't see what she gave him. It wasn't till he stopped in the woods I saw the papers.'

'We should pick this girl up straightaway,' Jericho says from behind me, and I'm aware he's got up out of his chair already.

'No.' I crane my neck round to look at him. 'No, don't do that. Wait till I've told you all of it.'

McNaught nods. 'Sit down, Jay. Let her finish.' And then, to me, 'Why didn't you tell Mr Anderson about her attachment to Fisher?'

A question I was dreading. If I tell them about my suspicions that Mr Anderson might not be impartial about Anita, I may get myself out of trouble but I'll put him firmly in it. It would make them suspicious of him forever, long after I've gone back to ordinary life. And in any case, as Bram said last night, I've gone soft on her myself.

'Report a love affair to him? Why should I? That was all I thought it was until I heard the quarrel. Then it was too late, Mr Anderson was gone. I didn't like the man, but I didn't suspect him of anything worse than black marketeering.'

'That's the problem of hiring civilians,' Jericho says. 'They get sentimental. They think.'

McNaught coughs out a laugh.

'All right. I probably deserve that. But you wouldn't know as much as you do if it hadn't been for me *thinking*.'

'Don't get upset, Miss Rennard,' McNaught says. 'You followed this chap Fisher into the woods, and you saw he had some papers. Then what?'

'I kept on following him. He came to a place in the woods, a house with high white walls all around. When he went inside, I couldn't go any further.'

'This house? You saw where it was?'

'I saw, but I didn't have any idea then where we'd come to. It was only later . . .' Now we're at the crux of it, the bit where I have to tell them about Bram. 'I ran back as fast as I could, I wanted to report it. But Mr Anderson was gone. I had no way to get in touch.'

'And?'

'I discovered the place was called Limeshard Gate.' I'm aware that the two men exchange a meaningful glance. I take a deep breath. 'The woman who lives there, Mrs Ilse Reed, is a Nazi sympathiser.'

There's a long silence. Then McNaught speaks. 'Interesting. And how, exactly, did you find that out?'

'Does it matter? It's true.'

Another look passes between them.

'Mr Nash, I presume?' McNaught says.

My face flames. I can't help it. I might have dyed my hair black, but my skin's still got the thin betraying transparency of a redhead.

'You were warned,' Jericho says. 'We told you not to contact anyone from Romsey. Especially him. You've put him at grave risk, Mrs Lester.'

'Shh, friend,' McNaught says. 'Walls have ears. But, as my colleague says, *Miss Rennard*, that was most unwise.'

'I haven't told him anything I shouldn't,' I say. 'And if you're any good at all at your jobs, you'll know he'd been investigating David Hine's death for himself. He's a friend of David's father. I've told him nothing about what I'm doing in Hursley, the leak. I didn't have to, there are enough rumours flying around. And George Hine knew, because of the police enquiries. He told Bram. I never confirmed it, but we were working on the same case from different ends. Even if I hadn't bumped into him that day in Winchester, they were bound to link up.'

'Well,' McNaught says, 'done is done. The question is, what now?'

'That's the thing,' I say, eager to move on. 'I know Fisher's got to take something to the same place tomorrow. I heard an argument about it, a man who works for Mrs Reed threatened him if he didn't deliver. I thought . . .'

'More thinking?' Jericho.

'Let her speak.' McNaught. 'She's been quite useful till now.'

It sounds ominous, but in some ways I don't care. The sooner they dispense with my services, the better I'll like it.

'What if I could persuade Anita the way to free herself from him and avoid getting herself arrested would be to help us catch him? If she'd agree to pass him one last lot of documents, tell us when, you could be at Limeshard Gate to pick him up when he delivers them. That way you'd catch Mrs Reed too.'

'You can't promise her immunity. If you're right, she's in serious trouble.'

'I know. But surely, if she co-operates . . . ?' I don't tell them she's pregnant by Fisher, it seems like something they don't need to know; something that would weigh against her if they did.

'Go downstairs and wait,' McNaught says. 'We need to discuss this.'

I hate his peremptory manner, but I do what he says.

In Romsey, Nash meets the doctor who treated George, arranges for a post-mortem to be carried out. He talks to Sergeant Tilling, too, persuades the policeman he doesn't need to ask Miss Stone for formal identification.

'I can vouch for that,' he says.

'That wouldn't be a conflict of interest?' Tilling asks. 'You being his solicitor.'

'Not at all,' Nash responds firmly. As a local man, he often knows the deceased, or the deceased's family. But privately, he thinks he will need to consult his colleagues about the ethical issues involved. Pity he can't ask Brown, but that would be a complication too far.

'Will you get more resources,' he asks Tilling, 'now the attack on George has become a case of murder?'

Tilling shrugs. 'I'd like to think so, but I don't know what the Super will say. We never had much of a lead in the first place, and now Mr Hine's dead without gaining consciousness, the hope we had he'd be able to identify his attackers is gone. You haven't got anything for us, I suppose?'

'Don't I remember you telling me I shouldn't get involved?'

'Ah.' Tilling has the grace to look embarrassed. 'But I didn't think you'd take any notice.'

'That's wanting to have your cake and eat it,' Nash says. 'But you never know. What do they say? Watch this space.'

Leaving a startled Tilling staring after him, Nash makes his way out of the hospital. On a morning that's gone from joy to great sadness, it's just his luck to top it off with hostility. Old Joseph Fox, seemingly lying in wait for him at the porter's lodge, pops out like a malevolent goblin as he passes.

'Oi, Nash. You seen that granddaughter of mine yet?'

'I thought you'd washed your hands of her years ago, Mr Fox. Why the sudden interest?'

'Family business,' Joseph Fox says. 'None of your beeswax.'

If Nash didn't feel sick at heart, he'd laugh. He hasn't heard that childish response since he was in the school playground.

'She'd be surprised to know you think of her as family,' he says.

'Pah.' The old man spits. 'You think you're clever? I told you before, there'll be trouble if she don't get in touch.'

'I'll remember. Now, excuse me.'

As he cycles away, he thinks he should ask Bill or Jim Fox, Jo's uncles, if they know what's biting the old man. But a turn or two more of the pedals extinguishes the thought as he wonders how Jo's got on in Winchester: whether McNaught and Jericho have bought her plan.

24

Sunday, afternoon

I T FEELS ODD TO BE back at the Hutments, and not be going to the Andersons. Not that I'm missing Hilda, but I'd welcome the opportunity to sit with Mr Anderson in his warm, sawdusty shed, drink another of his cups of tea fortified with rum. The meeting with McNaught and Jericho has unsettled me. After the initial game-playing, they agreed to my plan. They hadn't even suggested any changes. I was expecting more of a fight. Perhaps I'm overly suspicious but they seemed almost too pleased, too willing to go along with what I suggested. Not that I can do anything about it now. It's settled. All I have to do is persuade Anita to play her part, let them know what time to be ready to pick up Fisher, Mrs Reed and her crew.

I don't know Anita's parents, her family. All I remember is that her brother is in the Army, in the same company as Fisher. I have to hope he's not got time off this afternoon, because that will make what I have to do even more difficult. As it is, I'm not sure how I'm going to persuade her to talk to me, or even where we can go if she agrees. There's nowhere inside these buildings that's private enough.

Number 90 the Hutments is much nearer the main road than the Andersons' place, alongside the footpath out to the bus stop where I first saw the girl. It's as neat and tidy as all of the properties around, as if there's a competition to make sure the temporary development has an established, respectable feel.

I prop the Cyc-Auto where it won't annoy anyone. The gate squeaks as I open it, and a curtain twitches in the window overlooking the path. A pink curtain. Remembering what Mr Anderson said about Anita's choice of colour, it seems a fair guess that the room behind the window is the girl's. I'm half expecting she'll be reluctant to see me, so it's a surprise to find her opening the door before I can knock.

'What do you want?' she says. 'My parents are out. It's no use turning up thinking you can split on me about the baby.'

One problem solved. 'I haven't come to see them. It's you I want to talk to.'

'What for?' It's sullen, almost aggressive.

'You're on your own here in the house?'

'You needn't think you can bully me.'

'I don't want to bully you. I came to help. Good afternoon.' This, to a woman with a pram who's passing by, taking more interest than I'd like in the two of us on the doorstep. Though Anita's obviously tried to cover her bruises with makeup, they're still noticeable, even from a distance. 'If you don't want everyone to know your business, wouldn't it be better to ask me in?'

For a moment I think she's going to refuse, but then she relents, pushes the door wide at her back. 'Oh, you can come in. But you'll have to go when Mum and Dad get back.'

'What time are you expecting them?'

She shrugs. 'Three o'clock, maybe. Unless they get talking at church.'

A look at my watch shows it's not quite two. 'We've got plenty of time.'

'Oh, all right,' she says, sighing. 'Go on through.'

The layout's exactly the same as the Andersons', but while the sitting room there is the perfect showcase for Hilda's dour tastes and chilly personality, here it's cosy and cluttered, warm from a good fire in the hearth.

'Sit down,' she says grudgingly, as she perches on the edge of a chair. 'Clear yourself a space on the sofa.'

I make a space on the side furthest from her. I don't want to crowd her, frighten her into clamming up altogether. And it's nicely placed, squarely between her and the door. 'Thank you.' I let the silence fill with her unease, her curiosity, a cat-and-mouse game. But I know if I can get her to make the first moves to a dialogue, I'm winning.

'Go on, then,' she says. 'What's it about?'

'Your boyfriend Fisher. Adam, isn't it?'

Her composure breaks at the name, and she bursts into tears. 'Addy,' she wails. 'Addy, Addy.'

I'm shocked at the suddenness of it, the violence of her emotion. There's nothing to do but go to her. I kneel beside her chair, put a tentative arm around her. For a moment she resists, then huddles into my shoulder, crying as if she'll never stop. 'What is it?' I say. 'What's happened now?'

'Yesterday, he came yesterday. He says . . . he wants . . . oh, I can't tell you.'

'He wants you to get another lot of papers out of the Experimental Hangar for him, doesn't he?'

A fresh storm of weeping. She chokes out some incoherent words, but I don't get any sense of what she's said.

'Shh, shh.' I try to soothe her, but it's as much for my own selfish reasons as for her sake. 'Try and calm down.'

A hiccuping gulp, and she palms the tears from her eyes, rubs her sleeve across her nose and mouth. 'I need a hanky.'

'Here.' I fumble the necessary from my pocket, hand it over. It's crumpled, but clean enough. She wipes her face, the last of the powder making beige streaks across the fabric. The bruising round both eyes is bad, and I wonder if Fisher broke her nose when he hit her on Friday. 'That looks sore,' I say. 'Whatever did you tell your parents when you got home?'

'They think I walked into a piece of machinery,' she sniffs. 'My dad's really mad. Says he's going to go in and speak to the foreman.' She starts to sob again. 'Oh, what am I going to do?'

'The first thing,' I say, 'is we'll have a cup of tea. Then we'll talk. I'll do what I can to help. But you'll have to help me too. Now, show me where to find things in the kitchen.'

The move to another room, concentrating on the simple domestic task, seems to help Anita quite a lot, calm her down. When we get back to the living room, she sits more easily in the chair, and the tears, at least, have dried up.

'I'm right, aren't I?' I say as gently as I can. 'Adam does want you to get plans from the hangar?'

She hangs her head, nods. 'Yes.'

'It's not the first time?'

'No.' She looks up, a spark of defiance in her face. 'The first time, it was OK. He said it was. It was a test for the Army.'

'Right. Tell me about it, Anita.'

'It was before Christmas. We'd been walking out together for ages, I was . . . he's so handsome, I was . . . He said I was beautiful, he'd always love me, and I loved him so much. It didn't seem wrong.'

'You slept with him?'

'Yes, yes. You don't understand.'

Oh, but I do. If only you knew.

'So, what happened then? About the papers, I mean?'

'He said, it was a security exercise. The army wanted to see if . . . if anyone could get stuff out of the hangar. He said he'd been chosen because he knew people.' The defiance strengthens. 'He does, everyone knows him. He can get anything . . .'

'All right. He asked you to take the papers from the hangar. What project were they for? Some particular aspect of a design?'

'No, that was it, you see. It didn't matter what I took it was just to see if I could. I thought it couldn't possibly be wrong because . . . well, an enemy would want something special.'

'And you took them, gave them to him?'

'I smuggled them out down the front of my knickers. He said . . . he kissed them when I gave them to him, said . . . it made him feel randy to know where they'd been.'

The idea makes me feel queasy, but I try not to show it. 'You're doing fine, Anita. Go on.'

'I thought he'd give them back to me, but he didn't. He said he'd have to pass them to his superior, to prove it had happened. Oh, Miss Rennard . . .' Her eyes fill, spill over. 'And then . . .'

'Better call me Jo,' I say, though I shouldn't. But I can't bear to lie to her about it. Right now, she needs the truth every bit as much as she needs a friend. 'What happened next?

She shakes her head. 'I found out I was pregnant. I told Addy, I thought . . . I thought he'd be angry, but he wasn't, not then. He said, we'd be married, but he needed . . . he said he'd had to lie about the papers, because he'd wanted to get in with this bloke he knew. He was offering good money for anything Addy could get him from the hangar. Even components, but I told him, that was too difficult. It had to be papers I could hide. Addy said if we could go on a bit longer, he'd have enough put by to look after me and the baby properly.'

'Do you know who the man was who wanted the papers?'

'No. Some weird name.'

'Bertholdt?'

'That's it. He worked for this woman . . .'

'I know about her.'

'And then it started to go wrong. I wanted to stop, but Addy got angry, said we had to go on, because otherwise . . .' A sob comes from nowhere, derails her.

'Otherwise?'

'He said this bloke would kill him if we didn't keep passing him stuff from the hangar. I couldn't let Addy get hurt, could I? I didn't want my baby to be fatherless. So the papers . . . I went on getting them, but I was drawing things wrong, putting in mistakes.'

'That was clever,' I say, though inwardly I think it was probably asking for trouble. But it does explain why McNaught and Jericho couldn't trace the fragment of blueprint in David Hine's hand. It might even help her in the end, that she'd given them fake drawings. That, and her youth and her pregnancy might make a difference to the charges they'll want to bring. I'm thinking Bram might be willing to advise her when she spoils it, tells me what happened the night David Hine died.

'It was David's fault. Everything would've been all right if it hadn't been for him. It was an accident, anyway . . .'

*

Winter Solstice

Sunday 21ˢᵗ– Monday 22ⁿᵈ December 1942, late evening

She's excited, the girl in the gauzy pink dress with the full skirt and beads on the bodice. The sweetheart neckline shows off the top of her breasts in a way that excites her: she knows how much Addy will love it. It's the one good thing about having a baby, the way her bust has grown. She's never had much up top before.

It's a night of firsts for her: this dress, this party. She's not a child anymore, she's a woman. Everyone will see it.

Addy. It's all for him. All because of him. He's the one she has to please. The one she wants to show. He'll be so happy she's brought the stuff. It was a lot harder to hide the papers under the thin material of her dress tonight, but somehow she's managed.

A cold little shudder runs down her spine. It's nothing to do with the cold, though the mohair stole her mother lent her won't do much to keep out the winter chill once she gets outside. But it will be all right, with Addy's arms round her. If only he could be at the party, if he didn't have to . . .

The grandfather clock in the hall strikes midnight, and everyone cheers. She feels like Cinderella as she slips out into the garden, but she's not running away from her prince, but towards him. The thought makes her feel as if she's flying, she's so light and airy with excitement fizzing in her belly, thrumming through her veins. It's all going to be all right.

In the sunken garden, the moonlight makes the water into a puddle of silver, casts black shadows as solid-seeming as walls across her path. She skips down the steps, expecting to see her lover any moment.

But the fizz begins to leak out as she sees he isn't there. Another cold little shiver. He'll come, he must come. He must see her in her dress.

He must collect the papers she's so carefully prepared for him, so daringly brought with her. She wriggles them out from under her waistband, holds them close to her body to keep them warm. He likes to think how they've been touching against her skin.

Footsteps. She turns, eager. But it isn't Addy, it's that horrible little sneak, David Hine. He's always following her about. If Addy catches him here, he'll be furious. He's warned him off loads of times, even had a fight with him last week. If you can call it a fight. David's such a weakling, he didn't even get a punch in. He must be dopey if he thinks she'd want him when she can have Addy . . .

'Anita. What are you doing here?'

'What do you think? I'm meeting Adam, of course. Better not let him catch you, if you don't want another beating.'

'What do you see in him, Anita? He's a bad lot.'

'And you're a prig and a bore. Push off.'

He comes close. He's not a patch on Addy, so lanky and shambling. He's like one of the weeds he's supposed to dig up. She can even smell the earth on his clothes. 'Pooh,' *she says, stepping back.* 'You stink.'

He grabs her arm, and she drops the blueprint. She darts forward to pick it up, but he's too quick for her. 'What's this?'

'Nothing to do with you,' *she says.* 'Give it back.'

The lankiness she disparages means she can't reach to take it out of his hand as he holds it high in the air. She jumps to grab it, hears the paper begin to tear. 'Give it to me.'

353

'Yeah, give it to her, Hine.' It's Addy, and she turns to him with a cry of joy and frustration.

'He took the papers,' she says. 'He won't give them back.'

'Oh, he'll give them back all right,' the soldier says. 'Won't you, Hine?'

But David doesn't get a chance to say anything, do anything. A fist like a hammer connects with his jaw, and he goes down. There's a sickening second thud as the boy's head connects with the raised edge of the pond.

'Oh, Addy,' Anita whimpers. 'I think you must have killed him.'

'Hold this.' Fisher rips the blueprint out of the boy's hand, hands it to her. 'Nah, no such luck. He's breathing.'

He stands up, looks at her. His face is unreadable in the cold glimmer of the moon, full of strange shadows and hollows. So handsome, she thinks. So frightening.

'We'll have to get rid of him,' he says. 'Or he'll see us both at the end of a rope for traitors.'

'No.'

'Oh, yes,' he says. 'You're in it as deep as me.'

He lifts David Hine's unconscious form easily, drags him up against the low stone wall. 'An accident,' he mutters. 'Anyone can fall in drunk.' He pulls a hip flask from his pocket, unscrews the lid. Pours alcohol into Hine's mouth until the boy begins to choke. 'Good.' A push is enough now, submerging the boy's head and shoulders. A hand keeps them under.

'Addy, you can't.' A horrified whisper.

But it's too late. He has. There's no resistance, and before the soldier's even taken five breaths of his own, the bubbles stop rising from the water.

'He's had it,' he says callously, as he pushes the body more securely into the water, wipes his hands dry. 'Now, where's that plan?'

She shrinks back as he approaches. 'Addy . . .'

'Better give it to me,' he says. 'Like I said, you're in as deep as me. Pinching secret stuff from work. Now you're an accessory to a murder, too.'

She hands it over, trembling. 'Addy.'

'Ah, shut up,' he says. 'Go back to the party before someone misses you. Keep your mouth shut, and we'll both be all right.'

25

Sunday, afternoon and evening

BACK AT BASSWOOD HOUSE, FAN's eagerly waiting for him. The early morning telephone calls from the hospital alerted her to his absence overnight, set her guessing that George Hine had died.

'It's so sad,' she says when he confirms his morning visit to the hospital, the news of George's death. 'Poor Edna. Don't know what she's going to do now.'

'I'll try and sort something out. It may not be too bad if George has left provision for her in his will.' If he can find it, that is. It wasn't with the papers he brought home from George's desk.

'Would you mind if I popped round to see her for a while?'

'Of course not. Tilling will have informed her about the death by now. Give her my condolences, tell her I'll be round to see her in a day or so.' He straightens his shoulders, feels the pull of muscles from the morning's work on the farm. 'What I could do with is a good cup of coffee and a bath.'

'I'll get the coffee right away. And a sandwich? For a miracle I've got some ham.'

'Sounds good. Plenty of mustard.'

An hour later, hot water, caffeine, starch and protein have worked their restorative magic. It's remarkable how different he feels once they've taken effect. Even the shock of George's death is smoothed over, a problem for another day.

The doorbell rings. For a moment, he thinks, *Jo*? But he knows it can't be. Miss Stone, perhaps.

Fan's voice in greeting, a deeper response. A man. A second strange voice, and though he can't hear the words, Fan sounds anxious. He gets up from his chair, goes to the study door. Looks down into the hall. Two men he vaguely remembers, more from their voices than what he can see of them. As he makes his way downstairs, he nails the memory. The short one with the balding head is Jericho. The other must be McNaught, though Nash doesn't recall the beard.

'Mr Nash,' the taller man says. 'We've come wanting your help. I expect you can guess what it's about.'

'I expect I can.'

What he can't guess is why they're here. Whether they really want his help, or if they're planning to administer a slap on the wrist for his interference. If it's the latter, there's no need for Fan to be witness to it. 'Come up to the study,' he says. 'We can talk there.'

'Actually, sir, we'd like you to come with us if you wouldn't mind.'

It sounds ominous, but there's nothing he can do if they're about to arrest him. Better to go willingly. If he appears to co-operate, he may find out more than if he makes a fight of it. 'I'll get my coat.'

'No problem, sir,' McNaught says, with every appearance of affability, though Jericho frowns, fidgets with impatience.

'I don't know how long I'll be,' Nash says, casting an enquiring glance at the men.

'Couldn't say, sir,' the fat one responds.

'Very well. Fan, you'll have to expect me when you see me.'

'Sir.' She eyes the two men suspiciously. 'Is there anything you want me to do?'

Perhaps he's imagining it, being melodramatic, but it feels as if he should somehow alert her to the fact he's not entirely willing to go with these men. But how? 'If anyone rings,' he says, thinking, Jo surely will, 'let them know I've had to go out rather unexpectedly with these gentlemen.'

'Of course, sir.'

He doesn't miss the fact that the men each take one of his arms as they go through the door and down the steps to the road. There's a black car waiting, the engine running. Not imagination, then. It is a melodrama after all.

When Anita finishes her story, admits that ever since David's death, Fisher has kept her in line with his fists and his threats, I want to weep myself. For the pity of it, and because I'm so angry. Her adolescent passion for Fisher has caused so much trouble, led directly to David Hine's death.

But I feel sorry for her too. And for her baby. I know only too well what it is to be born a bastard in a world that turns its back, blames the child for the mother's sins, the father's criminal acts.

'Do you want to get out of this, Anita? Because if you do, I'll help you, but if not . . . well, it's up to you. If you want to be free to look after your baby when it's born, it's your only chance.'

She puts her hand on her belly. Her pregnancy's barely showing to the outside world, but I suppose she can feel it all right. 'I've got to help you, then, haven't I? My baby's started to move. I have to take care of it. What do you want me to do?'

'First, I need to know when Fisher's coming for the papers from the hangar. Where are you going to meet him?'

She fidgets, looks uneasy. 'Morning tea break, he said. The usual place, but it can't wait till lunchtime.'

'OK.' One eye on the clock for her parents' return, I run through what we want her to do. 'In fact,' I say, 'don't do anything different or say anything to make him suspicious. Give him the documents, and let him walk away.'

'Will you be there?' she asks.

'Yes, of course. Just in case.'

She doesn't ask, *In case of what*? and I don't tell her.

'And I haven't got to do anything else? I don't have to . . . see, when they arrest him?'

If she's angling to find out where the trap will be sprung, I don't bite. The less she knows, the better. Let her think I'm the only watcher, and Hursley Park will be the scene of the trap, if she likes.

I'm glad she's past crying anymore. When her parents come home, she's looking pale, but composed enough. They seem like nice people, pleased that Anita's had a visit from a friend. Though the girl hangs her head a bit at that, she doesn't break down.

'I'll see you in the morning,' I say as I take my leave of her. And then, because she still doesn't meet my eye, 'Anita?'

She nods, looks up. 'Yeah, see you.'

It's not quite the wholehearted agreement I would have liked, but I can't pursue it with her parents there. And there's nothing to be gained by badgering her. She'll do it or she won't. Only time will tell.

It's still daylight when I get to the main road. Time to go back to Sam's. But before I get back on the bike, I ring the number McNaught and Jericho gave me, to let them know what time Anita's handing over the documents to Fisher. I'm told that neither are available to speak to, but a helpful, if anonymous, male voice assures me he'll pass on the message.

I try Bram's number, but it rings and rings. I'm oddly annoyed. Though he's every right to go out if he wants to, I thought he'd be waiting for my call.

As the powerful car hums along the back roads, Nash thinks that here's another big black car, a candidate for knocking him off his bike. Not very likely, of course, it's all a bit too ad hoc for them.

'So,' he says, 'what *is* this all about? I take it you don't actually want my help.'

McNaught settles back in his seat. 'Oh, but you are helping us, Mr Nash, just by being here. We appreciate your co-operation.'

'Uh huh. And how long am I expected to – *co-operate*?'

'As long as it takes. Once our little clean-up operation is over tomorrow, it should be possible to let you go home.'

'Ridiculous. What do you think I'm going to do? You can't suppose I'd want your mission to fail.'

'The problem is, Mr Nash, you should never have been involved in the first place. We did tell Mrs Lester to avoid contact with you, but we should have known she wouldn't listen. That's the problem with employing amateurs. And, of course, we know you've been in touch with the press.'

'Laidlaw? That's a joke. I've been getting information from him, not giving it.'

'We can't take the chance of this affair becoming public. Your co-operation is, shall we say, damage limitation.'

'And what do you propose to do with me? Got a nice little cell all lined up?'

'Really, Mr Nash, we're not savages. A night in a hotel. Perhaps less privacy than you're used to, but no more than an inconvenience for you. As it goes, you're altogether a more serious inconvenience to us. Now, no more questions. Settle back. Enjoy the ride.'

*

It's as well that I can do the farm work without thinking these days, because my mind is not on what I'm doing. It's too full of what Anita's told me. Though I've promised to help her, I don't know if I can. Bram certainly won't get involved when he knows she's kept quiet about David's death all this time. When everything's done, I get myself what passes for a meal until tomorrow, when I can have fresh rations. And vegetables, I think. I should have thought of that the other day. Serve me right if I get scurvy.

It's almost eight by the time I'm knocking on the door at the post office. Bram will be back by now, surely? The long-suffering Della lets me in.

'Don't mind if I leave you to it, do you, my dear?' she says as she shows me into the telephone room. 'Only I've just this minute got tuned into *Melody Mixture* on the wireless.'

'I'll be fine, thank you.'

Couldn't be better, in fact. But it doesn't last. The phone's picked up almost before it's had a chance to ring at the other end.

'Mr Nash, is that you?' Fan's voice, sounding worried.

'Fan? It's not Mr Nash, it's me. Jo Lester.'

'Oh. I was hoping it was him.'

'So I gather. He's out?' I say like an idiot. Of course he is, or she wouldn't have thought I might be him.

'It's been such a horrible day, Mrs Lester. I woke up this morning to a telephone call from the hospital wanting to speak to him but he wasn't here. He must have been out all night. Oh, forgive me, I shouldn't have said that.'

'Don't worry. Go on.'

'It was lunchtime before he got home. He'd already been up at the hospital. I guessed from the call it must mean Mr Hine had died, and sure enough, that's what it was.'

'I'm sorry about that. Mr Nash must have been upset.'

'Yes, he was a bit shaken, I think. He'd had all that to deal with, then hardly time to eat a sandwich before a couple of men were at the door. Said they wanted his help, drove off in a big black car.'

A giant hand squeezes my guts. God, what if it's Ilse's men?

'What were they like?' I say urgently. 'Did you get their names?'

'They didn't tell me. It was a tall man who did most of the talking. He had a beard, like he might be in the Navy. The other one was a little fat fellow with no hair. They seemed respectable enough, but I thought it was a bit of a cheek coming along like that on a Sunday afternoon.'

McNaught and Jericho. No doubt about it. Better than the Blackshirts, but maybe not by much. What the hell do they want with him?

'I think I know who they must be,' I say. 'Did they say where they were going? What time they'd be back?'

'No. He said to expect him when I saw him, but I thought it would be before this.'

'Right.' The iron hand squeezes again. This is my fault. If they've arrested him, it's because I ignored what they told me. If I'd walked away from that first meeting in Winchester, he'd be safe at home.

'It'll be official business, Fan. You know, legal stuff. I'm sure he'll be back as soon as he can get away.' I get a grim kind of satisfaction from knowing I haven't told her a lie.

'Oh.' Fan sounds relieved. 'War work, you mean?'

'I expect so.'

'All right. I'll tell him you called when he gets back, shall I?'

I force a smile. Though she can't see it, I know it will reflect in my voice. 'That would be good. Thank you, Fan. Bye for now.'

'Bye.'

I'm shaking as I put the telephone receiver down. Some of it's fear, but mostly it's anger. Pent-up rage from all the things the secret service men have done. I could tolerate the disruption to my life in a good cause, but this . . . hauling Bram off who knows where without a word, without a reason, is going a damn sight too far. I don't care about tomorrow, or Fisher, or anything else either. They can't get away with this.

I dial the number I'd rung earlier. I've never used the same number twice before, I don't know what will happen. But if somebody doesn't answer, give me some answers, I'm off to Winchester, throwing stones through Brown's windows till I find out what I need to know.

The same anonymous voice answers, though he doesn't sound happy this time when I tell him who's calling.

'Is there a problem, Miss Rennard?'

'You bet your life. I want to speak to McNaught or Jericho. And don't tell me I can't, or I'll make such a row you'll never hear the end of it.'

A hissing silence, in which I think I hear whispered voices. Then: 'You'll have to give me a minute to find them.'

'Not even half a minute,' I say. 'I mean it about the fuss.'

'Very well.' The voice is sulky now. 'Putting you through.'

A whole battery of clicks, a different ambient noise. I think I can hear the sound of traffic. Not a car, but a bus, perhaps.

'Yes?' McNaught.

'Where is he?'

'Who?'

'You know very well who. Where's Bram? What have you done with him?'

'Why do you think it's anything to do with us?'

'A tall man with a beard and a short, fat, ginger baldy? Who else?'

'My colleague would be distressed to hear you call him ginger.'

'Boohoo. Where's Bram?'

'He's quite safe, my dear. Quite comfortable. Nice little hotel room.'

If I can believe him, that's somewhat of a relief. At least it's not a prison cell. 'Why?'

'Insurance,' McNaught says. 'Against tomorrow's little show. Don't want the wrong people hearing about it, do we?'

'You bloody fools. He wants Fisher as much as you do. And Mrs—'

'No names,' McNaught cuts in. 'You've been foolish enough yourself.'

'Yes. I don't dispute it. But it's not his fault. If you want insurance, you can have me.'

He laughs. 'You're not my type.'

'I didn't mean—'

'Enough. I know what you meant. Very heroic. I'm sure he'd be flattered.'

'You can't keep him as some kind of hostage.'

'No intention of it, beyond what's necessary. He's not my type either.'

'Very funny. Just let him go.'

'All in good time. If everything goes as planned. You can have him back tomorrow if you play your part, and he's sensible about signing a few papers. Now, off you go back to your goats, and keep your mouth shut.'

The phone cuts out before I can reply. I sit a long time with the receiver still in my hand, listening to the purr of the disconnected line. Long enough that Della pops her head round the door to check on me.

'You OK?' she says when she sees me. 'Not bad news, I hope?'

'No.' My hand is so stiff it hurts as I release the receiver into its cradle. 'I don't know what I owe you. Two calls, both local. But I was on the second call longer than three minutes.'

'Call it a bob,' she says. 'If it turns out to be more, I'll let you know.'

I hand over the shilling, thank her again. As I ride back to my goats, I'm still hearing it. Thinking I can hear it. The sound of my name, *Jo*, a whisper, less than a whisper under McNaught's patronising tone.

Bram.

There in a room with McNaught. And for all I know, Jericho too. A room where there's traffic outside. A bus, labouring up a hill. Not a prison cell, but he's not free.

Oh, Bram.

26

Monday 18th January, morning

THE NIGHT PASSES ON LEADEN feet. Despite a weariness that feels bone-deep, I don't sleep more than a few minutes at a time. Doze, start awake, heart pounding as fast as if I've run that mile through the woods again. Glance at the clock. Five minutes passed. Glance again a lifetime later, and it's only three minutes more. The tick tells me the clock hasn't stopped, but the hands move so slowly, so stubbornly.

At just after four I can't bear it any longer. I drag myself out of bed. I can't make myself tea, there's not even dust left in the caddy, and the used leaves I've been saving are exhausted. A cup of hot water is better than nothing, but not much. Lady looks a little surprised at my early appearance, but she trots out into the freezing morning with me good-naturedly enough. The moon's still up, almost full. Though it's nearing the horizon, there's enough light to guide me without a torch.

The first chore is to take food and water, and some more straw, up to the goats in the top field. But the pump in the yard's frozen. I have to boil a kettle to pour over the handle, free it before I can get the water flowing. I should have covered it last night, of course, but I was too upset, too angry to think of it.

When that's done, the moon's almost down. I light the lantern, go into the indoor pens. And there's that same air of expectancy as before, when the first doe kidded. Now, by the looks of them, there are two in the first stage of labour. I can't stop with them this morning, I mustn't be late. Too much rides on it. I'd give every secret in Supermarine away to get Bram back, but his return relies on this morning's exercise to catch Fisher and Mrs Reed going to plan. And small part though I have in it, I have to play that part.

But right from the beginning, it goes wrong. When it matters so much that it shouldn't.

At half past five, almost a decent hour for farmers, I shoot down to Mr Evans's place, throw myself – or more accurately, the goats – on his mercy. He comes willingly enough. I have to hope all the kids will be female.

I start the milk round as early as I dare. It's Sod's Law that everyone who has milk this morning wants to talk, or they've forgotten it's Monday and don't have their jug ready, or they don't answer the door and I'm hanging about, trying to decide whether to wait for them or go on. It's dark as midnight now the moon's set, and time's started to speed up, no longer leaden-footed. I'm getting anxious now about being late as I set off for the shop at the south end of the village, my last call this morning.

And then it decides to rain. A sleety, determined downpour that has me soaked through in seconds. Worse, the Cyc-Auto's engine sputters, dies. There's fuel, not much, but enough. It just won't go. I could scream with frustration.

I push bike and cart along to the shop, where at least the shopkeeper's waiting for me.

'Oh my,' she says. 'You look like a proper drowned rat.'

'I feel it too. And the damn bike's given up on me.'

'Not your morning.' She smiles sympathetically. 'But look on the bright side. You can have your rations today.'

'Yes. Could you be a darling and put them up for me? I'll collect them later.'

'Course I will, love.'

'And . . . is there anywhere I can leave this?' I kick the bike wheel. 'I don't fancy dragging it all the way up to the House in the wet.'

'Stick it down the side. It won't be in anyone's way there.'

I do as she says. Begin the trek up to Hursley Park House. People have started to arrive for work, collars up, heads down in the rain. The charter buses don't come through by Southampton Lodge, so there's only a trickle of folk, all intent on getting into the dry as soon as possible.

I trudge along the fence by the Experimental Hangar, find myself the only person on the path. Everyone else has gone into the hangar. There's a welcome bit of shelter from overhanging trees as I round the curve in the road, and I slow, wipe the rain out of my eyes.

And there's Anita, ahead of me. I'd recognise that coat anywhere. God, what's she doing? Out in this rain, and hurrying away from the hangar, not towards it. But I know, really I know before ever I see the figure step out of the trees.

Fisher.

She's double-crossed us.

Outrage sweeps through me as I catch a flash of yellow passing from the girl to the soldier: one of the oilskin envelopes I know only too well from my post room duties. It's too early. Much too early. Fisher's going to escape, deliver the package to Limeshard before McNaught and Jericho are ready. Will they even be there at all?

I'm not thinking about anything except the need to stop him as I break into a run. Anita looks over her shoulder in alarm, and I hear Fisher shout. 'It's a trap. You bitch.' He pushes her and she stumbles, as he turns away and begins to run.

My focus is on Fisher and I keep running, but out of the corner of my eye I see Anita fall. I'd ignore it, her, but she calls out 'Jo', and there's something in her voice that I can't ignore.

I halt mid-stride, glance across at her. She's holding her side, and there's red running between her fingers. Dear God, he's stabbed her.

One more glance at Fisher's retreating back. There's nothing I can do. No one else around. I have to help her.

I'm shouting for someone to come as I kneel next to her in the rain, as I pull her coat open. The wound is low on her side, the blood running freely but not pumping.

'My baby,' she whispers.

'Yes.' I pull off my scarf, make a pad of it. Press it hard against her side, hear her yelp in pain. I shout again. If no one comes this time, I'll have to leave her, go back to the hangar for help.

But now there's the sound of running footsteps from that direction, the noise of a vehicle moving towards us from Hursley Park House. In moments, it seems as if half the workforce is standing round. 'She's been stabbed,' I yell at their gawping faces. 'Get an ambulance, quick.'

'Calm down, miss.' One of the security guards. He's got a first aid bag over his shoulder. 'Now, let the dog see the rabbit.' His hands are blessedly competent as he takes over, his voice steady as he issues orders to the bystanders.

'She's pregnant,' I say as I kneel back, push to my feet. 'Make sure they know.'

He nods. 'Get this crowd out of the way. And tell that fella to shift the van or the ambulance won't get through.'

'But . . .' I can't wait around. I have to warn McNaught, get after Fisher.

'Look sharp,' he says. 'They'll be bringing the ambulance down from the army camp.'

Desperate, I shoo the crowd. I'm about to cross to the van when Hilda comes panting up. 'Anita?' she says to me. 'What happened?'

'Fisher stabbed her.' No time for finesse. I grab her arm as she tries to move forward. 'Leave it. They're taking care of her. If you want to help, there's something I need you to do.'

Her eyes are on the girl lying in the road, the guard beside her. 'How bad is it?'

'Listen, Hilda.' I shake her. 'It's important. I don't know how much you know, but if Mr Anderson were here he'd tell you to do what I say. Ring Winchester 31. Tell the person who answers you're calling for me. Say Fisher's already on his way, and I'm following. Do it now.'

'Anita . . .'

I shake her again, and she looks at me. 'You must tell them.'

'Winchester 31,' she says. 'Fisher's on his way.'

'Right. Do it.'

She turns back in the direction of the hangar, falters. Looks back longingly at Anita.

'Go,' I shout fiercely. But I can't wait any longer to see if she will. I start towards the House, to where the path runs out towards Ampfield wood.

'Here.' It's the van driver. It's Reg. 'Was it that bastard Fisher?'

'Yes. Can't talk. I've got to go after him.'

'Get in.' He flings open the door. 'We'll catch him.'

I'm hardly in my seat when he's got the engine going.

'Which way?'

'He'll have gone up through the woods. Heading for a place called Limeshard Gate. You can't . . .'

'Bloody well can.' He swings the van round in the road. 'That poor kid. I'll have the bastard.'

'He's got such a start. We'll never get there in time.'

'Don't you be so sure about that.'

With his foot to the floor, the old Austin van shudders and rocks as he turns sharp left off the drive to Hursley Park House.

'It's back that way,' I shout as we cross the path I followed last week, chasing Fisher.

'I'm Hursley born and bred, love. I know a trick or two worth more than one of his.'

We rattle through a farmyard, turn sharp left again. Now I can see we're travelling parallel to the woods' edge. Water sprays up from the road as we pass a couple of cottages, and I hold on for dear life as Reg pushes the van sharp left again and down a well-defined track between an avenue of trees.

'This'll bring us up by Limeshard,' Reg yells over the engine noise. 'It's the Coopers' carriageway to Outwood Lodge. Not supposed to be used by peasants like us, but . . .'

We skirt the edge of a disused chalk pit, and then we're into the woods proper. Reg is concentrating on keeping the van going, peering out through a windscreen obscured by the pouring rain. He's had to slow right down, because the surface of the track isn't good here, and I'm guessing it hasn't been maintained for a while.

'Got to take it a bit easy,' he says. 'Don't want to bust the sump.'

With the lessening of speed, it's easier to hear. 'We'd better stop a bit short of Limeshard anyway,' I say. 'I need to explain.'

A couple more minutes, and the white walls begin to show through the trees. We're crawling along now. He turns right off the path, bumps the van cautiously forward till it's nosed in under a stand of pines, switches off the engine. Ahead, through the trees, we can see bigger sections of the white walls, a dark corner of the gate. Behind, the junction of paths through the woods. After the chaotic churning of the drive, there's a shocking lull of movement and sound. Only the rain battering down and the click of the overstretched engine as it cools break the silence.

'What do we do now?' Reg says. 'Go and knock on the door?'

'No.' I put my hand on his arm. 'We should wait.' I've worked it out. If Fisher's got here before us, we'll see him when he comes out. And if by any chance he's not arrived yet, we'll see him coming. For the first time since I saw Anita running towards Fisher, I look at my watch. Only twenty minutes ago, it's not even nine o'clock.

What hope is there that McNaught and Jericho might be here? If they are, they haven't reacted to our arrival. If my guess is good that they were in Winchester last night, they could have set out before Hilda rang. Then they wouldn't be expecting anything to happen before 10.30, when Anita said she'd pass the documents to Fisher in the tea break.

Would Hilda have rung at all?

I have to work on the principle there's no help to be had. That there's only Reg and me to do whatever we can. It won't matter, as long as Fisher doesn't get away.

There's a stone in my gut. This is not looking much like a plan that's going well.

Oh, *Bram* . . .

I don't believe McNaught and Jericho will harm him directly, but they've got the power to hold him if they see fit. And with the stabbing, it's not going to be easy to hush up. It's a horrible mess, and I can't see how we're going to get out of it.

Reg stirs, breaking me out of my thoughts. 'Going to tell me what it's all about, then?'

It's only fair. I've dragged him into this. He needs to know what's going on. I skip some bits, gloss over others, wondering how much he might know anyway, since he's a friend of Mr Anderson's. And as the rain drums on the roof, he listens, doesn't ask any awkward questions.

Nine o'clock. Inside the big car, the tension is high.

'Turn here,' Nash says as the burnt-out shell of George Hine's house looms up out of the rain. His voice is harsh with sleeplessness, the cumulative effect of anger at McNaught and Jericho's incompetence.

They've not prepared the area, put men in overnight to watch for Fisher. It's just the two of them, and they don't even seem to know where to go.

And Jo's out there, unsupported, following a man who's already stabbed one woman.

'This isn't the place,' Jericho says. 'This isn't Limeshard Gate.'

'No. It's about half a mile through the trees. But if you think you're going to drive up there, announce your presence to all and sundry when Fisher's a desperate man and Ilse Reed's got at least two thugs inside the walls, you must be mad. Come on.'

Waiting. Waiting. Surely Fisher should have come by now? Have I got it all wrong? If he's gone inside, given up the papers he's carrying, what evidence will there be he's ever had them? Only my say-so, and Anita's . . . Anita. There was such a lot of blood. I don't even know if she's alive.

I'm beginning to think that Reg was right, that I should go up to the door and knock, when a figure appears through the rain. He's at the junction of the paths, but it's not Fisher, not from that direction.

Bram. It's *Bram*. Dimly, behind him, I see two others. McNaught. Jericho.

I'm shouting as I scrabble to get out of the van, my right leg dead from the knee down with pins and needles. So slow, too slow.

Bram's at the gate, ringing the bell.

I call again, stumbling over the rough ground beneath the trees towards him. He turns as the door in the gate opens behind him.

Another shout. Reg. 'Miss Rennard. Look out.'

But it's too late because Fisher's coming at me like an express train. Fisher, monstrous, dripping wet, covered in mud, knife in hand. He grabs at me and I pull away, but a hand twists in my hair. 'Stand still,' he says, 'or I'll stick you.'

If time has been playing games all morning, now it's decided on 'Statues'. In the stillness that follows, I'm aware of the knife, not at my throat, but at my side, like Anita. Of Reg, close by, his breathing harsh. Of McNaught and Jericho, stock-still, staring. Of Bram, and a young man in a black shirt behind him in the open doorway.

Like a child at a pantomime, I yell, 'Bram. Behind you.'

Fisher jerks my head and I feel a great strand of hair pull out of my scalp. I'd run, but the knife pricks fiercely at my side as he locks his free arm round my neck. 'Shut the fuck up.'

The Blackshirt in the doorway calls across the clearing. 'What the hell's going on?'

'It's all gone tits up,' Fisher yells. 'You've got to let me in.'

'You got the stuff?'

'Course I bloody have.'

'Better come in then. Bring your little friend with you. Mrs Reed's not going to be pleased.'

'Move,' Fisher says in my ear. 'No tricks.'

The threat of the knife and the choking arm round my neck means there's no trick I can play. But I resist as best I can, aided by the slippery ground, the rain half blinding both of us.

Fisher drops to one knee as his foot goes out from under him, drags me down with him. His arm loosens round my neck, but the knife is still hard against my flesh. In my peripheral vision, I'm conscious of someone moving. McNaught, perhaps, or Jericho. Fisher's seen it too.

'Stay where you are,' he shouts as he staggers to his feet. 'I'll kill her, and happy to do it, the bitch. A gut hit, it'll take her all day to die.' He yanks at me. I slither, slide, manage to rise. 'Now, get going.'

It seems like an enormous distance to cover, but it still happens too fast. We're almost in touching distance of the gate, the young man in the gateway, Bram. 'Out of my way,' Fisher growls. 'I'm warning you.'

It's meant for Bram, of course. But it's the young man who moves first, stepping unwarily out of the doorway. Fisher drags me past him, in through the gate, but not before I see Bram draw back his fist, hear the crunch as the blow lands.

'You stupid bastard,' Fisher yells as first Bram then McNaught and Jericho follow us in. But he's still got hold of me, and we're on a good, paved path now, solid underfoot. 'I told you. No nearer or she gets it.'

A stand-off.

He turns, pulls me round to face the house. I can't see Bram anymore. And I know my life's only worth something to Fisher as a shield as long as we're outside. If he gets inside, I'm finished.

A few steps more, though I do my best to hang back. The door opens, and there's a woman. A tall woman in a fur coat, blonde, icily perfect. Beside her, the young man I saw threaten Fisher in Hursley.

'What is this uproar?' she says. 'Fisher?'

'It's all gone wrong,' he says. 'You've got to help me. Get me away.'

She studies Fisher and me from her place in the doorway. 'And this is? Not the compliant Anita, surely?'

'She's nobody. An interfering bitch from Hursley Park who's been dogging my footsteps for weeks.'

She moves her gaze beyond us, to the men I know must be standing inside the gate. 'Mr Nash doesn't look as if he thinks she's nobody. A pretty little puzzle. I wonder, could she be his elusive assistant from Romsey? I'd heard she'd gone missing.'

'I don't care who she is,' he says. 'I'll stick her as soon as look at her.'

'And lose your insurance? Don't be foolhardy.'

'I've brought the papers,' he says. 'The right ones. I swear.'

She nods. 'So I should hope. Bertholdt, get the car.'

'Yes, madam.' He reaches back into the house, takes out an umbrella and opens it, hands it to her.

'I do so hate to get wet,' she says as she steps outside, moves towards us. But I can see she's being careful not to get too close.

A car, a sleek black Wolseley, moves from behind the house, round the curve of the drive until it's at its closest point to us. In a voice like iron, she calls out, 'Open the carriage gates, Mr Nash. Right up. You wouldn't want me to ask Fisher here to stab your girlfriend. He's very eager.'

The way Fisher's holding me, I can't look to see what's happening. But I hear the sound of bolts disengaging, the crunching sweep of wood on gravel.

'Very good. Now. The papers, Fisher.'

'You'll take me with you?'

She smiles. 'Why not? It would appear I've lost a member of my household. Poor Yan was always rather dim. But I need to see those papers first.'

I wouldn't trust a word she says, but Fisher seems to. He hesitates for a moment. If he wants to get the papers out, he'll have to take his arm from my neck, or move the knife from my side. I see him think about it. Hope he won't decide to solve the dilemma by stabbing me anyway.

'Hurry up,' Mrs Reed snaps.

In one quick movement, he takes his arm from my neck. Pushes me hard off the path, so I spin out of control, spluttering and falling onto the sodden lawn. When I drag myself up, I see the woman is climbing into the car, yellow envelope in hand. Fisher's following, hand reaching for the rear door handle, when Bertholdt lets in the clutch. Tyres screaming, the car pulls away in a spray of gravel and water. Fisher reels alongside for a few steps, still holding the door handle, then trips, falls with a scream. McNaught and Jericho rush towards him, but Bram's coming for me.

She'll get away . . .

But there's a crash, the sound of metal meeting metal. Glass shattering. McNaught and Jericho leave Fisher handcuffed and groaning on the ground, sprint out of the gate.

As Bram helps me to my feet, hugs me to him despite the mud that plasters me head to foot, Reg comes in through the gate, a shamefaced grin on his face.

'Dunno what they'll say back at Hursley,' he says. 'Poor old van's a write-off, I reckon.'

27

Wednesday 20ᵗʰ January, morning

NASH LOOKS OUT THROUGH HIS office window. On another day, the view might seem dreary, but today there's a dreamlike quality to the huddle of rooftops. His morning appointments are done, and in less than an hour, Jo will be back. Her job for Supermarine is over, and McNaught and Jericho have released her. Not willingly, perhaps, but it's the price they've agreed to pay for her silence, and his. David Hine's killer will never be formally named, but Fisher's on his way to the gallows nonetheless. George's killers, Bertholdt and Yan, plain Herbert and John, will join him, though the case will stay on Sergeant Tilling's books, marked down as unsolved. But Superintendent Bell won't be able to reproach him for it. He's disappeared, vanished in the wind blowing chill from Limeshard Gate.

Nash would rather have seen them all named, imprisoned, but it's been made plain he doesn't have that option. And no one will tell him what's become of Ilse Reed.

He chafes the scraped knuckles of his right hand against the palm of his left, taking an odd schoolboy satisfaction in the soreness, remembering the surprise on Yan's face as the Blackshirt thug had gone sprawling to his blow.

Jo will need to stay at Sam's for another week or two. They've agreed to adjust her hours, give her time to make the journey to Romsey without having to get up before dawn. It's not as if they're so busy she can't be spared till nine or half past.

A knock at the door. He turns from the window. 'Come in.'

It's Aggie, a wheeze in her breath and a look of grim determination.

He shakes his head at her. 'I've told you, Aggie, don't come flogging up the stairs if you need me. Use the phone to call me.'

She hauls in a breath. 'I didn't like to, Mr Nash.'

He takes in her sombre expression, the worry in her voice. It's something more than her usual grumpiness. His mind flies to the worst possibility. *An accident? Jo?* 'Bad news, Aggie? Tell me.'

'There's a man to see you. Personal business.'

'Is that all?' He tries not to snap at her for frightening him. 'Send him up, then.'

'I've seen him hanging around several times the last week or so. Thing is, he says his name's Lester. Dr Richard Lester.'

He stares at her as the words sink in. It's almost a surprise to find he's still standing. He feels as if he should be down on his knees, felled by a single blow. He and Jo have been on the brink of something new. And now it's over before it can begin.

Her husband.

Not dead, not interned far off in Germany.

Downstairs.

'Sir?'

'All right, Aggie. Send him up.' In some remote corner of his mind, he's pleased to note his voice sounds almost normal.

'If you're sure?'

'No point putting it off. Oh, and Aggie?'

'Yes, sir?'

'If . . . *when* Jo comes in, ring me. Don't let her come upstairs. Tell her I've got a client, but don't, whatever you do, tell her who it is.'

'No, sir.'

'I'll come down when I've seen him. Speak to her myself.'

'Yes. I'm sorry, Mr Nash.'

She's seen it then. Seen how he feels. *That* he feels. And now it's too late.

'All right, Aggie,' he says again, the words meaningless. Not all right at all. 'Thank you.'

When she's gone, he makes his way to his desk, sits down behind it, a tangible barrier.

Lester.

He's no idea what he's going to say, what he can do. All he can think is, *how can he be back?* And overriding even that, *why now?*

Another knock at the door. Too soon. 'Come in.'

He stands as the door opens, and Richard Lester enters. It's no surprise to see it's the man he noticed in the alleyway on Saturday.

'Nash?' The Oxbridge accent strangles the single syllable into something that sounds like *Nesh*.

'That's right. Please, sit down.'

'I'm sure you can guess why I've come, old boy.'

Nash winces at the public school expression, the patronising assumption of superiority. 'Yes?'

'I'm trying to track down my wife. I'm told you know where she is.'

A week ago, Nash thinks, he could have claimed ignorance. But now?

'The last she heard, you were a prisoner in Germany.'

Lester shrugs. 'It's a long story. Suffice it to say, I got out. I suppose Josephine was hoping I was dead?'

'You must know her better than that.'

'Question is, how well do *you* know her?'

Nash meets Lester's stare, says nothing. He doesn't feel guilty, it's too deep for that.

'Oh, ho. Like that, is it? Well, we'll call it water under the bridge, shall we?' Lester grins. 'I haven't always been a good boy. And Josephine, she's *never* been a good girl.'

The new scabs on Nash's hand break as his fists clench. 'If you feel like that, I'm surprised you've come looking for her.'

'But she's my wife, old boy. Time for her to come home.' He laughs, a derisive snort of sound. 'I've been to see that woman Dot, where she's been staying. What a dump, one poky little room. D'you know, at home, Josephine's the mistress of a six-bedroom manor house.'

Mistress? Nash is sure Lester's chosen the word deliberately. Jo's never talked about her life with this man, beyond saying she considered her marriage over before he'd been captured at Dunkirk. And she's far from having any kind of airs and graces. If Lester thinks Dot's is a dump, whatever would he make of Sam's? Seeing Jo do a land girl's job without pay, living on bread and scrape.

'Nash?'

He blinks back to the here and now. 'Yet you should consider she chose where she wanted to be.'

'You know, her grandfather's told me about you. The rumours about you and her. Quite a character, old Joe. Says he wishes he'd known about me before. Apparently, I remind him of Josephine's father. He was a doctor too, I understand.'

Nash can't believe what he's hearing. 'And you think it's a compliment to be like him?'

'Frankly, old boy, I don't care. I want to know where Josephine is. Her grandfather says nobody's seen her in Romsey for weeks. They think you've got her stashed away in some little love nest.'

'That's not even close to true.'

'You know where she is, though.'

On her way here, Nash thinks. *Oh, Christ.*

The phone rings. What little hope he might have had of getting rid of Lester before Jo arrived is shattered. It's too late. She's here.

'If you'll excuse me?'

Lester shrugs.

'Yes, yes,' Nash says, as he listens to his secretary's hurried whisper. 'Thank you.'

He puts the phone down. 'If you wouldn't mind waiting here a few moments,' he says to Lester, 'there's a small matter I need to attend to downstairs. I won't be long.'

Lester takes a packet of cigarettes out of his pocket. 'Mind if I smoke while I'm waiting?'

Nash pushes an ashtray across the desk. Though he's longing to get downstairs, he can't show his impatience. 'Be my guest.'

He crosses to the door, opens it. 'Would you like my secretary to bring you refreshments? A cup of coffee? Some tea?'

'Don't bother.' Lester exhales a long breath of smoke. 'I don't envisage us having much more to say to each other.'

Nash closes the door firmly behind him, takes the stairs at a run.

I'd been looking forward to this moment, being back in the office at Nash, Simmons and Bing. Seeing Cissie again, even Aggie. I know we don't see eye to eye, but after Hilda, even her brusque manner will seem like geniality itself.

But when I pop my head round the door of her office, expecting the minimum of fuss, I'm surprised. Because she gets up to greet me, takes my hands and pulls me into the room. Shuts the door behind me.

'Mrs Lester.' She half coughs, half chokes, flushes scarlet. 'Please, excuse me. How good to see you. After that terrible experience on Monday. A madman with a knife. You were cut, Mr Nash said.'

'Just a scratch.' Luckier than Anita, I think, though she will recover. And her baby's unharmed. 'What about you, Aggie. Are you all right?'

'Yes, of course. Now, let me tell Mr Nash you're here. He's with a client.'

'No hurry,' I say. 'I can wait till he's finished. Why don't you tell me all the news? What's been happening in Romsey?' It's a fair bet, after McNaught and Jericho's cover-up, it won't include any further details of the madman and his knife.

She coughs again. 'No, no. I must do as Mr Nash asked.'

While she's talking to Bram, I roam across to the window, look out into the alley. Even the smell of the office is friendly: beeswax polish, old linoleum and an afternote of coffee. It's good to be back. It feels like home.

'Now then,' Aggie says when she puts down the phone. 'A cup of tea?'

She doesn't wait for an answer, but goes through to the little kitchenette, leaving the door open this time. Even though I know he's busy, I find myself watching the hallway, waiting for Bram. I don't know how it's going to work: our personal relationship running alongside that of employer and employee, but at this moment I don't care. If I can be with him, that's all that matters.

Footsteps. To my view, limited to the bottom half-dozen steps, he appears as if in sections as he descends: feet, legs, body, finally the whole of him. I can feel the smile that has been on my face all morning vanish. Even from here, I can tell from his expression something's wrong.

'What is it? What's happened?'

'Jo, listen to me. Don't ask questions, just go. Not Dot's. My house. Fan will let you in.'

'What?' I can't make sense of it. 'Why . . . ?'

Aggie bustles into the hall, teacups on a tray. 'Tea's ready.'

'Please, Jo.'

Upstairs, a door opens. Footsteps sound on the stairs. Bram and Aggie seem to freeze. It's like a tableau, Aggie with her head cocked and her mouth open, Bram as pale and grim as death.

'It's going to be a shock,' he says. 'It's—'

But I can see what it is. *Who* it is. Beyond Bram, beyond the shape of Aggie in the doorway, I see the unmistakable figure of my husband.

'Steady.' Bram reaches out his hand towards me, lets it drop before it touches me. I retreat into the secretary's little room, feel the brush of the client's chair against the back of my knees. I skirt round it, feeling my way. The movement seems to draw everyone else into the room with me, so it's crowded, suddenly airless. This is worse than anything that happened on Monday.

'Richard.' I don't recognise my voice, though I know I've spoken. 'Where did you spring from?'

'Out of durance vile, my lovely,' he says, elbowing past Bram, giving me the lopsided grin that used to charm me. 'You don't look very pleased to see me.'

'I'm pleased you're safe,' I say, through numb lips. But it's not only my lips. My body, brain, everything is numb.

'Had the devil of a job tracking you down,' he says. 'Yet here you are, just as Nash was going to tell me he didn't know where to find you.'

'What do you want, Richard?'

'I want you to come home with me, of course. Back to Silverbank.'

I shake my head. 'Not my home. Not since I caught you in our bed with Sophie. Or was it Carol? No, that's right, it was Amy. Schmooze one of them if you like. I'm not coming back.'

'You'd rather stay with a man with half a face?'

Nausea rises in my throat. 'Better than having two, like you.'

I push him out of my way, see him stumble over the chair the way I had. Push towards the door, past Bram, past Aggie.

'Josephine. You're my wife.'

I turn. One last look. 'No. Not anymore. Don't bother to come looking for me again, Richard. The answer's always going to be no.'

Out in the street, the rain's falling steadily. I look at my watch. Not quite one o'clock. Less than half an hour since I went through the door, full of hope. Now, everything's changed.

I start to walk. I have to get away.

Where? Where can I go?

Not with Richard, never with Richard. Oh, God, why did he have to come back?

I should have gone to Bram's house. If only I'd . . .

I walk on, not thinking where anymore, only *away*. I must get away.

The rain turns warm on my face, salty on my lips. Though the streets are mercifully deserted, I can't cry here.

Round and round it goes. What could have been. What almost was. A future, unfurling. A true partnership.

Shattered in an instant, and for what? If I were to go back to Richard, he'd betray me before the week was out.

Anger rises inside me, a fiery heat that scorches out tears. Twice, I've been made to leave Romsey. Damned if anyone will make me go a third time. Everything that's alive in me, everyone who matters to me, is here. And that won't change.

Epilogue

Wednesday 20th–Thursday 21st January 1943, after midnight

TIRED WOMAN, HEELS BLISTERED FROM walking in the rain. Away from home, but in a homely place. A warm kitchen, a sleeping black and white dog, paws twitching with dreams. The Tilley lamp casts a soft white light across her face, the tiger stripe of hair where red is growing out through harsh black dye.

A cup of precious tea has gone cold at her elbow. She should go to bed. Morning will come all too soon, and with it, chores that can't be put off: goats to see to, milk round to do. But too much has happened for her to sleep yet.

She turns a small piece of paper in her hand, hardly more than a scrap. Two words and a name. She'd found it, weighted down with a stone on the table when she'd come in from tending the animals this evening. An hour each way to deliver it, but he hadn't taken his own invitation.

Please stay.
Bram.

Historical Note

THE STORY OF *TREACHERY AT Hursley Park House* is just that – a story. The events and characters described in it are entirely fictional. Although I have used the real names of Lady Cooper; Theophilus E. Brown, the Winchester coroner; and Mr Wakeling, the ex-Scotland Yard policeman assigned to security at Hursley Park House; the roles they play in this story and any characteristics ascribed to them are the product of my imagination.

However, the history of Supermarine's presence at Hursley Park House is factual. In September 1940, at the height of the German air offensive against strategic targets in southern England, the Vickers-Armstrongs (Supermarine) works at Woolston and Itchen in Southampton were effectively destroyed in a series of bombing raids. The factory was, at that time, the main production centre for the Spitfire, and while the actual manufacture of the aircraft was swiftly dispersed into a multitude of small 'shadow' factories in the area and elsewhere, the Design and Production Departments needed a home. The recently widowed Lady Cooper, owner of Hursley Park Estate, some nine miles outside Southampton, had offered Hursley Park House for use as a hospital, as in WWI. Instead, it was requisitioned by the Ministry of Aircraft Production. In December 1940, Supermarine moved in to occupy the main part of the House, welcomed by Lady Cooper with a Spitfire made of flowers. Meanwhile, the estate grounds had become the site of a number of variously purposed army encampments.

Lady Cooper continued to live in part of Hursley Park House, and she and her staff coexisted there with Supermarine for some time. But in December 1942, after a number of concerns regarding security, she moved out and Supermarine was left in sole charge of the house and immediate grounds. Numerous buildings were erected to meet the increasing needs of the firm's design teams and craftsmen building aircraft prototypes.

The personnel needed to staff Supermarine were brought to work daily by a fleet of buses, or accommodated in lodgings in Hursley and nearby villages. Additionally, a group of prefabricated buildings known as the Hutments was built by Vickers in nearby Chandler's Ford to house Supermarine personnel and their families.

After the war, Vickers continued to occupy Hursley Park House until 1958, when they moved their design team to Swindon. A survey of the house at this time, carried out for Sir George Cooper, Lady Cooper's son, revealed it was not economically viable to restore it as a private residence. It was leased to IBM from 1958, and subsequently bought by them following the death of Sir George in 1961.

Some resources used for the background of *Treachery at Hursley Park House:*

Historic maps of Hursley and the surrounding area: https://maps.nls.uk

History of Hursley Park House: https://hursleypark.wixsite.com/history

Supermarine history: https://supermariners.wordpress.com/

Chandler's Ford Hutments: https://chandlersfordtoday.co.uk/chandlers-ford-the-hutments/

Brenton, Howard. 2018. *The Shadow Factory*, London: Nick Hern Books

Farmer, David. 2000. *A Brief History of Oliver's Battery*

Goodall, Nick, ed. Peach, Len D., comp. 1995. *Merdone, The History of Hursley Park,* Hursley Park: IBM UK

Rutter, Stella. 2014. *Tomorrow is D Day*, Stroud: Amberley Publishing

Tate, Tom. 2018. *Hitler's British Traitors*, London: Icon Books

Acknowledgements

I'D LIKE TO THANK EVERYONE who has supported me through the process of the writing *Treachery at Hursley Park House*. In the exceptional conditions brought about by Covid-19, there have been gains as well as losses – for me, being forced to stay home was not altogether a bad thing!

Thanks to my agent, Rowan Lawton, and her assistant, Isabelle Wilson, at The Soho Agency. To the editorial team at Bonnier Zaffre, especially Kelly Smith, my amazing new editor; Ben Willis, publishing director, who kept me so well informed over the changeover period; and also Ciara Corrigan, editorial assistant, and Eleanor Stammeijer, press officer. A shout-out, too, for Katherine Armstrong, my previous editor at Bonnier, who believed in me enough to ask for more books about Jo and Bram.

I owe so much to the generous encouragement from my fellow writers. Rebecca Fletcher, who has been a wonderful friend and advocate for the book throughout – thank you so much. Anne Summerfield, Adelaide Morris, Corinne Pebody, Jan Moring, John Barfield and Steve Scholey of Chandler's Ford Writers have been as amazing as ever in their friendship and support. Also to new friends at Taverners, thank you for inviting me to join you. Last but by no means least, all at Dovetail Writers – the AE class I take on a Thursday. I often wonder who's teaching who! While Zoom is not the same as being able to meet in person, I'm so grateful to it for allowing us to keep in touch and working together.

Most special of all, I want to thank my family. Nick, my husband – what can I say except you're the best! I couldn't have done any of it without you. Will and Abbie, Phil, Kat and Danny – you are each so important to me. You've been an inspiration for your courage and resilience in the face of unprecedented challenges over the last year.

I should also mention everyone who talked to me – and let me talk – about the local history underlying this story. The website https://supermariners.wordpress.com/ run by David Key is a marvellous resource for everything to do with Spit-fires at Hursley.

To everyone who helped – the good stuff is yours, the mis-takes, all mine.

Read on for an exclusive first look at the next
Josephine Fox mystery

Prologue

The night of 4ᵗʰ June, 1944

FROM HIS POST HIGH ON Romsey Abbey's clock tower, Bill Fox raises his binoculars as a pinprick of light appears towards the south-east. A pinkish glow, it might almost be the first touch of dawn, except dawn doesn't begin in Hampshire at 3 a.m., even in midsummer.

The light strengthens, the pink streaked with gold, quickly eclipsed by it, a growing haze somewhere off in the direction of Southampton. It reminds him of the way the sky would brighten at the start of an air raid back in 1940 or '41. But though he can see flames now, flickering into the night sky, they don't spread the way they had done then, eating across the horizon.

The fire's not as far off as he first thought. He stares, trying to work it out. Something domestic, perhaps? A hayrick? Except it looks as if it's burning too hot for that. There haven't been any bombing raids, and though there have been plenty of their own aircraft over, there's been nothing untoward. No hint of a concussion that would signify a downed plane: that deep vibration of sound that shakes the belly more than the eardrums.

He reaches for the field telephone, turns the handle to alert his colleagues in the ARP post below. Whatever it is that's burning, it needs investigating. Tensions are high, rumours everywhere about the sudden emptying of the army camps, the disappearance of the lorries and tanks from the lanes where they've been parked up for so long. Whispers about invasion, though no one dares to speculate aloud.

The first firemen to reach the scene find a vehicle burning in a ditch. The leaping conflagration that alerted Bill Fox has settled to a steady blaze that has set the hedgerow alight, despite last night's rain. There's an acrid stench of chemical combustion: petrol and rubber, the flammable materials from the car's interior. Overlying that, woodsmoke from the hedge, and something other, more sinister: the unsettling whiff of roasting flesh. With horror, they make out the shape of someone slumped in the driver's seat, but there's nothing they can do. The heat's too intense for heroics. Whoever the poor bastard is, he's a goner for sure. All they can do is try and control the flames, keep the fire from spreading into the crop of ripening wheat beyond the hedge.

THE UNEXPECTED RETURN OF JOSEPHINE FOX

**Winner of the 2018 Richard and Judy
Search for a Bestseller competition**

April 1941, Romsey, England.
Josephine 'Jo' Fox hasn't set foot in Romsey in over twenty
years. As an illegitimate child, her controlling grandfather
found her an embarrassment. Now, she's returned to
uncover the secret of her parentage. Who was her father
and why would her mother never talk about him?

Jo arrives the day afterthelocalpubhasbeenbombed.
When an unidentifiedbody–thatofateenagegirl–is
discovered in the rubble, rumours are rife. Who is she and
how did she get there? When it becomes clear that the girl
was murdered, the hunt is on for the killer in their midst.

Teaming up with local coroner and old friend Bram Nash,
Jo sets out to establish the identity of the girl and solve the
riddle of her death, whilst also seeking to unravel
the mystery of her own past.

Available now